ABOVE ALL

JOHN W. HUFFMAN

ACKNOWLEDGMENTS

My deepest appreciation to my hardworking readers circle for all their invaluable feedback and suggestions on the early drafts of this manuscript, with explicit thanks to Jerry Nealy, Louis Smith, Leonard Jordan, Whitney Brock, Jackie Neely Jansen, John Morgan, Captain, U.S. Army, (Ret.) and Doug Meadows, Lt. Col., USAF (Ret.)

To my charming wife, Misty,
whose love of my stories spurred this novel to print.

CHAPTER 1

With some irritation I set my book aside and picked up the ringing phone on my end table.

"Hello?"

"Professor Hess?" a soft voice inquired.

"Yes?"

"Are you the former Captain Randall Hess who served with the 120th Aviation unit in Vietnam?"

"Yes," I replied, somewhat mystified.

"I'm Mary Ellen Jones," the gentle voice advised. "My father was John Joseph Sharpe."

"Y-Yes, I ... I remember Lieutenant Sharpe," I replied tentatively, a rush of adrenaline sweeping through me.

"My father was in a fatal accident."

"I'm ... sorry to hear that."

"His memorial service is tomorrow afternoon in the chapel at Fort Sam Houston. I thought you should know ..."

"Yes ... yes, I appreciate you calling."

"Goodbye, Professor Hess."

I hung the phone up slowly. After forty years, I hadn't expected such a call and thus experienced a sinking phenomenon similar to each time I watched the victorious North Vietnamese Army storm the South Vietnamese presidential palace in Saigon on the History Channel. I looked to the wall where a color photograph of a much younger version of me in Army dress blues hung, my expression grim as President Nixon placed the Medal of Honor around my neck in the Rose Garden on the White House lawn. Two other heroes stood rigidly beside me, my crewmembers in the incredibly valorous exploit that merited the highest award our nation could offer, each wearing the Silver Star, each knowing I was the least worthy of the trio, an embarrassing reality further accented by the fact that the man who truly deserved such noble distinction was discreetly missing.

As the familiar wave of guilt engulfed me, I picked up the phone and dialed, determined to do what I should have done many years ago.

"Department of American History," the voice greeted.

"Connie, I'm taking a leave of absence for a few days. Please notify the faculty and book me the first available flight to San Antonio, Texas."

"Is there a problem, Professor Hess?"

"No, Connie, I'm just going to … say goodbye to an old friend …"

I hung up the phone and searched through my closet for the worn journal I'd kept during that era and the case that held the medal I'd never worn after removing it from my neck the day it was awarded. I then sank into my easy chair to review the incredible chronicle of that unbelievable man in those unusual times and the implausible adventure he took us on ... which was above all, a most bizarre tale ...

It all began for me in the early morning hours at the 21st Replacement Depot outside of Saigon. I'm not at my best in the morning, and being temporarily attached to that rather dismal holding unit while I awaited orders for my permanent in-country assignment didn't help my disposition.

Once a sprawling complex supplying a constant source of replacement raw meat to the huge Vietnam war machine, the depot was now a shadow of its former glory comprised of ragged, rusted strands of sagging concertina wire surrounding a tiny cluster of dilapidated tin Quonset huts in a small corner of the once huge compound. On this end of the lagging war effort, the depot now fed us few stragglers into the backwash of the Vietnamization program, our new national strategy designed to turn over the fighting to the Vietnamese in order to allow us to withdraw with some semblance of dignity after getting our asses kicked over here for the last ten years.

In this instance, a cadre sergeant permanently assigned to the replacement depot shined a flashlight in my face as I lay sleeping in the bay of the transient officers' quarters.

"Captain Hess? We need you in the orderly room right away, Sir!"

I scowled at the luminous dial on my watch. "Sergeant, do you know what time it is?"

"Yes, Sir, it's 0200 hours," he replied anxiously. "Please hurry, Sir."

The sergeant dashed out the door as I swung my legs over the side of the bunk with spots swimming before my eyes and searched for my trousers in the renewed darkness. It was cool in the damp night, unlike the woeful blazing heat of the day. I shivered into my shirt, quickly laced my boots, and headed for the orderly room in some alarm, anticipating an emergency back home.

Nancy, whom I had tearfully departed from two days previously, was five months pregnant with our second child. Even though we were both excited about the prospect of a hoped for little boy to go with our perfect two-year-old daughter, the tension of my being assigned to Vietnam just as my nondeployment date approached had been a strain on her. A week before I left, the doctor pulled me aside to warn me she was showing signs of miscarrying, which only added a heavy layer of guilt to my already existing remorse of my not being there with her for the birth of our new child.

Nancy wasn't the strongest of women, but I loved her nevertheless. As an adamant supporter of the anti-war protests occurring back home, she and her good-intentioned but misguided peacenik friends and their legion of sleazy, opportunistic politicians had fervently ground all patriotic support for the war effort into silence. To leave my family to serve in such an obviously lost cause was senseless in her view. The argument that my only alternative as a soldier was imprisonment for refusing to deploy didn't seem to have an impact on her—if necessary I should desert the Army rather than abandon my family.

My only consolation as I hurried into the orderly room was that after this one-year tour of duty in this godforsaken place I'd be out of the Army with my debt to the ROTC paid in full.

The sergeant who had awakened me sprang up from his seat. "*Attention!*" A staff sergeant and a specialist fourth class seated at different desks braced up quickly as well.

"*Carry on!*" I called as I paused before the staff sergeant. "What's the problem?"

"Thanks for coming, Sir. My apologies for having to wake you, but our commandant got stranded in Saigon tonight and our executive officer is home on emergency leave."

"Which means?"

"We're, uh, having a problem in the O Club, Sir."

Relief surged through me with the apparent lack of an emergency back home. "What does a problem in the Officers' Club have to do with me, Sergeant?"

"Well, Sir, technically you're the ranking officer here until new orders are cut reassigning you to your permanent unit. I'm sorry to have to request your assistance, Sir, but unfortunately it's an officer who's causing the problem, and so you see, Sir, with our commandant away for the evening and all …"

"Damn, Sergeant!"

"Yes, Sir, I agree, Sir, but in this instance I feel it best if we involve an officer to assist us in stabilizing the, uh … unfortunate, uh … *situation* …"

"And exactly what *is* the situation, Sergeant?"

"We've got a lieutenant in the O Club with some Army nurses who are, uh, well, uh …"

"Yes, Sergeant?"

5

"Uh, well, you see, Sir, they're uh … *inebriated*, Sir."

"They're what?"

"Intoxicated, Sir."

"They're drunk, Sergeant?"

"Yes, Sir, and our standard operating procedures require we close the O Club at 0200 hours."

"Did you inform the club manager to close the club per your SOP, Sergeant?"

"Well, uh, not exactly, Sir, you see, they've got the club manager drunk with 'em, Sir, and, uh, you see, Sir, we … can't get 'em out of the club …"

"Did you inform the lieutenant and the nurses that it was closing time?"

"Uh, yes, Sir, we told 'em it was quitting time, Sir."

"And?"

"The lieutenant, uh, suggested I go piss up a rope, Sir."

"Damn, Sergeant!"

"Yes, Sir, I agree, Sir. Maybe you could have a word with him, Sir?"

I sighed. "Lead the way, Sergeant." I tagged along, greatly annoyed, as the staff sergeant hurried out the door, thinking *damned lieutenants are dumber than rocks! Six months of Officer Candidate School and they come out full of themselves thinking they own the Army.*

The sergeant snatched open the door and stood stiffly aside as I strode purposefully in acutely aware that while my six-foot two-inch frame could appear menacing at a distance, up close my receding hairline tended to give me a mild-mannered geek look. To offset this dismal effect, I knitted my eyebrows together above my pencil-thin lips in order to project my best glower—and stopped so abruptly the sergeant ran into me.

My fierce look melted to one of astonishment as my jaw unhinged and my eyes bulged at a sexy blond gyrating on a table slowly unbuttoning her blouse while staring down with half-lidded eyes at a lieutenant with a lecherous grin who had an attractive brunette in his lap. I quickly took in the jukebox blaring at maximum volume, the bartender passed out on top of the bar with a bottle of vodka cradled protectively in his arms as he snored in open-mouthed bliss, and two other nurses flanking the lieutenant and his lap-mate, one with his hat on her head backwards. As I gaped, the lieutenant whistled raucously and pointed a small aviator flashlight up the dancer's skirt as she squealed and covered her patch of heaven with her hands in mock alarm.

I grimaced as the staff sergeant, leaning wide-eyed around me to take in the scene, fell over on his face. I took his arm and yanked him to his feet as the dancer on the table sensuously twirled her bra above her head and tossed it at the lieutenant, where it wrapped around his face. I turned to the foolishly grinning staff sergeant as she dropped her palms along the edge of her skirt to slide it teasingly up her thighs. Unable to make myself heard over the din, I mouthed '*Pull the plug!*' as I pointed at the jukebox. He sidled over to the apparatus, never taking his eyes from the dancer on the table, and reluctantly yanked the cord from the wall socket. As the music fizzled out, all eyes turned to the guilty-looking sergeant standing sheepishly with the cord in his hand.

"Lieutenant, the Officers' Club is closed!" I called out briskly.

All eyes swung from the sergeant to me. Well, not exactly every eye. The startled bartender sleeping on the bar attempted to sit up and drunkenly toppled over backwards onto the floor behind it in a crash of debris. The nurse on the table hastily began buttoning her blouse as the one on the lieutenant's lap scrambled up smoothing out her skirt modestly and the other snatched his hat off her head.

The lieutenant lifted his cat-like agile five-foot nine-inch slim frame dressed in a tailored khaki uniform bloused into the tops of gleaming black Cochran jump boots from the chair and locked daunting, cold blue eyes on me. A thin gash decorating his right cheek just below his short, silky blond hair gave him an air of impious defiance, his intrepid, bold stance suggesting a wicked, rakish nuance women inevitably found appealing and us merely mortal men slightly intimidating.

Unnerved by his direct, calculating stare, I shifted my eyes to the rows of ribbons covering his left breast, taking special note of the Combat Infantry Badge, Paratrooper Wings, Aviator Wings, Silver Star, Bronze Star with Cluster, Vietnamese Cross of Gallantry, and Purple Heart with two Clusters among various other campaign ribbons and sundry decorations. The man, even discounting his youth, which I gauged to be roughly twenty-two or so years, was obviously a highly decorated combat veteran who had been there and done that. So what was a hardcore, battle-tested, junior-grade lieutenant with a chest full of hero confetti doing back over here in this dreadful place? Luck of the draw wasn't likely. A volunteer was more probable—possibly a nut case or perhaps a war-crazed sociopath? His casually arrogant countenance as he faced me with narrowed, watchful eyes suggested he had already pegged me as a greenhorn, which I found disconcerting.

He lifted his glass in the deafening silence. "The night's still young, Captain. Buy you a drink?"

I suppressed an involuntary quiver. "M-Maybe tomorrow, Lieutenant." *Damn*, I sounded like a reticent schoolboy standing before his headmaster. I was a *captain*, for *christsakes*. I had the upper hand here. Didn't I?

"There are no tomorrows, Captain," he replied with a trace of mockery.

I glanced around the club in an effort to break his unsettling stare and gather my scattered wits. "The sergeant needs to close this place down. Sorry to have to spoil your, uh, party."

He lifted his glass in a scornful toast. "Aye-Aye, Captain. The bar is closed."

He tossed his drink down, deliberately placed the glass on the table and looked up at the blond still standing on top. "Ellen, darling, the party seems to be over." He offered her a steadying hand as she stepped down gracefully onto a chair and to the floor, and then extended his elbow in a gallant gesture. "May I escort you home?"

She giggled as she slipped her hand through the crook of his arm and they walked out without a glance in my direction as the other women straggled out behind them in a tittering group.

Somewhat relieved, but rather pleased with myself, I turned to the sergeant still standing by the jukebox with his mouth open and the cord in his hand. "Sergeant, check the bartender to see if he's still alive and close this place down."

"Aye-Aye—uh, *sorry*, Sir—I mean, *Yes, Sir!*" He dropped the cord and scurried around the bar to pull the bartender from the rubble.

9

I returned to my hooch, undressed, and lay down on my bunk shivering as I pulled the sheet up to my chin, allowing my mind to drift as I longed for the warmth of Nancy beside me.

This was our first separation. We dated for two years while I fulfilled my schooling in the ROTC and my military flight training requirements, which corresponded with her graduation from college. In the intervening four years since our marriage, mainly due to my advanced educational degree, I'd fortunately been assigned stateside classroom training duties at Fort Rucker, Alabama, to help fill the huge demand for pilots at the height of the war effort. With fourteen months left on my five-year service obligation, the system, determined to get a return on its investment for the four years of college and one year of flight school it had funded on my behalf, caught up with me in the form of orders for Vietnam a mere two months short of my nondeployment date.

Though I considered myself a patriot, I was glad to be near the end of my service obligation and looked forward to returning to civilian life, where I planned to continue my education and obtain a Ph.D. My biggest objective in the next twelve months was to do nothing stupid to alter that plan as I suffered through the agony of my separation from my family. Though the days stretched interminably before me from this end of the spectrum, at least the personal risk would be minimal since our new mission of supporting the Army of the Republic of Vietnam as we disengaged and pulled out meant the ARVNs would carry the brunt of the war effort while we kept out of harm's way.

I had but one desire—to return safely home to my wife and children.

A half-hour later, I was neither awake nor asleep as I lay mulling over my sad fate when the sergeant rushed back into the hooch and again shined his flashlight in my face.

"Captain Hess, wake up, Sir! We've got a penetration, Sir!"

I fought through the layers of consciousness as I held my palm up to shield the harsh beam of light. "A what?"

"A penetration, Sir! One of our sensors has gone off. Probably just a false alarm due to an animal or something, but we still have to check it out, Sir. It's SOP."

I pulled on my trousers and stuffed my feet into my boots. "Why do you need me if you know what to do?"

"'Cause we have to issue live ammo, Sir. That requires an officer's approval."

"Approved, Sergeant," I mumbled groggily. "Now can I go back to bed?"

"But, Sir, what if it ain't a false alarm? What if it's the real thing?"

"The real thing, Sergeant?"

"What if it's a *Vietcong*, Sir?"

My heartbeat kicked up a pace. "Damn, Sergeant!"

"Yes, Sir, I agree, Sir."

"When's your captain coming back?" I demanded. "I'm getting damn tired of doing his job for him."

"We never have any trouble around here, Sir. I don't know what's going on tonight. It must be the full moon or something. I'm sure sorry about this. My captain would have already been back, but he flew to Saigon in a chopper for a briefing at MACV and his flight back got cancelled for some reason."

I sighed. "Good grief!"

"It's those damned aviators, Sir! You're new over here, but you'll find out they're just a bunch of jeep-stealing, womanizing cowboys, is all they are. Know what I mean, Sir? Just like that aviator lieutenant causing all the trouble tonight!"

"Sergeant, it so happens *I'm* an aviator."

"Oh, uh, present company excepted of course, Sir!"

"What are the standard operating procedures for a penetration?" I asked as I laced my boots.

"Well, Sir, first we alert the Reaction Force. We've done that and they're on standby. Then we go check it out. If we don't find anything, then we call the Reaction Force and they stand down."

I nodded appreciatively. "Sounds reasonable, Sergeant. What if you find something?"

He hesitated. "Gee, I don't know, Sir. We've never found anything before."

A sinking sensation occurred in my stomach as I followed him out.

The staff sergeant sprang up when we entered the orderly room. "Request permission to issue rifles and ammo, Sir!"

"Permission granted, Sergeant!" I looked around expectantly. "Who are you issuing them to?"

"You and me, Sir." The staff sergeant unlocked a cabinet and pulled out two M-16s and two clips of ammunition, extending one of each to me.

I blinked. "You and me?"

"But I leave the keys to the cabinet for Sergeant Mullins here and the specialist. If we come under fire, they're authorized to draw their weapons and ammo."

My gut clenched. "Just how far away is this reaction force, Sergeant?"

"No more than thirty minutes, Sir."

"Thirty minutes! How are the two of us supposed to block a penetration for half an hour with one clip of ammunition each until they get here?"

"I don't write the SOPs, Sir, I just follow them."

I glowered. "Your standard operating procedures leave a lot to the imagination, Sergeant."

"Yes, Sir."

"Okay, what's the situation?"

"See this board, Sir?" The sergeant pointed to an electrical board with three red lights blinking in a line. "About ten minutes ago first one and then the next two lights lit up in sequence leading to this point here indicating that something moving through the area set them off."

"What is located in this area where the sensors lead?"

"The helipad, Sir."

"The helipad? Are there any aircraft parked there?"

"No, Sir. It's only a small pad for one aircraft to land and take off from at a time. There's nothing there tonight."

I stared at the board. "Why would anybody want to go there with all the other targets in the area?"

"Maybe they're trying to ambush our commandant when he returns in the morning, Sir," Sergeant Mullins offered.

"Do we have any lights in that area, Sergeant, or any other form of illumination?" I demanded, ignoring Sergeant Mullins.

"No, Sir. But we've got a spotlight on the jeep."

"How far is the helipad from us?"

"About fifty yards, Sir, straight down the road there on the right."

I locked the magazine into my rifle and chambered a round grimly. "Well, let's go have a look."

Dead silence prevailed as the three of them stared at me in frozen horror.

"*What?*" I demanded.

Sergeant Mullins, aghast, stared at the rifle in my hands. "Sir, you can't lock and load unless you come under fire."

I blinked. "You're kidding!"

"No, Sir. That's SOP, Sir. I don't write them, I just—"

"I know, I know, Sergeant, you just follow them!"

I reluctantly released the magazine from its well and jacked the chamber to the rear to flip the round onto the floor. I scooped the cartridge up and shoved it back into the magazine, figuring with a possible thirty minutes of combat facing me, I needed every one of the twenty rounds in the load, and that by damned if I lived through this, I was going to rewrite their SOPs for them, damn it!

When we climbed into the jeep I studied the spotlight on its post above my head, located the switch mounted on its side, and aimed it directly in front of the jeep.

"Sergeant, drive down the road and turn into the helipad. Stop the jeep and get away from the vehicle quickly. I'll turn the light on and exit on my side. Be prepared for anything. Are you ready?"

He cranked the jeep and slid it into gear. "Yes, Sir."

"Have you got your ammunition handy?"

"Oh, shit! Sorry, Sir."

He cut the engine, hopped out, scurried back into the orderly room, and dashed back out carrying the magazine aloft enthusiastically as I watched in dismay, thinking *this is really going to be interesting … where's that hotshot lieutenant with all his fancy combat ribbons when you need him?*

The sergeant restarted the jeep, lurched off, and made a left turn on the road with our headlights off. Thanks to Sergeant Mullins' full moon, we had no trouble picking out the thin ribbon of asphalt leading down a slight incline. Off to my right front I saw a dark patch that was the helipad. As we drew abreast, the sergeant swung the jeep hard to the right, slammed on the brakes, and dove out the left side. As I flipped on the spotlight and rolled out the right side, I saw his magazine on the seat where he'd left it. I hit the ground in a heroic bruising tumble that would have made John Wayne envious and popped up unsteadily on one knee with my rifle pointed at the helipad, the magazine close to the well ready to load.

The beam of the spotlight illuminated a gyrating bundle of blankets in the middle of the helipad. Flanking one side were a pair of khaki pants and a shirt neatly folded on top of paratrooper boots, with white cotton briefs and a T-shirt draped over them. Strewn about on the other side were a nurse's uniform, a pair of women's shoes, a brassiere, panties, and some stockings. The rippling of the blanket froze, and the top blanket flipped back to reveal two blonde heads staring out at us in bewilderment.

I leapt for the switch, cracking my knee against the side of the jeep in the process, and flipped off the spotlight, again enshrouding us in darkness. "Sorry about that, Lieutenant!" I panted. "I thought we had a penetration."

A low chuckle emanated from the blackness. "Aye-Aye, Captain. We definitely *had* a penetration." A female giggle stung my humiliated ears.

"Get in the jeep, Sergeant!" I ordered as I jumped into the passenger seat. "Get me the hell out of here! *Now!*"

The sergeant started the engine slipped the clutch, and we lurched as the engine died. After an agonizingly long grinding of the starter, it again fired, we lurched, and the engine again died as I about died with it.

"*Damn, Sergeant!*"

"Sorry, Sir!"

The engine fired and we shot backward, turning rapidly in reverse down the road. The sergeant ground the gears in a ripping tear and popped the clutch, snapping my head to the rear sharply and then pitching me forward again as the engine died. He re-fired the engine and we finally bolted off as I seethed.

After turning in the rifles and magazines and signing the charge of quarter's log attesting to the fact that we had turned in the rifles and ammunition per the unit SOP, I then dumped my tired, besmirched self into my bunk for the third time that night and pulled the sheets up over my head …

…despairing of my ignoble start to this long, miserable year of war.

CHAPTER 2

I awoke more tired than when I first went to bed the night before, or for that matter, the second or third time. In the shower, I painfully discovered through various stings I had skinned both my elbows, my right knee, and had sustained a large bruise to my right shoulder during my commando roll out of the jeep at the helipad. I put on a flight suit and made my way to the mess hall, where I filled my tray. As I turned to the officers' dining section, I blanched at the sight of the lieutenant sitting with two nurses at a table. Instant envy quickly replaced abrupt despair as I noted his silver one-piece Air Force flight suit with zippers all over the chest, arms, and legs exuding the perfect image of the devil-may-care flyboy.

"Captain, please join us," he invited before I could dodge him, feeling dowdy by comparison in my own baggy Army issue olive-drab, two-piece, Nomex flight suit.

Even the way he extended the invitation tended to irritate me, but since I had no respectable way out, I graciously slid into the empty chair at the table. "Good morning, Lieutenant. Slept well, I presume?"

He grinned. "Aye-Aye, Captain, like a baby after all the traffic died down."

I flushed and picked at my eggs, thinking he looked fresh as a daisy compared to my own haggard countenance, drawing some comfort that the blond who had been with him the night before at the helipad was conspicuously absent, obviously sleeping off her hangover.

"Nice flight suit," I complimented sullenly.

"Thank you, Captain, I'm fortunate to have several of them. I'd offer you one, but you're such a tall drink of water, I don't think it'd fit you."

"Several?" I asked, seething silently.

"I could probably get you a couple your size by tomorrow, if you'd like?"

I stared at him with scrambled eggs hanging out of my mouth. "And how would you do that, Lieutenant?"

"I've got an Air Force friend I do some trading with. Tall and slim, right?"

I stiffened. "Black market?"

He shrugged. "Military issue for military personnel, Captain."

"No thanks, Lieutenant, I'm sure those suits are out of the price range of a married man with kids."

"I'll cut you a deal, Captain—two your size for a future favor."

"What kind of favor?" I asked carefully, greed beginning to get the better of me.

He chuckled. "Don't know until I need it, Captain, whatever I want within your power to grant, I suppose."

I studied him suspiciously. "And *legal?*"

He stood. "Agreed, Captain, the favor must be *legal* before it's granted. Are you ladies ready?"

I flushed and focused on my breakfast, deeply resenting the inferiority complex this cocky little lieutenant instilled in me as he and his coven of nurses departed in a cavalier group.

I spent the rest of the morning writing Nancy a brief account of the highlights of my troublesome night with the maddening lieutenant. Afterward I ate lunch alone in the dining facility and then dozed the afternoon away in boredom listening to popular tunes played on the Armed Forces Radio Network, which filled me with nostalgia for home.

In late evening I sat alone at the evening meal, lonesome and homesick. The lieutenant and two of his female sidekicks entered, filled their trays, and joined me without being invited. I wasn't in a particularly good mood and their gaiety annoyed me even further.

"Get the deal worked out on my flight suits, Lieutenant?" I pricked at him for no other reason than I wished him gone so I could enjoy my solitude and wallow in my despair.

"Aye-Aye, Captain. They're due in any time now, but there was a glitch."

My heart pounded in near excitement, but I quickly calmed myself and set my antenna for danger. "What's the glitch?"

"The idiots sent four of the things. I'll never be able to trade them because you're so tall, so I'll make a new deal with you. You can have all four, but I get *two* favors instead of one, and I need one of the favors granted tonight."

He measured me as I contemplated the offer. He was a sly one all right. Still, he was apparently delivering more than he said he would and ahead of schedule.

I prayed the favor was in my power to grant—and would net me no more than a couple of years in the stockade. "Two *legal* favors, *one* to be granted tonight, for *four* of those silver flight suits?" I confirmed, trying to keep my voice steady as heady anticipation built in me.

He nodded solemnly as the two missing nurses, one of them the blond, table-top-dancing Ellen from the helipad fiasco the night before, came through the door, each carrying a brown paper bag. "The suits to be delivered to you now, Captain."

The brunette who had been sitting in his lap the night before slid in beside him. "Hey, sweetie, sorry we're late. The chopper had to stop to refuel. Running errands for you is such fun!"

"Things went well, I take it?" he asked.

"No problems at all," she affirmed. "While we were in Saigon we saw two full-bird colonels waiting for a flight. You should have seen the looks they gave us when our own private helicopter flew in and whisked us away right in front of them."

"Hey, handsome." Ellen pecked his cheek and pulled up a chair beside him. "I wanna join the mile-high club! Those aviator friends of yours said I could. Would you indoctrinate me, sweetheart?"

I gulped. The mile-high club was allegedly a secret society in Vietnam I had always thought was more myth than fact. Supposedly you took a woman up 5,280 feet in a Huey, one mile to be exact, and had intercourse with her. The pilots in front, at the moment of penetration—*ouch*, that word still stung my psyche—chopped the throttle, kicked in left rudder, and stood the aircraft on its nose, causing it to drop like a rock and thereby lifting the participants in the cargo bay in a free-floating zero-gravity experience. Obviously only aviators could indoctrinate a woman into the guild, but she was free to select any aviator of her choice for the event. Afterwards the chosen aviator awarded her a tiny set of silver wings engraved with his designated call sign on the back. From that moment forward, she was a member of an exclusive society, which every aviator in Vietnam honored, and given all the benefits the aviators gave themselves, which were legendary in Vietnam.

The lieutenant bowed gallantly. "I would be honored, Ellen."

Ellen clapped her hands in anticipation. "Really? *When?*"

"Soon," he promised.

She draped her arms around his neck and nibbled his ear. "Oh, I'm so excited! Can we practice tonight?"

I looked around uneasily to see who might be listening to all this, reminding myself not to pull another commando raid on the helipad if the sensors went off.

"Practice makes perfect, darling. Are those my packages?"

She handed the sacks to him. "Those Air Force guys were so nice. They let us sit in one of their jets. It was so much fun! They tripped all over themselves helping us up the ladder into the cockpit."

The lieutenant chuckled as he inspected the parcels. "They just wanted a peek at your panties while you were climbing up."

My heart hammered as I watched him expectantly, my eyes glued to those bundles in his hands.

Ellen giggled. "Well, they're probably disappointed then, because I wasn't wearing any!"

"Poor slobs," the lieutenant mused as he looked inside the bags to check the labels for the correct size, nodded in satisfaction, and passed them over to me.

I peeped inside as my hands shook, where I found four silver, neatly folded, extra long, one-piece flight suits covered with transparent plastic wrappings. I looked up at the lieutenant as he watched me closely. "What's the first favor?"

"Captain, I want you to party with us at the O Club tonight."

"That's it? That's the favor?" I swallowed nervously. "Lieutenant, I-I need to tell you I'm a happily married man … I've got a wife and daughter and … and a little boy on the way … at least I hope it's a boy …"

He grinned. "I didn't ask you to compromise your marriage, Captain, although technically it wouldn't be *illegal* if I had."

Though he still hadn't used the "Sir" word with me, from some inner depth I sensed I had just passed a test with him, and that it was important for me to have done so. "Well, uh, okay then, and thank you, Lieutenant! I'll see you later at the club!"

I hurried out with as much dignity as I could muster, unable to believe my good fortune of having four of the most sought-after flight suits in the world, each perfectly my own size, which was hard to do even with normal clothes due to my height. What kind of man was this weird lieutenant with all the heavy hardware on his chest?

I tried on the first flight suit, which fit as if tailored for me. In pure ecstasy, I quickly tried on the remaining three, even though they had the same size labels. Each fit perfectly, I saw as I admired myself in the mirror. After showering, I slipped one on and admired myself again, fearing any minute I was going to wake up and find this was only a dream. I folded the remaining three flight suits carefully, placed them gently back in their wrappings, and set out jauntily for the officers' club.

The lieutenant was holding court with his coven of lovelies when I entered. He waved and made room at the crowded table for me as I ignored the envious stares of the non-aviators around us, feeling positively dashing as I pulled up a chair to sit down in the middle of his group.

"Now that's the style, Captain!" he praised as he motioned for the bartender. "What's your pleasure?"

"A screwdriver, thanks, Lieutenant," I replied gaily.

"Barkeep, bring the captain here a double screwdriver, and put one for yourself on my tab, if you please."

"Thank you, Sir." The bartender hurried off to fill the order.

The lieutenant lifted his drink in toast as the bartender sat mine in front of me. "To your wife and one and a half kids back home, Captain!"

Ellen nuzzled up to him and hooked her arm through his as one of the other nurses leaned over and breathed in my ear. "Hi, I'm Rebecca. I *love* tall men. They say you can measure a man's masculinity in direct proportion to his legs. You've got *really* long legs!"

I gulped my drink and lurched as her fingers slid down my thigh.

The lieutenant laughed as he draped an arm around Ellen and pulled her close. "I can't control them, Captain, you'll just have to be firm with them, no pun intended."

The night became a haze. I do know I went back to my quarters alone—somewhat reluctantly maybe, but alone. I also know that at some point I was up on the table dancing some gyrating dance with Rebecca's backside pressed to the front of me while Alice hugged me from the rear. At the time it all seemed perfectly natural, but in the light of morning, with my pounding headache and pulsating flashes of guilt for my near betrayal of Nancy, I wondered if I had lost my mind.

And so, being the morally weak, easily corruptible man I am, I became an unsuspecting disciple of U.S. Army Second Lieutenant John Joseph Sharpe, blissfully unaware that my life would never be quite the same again.

Orders assigning me to my permanent unit awaited me when I checked in at the orderly room after breakfast.

"The 120th Aviation Company?" I mused. "I don't think I've ever heard of them."

"The Deans are about as good as it gets over here, Sir," the specialist advised. "They're a renowned VIP unit that flies all the top brass around. Only the best pilots get assigned there. Pardon me, Sir, but you need to hustle on over to the helipad or you're gonna miss their chopper inbound to pick you up."

I rushed back to my temporary quarters, grabbed my gear, and set out for the helipad to catch my flight, happily anticipating my assignment to a VIP unit, which in essence meant I'd never be expected to fly into harm's way with such precious cargo aboard. When I reached the helipad, the lieutenant and his bevy of nurses were there.

"Morning, Captain," he greeted, tossing a haphazard salute in my general direction. "Was beginning to wonder if you'd make it."

"Good morning, Lieutenant," I acknowledged, snapping a crisp salute back at him. "Got your orders too, I see. Where are they assigning you?"

"I'm going with you of course, Captain, where else, since all the *good* units are standing down? From what I hear, the 120th is a little suck-ass rear echelon unit located in Long Binh, but on the bright side, our lovely ladies here have been assigned to the field hospital there, so things aren't all bad, I guess."

I experienced a slight sinking sensation as a helicopter descended to pick us up on the fabled helipad at the 21st Replacement Depot. The lieutenant ushered nurses Ellen, Rebecca, and Alice aboard before climbing in after me, and we were flown bag and baggage a short distance to the Long Binh airfield located within the huge, sprawling perimeter of the base camp. The aircraft deposited us in front of the flight operations center, where the lieutenant and I received an inordinate amount of attention from the other aviators as we dismounted due to the finery of our silver flight suits. A waiting jeep whisked the three nurses away to the field hospital as I surveyed the airfield, which was small by most standards and more of a helicopter base than a fixed wing facility, with one narrow, short runway on the far side of the fifty or so scattered helicopters parked in their sandbagged revetments before us. Three medium-sized hangars flanked two small metal Quonset huts behind the revetments. Concertina wire encircled the whole airfield, with sandbagged bunkers crouching at intervals just inside the wire forming a small defensive perimeter within the larger base camp stretching around us. I found it a dismal, squalid place squatting in shimmering heat waves rising from the green metal engineer strips forming a base over the red clay underfoot.

Sharpe and I met individually with Captain Nichols, the Dean flight operations officer, who scheduled us for in-country check-rides the following morning after depositing our flight records with him. Captain Nichols then had us transported, courtesy of his jeep and driver, to another miniature enclosure within the Long Binh base camp called the RMK compound, which quartered the aviators of the Deans. The billeting sergeant assigned us individual rooms consisting of a relatively bleak ten-by-twenty-foot space within one of the five barracks, the center of each housing a community shower facility with accommodating commodes and stalls for the occupants. Across from the row of barracks stood a large officers' dining facility, and beside this, an officers' club.

We deposited our gear and drew our bedding before Captain Nichols' driver again carted us from the RMK facility to the company orderly room located among the barracks of the NCO and enlisted men of the company situated a short distance away. We formally signed in on the duty roster, deposited our personnel files, and filled out various personal information forms. With these tedious tasks finished, we were ushered into our new commander's office for formal interviews.

Major Crystal directed us to two overstuffed chairs in front of his desk. As he studied our career sheets in front of him, we studied him, finding a slim, medium height chap with well-groomed black hair turning to a dashing gray at the temples, wearing tailored jungle fatigues. He lifted speculative brown eyes to assess us, bringing *martinet* to mind as I shifted uneasily when his focus rested on me.

"Captain Hess, I see you have spent extensive time, some four years I believe, at Fort Rucker, Alabama, as a ground instructor. I believe you will be a valuable asset to the Yellow Platoon." He smiled as though he had just bestowed an honor upon me.

I smiled back. "Thank you, Sir. I'm sure I'll find the assignment most rewarding." *Just the right touch of kiss-ass,* I congratulated myself.

His eyes soften pleasurably before assuming an air of delicate distaste as he shifted to the lieutenant. "Lieutenant Sharpe, you are a Mustang, I see."

Sharpe's eyes narrowed. "A '*Mustang*', Major?"

The commander's lip curled in disdainful amusement. "You are unfamiliar with the term, Lieutenant?"

Sharpe shrugged. "Back in Texas where I come from it means a scrawny little wild range horse that nobody wants, Major."

It was obvious the lieutenant's refusal to use the *Sir* word was annoying the commander, as it had me, though Sharpe seemed very skilled at avoiding the simple courtesy without crossing the line of outright insubordination.

"The term, Lieutenant, in Army vernacular, refers to a former enlisted man who aspires to be an officer," the major replied as if lecturing a retardant student.

"If it's all the same to you, Major, I *am* an officer, and don't *aspire* to be anything less," Sharpe challenged.

The major flushed. "As you prefer, Lieutenant, as you prefer. Now let's see, due to your, uh ... *background* ... I think you'll be well suited in our Red Platoon."

"If that's the gun platoon I requested over at flight ops, then I'm delighted, Major," Sharpe replied.

Major Crystal blinked. "You *requested* the Red Platoon? Surely you jest? Why would you want to be assigned there?"

The lieutenant shrugged. "They're the only thing you've got capable of fighting, Major."

Major Crystal smiled. "But they don't have a mission now, Lieutenant. Apparently you haven't gotten the word—we've stood down from direct combat operations."

"Mission or no mission, Major, I didn't volunteer to come back over here to be a high-priced taxi driver for a bunch of REMFs."

"REMFs, Lieutenant? Exactly what does that term mean?"

Sharpe looked him in the eye. "The term, Major, in *Army vernacular*, means *Rear Echelon Mother Fuckers*."

The color changed three shades in Major Crystal's face. I had an urge to duck as the corners of his lips twitched and his left eyelid fluttered, keeping rhythm with a throbbing vein in his neck, which appeared to be growing larger by the moment.

"Th-That … is *all*, Lieutenant! You are *excused!*"

The major's whole body was twitching now, I noted apprehensively. Sensing an opportune time to make my own escape, I stood with the lieutenant, saluted, and made a hurried departure with him.

Once we cleared the orderly room, I expelled my breath. "You were really pushing it in there, Lieutenant Sharpe."

He grinned. "He's a little smart ass, ain't he, Captain? It's fun to bust their balls when they're so full of themselves."

"Lieutenant, you have a tendency to play a very dangerous game with superior officers."

"I've never met an officer *superior* to me, Captain, only ones senior in rank."

"It's been my experience that when you deliberately crush someone's nuts it eventually comes back to haunt you."

He scowled. "I appreciate the advice, Captain, but I could care less about that pompous little asshole. He insulted me twice in there, which was one over his lifetime allotment. For the record, he's now on my shit list."

"Lieutenant, you just insulted his *whole command* and their *entire mission* over here," I explained in exasperation. "No doubt you just made the top of *his* list too!"

"I meant no personal disrespect to the other aviators in the company, Captain. Somebody has to perform their little pussy mission, but personally it's just not my cup of tea. I'm honored to fly gunships because frankly, if it's not combat related, I'm not too interested in dealing with it. But for him to insult me because I came up through the ranks was unpardonable. Who the hell does he think he is anyway?"

"He's a *field grade* officer and our *commander!*" I scolded. "You can't insult him to his face like that!"

"Wrong, Captain. He's simply a little eaten-up-with-himself miniature field-marshal-aspirant who doesn't know the first thing about real soldiering. Unfortunately some dumb-ass pinned a major's oak leaf on him and put him in charge, so we'll just have to deal with the situation as best we can."

"If you don't mind my asking, why did you volunteer to fly in the Red Platoon?"

"Just like I told that little pristine despot back there, Captain, I don't want to be a taxi driver for a bunch of rear-echelon pukes. I want to be where the action is."

"But the war's virtually over for us, Lieutenant. Like he said, we've turned the fighting over to the South Vietnamese Army now. What are you going to do with a *gunship?*"

He looked at me as if I were a dimwit. "I'm going to *kill* something with it, Captain, what do you *think* you do with a gunship?"

I shook my head in frustration. "Okay, Lieutenant, have it your way. But that's a damned good way to get yourself killed, if you ask me."

He swung into the jeep. "I'll meet you at the O Club later on, Captain. I've got a promise to keep to a pretty little lass in half an hour."

I drew back, repulsed. "The mile-high club?"

"Yeah, want to tag along?"

"*No!*"

"Aye-Aye, Captain. Catch you later then." He threw me a half-hearted salute, flicked his hand to the driver, and off they sped.

They were two blocks away before it occurred to me he had just commandeered our borrowed jeep and that I was going to have to walk back to the RMK compound.

Damn!

CHAPTER 3

That evening I sat despondent at a table in the RMK officers' club nursing a scotch and water after deliberately changing into one of my old flight suits before I came over so as not to attract attention. After introducing myself to several aviators around me and receiving a cool reception on each occasion, a first lieutenant approached my table.

"Captain Hess, Sir?"

I looked up eagerly. "Yes?"

"You probably don't remember me, but you were one of my instructors in air navigation back at Mother Rucker two years ago."

"I think I do," I replied hesitantly, trying to put a name with the face. "Lieutenant Carmichael, right?"

He pulled out a chair at my table. "You got it, Sir. Welcome to the Nam. Buy you a drink?"

I held up my half-empty glass. "Thanks, but I was headed back to my room after this one. I'm not much of a drinker, I'm afraid."

"When did you get in, Sir?"

"This morning. How long have you been here?"

"Almost a year, Sir. I'm heading back to the land of the big PX in a few days."

Waves of envy enveloped me. "Congratulations, Lieutenant."

He looked around warily. "Have you got this place figured out yet, Sir?"

I scowled. "Not really. The aviators here don't seem very friendly."

He smiled lamely. "These guys choose their friends carefully. They view you as a potential threat to their established pecking order. They're waiting to see what you might have to offer them in the way of their personal advancement before they're willing to commit to a friendship. Let me give you an initial understanding of how things work."

He indicated the bar behind him. "What you see there at the bar is nothing but green hats sitting in casual splendor, talking quietly as they display their royal selves."

I looked at the half dozen aviators sitting at the bar, each with a green baseball hat on the bar in front of him.

"The first tier of affluence within the hierarchy of the Deans is the Green Platoon," he continued. "You simply aren't shit unless you're in the Green Platoon. They fly all the high-level brass and diplomats. Only the most skilled pilots and the best aircraft are assigned to their exclusive VIP section. They have graduates' mortarboards painted on the sides of their highly waxed and painted UH-1H aircraft, which also sport plush leather seats and noise-absorbing padding. The pilots themselves are mostly the salty old master aviators composed of chief warrant officers. They rarely associate with the rest of us in the company. They are the elite of the elite, and you're expected to know it and act accordingly when you are perchance in their majestic presence."

He nodded at the grouping of tables in front of the bar. "That is where the yellow hats hang out, who you'll note are drinking lightly and talking animatedly, hoping to catch the ear of one of the Green Platoon pilots and be invited over to have a drink with him in order to showcase their potential."

I looked at the dozen or so aviators sitting at tables near the bar, each with his yellow baseball hat on the table in front of him.

Lieutenant Carmichael leaned toward me and lowered his voice. "The second tier within the Dean hierarchy is the Yellow Platoon. They're the wannabes who fly the full colonels and lesser diplomats. The Yellow Platoon is basically a proving ground for pilots aspiring to reach the exalted ranks of the Green Platoon. They have Snoopy emblems painted on the sides of their UH-1H aircraft, but they don't get the wax, special paint, leather seats, or sound-absorbing treatment. The prima donnas in the Yellow Platoon take themselves and their mission seriously—which basically is to look for an opportunity to kiss ass and climb up the ladder to the Green Platoon."

He took a sip of his drink and motioned for the Vietnamese waitress to bring him another before continuing. "The area to the right of the bar here where we're sitting is no-man's land. This is where you and the other four or five newbies are expected to sit until you are invited into the ranks of the Yellow Platoon. That takes a week to a month, so be patient."

He took his drink from the waitress and paid her, leaving a small tip. "At the far right of the room in the back corner there is the riff-raff of the Red Platoon, drinking fugitively and pretending to belong here at all."

I turned to my right to observe a large group of somewhat subdued aviators with red baseball caps on the table before them.

"Now they're a story unto themselves, Captain. No one is real sure where they came from or what to do with them since they are, regrettably, *here.* It was some sort of a system glitch or something in all of the confusion of our screwed up Vietnamization program. During the stand-down they got assigned to the Deans, but nobody knows how or why. The Deans for the most part are a tad embarrassed by that lowly gaggle of roustabouts who fly the old antiquated Charlie-model gunships. Even more distressing, they have a fierce Arkansas razorback *pig* with huge tusks painted on the sides of their aircraft as their emblem. The pilots of the Red Platoon are astutely aware of their unloved step-child status within the company, and a few work hard to climb up the social ladder to Yellow Platoon status. Most don't give a damn and ignore the rest of us, who just as judiciously ignore them back. If you ask one of them their unit, they invariably reply 'The Razorbacks,' instead of the more correct 'The Deans' or the more formal '120th Aviation Company.'"

He sipped his drink and chuckled. "There you have it, Captain. It's all a perfectly organized social circle with everything in its proper perspective, with every-one knowing his proper place in the overall scheme of things." He toasted me grandly with his drink. "And I'm sure as hell glad to get out of here, Sir. If I had a whole year left like you do, I'd just slit my throat and be done with it."

I nodded glumly. "Thanks for the encouragement."

The low murmur of drinking men faded as completely as if someone threw a switch as every eye in the place stared with envy at the silver flight suit Lieutenant Sharpe wore as he sauntered into the club. He stood near the door allowing his eyes to adjust to the dim interior as he absorbed the distinguished surroundings, then walked jauntily over to the bar to the rhythm of the soft background music and carelessly moved the green cap of a chief warrant officer sitting there to clear a space for himself. He ordered a Jim Beam and Coke as everyone watched in shock.

He glanced at the glaring chief warrant officer beside him as he waited for his drink. "Hey, Chief, how you doing?"

"*Indians* are *chiefs*, I'm a '*Mister*,'" the chief warrant officer growled, referring to the well known status of warrant officer, a rank between a noncommissioned officer and a commissioned officer, who all knew resented being called "Sir," a rendering reserved exclusively for the commissioned officer corps. It was common knowledge they were very particular about being addressed as "Mister," which is their proper title, especially the highest-ranking warrant officer fourth class, referred to as chief warrant officer. Only close friends dared call them "Chief," however. Though technically a lieutenant outranks a chief warrant officer, due to the latter's years of experience and training required to reach that level only majors and above, or field grade officers, were considered their equal. It was also widely known that chief warrant officers loved to humiliate smart-assed second lieutenants and put them in their place. Even first lieutenants and us captains, referred to as "company grade officers," were wary of their legendary wrath. Basically, they were just grumpy old bad-assed dudes, and you were generally ahead of the game if you didn't screw around with them.

Sharpe glanced at the man. "So how long have you been suffering through menopause, Chief?" He turned his back to the bar, propped his elbows on the edge, and studied the plethora of yellow hats on the tables before him as their owners watched him in gleeful anticipation waiting for the hammer to fall. "Now who in hell would want to wear a puke-yellow hat, Chief?" he asked loudly as several of the Yellow Platoon aviators stiffened. "*Soooooooouiiieee!*" he yelled in the thick silence as several of the Razorback pilots stiffened. "Where the hell is *The Hog?*"

I was amazed. In less than two minutes he had managed to offend every pilot in the room. The silence was deafening as I studied my half-empty glass closely, avoiding eye contact with him, praying he wouldn't come over to sit down with me and Lieutenant Carmichael.

One of the Razorback pilots in the back of the room stood, walked deliberately through the penetrating silence, and stopped before him menacingly. "Are you inquiring about the *Razorbacks,* Lieutenant?"

Sharpe looked him up and down insolently. "Hell no, I'm not *inquiring* about the little *piglets,* and pardon me for not having the fucking patience for parlor talk, but I'm looking for the nastiest son-of-a-bitching *gun-pilot* in Nam. I'm a *hog* now, and I'm here to kick some *gook ass*! Let it be known that from now on I want all of those friggin' little slopes for myself, because I *don't* like to *share.*

That makes *me* the meanest hog in the Razorbacks! Now where's your *Top Hog*? I'm going to elbow his ass away from the trough so there'll be *more* for *me!*"

The Razorback pilot grinned and swept his hand to the rear of the room where the dozen or so pilots from the Red Platoon were watching intently, with most breaking out into wide grins because this crazy little lieutenant spoke their language. "Lieutenant, the Razorbacks are located back there."

Sharpe scowled. "That's the *first* thing we're going to change! The lights are bad back there, the music is distorted, and the service sucks. If we're the best, we deserve the best. Get off your asses and get up here in front where you belong, Razorbacks! The next round's on me!"

The startled Razorback pilots eyed each other uneasily. And then, hesitantly at first and then in a laughing clamor, the insurgents stood and moved as a group to the front of the bar to cluster around their strange new lieutenant and greet him individually as the bartender hurriedly filled their glasses.

Just that quickly Sharpe upset the whole social balance of the mighty Deans and in a stroke bestowed a measure of pride to a browbeaten, demoralized group. Within minutes he had the jukebox cranked up to maximum volume and the Razorbacks grouped at the front tables around him as the Yellow Platoon eased away cautiously and the Green Platoon fled for the door to escape the disrupted harmony of their former domain.

Members of the Red Platoon were soon partying hard with their newfound hero, who won them over completely as they drank and toasted and whooped and hollered. Early on after the power shift I eased out the door, slipped back to my room to unpack, and dashed off a quick letter to Nancy filling her in on the latest adventures of the indomitable Lieutenant Sharpe.

Well, most of them anyway … I left out the mile-high club part.

The next morning I weathered a grueling oral exam followed by an exhausting two-hour check ride covering all emergency procedures involving a series of running landings and auto rotations with a stern, aloof unit standardization instructor pilot. Although rusty and somewhat shaky at the controls, he reluctantly certified me as a mission ready copilot in the Deans. Following a short break for a quick lunch, I made my way back to the airfield for my in-country orientation flight, where I was introduced to a red headed warrant officer named Daniels.

"Captain Hess, welcome to the Deans," he greeted as we shook hands.

"Wish I could say I was glad to be here," I replied contritely.

"The first six months are the toughest," he advised. "The last six go considerably faster. I'm rotating back to the real world in two weeks, I'm happy to say." He handed me a map sealed in plastic with different colored circles drawn on it. "We're located here in Long Binh, just outside Saigon, in the heart of the III Corps area of operations. Our AO has the most diversified topography in the entire country. North of us is dense forest and the Central Highlands. East is Saigon and the sea, south is the Mekong Delta, and west is mostly triple canopy jungle bordering Cambodia. In the center are the vast rice fields. Grab your helmet and I'll point out the key terrain features and friendly outposts."

My stomach fluttered. "You mean we'll be flying over enemy territory all by ourselves?"

He shrugged. "Everything outside our base camp is enemy territory, Captain."

After preflighting our helicopter, we were soon airborne with Mr. Daniels at the controls and me trying to stay orientated on the map. He climbed to two thousand feet and flew over a scattering of narrow paved roads with sporadic clusters of tin roofed houses, fenced in storage facilities, and groupings of petroleum storage tanks toward the huge capital city of Saigon in the indistinct, hazy distance.

"Not much to see here," he advised. "This is mostly an industrial district. Not much happens in this area."

He turned eastward as we approached Saigon and skirted the dingy, smog covered city below. I sat forward to curiously study the crowded streets filled with throngs of sarong clad people and multitudes of motor scooters, three wheeled Lambrettas, overloaded trucks, and chugging buses, all scurrying about in disorderly chaos amid the permeating stench of rotting garbage hanging in the humid air.

"There are three million refugees down there, most of them living in alleys and on the streets," Mr. Daniels briefed as we skimmed overhead. "The kids beg, the young women prostitute themselves, the young men steal, and the old folks do whatever they can to survive in their desperate little world."

He swung out over the harbor filled with huge cargo ships and hundreds of tiny sampans and turned south, skirting the coast as he called out meaningless names of scattered settlements while I tried to track them on the map. Below my feet, the mostly barren scrub brush of the coast soon gave way to a vast swampland stretching off into the horizon with glints of water reflecting from its muddy mass broken by occasional thick clusters of vegetation surrounded by a multitude of streams and narrow waterways running in a myriad of untraceable directions.

"This is the Mekong Delta, Captain," Mr. Daniels pointed out as I stared down with misgivings at the uninviting tangle of water and weeds. "This region is a major supply route for the Vietcong. Those gunboats are the Vietnamese Navy who patrol the waterways in an attempt to stem the flow of war materials to the VC. Those little wooden sampans house whole families who rarely set foot on dry land. They primarily fish and smuggle to survive. Off to our right is one of the South Vietnamese Army outposts which dots the whole country, each manned by approximately two hundred ARVN soldiers and a couple of American advisers. I'd hate to be one of those poor bastards— they're nothing more than live bait. One or two a month get overrun and destroyed."

I studied the strange, isolated triangular earthen and mud enclosure surrounded by a dry moat filled with sharpened bamboo stakes proudly flying the yellow flag with three red stripes of the South Vietnamese government.

He swung the aircraft back to the northwest and we were soon flying over a thick, uninviting mass of greenery, which sent an ominous shudder passing through me as I instinctively shrank down in my armored seat.

"This is War Zone C, Captain, pure Indian country," Mr. Daniels reported as my heart rate increased tempo. "That mountain over there is called Nui Ba Den, or Black Virgin Mountain."

I studied the solitary mound rising out of the otherwise flat terrain protruding some twelve hundred feet into the air.

"We have a Special Forces camp on the very top, and one of our major bases located at the bottom, called Tay Ninh, but the VC owns the area in between. You'll notice on your map that part of Cambodia juts into South Vietnam here, which is called the Parrot's Beak due to its shape. The Ho Chi Minh Trail, the main supply route from North Vietnam, empties into South Vietnam right here."

"I wouldn't want to go down in this area," I observed fearfully.

"No you wouldn't, Captain. They say it's so dark under that triple canopy jungle it's like moonlight, the temperature hovers around a hundred and ten degrees because there's no air circulation, and the vegetation is so thick you can hold your arm out in front of you and lose sight of you hand. If you ever have the misfortune of crashing in this shit, chances are they'll never find you." I inhaled the heady smell of decaying vegetation as I imagined the deep gloom below the thick foliage flashing under us.

Thankfully, he swung the aircraft back to the east and we were soon flying over perfectly spaced trees on the fringe of the trackless jungle.

"This is the Michelin Rubber Tree Plantation," Mr. Daniels informed me. "A good part of the world's rubber comes from this area. That darker patch of forest to the north is the Bo Loi Woods, which is part of the Iron Triangle, a Vietcong stronghold we've fought over for years. If you don't mind, we won't fly over that area because it's loaded with anti-aircraft guns and bad guys."

"Fine by me," I agreed readily.

"Off in the distance, you can see the coast and Saigon, where we started. Now I'm going to turn south and show you the breadbasket of the country."

I stared down at the vast network of squares filled with water and stooped peasants tilling rice in the blistering heat as a humid stench assaulted my nostrils. Spaced throughout the area were small patches of dry land with groupings of mud and thatch houses. Thick lines of green shrubbery, which Mr. Daniels called *hedgerows*, divided the smaller mud and water squares into larger squares. Throughout the area were the triangular ARVN compounds, and at even more irregular intervals, small hamlets with strange names such as Trang Bang, Bam Me Tuit, Cu Chi, and My Ly, which I tried to locate on my map as Mr. Daniels pointed them out.

"The peasants live in those primitive hooches with dirt floors and no plumbing," Mr. Daniels continued. "They don't have hospitals, schools, electricity, running water, or even outhouses. As you can see, only narrow dirt roads and foot trails interconnect the area. Their whole livelihood is their tiny patch of mud and the rice they harvest. The middle class peasants might have a water buffalo and a wooden cart, but most don't even have that. They are taxed by both the South Vietnamese government and the Vietcong, leaving them very little to survive on themselves. They're a sad, pitiful lot, and suffer the harshest burden of this stupid war." He dropped down and flew low over one of the crude structures as the old men and women stooped over in the paddies nervously straightened up to shield their eyes and watch us pass.

The diversity of the area was overpowering, the strangeness of it all mixing in with my fear of coming under fire at any minute and brought down in flames. Mercifully, Mr. Daniels lifted us back up to five thousand feet and Long Binh soon appeared on the horizon.

After we landed, I thanked Mr. Daniels and hitched a ride back to the RMK compound, totally exhausted by my long day and filled with dread for the year stretching before me in this god-awful place. After dinner, I wandered over for a calming drink at the club, where I found the Razorbacks had taken over the front of the facility and had the music cranked up. The long bar stood all but empty as the Green Platoon had again fled from the crime scene. The Yellow Platoon now sulked in the back of the club where the Red Platoon had formerly gathered, but most shocking of all, eight nurses were scattered among the hard partying members of the Red Platoon.

Ellen, the newest member of the mile-high club, with her tiny silver wings notably pinned to her chest, cuddled up in the lieutenant's lap drunkenly playing with the zippers on his flight suit as he held court. He motioned me over to a chair beside him, where I hesitantly seated myself ignoring the dubious stares directed at me from members of the Yellow Platoon.

Sharpe motioned for the Vietnamese waitress and ordered me a screwdriver. "I was about to give up on you, Captain. Get all squared away on your in-country check ride?"

"All ready to go," I announced. "How about you?"

"I floundered through a four-hour transition and a two-hour check ride in the Charlie-model gunships to earn my in-country wings. Now I need to call in that favor you owe me."

My heart increased tempo. "Uh, okay, Lieutenant. What's the request?"

"I took the liberty of making an appointment for you with Major Crystal in the morning at 0800 hours. Tell him you want to be reassigned to the Razorbacks."

I sputtered, spilling my screwdriver down my chin. "*Do what?*"

He shifted Nurse Ellen on his lap, who was sleeping contentedly with her head on his shoulder now. "We need you."

I swallowed my panic. "Lieutenant, are you crazy?"

He grinned evilly. "Captain, it *is* a *legal* request, right?"

My stomach lurched. "Why do you want *me?*"

"Look around you, Captain. We ain't got a lick of clout in this platoon. All of the Razorbacks are warrant officer ones and twos. The only commissioned officers in the whole platoon are First Lieutenant Owens over there and myself, and that little pussy wants to join the Yellow Platoon. By the way, get him reassigned in exchange for your transfer and then I can be your second in command."

My mind raced considering escape routes from the trap. "And why is it so important to have me in the platoon?"

"These poor bastards have been at the bottom of the shit barrel long enough. They've got twelve aircraft in their platoon, but only four are flight-worthy because they're at the end of the priority list for maintenance. Half of their guns and rocket pods don't work because they can't get spare parts. They haven't flown a real mission in five months. They go out and fly around Long Binh in circles, supposedly looking for the enemy. Nobody gives a damn about them and they're just wasting away. You and I are about to change all that."

I sucked in a deep breath to fight off the hypertension threatening to suffocate me. "*We* are? *How?*"

"Captain, we need your rank. I did a quick check with the company clerk. You happen to be the third-highest-ranking officer in the company behind Major Crystal and Captain Nichols. As such, you outrank the Yellow Platoon leader by two weeks."

I cleared my throat. "Really? Nobody told me that. And if Major Crystal denies my request for transfer?"

"Captain, they assigned you as a *pilot* in the Yellow Platoon. They should have made you the *platoon leader* because of your seniority, but it's well known the Yellow Platoon leader is one of Major Crystal's little favorites, so he's trying to pull a fast one on you. If you push it, Crystal has only two choices—give you the Yellow Platoon, as is your right, or allow you to transfer to the Red Platoon to get you out of the way."

I nodded uneasily. "Okay, but once I'm assigned to the Razorbacks, what then? I don't know the first thing about gunships or their mission. Hueys are all I've ever flown, and sparingly at that to maintain my flight status. I'm afraid I'm not much of a pilot and wouldn't be much help to you because I don't know my butt from a hole in the ground."

"Not to worry, Captain. A helicopter's a helicopter. Hell, before today I'd never flown a gunship myself. Basically it's just a souped-up slick with some rockets and miniguns strapped on the sides. I'll teach you everything you need to know about guns as I learn myself. And their mission is pretty simple—find the enemy and destroy him."

"But you just said two-thirds of their aircraft can't fly, half of their guns and rockets won't shoot, and they don't have a real mission!"

"I *also* said you and I were going to *change* all that." He bent down to Ellen in his lap. "Darling, you need to wake up now, my leg's going to sleep." When she awarded him with a drowsy moan, he lifted her in his arms, walked over to one of the warrant officers at the next table, and deposited her gently on his lap, where she snuggled up to the startled aviator in contentment and rested her head on his shoulder.

"Keep an eye on her for me, if you don't mind," the lieutenant instructed.

"Lieutenant Sharpe, please don't ask this of me," I begged like a puppy as he sat back down. "I've got a wife and a kid and another one due in a couple of months. I'm not a career man. I'm getting out of the Army after my tour over here is up. I just want to get home safely. I don't want to kill anybody, and I sure as hell don't want to get killed. I'll help you find another officer who will better suit your needs."

He shook his head decisively. "Sorry, Captain, but most of those reasons are exactly why I want you. I guarantee you I'll keep you out of harm's way. You have my word on it. Hell, I don't care if you don't even fly. I need to get these guys whipped back into shape and instill some pride and fighting spirit back into them. The thing is, I can parlay your seniority into enough power to overcome all the obstacles we currently face in order to reach that goal. I'll build you the best gun unit in Nam before I'm through—something you'll be damned proud of."

"But the war's almost *over*, Lieutenant! We're standing down and turning things over to the Vietnamese. In a year we'll all be out of here and safely back home. Why would you even *want* to do something like that?"

He fixed me with a level stare. "Because that's what soldiers do. They fight. I want to fight, and these guys around me here want to fight. That's why they're gun pilots to begin with. We've got to give them the opportunity to do their job." He stared hard at me as I hung my head.

The Razorback pilots and the nurses around us were perfectly still and watchful as I pondered the situation. This little lieutenant was treacherous. He was smart and a master manipulator. But damn it, he was also fascinating to be around. It would be interesting to watch him operate. Besides, a deal was a deal. What he was asking of me certainly wasn't illegal, and I really had no honorable way out of accepting his request. I looked at all the eager faces staring hopefully at me, each wanting to believe the lieutenant could really pull this off for them, as a little voice inside me shouted *run*!

Instead, I sighed. "I'd be honored to serve as your platoon leader."

The guys and dolls around us burst into cheers as the lieutenant smiled.

Major Crystal was stunned the next morning when I met with him to request the transfer to the Razorbacks. He seemed initially inclined to disapprove the request until I pointed out my seniority to the Yellow

Platoon leader, at which time he quickly granted the reassignment and ushered me out of his office before I came to my senses. He even approved the transfer of Lieutenant Owens from the Razorbacks to the Yellow Platoon. When I cleared the door to the orderly room, Sharpe was waiting in a jeep.

He tossed a sloppy salute in my direction. "Any problems, Captain?"

"No, you pretty much had the situation read—I'm your new platoon leader. Now what?"

"Now, Captain, hop in and I'll drive you to the airfield to meet your new platoon. They're a pretty ragged and demoralized group, but give me a few days and I'll get them straightened out for you."

"How many men are there?"

"About fifty, Captain. We're a little short-handed, but we'll get the rest of them back before the end of the day."

"And how will we do that?"

"By applying a little judicious blackmail, Captain."

"*Blackmail* is *illegal*, Lieutenant! We have an *agreement!*"

He cut his eyes at me as he hit the starter. "I'll tone it down a bit to more along the lines of *judicious intimidation* then, Captain, if that'll make you happy. Just let me handle things."

"Who did you borrow the jeep from?" I asked as I settled into the passenger seat.

"I didn't borrow it, Captain, it's yours, and we've got five more coming."

"*What?* There aren't five jeeps in the whole company!" I protested.

"They're not company jeeps, Captain. I traded for them."

"You did *what?* With *who?* What did you *trade* for them?"

"Now, Captain, if I'm going to be your assistant platoon leader, you're going to have to let me handle the insignificant little details while you focus on the bigger picture. Knowing too much can hinder our operations."

I glared at him. "Sharpe, you've already got me doing something illegal, haven't you?"

"Of course not, Captain," he reassured me righteously. "Besides, if you think about it, nothing's illegal unless you get caught. That's another reason you don't need to be personally involved in the details—you can maintain deniability if I ever need you to bail my ass out of a jam."

My heart pounded against my ribcage in an unhealthy stutter as he smiled complacently and lurched off.

CHAPTER 4

We wheeled into the airfield complex where the Red Platoon stood neatly drawn up in three different formations awaiting our arrival. Nineteen warrant officer pilots stood in the first formation, with Sharpe and me making twenty-one in total, leaving us three short. The second section consisted of twelve crew chiefs and twelve door gunners, one of each assigned to the twelve aircraft, which was the full complement authorized. The first echelon maintenance crews made up the last section—fifteen of them where a total of thirty were normally assigned.

After Sharpe and I walked the line greeting the men individually, he dispersed them back into the hangar as the maintenance sergeant handed him two sheets of paper.

"Now I'll go get the rest of our maintenance crew, Captain," Sharpe informed me.

"Where are they?" I asked.

"They're temporarily reassigned to the Yellow Platoon to supplement their maintenance effort ... can you believe that shit? But I'll go get that shit straightened out right now and pick up the spare parts we need as a bonus."

"Um, is this by chance where the blackmail part comes into play, Lieutenant?" I questioned.

"*Judicious intimidation,* Captain," he corrected. "I'll be back in a few minutes."

"I somehow feel this driving need to accompany you," I advised.

"It'll go a lot smoother if you just let me handle things, Captain."

"*I'll* feel more at ease if I *go with you,* Lieutenant," I insisted.

He grimaced. "Well, okay, if you insist, Captain, but just stand off to the side and scowl while I handle the situation. Understand?"

"Scowl?"

"Yeah, Captain, they need to know we're pissed and mean business."

I hurried after him as he turned on his heel and tromped off toward the Yellow Platoon hangar. There one of the maintenance personnel pointed out the platoon sergeant.

"Yes, Lieutenant?" the sergeant asked when he shuffled around after Sharpe tapped him on the shoulder.

Sharpe handed him the two sheets of paper the Red Platoon maintenance sergeant had given him. "Assemble all our men temporarily assigned to you on this list here for me, Sergeant, and then gather up all the parts on the other list here so they can transfer them over to our place on their way out."

The maintenance sergeant glanced at the two lists, eyes narrowing. "I think you need to take this issue up with my platoon leader, Sir."

Sharpe nodded. "Fine, go get him then, Sergeant, time's a wasting."

Within minutes Captain Rawlings, the Yellow Platoon Leader, approached us with his maintenance sergeant in tow. "Captain Hess, what is all this foolishness?"

"Simple, Captain, we want our men and spare parts back," the lieutenant replied.

"I was addressing your Captain here, Lieutenant!" Rawlings snapped.

"My Captain is too pissed to discuss the situation with you, Captain. He's agreed to let me arbitrate things before they get out of hand."

Captain Rawlings glanced at me, whereupon I knit my eyebrows together in what I hoped was a scowl, and then focused back on Sharpe curiously. "What seems to be his problem, Lieutenant?"

"My Captain outranks you and should by rights command the Yellow Platoon. I've convinced him that if he'll let matters stand and accept the command of the Red Platoon instead, we'll get back all our men and all the maintenance items on our list—now, today, right this very minute—and together build the Razorbacks into something he'll be proud to call his own. Luckily he prefers guns to slicks, so if you'll just assemble all the men and parts on those two lists, we'll be on our way."

"Does Major Crystal know about this?" Rawlings demanded.

"That's where my Captain was headed when I cut him off," the lieutenant advised. He then glanced over his shoulder at me and leaned forward to whisper something to Captain Rawlings, who stiffened and glared at me.

"Sergeant, get these men and parts together immediately!" he directed before hurrying off without a backward glance.

It took us the remainder of the day to get our men rounded up and truck all the parts over to our hangar. Our pilots showed up with cases of beer, which they spread around joyfully, and then pitched in to help the maintenance crews sort the parts as the crew chiefs and gunners eagerly set to work on their birds.

"What did you whisper to Captain Rawlings back there in the hangar?" I asked as we stood watching the men work.

He shrugged. "I just informed him that my intervention in the matter wasn't personal, that in fact I was looking forward to serving under him in the Razorbacks, and that I thought he and I would make a great team as soon as we got our mutton-headed commander Major Crystal out of our way. Why?"

The men joyfully toiled until 0200 hours that morning, when I finally insisted they quit. Before surrendering to the day's fatigue, I dashed off a quick note to Nancy telling her about the dramatic change of events concerning my new position as the Red Platoon leader.

We spent the next four days in the hangar with our aircraft, where the maintenance crews and crew chiefs supervised the pilots and gunners as they worked almost nonstop to bring our platoon out of the doldrums. Sharpe encouraged me to assign aviators to their own birds and have their names stenciled on the doors to generate pride of ownership. The crew chiefs and gunners followed suit with their names stenciled by their bay doors. It was an intensive period when rank was meaningless and the job at hand came first. Sharpe was in the middle of everything and once stoically withstood a blistering ass-chewing from his crew chief for dropping some foreign object into the transmission sump pump, which required over an hour to fish out. By the evening of the fifth day, we had ten of our twelve aircraft air-worthy, all with working machine guns and rocket pods. Though forced to cannibalize the two remaining birds to get there, which Army regulation strictly forbade, the men just took what they needed without asking and pushed the two aircraft to the rear of the hangar for the maintenance crews to bring up as the back-ordered parts arrived.

I still knew little to nothing about Charlie-model gun-ships, and what I'd heard was not encouraging. I walked slowly around our ten flyable aircraft inspecting them with some trepidation, assessing what I had learned over the last few days. They looked similar to the Hueys in their physical appearance but in fact were vastly different. Though they possessed more powerful engines to carry the extra load of guns and ammo, they were still considered greatly underpowered for their close air-support mission. The pilots sat side by side as in the slicks, one flying while the other handled the gun system. The crew chief and door gunner each had a free mounted M-60 machine gun located on opposite sides of the bird at the rear of the cargo bay mounted on posts to fire out the sides as they flew past the target area in a gun run. Below their feet on each side of the aircraft were two modified belt-fed M-60 machine guns and two rocket pods that held seven rockets each in individual tubes that the pilot-gunner controlled from his cockpit firing position. They were reportedly appallingly slow and ponderous, their antiquated weapon systems experienced frequent jams, and the gun-sights were notoriously unreliable.

Why anyone would want to fly one of them under combat conditions was a total mystery to me. They were at best irritants to the enemy and at worst mobile death traps for their crews. I concluded it took a different breed of man to be a gun pilot—one the rest of us normal pilots could rarely identify with. Now I had some twenty of them looking to me for leadership—a most peculiar situation, indeed.

Lieutenant Sharpe moved up beside me. "You look worried, Captain."

"I'm scared shitless, Lieutenant," I admitted ruefully. "I'm in over my head. I don't know guns. Hell, I don't even *want* to know guns. And you bunch of crazy gun pilots petrify me. You're all nuts! I'm even crazier for agreeing to be your platoon leader. You've got to let me out of this! I'll help you find a new platoon leader, one who's worthy of these men and machines. I'm just not the man for this job."

"You worry too much, Captain," he soothed. "We'll be just fine. We might have shitty equipment, but we'll make do with it for the time being. The main thing is these are all good men. All you need to do is run interference with the brass and the petty politicians. If you keep them off our ass and out of our way, we can handle the rest. Trust me."

I sighed. "Please, Lieutenant, I'll even give the flight suits back …"

"We need to throw a party, Captain. That'll lift your spirits!"

"A party?"

Soon a convoy of our new jeeps ferried cases of iced beer out to our hangar, and the men indeed threw themselves a hell of a victory party. As the festivities reached critical mass, a new convoy of our jeeps pulled up in front of our hangar and unloaded Ellen and six other nurses. Somebody set up a stereo, and each nurse soon had five men at a time dancing with her on the hangar floor. The result was a laughing, flirting mass of gyrating gaiety. Eventually a loud booming drew everyone's attention to Sharpe, who stood on a platform banging on the side of a drum with a wrench.

With the music turned off and everyone's attention on him, he called each aviator in the platoon up one at a time to the platform, where the nurses stripped each down to his underwear as the rest of the men hooted and clapped in glee. When all nineteen of our pilots stood in a near nude line grinning sheepishly, the nurses then dressed each in a silver one-piece flight suit, two of which Sharpe had procured for every pilot in the platoon. Sharpe then called the crew chiefs and door gunners up, where the nurses stripped and issued each a silver flight suit as they stood in awe. Afterward one overly emotional aviator chased Sharpe around the hangar insisting he was going to kiss him, but the nurses eventually saved the lieutenant by sacrificing themselves to his pursuer's gratitude as the rest of the platoon applauded in a howling, foot-stomping mass. Sharpe banged on his drum again to restore calm.

"Men of the Red Platoon! *Razorbacks*! Today we are again combat-ready. Tomorrow we sally forth to *kick ass*!" He held his arms up as the men cheered.

"I've watched with great pride how hard you've worked, how each of you have pitched in to make this moment possible with your time and energy and knowledge. In the last five days you've accomplished what many thought impossible. I never doubted you. I knew you had the heart and the desire to be more than you were allowed to be. You have proved me right. We are more than a platoon now. We are a *family*." He again held his arms aloft as he waited through their cheers.

"Lest we forget, I would like to take this moment to recognize the one man who made this all possible. To this man I ask each of you to raise your drink in grateful toast, for he alone pulled us up from the gutter and restored our pride and dignity. He alone believed in us when no one else did. In the days ahead, let each of us remember his gift to us. Let not one of us ever bring shame on him for our actions as we go forth to engage the enemy. Gentlemen! To our leader, *Captain Hess*!"

Well, hell, I just watered up like a baby as I stumbled through the joyous men to mount the platform among their hearty cheers that I was certain could be heard all the way to Hanoi. I stood before them humbly as Sharpe backed away raising his hands to settle them down.

I wiped at my eyes in embarrassment. "When I was assigned to Vietnam, if anyone had told me I was going to command a gun platoon, I would have thought them insane. Hell, I've never even *been* in a gunship before." I waited until the laughter and renewed cheers died down.

"I've got a lot to learn about them. I need every man here to help me make the adjustment. I will be as good a platoon leader as you make me or as bad as you allow me to be. But whatever the future holds, on this day, at this moment, I am the proudest captain in the United States Army to call this platoon *my platoon*! I thank you for the support you have given me and the confidence you have placed in me. I pray I do not fail you!"

The men cheered as I descended the steps of the platform and whooped with glee as every nurse there lined up at the bottom to greet me. I passed through them and came out at the end smeared with lipstick, my face beet-red.

And so the Razorbacks rose up out of the slagheap and were reborn due to the determination, spunk, and manipulations of one little second lieutenant who was spoiling for a fight ...

... and the rest of us followed meekly where he led like little lost sheep.

We made an incredible splash at the club the next evening, causing every jaw in the house to drop when our group swaggered in wearing our new silver flight suits. But, alas, it seemed we were all dressed up with nowhere to go. In our haste to become flight-worthy, we had somehow forgotten we did not have a mission. Unbeknownst to me, the lieutenant had implemented a plan to remedy that.

Things would have gone a lot smoother if he had warned me first so I could have advised Major Crystal. But my little lieutenant didn't seem concerned with such mundane things as using his chain of command, nor inclined to bother with simple, long-established Army precedents such as seeking prior mission approval or even, heaven forbid, of bothering to receive command authorization and the like.

Major Crystal spent a very long time in a one-sided discussion of these issues with me three days later as I stood at rigid attention in front of his desk with my eardrums aching from the shrill assault emanating from his screeching voice.

"Do you *realize*, Captain, that your Lieutenant Sharpe has dispatched your pilots and your aircraft to every outlying ARVN post within a hundred miles of here and left *business cards* with our call signs, radio frequencies, and the slogan *'For an immediate attack— call a Razorback!'* in both English and Vietnamese? Are you *aware* of that, Captain?"

"Well, Sir, I—"

Major Crystal pounded his desk with his fist for emphasis as I flinched. "And did you *know*, Captain, that the American advisers in those outlying ARVN posts were so grateful to now have air support that they personally *thanked* the MACV commander, *who didn't know what the shit they were talking about?*"

"Well, Sir, I—"

He slammed his palm down again. "And did you *know*, Captain, that when the *MACV commander* asked the *corps commander* for a briefing on the new operational mission, *the corps commander didn't know what the shit the MACV commander was talking about?*"

"Well, Sir, I—"

His voice raised another octave. "And, *Captain*, would you believe that when the *corps commander* asked *me* for a briefing, *I didn't know what the shit the corps commander was talking about?*"

"Well, Sir, I—"

"And now, *Captain*, you want to stand there and tell me *you don't know what the shit I'm talking about?*"

Sweat trickled down my cheeks. "Well, Sir, of course … I was sort of … uh, Sir … could I get back to you on this?"

"We're not a *fighting* unit, Captain. We're the *Deans*, a *VIP* unit. Do you understand me? The *Vietnamese* fight. We're turning the war over to *them*! We're in an *advisory* and *support* role. Do you *understand*, Captain?"

"Well, Sir, I—"

"Where's your Lieutenant now, Captain? I want him in this office immediately! I want to *personally*—"

A loud knock at the door interrupted his tirade, and the executive officer thrust his head in. "Sorry, Sir, but we have an emergency."

Major Crystal blinked. "What kind of emergency?"

"One of our aircraft has called for crash landing instructions at the airfield, Sir. He's shot up pretty bad and trying to make it home. The fire and rescue teams are standing by. I thought you'd like to know, Sir."

Major Crystal stared in stunned confusion. "Shot up? How? Who'd shoot *us*? Which aircraft?"

"Call sign of Red One-Seven, Sir," the XO reported. "A Lieutenant Sharpe, I believe."

My heart sank to my boots as Major Crystal grabbed his hat. "*God damn it*! Get my jeep! Well, we sure as hell know where your Lieutenant is now, Captain, don't we? Tearing up my goddamned aircraft, that's where! Come with me!"

We clamored aboard the major's jeep and tore off to the airfield in a roar, arriving just in time to see four Charlie-model gunships appear on the horizon.

Major Crystal turned to the flight operations officer as he hurried up to the jeep and saluted. "What's their platoon frequency, Captain Nichols?" He dialed in the frequency hurriedly on his jeep radio, which crackled to life as we watched the four aircraft approach with one out in front and the other three closely trailing him home.

"How's it going, One-Seven?" a voice inquired from the receiver.

"Well, hell, the bitch's still flying, so I guess I can't complain, One-Six," Sharpe's voice answered. "These hogs do auto-rotate like the slicks, right? The one I got checked out in didn't have all the guns and shit on board."

"You're much heavier now, One-Seven. You gotta pull more pitch at the bottom and flare a lot lower than normal," another voice advised.

"Thanks, One-Four."

"One-Seven, this is One-Three. I recommend a running landing, buddy. Make sure your weapons systems are off and on safe. You're trailing smoke now."

"Yeah, my temperature's going out of sight and the controls are getting a bit sluggish. I can see the airfield now. I'll make a wide loop and bring her straight in."

"Okay, buddy. You've only got one shot at it, so make it a good one."

"Roger, One-Three. We ain't got enough hogs for me to go screwing one up."

We watched the slow turn of the crippled aircraft with the lieutenant's three shadow birds covering him. I held my breath as he began a gradual descent with a thin trail of vapor curling from his engine compartment.

"Easy now, One-Seven, you're almost home. Smooth now, easy does it. Drop the nose, Lieutenant! You're coming in too high. Keep your airspeed up, push the nose down, and just ride her home. Easy ... easy ... easy, now. Okay, flare, pull back and set her down. *Flare, One-Seven, you're too hot!*"

The aircraft set down hard, bounced back into the air, and then wallowed down again in a grinding half-crash as it tore down the runway with sparks curling up from the skids and the nose fishtailing back and forth. The other three aircraft streaked by the wounded bird as it groaned to a halt amid the shrill sound of grinding metal. A fire truck raced up as the engine shut down and the crew members jumped out to rip open the pilot's doors on each side.

"Get me out there!" Major Crystal ordered his driver, and we lurched off with tires spinning.

"Good job, One-Seven. Now un-ass that bird, she's starting to burn," the radio crackled.

We skidded to a stop as Lieutenant Sharpe jumped out of the cockpit, jerked his helmet off, and ran to the rear of the aircraft to direct the fire team as they sprayed foam on the burning engine compartment.

Major Crystal watched in fury. "Captain, go get your Lieutenant! Bring him to my office immediately! He's grounded for the rest of his tour! In fact, he may never fly again! Just *look* at my *aircraft*!"

I jumped out of the jeep and hurried toward the stricken bird as Major Crystal and his driver drove off in a rage.

Numerous jagged holes sprouted throughout the gunship, at least five the size of a fist. One side of the Plexiglas windshield was shattered. The top of the aircraft blazed as the fire crews fought the flames. One skid had pushed out from the hard landing, and the left side sagged lower than the right side.

I eased over to Sharpe. "Are you and your crew okay, Lieutenant?"

He turned to me. "Hey, Captain. Yeah, we're good to go. But I think my bird's screwed. I can't believe those dirty little bastards set me up like that! Now I'm really pissed! Can you believe this shit?"

I cleared my throat. "Uh, speaking of being pissed, Major Crystal wants to see you in his office pronto."

He scowled. "Hell, I'm busy, Captain. Can't you handle it?"

"Uh, no, I don't think so, Lieutenant. He's sort of upset about you going out and advertising to the ARVN outposts that we're available for gun support."

He turned to me wide-eyed. "How else were they supposed to know we're here? Damn, I ain't got time for this shit, Captain! I've got more important stuff to do than trade barbs with that numbskull. I've got to try and get my bird flight-worthy again. Just look at my pretty baby! They shot the shit out of her! The rotten bastards!"

I nodded sympathetically. "It's in pretty sad shape. I don't think you'll get it flyable again. And since we're on that subject, Major Crystal did mention the damage to the aircraft as well. In fact, he seemed quite peeved about you getting it all shot up. He wants to discuss that issue with you also."

He glared at me. "Damn, Captain, there's not a lot to discuss! Why can't you go dilly-dally around with the little shit while I see what's salvageable here? Maybe I can recover enough parts to get one of our hangar queens parked out back flyable."

"He specifically asked to see you."

"I can't get much done around here if I have to run up to that asshole's office every few minutes and chat with him about shit, Captain."

I drew a deep breath. "I suspect this is going to involve more than a little chat, Lieutenant."

His eyes narrowed. "What's that supposed to mean, Captain?"

I expelled my breath. "He said you're grounded."

"Grounded! *Me?* Are you shitting me? For what? You're damned right I want to go see that little son of a bitch! Come on, Captain!"

As he stormed off I hurried after him, thankful I had decided not to make a career of the Army.

CHAPTER 5

The lieutenant and I stood at attention in front of Major Crystal's desk, where we had waited for several long minutes without a word spoken as he wrung his hands, cracked his knuckles, and muttered to himself.

He finally broke the silence, a thin edge to his voice. "Lieutenant Sharpe?"

"Yes, Major?"

"Do you know how to say *Sir*, Lieutenant?" Crystal demanded.

"Of course, Major."

"Would you care to tell me why one of my aircraft is destroyed, Lieutenant?"

"Sure, Major. The Vietcong shot it all to hell with a big gun."

Major Crystal leaned forward. "And *how* did they come to shoot it with their big gun, Lieutenant?"

Sharpe pursed his lips thoughtfully. "Personally, I think they got lucky, Major, but it could've been because they had a pretty good gunner down there too. It's really hard to say."

"Are you being cute, Lieutenant? Do you think this is a joke? Do you realize this is the first Dean aircraft hit by enemy fire on my watch? *And I god-damned well want to know why it happened, Lieutenant!*" He slammed his open palm on his desk for emphasis.

Sharpe's tone grew icy. "Sorry, I thought I'd just explained it to you. The VC shot the shit out of me. Isn't that clear enough, Major?"

"*How* did they shoot you, Lieutenant?"

"With a .51 caliber anti-aircraft gun, Major."

"Lieutenant, the next time you open your mouth and the *first* time *every time* after that, the first word I want to hear out of you is *Sir.* Do you understand me?"

"Sir, I understand you."

Major Crystal smirked. "Thank you, Lieutenant."

"Sir, you are welcome, Major," Sharpe replied.

Crystal's jaw clenched. "Do not use 'Sir' and 'Major' together in the same sentence, Lieutenant. Now, *why* did they shoot you?"

"Sir, I strongly suspect they don't like me very much. They apparently consider me to be their enemy and, as such, are prone to attack me when the opportunity presents itself."

Crystal's jaw clenched. "Lieutenant, *who* authorized this mission?"

"Sir, flight operations did."

"Explain that, Lieutenant."

"Sir, a call came in for gun support. Flight operations called the mission down to the hot pad. I responded to the call. When I arrived on site with my wing man, I called for another two hogs for backup, Major."

"Lieutenant, please do not refer to my aircraft as *hogs.*"

"Sir, what would you prefer I call them?"

"Aircraft, Lieutenant."

"Sir, I called for two additional aircraft with guns."

"And how did this mission come to be called in, Lieutenant?"

"Sir, I assume by radio."

"You know what I mean, Lieutenant. *Why* was this call made?"

"Sir, because they needed gun support."

"I give up, Lieutenant. You are grounded! As of now, you will be the new unit mess officer. You got that, flyboy?"

"Sir, under what justification am I grounded?"

"Because I said so, Lieutenant!"

"Sir, I demand to be informed of the justification for my removal from flight status."

"You *demand*, Lieutenant? You *demand* to know the justification? Did I hear you right?"

"Sir, apparently you did hear me right."

"By what right do you *demand* anything of me, Lieutenant? I'm the *commander* of this unit! My decisions are final and go without *question*."

"Sir, is that all?" Sharpe asked.

"Why do you ask?"

"Sir, because I would like to be excused now," the lieutenant replied.

Crystal smiled pleasantly. "Oh, really? Do you have an appointment, Lieutenant?"

"Sir, I need to go to the Judge Advocate General's Office, if you are finished."

Major Crystal sat forward in his chair, eyes narrowing. "To JAG? Is that a threat, Lieutenant?"

"Sir, I don't threaten. Will there be anything else, Major?"

"And what is the purpose of your urgency to go to the JAG office, Lieutenant?"

"Sir, I intend to request a formal investigation into my removal from flight status."

Crystal exhaled a derisive snort. "You're joking, of course, Lieutenant?"

"Sir, will that be all?"

"You're *not* joking?"

"Sir, I request to be excused."

"Lieutenant, if you persist in this endeavor, I will personally see that you never reach the rank of first lieutenant. Do you understand me?"

"Sir, I take that as a threat. I formally request to be released now."

Crystal frowned. "Don't you care about your career, Lieutenant? Do you understand what impact this will have on your future in the Army?"

"Sir, my career is secondary to my rights as a soldier, an officer, and an aviator. I deem your actions to be unjustified, and therefore unlawful. The Department of the Army can decide if I am wrong, Major."

"*Unjustified* and *unlawful*, Lieutenant?" he bellowed. "Those are *serious* allegations. I hope you're *fully* prepared to back them up."

"Sir, I assure you it is my intention to fully back up those allegations."

Major Crystal sat back in his chair. "Lieutenant, you will wait outside in the orderly room until I release you. Is that clear?"

"Sir, that is clear." Sharpe saluted Crystal and departed.

"Sit down, Captain Hess," Crystal ordered in a subdued voice.

I sat as directed.

He pulled at his face with the palm of his hand and sighed. "In all my years I've never met anyone as impertinent as that lieutenant. He's borderline insubordinate and arrogant beyond reproach." He looked at me for confirmation as I sat silently without expression. "Please speak your mind, Captain."

"Sir, I think you may have a problem with grounding him."

He fixed me with a censorious glare. "How so, Captain?"

"When an aviator is grounded he must be given cause and he's allowed a board of review if he so desires. He was given no cause for the grounding, and I can guarantee you, Sir, he will not back down from the review board."

"Well, *give* me a cause to ground the little bastard then, Captain!"

I hesitated. "I … can't think of a legit cause for grounding him offhand, Sir."

Crystal impacted his fist on his desk as I flinched. "Are you implying that I've done something wrong, Captain? Are you implying that my decision is unjustified? That little bastard just destroyed a half-million-dollar aircraft!"

"Sir, I'm trying to help you understand how a board of review will see this. The aircraft was engaged in a mission against hostile forces. To our knowledge, the lieutenant has done nothing that would indicate he has contributed to the destruction of the aircraft other than fly an approved mission. If every aviator was held personally responsible for battle damage, we'd never get a mission flown."

Major Crystal jumped up and paced behind his desk. "But it was *not* an approved mission, Captain! *I* never approved that mission, and I'm the *commander* of this unit."

I selected my words carefully. "But the mission was called down from flight ops, Sir. That makes it a legal mission. I'm afraid, Sir, the flight review board will overturn your decision to ground him. They could even reprimand you for taking an unjustified action that's detrimental to the lieutenant's career."

"A *reprimand*! For *me*? *I'm* not the one who just flew an unauthorized mission and destroyed a five-hundred-thousand-dollar aircraft. A *reprimand*! You can't be serious!"

"Sir, how many aviators have you grounded in your career?"

"Well … none that I recall … never had a reason to until now."

"Sir, when you ground a pilot, you take away his right to perform his proper duties. It's similar to your commander telling you that you can no longer make command decisions in this unit. That is a step to be taken very carefully. It requires proper justification and cause. It's not something to be taken lightly."

Crystal's face turned ashen as he paced. "Then what should I do in this situation?"

"Sir, if it were my decision, I'd drop the whole issue," I advised soberly.

Crystal whirled around. "No! I'll *not* admit that my actions are unjustified! What other options do I have?"

"Well, Sir, at the risk of embarrassing yourself, you could temporarily ground Lieutenant Sharpe pending the evaluation of a flight review board."

"In other words, *I* ask for a board of review instead of the lieutenant? That makes me look like a concerned commander trying to do the right thing. I like that, Captain. You said I might embarrass myself? How?"

"Sir, I don't believe the review board will uphold the grounding. I think they'll reinstate him to flight status. Depending on how far you push this, it could still have an adverse impact on you personally."

"That smart-assed lieutenant needs to be taken down a notch!" he shouted. "I need to get his attention and show him who's in control here."

"Yes, Sir, but I caution you, the lieutenant's a fierce adversary."

"What are you saying, Captain?"

"Sir, when you fight a skunk, you get smelly regardless of who wins the fight."

Crystal's eyes bulged. "I'm a *field* grade officer and the *commander* of the most *prestigious* aviation unit in Vietnam. Are you telling me I need to be *concerned* about an *insignificant* little *second lieutenant*, Captain?"

"Sir, this is not just *any* second lieutenant. He came up through the ranks the hard way, as you are aware. He seems to know every regulation involved in this situation and appears capable of using them to his advantage. Sir, I've watched him operate and strongly advise you to proceed with caution. He's not only smart, he's cunning. In my opinion he can be a staunch ally or a relentless foe."

"So what are you advising, Captain?"

"Sir, he doesn't give a damn about his career. He wants to fight. Let him fight. If we get in his way, he'll think of us as the enemy and conduct himself accordingly. I think you'd be well served to just ignore him. Let me handle him. I think I can keep him under control to a degree."

Crystal slid slowly into his chair. "And if you *can't* keep him under control, Captain?"

Okay, he wants a scapegoat to cover his ass with, and it's to be me. I took a deep breath. "Sir, if he crosses the line, I'll be the first to ensure he faces the consequences."

"And you don't think he's crossed the line in this situation?"

"No, Sir. As you said earlier, he's borderline. But I don't think he has actually crossed the line to the point that we can discipline him for this incident."

"And how do we handle the situation from here, Captain? We've still got some very curious commanders out there waiting for answers as to how this all came about."

"Sir, you have a gun platoon assigned to you. Guns are a support mission. Has anyone ever told you not to deploy them?"

"Well, no, no one's ever told me anything to do with them since they've been assigned here. Until that stupid lieutenant started handing out his business cards, I don't think anyone even knew they were here."

"Everyone sure knows it now, Sir, and apparently it's being well received by the outposts in the field. Until someone tells you different, let them perform their assigned mission, which is to provide direct air support for the sector."

"But what about my destroyed aircraft?"

"Sir, in combat there are going to be losses. The Red Platoon is down to nine flyable aircraft now. There are no replacement aircraft available in our inventory, and the aircraft we have are so antiquated spare parts are almost impossible to come by. Most of them are used up and worn out. In another week or two, at the rate we're flying, we'll be down to two or three operational aircraft."

He smiled craftily. "So this thing could just fade away on its own accord?"

I nodded. "Sir, these aircraft are relics from the beginning of the war. They should've been out of the Army inventory by now. Maintaining them and keeping them flying will be next to impossible."

He nodded sagely. "I like your reasoning, Captain. But what about the lieutenant?"

"Use the situation to your advantage, Sir."

"My advantage?"

"Yes, Sir. Your executive officer approached me on my way in and asked me if I could get you and him one of these fancy flight suits. The lieutenant's the source of them. Make a deal with him that you'll drop this whole issue for two of the flight suits. It'd be a win-win situation. You'll save face in reversing your decision by letting him barter his way out of it. He's the type who would understand a deal like that. You come out as the good guy by giving him another chance, and you and the XO get one of these fancy flight suits."

Crystal's face flushed. "And all I have to do is eat shit, right?"

"Sir, you need to get all the mileage out of this situation you can—and maintain enough distance to hang him if it becomes necessary. The odds are the Razorbacks will fade away on their own. The point is, Sir, he's not someone you need to have as an adversary. Since he doesn't give a damn about his career or anything else, it's hard to win against someone who has nothing to lose. Let him focus on the enemy. Give him all the rope he wants. If he crosses the line, hang him. Otherwise, let him do his thing. He might even bring this unit some positive recognition, which would be to your advantage. Either way you win."

He frowned. "I'll take your advice, Captain, but I warn you, I hold you entirely responsible for his conduct from here on out. Do I make myself clear?"

My stomach did flip-flops. "I hold myself accountable for all of my men, Sir."

"Bring the little bastard in," Crystal ordered.

I opened the door and motioned to Sharpe, who entered and stood at attention in front of Crystal's desk.

"Lieutenant Sharpe, Captain Hess has persuaded me to reconsider my decision to ground you. He feels you deserve a second chance. He has assured me that if I'm willing to overlook this unfortunate incident, you will procure silver flight suits for my XO and me. Is that agreeable to you?"

"Sir, any agreements between you and Captain Hess are of no concern to me. My reinstatement to flight status is my only concern."

"And the flight suits?"

"Sir, if my Captain requests two flight suits, I'll do my best to provide them to him. What he does with them is his business."

"Sit down, Lieutenant. You and I seem to have gotten off to a poor beginning." Sharpe sat stiffly as directed as Major Crystal sat back in his chair. "Lieutenant, tell me a little about yourself."

"Sir, what do you want to know?"

"To begin with, why do you have this aversion to calling a superior officer 'Sir' as is the normal military courtesy?"

"Sir, I have no superior officers. The 'Sir' rendering is a military courtesy bestowed upon a senior officer as a form of respect. When I respect the man holding the senior rank, I am more than willing to show the proper respect to his rank."

Crystal's face darkened. "Do you imply you do not respect me, Lieutenant?"

"Sir, the first day we met, you intentionally insulted me as a commissioned officer. Respect goes both ways, Major."

"I don't need a *lecture* from *you* on *military courtesy*—"

"Sir, let me handle it from here, if you will," I interrupted hastily as the situation rapidly deteriorated between them again.

Major Crystal took a deep breath and pointed to the door.

We saluted and hurried out.

When we cleared the orderly room, I drew up at my jeep and turned to Sharpe angrily. "Lieutenant, I would think you'd know it's difficult enough to cover your ass in this man's army without antagonizing the commanding officer of your unit!"

He scowled. "With all due respect, Captain, he can kiss my bony little ass, and that's just the way it is!"

"You go out of your way to provoke him! For what purpose?"

"Captain, I've talked to that asshole twice. The first time he implied I was something less than a *real* officer, and today he attempted to destroy my career. You saved his ass in there by talking him out of his decision to ground me, but it was *his* ass you saved, not *mine*. Personally, I wish you hadn't bothered. I'd enjoy making a jackass out of him."

"Just calm down," I soothed. "Let me handle him in the future. Stay as far away from him as you can. Okay?"

"Captain, I'm going to do my job, and I'm going to do it well. If that shit-head gets in my way or threatens me again, I'd appreciate you letting me handle him myself. If that piece of shit is looking for a problem with me, I'm more than happy to oblige him."

I sighed. "I take it you don't intend to let me handle him?"

"I have the highest respect for you, Captain. I have zero respect for that little politician masquerading as an officer and a soldier. I will not go out of my way to 'antagonize' him as you call it, but I will not go out of my way to avoid him either, and I won't eat his shit for one minute. If I screw up, he can have my ass and be welcome to it. But he doesn't intimidate me just because he thinks in his own little piss-ant mind he's *superior* to me because he went through West Point and I came up through the ranks. As far as I'm concerned, I'd just as soon never talk to him again, so you're more than welcome to handle him … up to a point."

"Lieutenant, if you persist in this, he'll find some way to screw you over. He's a field grade officer, for god's sake. You can't possibly win."

"If he plays by the rules, I'll play by the rules."

"Since when?"

He grinned. "I always play by the rules, Captain."

"Whose rules?"

"The rules of right and wrong—I like the challenge of winning fair and square."

"And if he doesn't play by the rules of right and wrong to beat you fair and square?"

As Sharpe's eyes narrowed, chills laced up my spine. "Then he'll pay a price he can't even fathom, Captain, and at that point there'll be no rules."

"I hope that's not a threat, Lieutenant Sharpe," I advised uneasily.

He smiled brightly. "I don't make threats, Captain. Now, with all due respect, I'm through talking about that insignificant little piece of shit. I've got two men I want you to interview from the Yellow Platoon who want to transfer to the Razorbacks. They're waiting for us over at the Dean lounge."

I blinked. "*Two* pilots from the *Yellow Platoon* want to join *us*? I don't believe it. Who are they?"

"Captains Benedict and Everett."

"Two *captains* want to join us? Are they *crazy*?"

"They appear to be as sane as you and me, Captain."

"*That's* not necessarily a reassuring reference point," I allowed.

He shrugged. "Regardless of their mental status, we need them, Captain."

"But if they join the platoon, you won't be the assistant platoon leader anymore," I pointed out.

"No slight intended, Captain, but this assistant shit ain't what it's cracked up to be. You *real* officers need to handle all the administrative crap to free me up so I can do the important shit, like killing gooks. The point is these two jokers are crucial for our next phase."

I stiffened. "Our next phase? Um, and what would that be, Lieutenant?"

"I've got my eye on these fifteen Cobra attack helicopters sitting down in Vung Tau waiting to be turned over to the ARVNs. They're brand new suckers with all the latest armaments and the newest gun-sight technology. Do you realize we're marking our Plexiglas windshields with grease-pencil crosses to aim our rockets and machine guns with because our piece-of-shit gun sights don't work? Talk about primitive! If I'd had one of those high-tech Cobras today, I wouldn't have got my ass busted out there. I'd of—"

"*Lieutenant!*"

"Yes, Captain?"

I grimly attempted to swallow the lump in my throat down into the paralyzing pressure building in my chest. "W-What do you mean … fifteen Cobra gunships … ARVNs … you can't, I mean that's *illegal* … you have no authority … you promised … I've got a wife and kid!"

"Calm down, Captain," he soothed, taking my elbow to steady me. "Here, sit down in the jeep. Is it the heat? Do I need to get you to a hospital or something? Just take deep breaths. Think about something serene."

"S-Something s-serene?" I gasped.

"Envision a half dozen naked nurses frolicking around you or something wonderful and frivolous like that."

"N-N-Naked nurses?"

"Anything that tickles your fancy, Captain," he advised, hovering over me in concern.

I tried to focus on Nancy and my sweet little daughter, but Major Crystal's image appeared among all the spots swirling before my eyes and offered me a blindfold and a cigarette as a line of men chambered rounds into their rifles and looked at me expectantly. I blinked away the image and took several deep, ragged breaths. "Lieutenant, you can't … *steal* fifteen Cobra attack helicopters from the ARVNs … you-you *can't!*" My voice failed me completely as spots reappeared before my eyes.

"Steal? Oh hell no, that's not my style," he reassured me. "I'm actually trading for them, Captain."

The spots reappeared in greater mass. "Lieutenant, those are million-dollar aircraft! *Fifteen* of them? Fifteen *million* dollars! What are you going to *trade* for *fifteen million dollars* worth of *aircraft?*"

"Now, you don't need to be concerned with the details, if you get my drift, Captain."

"Those aircraft are *U.S. Government property*! They'll soon be the property of the South Vietnamese government! There's no *legal* way you can do this! I'll end up in *jail*! Besides, our pilots aren't trained to fly them, and our maintenance personnel aren't trained to work on them! Are you *insane?* What would Major Crystal say if *fifteen Cobra attack helicopters* suddenly appeared at his *airfield?*"

"Details, Captain, details," he scoffed. "*You* need to focus on the bigger picture and let *me* worry about the minor details of implementing the plan."

"These—these *plans* of yours scare the hell out of me, Lieutenant! I've got a wife and kid back home—"

"I know, Captain, I know, and one in the oven. That's why I promised to keep you out of harm's way and send you back home to them all safe and sound, right? And that's exactly what I'm going to do."

"Sending me home in *handcuffs* doesn't count, Lieutenant! This is crazy—don't you see, Major Crystal will … h-he'll *kill* us *b-both* …"

"Captain, you've got to learn to relax. Now, let's go interview these two men I've got waiting. Oh, and let me handle them. You just sit there and frown a lot. Okay? I really need these two yahoos, but I can't let them know how much I need them or it'll drive up the price."

"T-The *price?*" I gasped. "You're *trading* something for two *captains?* You can't do that! You can't *trade* for *people!* President Lincoln *stopped* all that—"

"I'm not *trading* for them, I'm *recruiting* them," he explained patiently as he got into the jeep on the driver's side. "But they need to think we really don't want them that badly. Do you see what I mean?"

"No."

"Just let me handle it, Captain, okay?"

Captain Benedict, a tall, handsome, well-built, blond-haired, blue-eyed individual, had a look about him that didn't feel right to me. Maybe it was the way he stared at me intently without blinking. Captain Everett, a short, wiry man with deep brown eyes and tight black curls closely cropped around his head, looked at my fake scowl and dismissed me immediately as he focused on my lieutenant. During the short interview, I quickly learned they were both former Cobra flight instructors from Fort Rucker, Alabama.

The lieutenant looked at them expectantly. "Well, gentlemen, if I can convince Captain Hess to accept you, would you be willing to transfer out of the pussy Yellow Platoon to the Razorbacks?"

"And we each get two of those fancy flight suits if we do?" Everett confirmed.

"And you're certain you're going to get the Cobras?" Benedict demanded.

Sharpe shrugged. "As good as done on both counts."

The two looked at each other and back at him.

"When do we get the flight suits?" Everett asked.

"And when do we get the Cobras?" Benedict interjected.

"The flight suits the day after you transfer, the Cobras within four weeks from today," Sharpe assured them as he held out his hand to confirm the deal.

Everett shook with the lieutenant. "I'll transfer."

Benedict crossed his arms, ignoring the lieutenant's outstretched hand. "Okay, I'm in. But if the Cobras don't show up, I'm out of here and I *keep* the flight suits. I refuse to fly those Charlie-model relics. They're death traps."

The lieutenant nodded. "Fair enough. Let's have a drink to seal the deal. Captain Hess can accompany you to see Major Crystal in the morning. Tonight party. I've got a couple of nurses coming over later this evening."

And so, as improbable as it seemed, we gained two more highly experienced pilots, if of somewhat dubious intellect and questionable distinction, for the Red Platoon.

CHAPTER 6

The transfer of Captains Benedict and Everett occurred the following morning with the somewhat skeptical but distracted approval of Major Crystal, who was more preoccupied with admiring his new silver flight suit I brought along than with the reasons the two captains wanted to transfer into the slush of the Razorbacks. I drove them to the airfield and introduced them around, where they viewed our poor Charlie-model gunships with disdain before pausing before the lieutenant's shot-up aircraft.

Benedict shook his head. "That's one lucky son of a bitch."

Everett nodded. "What possessed him to tackle a .51 cal.? I wouldn't jump on one of those with a Cobra, much less a sickly Charlie model. Is he just plain nuts, or what?"

Benedict frowned. "Either that or the fool doesn't know any better."

I shrugged. "It was a little of both, I guess."

"How long has he been flying guns?" Everett asked.

"That was his first mission," I explained. "He just transitioned to guns last week."

Benedict smiled. "He's got balls, I'll say that. I hope he's a fast learner. In my experience you only get one chance to face off against a .51 cal. When you find one, they generally zip you up in one of those black vinyl bags and send you home to your mother, or what's left of you anyway. Where is he? I'd like to hear his war story."

I swallowed. "Uh, he, uh, well, he took three more birds this morning and went back out there to try and get that gun. You see, he took it kind of personally."

Benedict stared at me in disbelief. "Well, now we *definitely* know he's not a fast learner."

Everett chuckled grimly. "I sure hope he got our flight suits before he took off."

I shuffled my feet. "Look, guys, I'm not a gun pilot. I'm trying to learn this stuff. I need you to teach me these things."

Everett scoffed. "It's easy enough to figure out— don't go screwing around with sons of bitches bigger and meaner than you are."

"Listen, can I be straight up with you two? Captain to captain? I need you guys to help me keep the lieutenant out of trouble. He's a good man in some ways, but he can take a hard left turn quicker than you can blink. He's a highly decorated combat veteran and a former Infantryman who views the world a little differently than the rest of us, if you know what I mean." I held my index finger up and circled the side of my head, signifying flaky.

Everett smiled. "Three captains to look after *one* second lieutenant? That's a bit of overkill on the supervision end, don't you think?"

"Actually, I think you'll find we're undermanned," I advised as my maintenance sergeant rushed by with several men in tow.

"Captain, we've got damaged birds inbound!" he yelled.

Benedict grinned. "I could've predicted that."

"Shit!" I rushed for the door and joined a growing crowd of men hurrying to the runway. Major Crystal's jeep skidded up a few minutes later and he switched on the radio as we clustered around to listen.

"Roger, One-Six, set her down in that paddy to your left," Sharpe's voice ordered. "She's smoking badly. I don't think you can nurse her back home."

"Let me try, One-Seven," the pilot begged. "We can't afford to lose another bird. Dean Six will shit a brick and ship us off to bum-fuck Egypt."

"I don't give a damn about the bird," the lieutenant countered. "It's the crew I can't replace. Set her down before you get yourself hurt. I'll follow you in and pick you up."

"But, Lieutenant, we can't just leave it in the paddy," One-Six argued.

"After I've extracted you, I'll put my last two rockets up its ass. It's cooked anyway. There's nothing worth salvaging."

"Roger that, Lieutenant, but Dean Six is gonna have a large chunk of your ass and ground you for life."

Major Crystal snatched the transmitter off its cradle and keyed the mike. "Red One-Seven, Dean Six, over."

There was a decided hush of the jabber as they realized Major Crystal was monitoring their frequency.

"Uh, Dean Six, this is Red One-Seven, over," Sharpe answered.

Major Crystal keyed his mike. "What's your situation, over?"

"Dean Six, Red One-Six is shot up and losing hydraulics. I've ordered him to ditch. I'm following him in to retrieve the crew. Recommend destroying the aircraft in place, over."

"Roger—just bring that crew home safe, One-Seven," Crystal ordered.

"Roger, Dean Six. Be advised Red One-Four also has battle damage. Red One-Three's following him home. I believe he can make it back safely, over."

"Roger, fire and rescue is standing by," Crystal apprised.

"Roger, Dean Six. Red One-Six is down and we're beside them." We waited tensely. "Dean Six, we're off the ground with crew intact. I'm coming around to make a run on the downed aircraft now." We waited another half a minute. "Downed hog is flaming!"

"Roger, One-Seven. Return to home base. What is your ETA, over?"

"Roger, Dean Six. Estimated time of arrival one-five minutes, over," the lieutenant replied as we watched two Charlie models appear on the horizon, make a gradual turn, and begin their descent.

"One-Four, I'm watching you all the way down, buddy. How's she handling?"

"Sluggish, One-Three, but what would you expect? I'll be fine."

"Roger, buddy, you're looking good."

He chuckled. "Thanks, One-Three. I know *I* look good. It's my beautiful little hog I'm worried about."

They bantered casually back and forth as they lined up with the runway and glided home. Red One-Four touched down gently in a running landing and skidded down the runway as One-Three streaked by. The fire-and-rescue crews moved out quickly as the crippled bird slid to a halt and the crew bailed out to open the pilot's doors.

Major Crystal turned to me with a smug grin and winked knowingly. "That's two more flight suits you owe me, Captain."

"Uh, yes, Sir. When do you want to see me and Lieutenant Sharpe, Sir?"

"You handle it, Captain. This might not take a couple of weeks after all." He laughed wickedly and motioned to his driver as I stared after him in shock.

The lieutenant's aircraft appeared on the horizon ten minutes later and taxied to its parking ramp after landing. He climbed out shaking his head in disgust.

"Sorry, Captain, he busted our ass again."

"You mean you didn't get him?" Everett chided wide-eyed.

The lieutenant hung his head glumly. "The little bastard was waiting for us and had a friend off to the side with a .30 cal. We came in on the .51 cal. in a V and the .30 cal. peppered two of us before we could even arm our guns."

"But you learned a lesson this time, right?" Everett pressed.

Sharpe nodded grimly. "Yeah, he's treacherous as hell and doesn't fight fair, so we've got to rethink our tactics."

"Do you want to know the best tactic to use against him, Lieutenant?" Everett persisted.

"Sure, Captain, I'm all ears. What we're doing now ain't working for shit."

"Take your map out, draw a red circle around the site about a half-mile out, and don't fly through his airspace anymore since it tends to piss him off."

Sharpe scowled at Everett as Benedict laughed gleefully. "Can't do that—he's shot down three of my hogs and it's personal now. I'm going to bust his ass even if I have to crash on him when he shoots my ass down again."

Everett locked eyes with him. "By my count you've lost three half-million-dollar aircraft trying to knock out one five-hundred-dollar gun—and you're damned lucky no one's been killed."

"It's a matter of principle," the lieutenant insisted. "He's controlling a piece of my sky, and it annoys the hell out of me to have to fly around him. Besides, he's proven himself to be a worthy opponent now. That makes him worth fighting." He turned to me. "Okay, Captain, take me to our fearless leader for my dose of humility and fifty lashes."

I grinned. "Crystal says he's too busy to be bothered with you. He figures at the rate you're going we'll be out of business in a few days anyway. But he did say to put a rush on the two new flight suits we owe him for this debacle."

"Damn, he's getting expensive. Maybe we need to renegotiate."

"Speaking of which, where are *our* suits?" Everett demanded.

"Buy me a drink, Captain, and I'll dress you in your finery."

"Where're my Cobras?" Benedict demanded. "At this rate I'll wager you won't last long enough to get them for us."

"I'll take that bet, Captain, and give you favorable odds," Sharpe scoffed.

"Only if somebody else holds the money—dead men don't pay their debts," Benedict countered coolly.

We drove off to the O Club, where the three of us settled into the empty interior and ordered drinks while the lieutenant stopped off at his room. When he rejoined us, he had two flight suits apiece for Everett and Benedict, and gave me two more for Crystal. He handed a note to my driver with instructions to give it to Ellen at the hospital and sent him off.

"Okay, guys, here's the plan," he advised as we leaned closer with drinks in hand. "Captain, here's a list of maintenance personnel and pilots for temporary duty assignment in Vung Tau for Cobra maintenance and transition training. It's important they depart on the correct dates. It's normally a four-week course, but we're going to cram it into two weeks. We start ferrying the Cobras to Long Binh in four weeks. Under this schedule we'll be half-trained at that time, but we'll bring the rest of the platoon along in the two weeks after that. Captain Benedict, you'll instruct the pilots in a ground school for the next two weeks. Captain Everett, you'll conduct a ground school during this same period for the maintenance personnel before they depart. In six weeks we'll be 100 percent mission-ready."

Everett shook his head as we stared at each other uneasily. "Are you nuts, Lieutenant? We don't have lesson plans, training devices, mock-ups, or anything. This can't be done in the time frame you're giving us."

"You both taught in Mother Rucker for three years before coming over here, so you should know the lesson plans by heart, and we'll use the real thing as our training aids. I have two Cobras flying in tomorrow we can use for six weeks—one for you to tear apart and put back together with the maintenance crews, and one Captain Benedict can use to teach us pilots how to fly." He drained his glass and motioned for another.

"The men can't take that kind of a cram course, Lieutenant," Benedict argued. "They can't absorb that much information in such a short time."

Sharpe met his gaze. "Stateside, I'd agree with you, Captain. But this is Nam and a war zone. The men are eager for this transition and highly motivated. They'll do just fine. You can cut out all the hokey crap and just teach them the important stuff."

I studied his rather ambitious list of names. "Assuming that's so, how are you going to slip those two Cobras by Major Crystal tomorrow? Not to mention how are you going to snatch fifteen more Cobras from the ARVNs in the first place?"

He smirked. "That's already handled, Captain. It's best you not concern yourself with the particulars."

My insides turned to jelly. "No, by god, not this time, Lieutenant! I want to know the particulars *before* it happens. I'm not going to jail!"

"Captain, at some point you're going to have to trust—"

"*Now*, Lieutenant!" I insisted. "I want to know everything *right now!*"

He sat back, crossed his arms, and studied me as I stared back at him. After several long minutes he slumped in resignation. "Would you two give us a moment?" He grimaced as Benedict and Everett moved off to another table. "I wish you'd reconsider this, Captain."

"*Everything*, Lieutenant," I demanded.

"Okay, Captain, here's the short version. My friend Ellen, whom I just sent your driver to fetch, has a sister working in MACV as secretary to a very married operations officer who has a serious case of the hots for her. Via this dilly-dallying around with Ellen's sister, another source who owes me a favor was able to assist this officer in seeing the merits of having the gunships of the Deans upgraded to high-tech Cobras in order to provide more effective gun support to the III Corps sector."

"T-That sounds suspiciously like *blackmail*, Lieutenant!"

He sighed in exasperation. "Not really, Captain. I mean, no direct threats were made, and furthermore, if you stop to think about it, it's a natural evolution thanks to all the great things the advisers are saying about having our air support, right? In fact, the word is the operations officer in question rather enthusiastically sold the project to the MACV commander and came away something of a brilliant tactician in the process, so where's the harm? The fact is, as of yesterday the Cobras were withdrawn from the ARVN list and orders were drawn up for their assignment to the Deans as replacements for our Charlie models."

"Is that it, Lieutenant?" I demanded. "You said this was the short version. Is there more you're not telling me?"

"Captain, I'd really rather not go there unless you insist."

I sat back in my chair as he studied me over the rim of his glass. So now I knew—and technically speaking he was right—nothing illegal had transpired. Just immoral, undermining, devious, self-serving manipulation that I wish I didn't know about.

He set his glass down. "Captain, this needs to be the last time I go through this kind of thing with you. I gave you my word in the beginning I wouldn't do anything illegal, and I haven't. But I *will* use the system to beat the system, and I *will* use unconventional means to achieve my goals. Please don't ask me for particulars again. I'd prefer you not know them. It could harm some of the people involved in helping me. Do you understand?"

I nodded bleakly. "Yes, Lieutenant, I understand. I just couldn't imagine how you were going to pull this off. So, out of the blue, Major Crystal will receive an order from MACV to turn in our Charlie models and pick up the Cobras?"

"Something like that, and it's important you be as surprised as he when it happens." He motioned my two new captains back to the table. "Now can we get back to drinking, Captain?"

Benedict seated himself. "All is well?"

I nodded reluctantly. "All … is well."

"And we're gonna get the Cobras?"

"I absolutely believe that to be so," I acknowledged glumly.

"Is anybody going to jail?" Everett asked.

I sighed. "Not this time apparently."

Lieutenant Sharpe lifted his glass. "Let's get our platoon transitioned, gentlemen. Time is short!"

And we drank to the devil as he leered at us.

Ellen and her freewheeling entourage of nurses came in a few minutes later, and the party started in earnest. I took the opportunity to slip out to write a letter to Nancy and turn in early, filled with misgivings.

The next day when summoned to Major Crystal's office, I slipped through his door on trembling legs with my best bland look, saluted, and took a chair as directed.

"You're not going to believe this, Captain."

"What's that, Sir?" I asked meekly.

He buried his face in his palms. "That god-damned lieutenant of yours has gotten so much attention MACV has decided to replace our Charlie models with Cobras. There's no way I could have anticipated this. I'm afraid we're stuck with those guns. There's nothing I can do."

"I understand, Sir."

He thumped his fist on the desk. "Damn! You're down to seven flyable aircraft. Another week and there would've been none!" He shook his head sadly. "We'll just have to make the best of it. If MACV wants air support, we'll give them air support. There are fifteen of those damn Cobras somewhere in the depot at Vung Tau. Make arrangements to bring them here and to turn in our Charlie models. I've instructed flight ops to provide whatever resources you need."

"Thank you, Sir. I'll get right on it. Anything else, Sir?"

"Have you come up with anything I can hang on that little bastard?"

"Not yet, Sir, but I'm watching him closely."

"Well, if he's being quiet, that means he's plotting something, so be alert, Captain!"

"Yes, Sir."

I sneaked out as he sat morosely staring out his window.

CHAPTER 7

The following four weeks were hell on the men as they spent ten-hour days maintaining the sickly Charlie models and an additional eight to ten hours a day cramming in the classes my two captains conducted.

True to Lieutenant Sharpe's word, two Cobras flew in the following morning. Two of our maintenance NCOs who had been to the Cobra maintenance school quickly became part of Captain Everett's training team. The lieutenant insisted on going through Captain Benedict's flight transition course with the first group, leading them to the limits of their endurance. Two weeks later he led the first contingent to Vung Tau to complete their formal Cobra transition training. They returned five days later as qualified Cobra attack helicopter pilots. My exhausted lieutenant promptly vanished into his room for sixteen hours upon his return—with a doting Ellen to care for him.

During this period our platoon flew nineteen sorties in the Charlie models in support of the war effort, resulting in one aircraft shot up and three more grounded for repairs awaiting parts, leaving us three flyable birds. On the optimistic side, the lieutenant stayed out of Major Crystal's way, and the corps commander positively beamed with the reports he received from the field concerning our support role as the platoon eagerly awaited our new aircraft and the increased combat capability they would give us.

We spent two days flying our prizes home and arranging for the non-flyable Charlie models to be sling-loaded out by Chinook heavy-lift helicopters. With the last of the Cobras picked up, we dropped off our last three Charlie models, placed our remaining pilots and maintenance personnel in the transition course, and flew home. That evening fifteen pristine Cobras stood arrayed before us at the airfield.

I walked onto the tarmac to stare up in wonder at one of the magnificent birds. Long and tall compared to our short, squat Charlie models, it was barely a yard wide when looked at head-on, posing virtually no target in the attack mode. The pilot sat high in the rear, and the gunner sat low in the nose directly in front of him with no crew chief or door gunner required. The nose sported a 40-millimeter cannon and a 7.65 minigun capable of firing four thousand rounds a minute. Rocket pods suspended on each side held 76 rockets in a potent mixture of high explosive and flechette rounds. Powered by the latest turbine engine capable of producing four times the lifting power of the Charlie model, it had more than twice the speed at 180 knots. The arms system was the most advanced available, providing deadly gyroscopic accuracy to its guns and rockets. Where the Charlie model gunship evolved out of the troop transport UH-1 filled with flaws and inadequacies, this hot rod was built from the blueprint up as a pure gunship designed for speed, deception, and destruction—a ferocious killing machine that carried more firepower than six Charlie models together or a whole company of Infantry. Even sitting idle before me, it appeared lean, mean, and hungry, seemingly spoiling for a fight.

Lieutenant Sharpe and Captains Benedict and Everett eased up beside me as I peered up at the intimidating bird of prey with the setting sun casting a golden halo around it.

"It looks mad or something," I observed dolefully.

"There's not another in the world more beautiful or proud and lethal," the lieutenant mused. "She steals my heart just looking at her."

"She's as fast as greased lightening and as deadly as a ... *Cobra!*" Captain Benedict observed.

"She's poetry in motion," Captain Everett added, shielding his eyes against the setting sun as he stared up at the aircraft. "Woe be it to any man who gets on her fighting side."

"Do they give you guys psychological tests to certify your insanity before they make you gun pilots?" I asked cautiously. When they stared at me inquisitively, I sulked back to the hangar in despair.

I broke the platoon into three sections of five aircraft, one section each under Captains Benedict and Everett and one under Lieutenant Sharpe, with seven pilots in each section. They spent the next three days on a free-fire range polishing their tactics and perfecting their gunnery skills, seemingly in heaven with the lithe Cobras after the cumbersome Charlie models. The crew chiefs painted our Razorback emblem on the nose— when they could get them away from the pilots long enough for the paint to dry.

Our arrogant little lieutenant had once again engineered the impossible. After a miraculous six weeks, we were a fully transitioned, combat-ready, cohesive unit with a bona-fide mission, and fast becoming the darlings of III Corps. As I sat pondering our fate, a hearty knock shook the door to my office in the hangar. I looked up to see a short, dark, beefy captain wearing a camouflaged boonie hat peering in at me.

"Come on in," I offered.

He eased into my tiny cubicle and plopped down in the only chair outside of my own beside my desk. "I'm Dan Harding. I need you to approve my assignment from the Yellow Platoon to the Red Platoon."

"Why do you want to join the Razorbacks?" I asked carefully.

"Mostly I want one of those silver flight suits," he replied. "I'm a fully qualified Cobra maintenance officer on my second tour of duty over here, and I understand you desperately need one."

"We do indeed," I replied cautiously. "But I warn you we're a little unconventional around here compared to the other platoons."

He grinned. "Hell, everybody knows that, and it's the second reason I want to join up with you guys."

"Um, well, welcome aboard, Dan. We'll go see Major Crystal this afternoon to get the transfer approved. I know my maintenance sergeant will be glad to see you. He's about worked himself to death over the last few weeks."

When I informed flight ops the following morning the Razorbacks were mission ready, Lieutenant Sharpe felt compelled to throw another hangar party. Under his supervision, by evening, music, tubs of beer, and plenty of nurses were on hand with barbeque pits smoldering.

During the height of the festivities as Captain Harding and I stood off to the side watching, Ellen waltzed by in the lieutenant's arms and laid a sizzling lip-lock on him amid the celebrating men.

"Ohooo, Sugar Bear, you make my toes curl," she cooed as she hung limply in his arms.

"*That's* what I'm looking for," Harding announced as he motioned to the lieutenant's crew chief on the crowded dance floor.

"You wanna see me, Sir?" the crew chief asked after threading his way over to him.

"Specialist, first thing in the morning I want *A/C: Sugar Bear* painted in script on the side of the lieutenant's aircraft just below the canopy. You got that?"

The crew chief eyed him hesitantly. "What does it mean, Sir?"

"It means *Aircraft Commander* and Lieutenant Sharpe's new nickname, *Sugar Bear*," he replied.

The crew chief grinned. "Done deal, Sir, but only if you promise not to let that crazy critter kill me for doing it!"

"And under his name, add *Crew Chief,* followed by your new nickname, *Critter.* Got it?"

"*Critter*? I sorta like that, Captain!"

"Then see to it, Critter!"

"Yes, Sir!"

As the newly christened Critter rejoined the throng on the dance floor, I turned to Captain Harding, who was now to my disquieting dismay wearing what appeared to be a huge purple sultan's turban with a big fake emerald attached to the front.

"What was that all about?" I inquired somewhat anxiously.

"Well, *Boss Hog*, since we work in such close proximity and are forced to trust one another with our very lives, I see no reason to continue tripping all over each other's rank. Using nicknames will help lighten things up a bit."

As I stood absorbing this bit of wisdom, Captain Benedict stumbled by with an attractive nurse tucked under his arm.

"Oh, you're a devilishly sly one, alright," she giggled as they passed.

Captain Harding immediately motioned Captain Benedict's crew chief over and directed he stencil *A/C: Sly* below the canopy of his aircraft.

Thus this newest custom initiated by my latest exigent officer acquisition bounded through the platoon like a herd of gazelles on a hot African plain. Almost overnight virtually every man in the Razorbacks answered to his own colorful moniker, which indeed did seem to heighten morale by reducing the strain of the many conflicting ranks. Captain Everett acquired his nickname the next day when, it seems, he left early for the airfield leaving behind in his bed a profoundly sated nurse. The lady awoke later and pinned a note to his door before she left. The Vietnamese hooch-maid who cleaned his room took the note to the aviator next door to read, assuming it was instructions left for her. That aviator promptly took the note to the airfield, keyed the transmitter on the Dean flight operations frequency—which every aircraft in the unit monitored at all times—and read it to Captain Everett over the air.

My Dearest One,
You are truly a dandy. I cannot express the joy you fill me with. Last night was the zaniest, most wonderfully frivolous, crazy, and incredibly exciting evening a

woman could lust for. I hope it's not our last and look forward to being your little love slave again soon. My body and soul await your beck and call.
Linda.

So *Dandy* Captain Everett became, to his chagrin amid the howls of laughter. I even joined the circus by dubbing Captain Harding the *Mad Hatter* partly due to the offbeat headgear he wore, but mostly to get even for his baptizing me *Chief Hog*.

Several nights later when our usual bevy of free-spirited nurses breezed into the O Club for the by now customary evening party, my attention was immediately drawn to a drop-dead gorgeous newcomer with white hair framing deep blue eyes above a perfectly proportioned figure on a small, exquisite frame.

"Everybody, this is Cherrie," Ellen introduced as she plopped down in Lieutenant Sharpe's lap with the newbie's entrance completely subjugating the entire room and stopping the low roar of chatter as eyes popped out and mouths salivated like hungry wolves. "Cherrie is the newest member to our hospital staff."

"Hi, Cherrie, have a seat," the lieutenant offered, raking her appreciatively from head to toe as she flushed under his bold appraisal. The rest of us quickly made room, elbowing each other aside in our haste to pull out a chair for her as she sat down across from him and Ellen.

"People are watching!" Ellen exclaimed, fighting Sharpe's hands from beneath her skirt.

"Let's give them a show then," he challenged as she squealed in protest.

"He thinks all women should be exploited," Ellen warned as she picked up his glass and sipped.

Cherrie frowned. "Is there any other kind of male beast?"

"I take it you're not an ardent supporter of free love?" the lieutenant challenged.

"I've found only things of intransient value are free," Cherrie countered.

Sharpe tipped his glass to her. "Good point."

Her eyes meshed with his. "I've heard some pretty incredible things about you guys."

He held her stare. "Welcome to The Nam … where you can believe only half of what you see and none of what you hear." They sipped, eyes locked across the rims of their glasses charging the air with electric intensity.

"This is Sly, Dandy, Mad Hatter, and Chief Hog," he introduced casually before indicating the other Razorbacks clustered around us gazing at her awestruck. "The rest of these, err, *gentlemen*, you can meet as we go along."

Cherrie's attention remained fixed on the lieutenant. "And what do they call you?"

"*Sugar Bear*," Ellen answered, "'cause he's sweetly dangerous!"

Cherrie glanced at Ellen. "I take it you two are, um … *together?*"

Ellen's smile slipped. "Not really—I claim no one and laying claim to him is like trying to lasso the wind."

The lieutenant grinned. "Consider us as more along the lines of *kindred spirits.*"

"Sorry … I didn't mean to infer …"

He shrugged. "No harm, no foul."

"I've sure missed you guys," Karen, a pretty brunette seated beside me, injected with a pronounced pout in the strained silence. "Did you miss me?"

"Of course we did, sweetheart," the lieutenant replied, turning to hug her. "Where've you been?"

"I've had night shift. So what have I missed?"

"Chief Hog here's been trying to kill us for the last six weeks," he complained. "He wants everything done yesterday. You know how that goes."

Karen slid onto my lap, wrapped her arms around my neck, and stared up at me with half-lidded eyes. "So maybe he needs a distraction so you guys can catch a break?" she teased.

"I … I'm a family man …" I choked out, squirming as she nuzzled my earlobe.

"And alas, as such, unavailable," she cooed sadly as everyone laughed.

"Doesn't availability tend to be a geographically dependent condition with most men?" Cherrie quipped.

Even I might be tempted under the right circumstances, I thought deep down in my lustful, degenerate soul before Nancy's image appeared in my mind to instill remorseful guilt for the moment of lecherous weakness.

"That's true enough, I suppose," the lieutenant countered. "Given that women generally get what they want and mostly want what they can't have." He turned to Captain Benedict. "Which reminds me, Sly, I'm going after that gun tomorrow. Want to tag along?"

The chatter instantly died out as everyone tuned in to the two of them in watchful suspense.

"Why?" Captain Benedict inquired coolly.

The lieutenant shrugged. "He's in my way."

Benedict's eyes narrowed. "Leave well enough alone, Sugar Bear."

The lieutenant shook his head. "Can't, he's made it a challenge."

Cherrie turned to Mad Hatter. "What are they talking about?"

"Apparently Sugar Bear's got this crazy fixation on this anti-aircraft gun that shot him down," Mad Hatter explained.

"Shot *three* of us down," the lieutenant corrected. "And we can't let him get away with that. It's a matter of pride and principle."

Benedict crossed his arms. "I'd consider taking your gun out for you for another fancy flight suit."

"No deal," the lieutenant scoffed. "He's mine and I'll take it out myself. You can fly my wing."

Benedict laughed. "Yeah, right, and if you miss, it'll be my ass too. You don't have enough experience yet."

The lieutenant rocked forward in his chair. "You get experience by *doing* it, Sly. I *won't* miss."

Benedict eyed him warily. "You truly are crazy."

Sharpe raised his glass. "Hell, I'll drink to that, but the deal is, you help me take out the gun for one flight suit. Are you in?"

Benedict raised his glass. "I guess that gun's going down then. We'll need Dandy too."

"Bullshit!" Captain Everett protested. "You two are nuts! Count me out!"

"A suit for you too, Dandy, if you'll join us," the lieutenant offered.

"I don't buy into this pride and principle thing, Sugar Bear," he insisted. "Besides, who would take care of my sweet little Linda here if I got my ass busted out there with you fools?"

"*I will!*"

"*No, me! I'll do it!*"

"*You can count on me being there for you, Dandy!*" a chorus of volunteers promised as Linda giggled nervously.

The lieutenant nodded. "It's all settled then! So what's the plan, Sly?"

A hush descended over us again as Captain Benedict smiled. "Simple, Dandy prances around out there and draws their fire so we can pinpoint their location. You go after the big gun, and I'll take out his little sidekick. It's not a problem as long as we coordinate our attacks ... and neither of us misses."

The lieutenant grinned. "Sounds easy enough."

"It is," Benedict assured him. "But it's even easier to screw it up, so I want the flight suit *before* we depart."

"Me too," Dandy echoed uneasily. "And just how much 'prancing around' am I expected to do out there anyway?"

"We'll cover the details before departure in the morning," Benedict replied.

"*Gentlemen and Razorbacks!*" Mad Hatter shouted as he scrambled up on top of the table holding his glass high. "I propose a toast to our three noble knights who go forth on the morrow to do battle with the forces of evil in order to redeem our daunted self-esteem! To *Sly*, the cunning tactician; *Dandy*, the designated target; and our own fearless champion who will be waving the twin banners of pride and principle as he dives into the fiery enemy stronghold to smote our adversaries, our very own *Sugar Bear*! May our three brave warriors' valorous endeavors bring forth the enemy Gideon to our fold!"

The lieutenant clinked glasses with Benedict and Everett as a rousing cheer shook the club and all stood to join in the toast—even, to my astonishment, the green and yellow hats.

What is this world coming to, I wondered as I lifted my glass to the three men staring calmly at one another. *This strange man has united us heart and soul, and bent us yet again to his forceful will!*

CHAPTER 8

When I arrived at the hangar the next morning the three aircraft had already departed and my small office was crowded with eager men clustered around my radio. I chased them out and set the speaker outside in the bay so everyone could hear, where they clustered around making wagers and laying odds as Ellen, Cherrie, Linda, Sandra, and two other nurses hurriedly joined the group. A moment later my stomach did a flip-flop when Major Crystal's jeep pulled up to the operations shack and he rushed inside. Almost immediately, my landline rang and Captain Nichols requested I report to flight operations, where I faced a glaring Major Crystal upon my arrival.

"Captain, I'm not stupid, regardless of what your little shit-for-brains lieutenant thinks!"

I tensed. "Sir?"

"I know about that little moron and those two idiotic captains! I should have suspected something when they asked to be reassigned to the Red Platoon."

A litany of our crimes flashed through my mind as my heart pounded—perhaps it'd be best to fall on his mercy. "Sir, I can explain—"

"Explain what, Captain—that you now have *three* degenerates assigned to you? I intend to put a halt to this ridiculous farce and court-martial that little wise-ass lieutenant in the process!" He turned to Captain Nichols. "Give me the particulars of exactly how this cockeyed mission came about!"

Captain Nichols quickly consulted his mission sheet. "S-Sir, a mission request came out of a fire base near Go Dau Ha at 0800 hours this morning for air support. I-I assure you I had no indications it was not on the up and up at the time! They reported a heavy machine gun attacking their compound sporadically. I advised the Red Platoon it was a probable an anti-aircraft gun and carried some risk. Captains Benedict, Everett, and Lieutenant Sharpe immediately responded as mission ready."

Major Crystal sneered. "How convenient! Especially since the three of them planned the mission last night in the O Club! I'm going to get to the bottom of this! Do we have communications with Go Dau Ha?"

"Yes, Sir," Captain Nichols confirmed. "We have a landline connection. That's how we received the mission request."

"Get their commander on the phone!" Major Crystal turned back to me cracking his knuckles in eager anticipation. "I think our arrogant little lieutenant has just crossed the line, Captain Hess! You were right about giving the little shit enough rope to hang himself!"

My heart rapidly increased tempo as sweat beaded my forehead. *Come on, lieutenant, surely you didn't do anything stupid like fabricating a bogus mission!*

"Yes, Go Dau Ha? This is Captain Nichols from Dean flight operations, Dean Six would like to talk to your Six. Yes, I'll hold." Captain Nichols placed a palm over his other ear as he pressed the receiver closer. "The connection's weak, Sir, but they're getting the … Yes, Go Dau Ha, I'm still here. Colonel Masterson, please hold, Sir. Major Crystal would like to speak to … No, Sir, I'm not his personal secretary, I'm his flight op … Yes, Sir, I realize that, Sir. Sorry, Sir. Here's Major Crystal, Sir!"

He thrust the phone at Major Crystal. "Sir, he's pissed because he was summoned to talk to a junior commander by a subordinate!"

Major Crystal lifted the receiver to his ear. "Colonel Masterson? Good morning to you, Sir! I'm sorry to bother you, but I've got this little problem here and I need to verify … Yes, Sir. My apologies, Sir, I was busy and asked my flight ops officer to … Yes, Sir, I realize you're busy too, Sir! I just … Yes, Sir! Yes, Sir! Uh, well, Sir, our aircraft are en route to you as we speak, Sir, and I assure you we're proud to be of service to you! Yes, Sir, that is correct, Sir, three of my best crews are on their way and if you need more you just let us know! I assure you I'm *personally* monitoring the situation, and if you need *anything* else, you just let me know, Sir. Yes, Sir, thank you, Sir. I appreciate that, Sir. Out here, Sir." Major Crystal hung up the phone and swallowed hard as he turned to us.

"Well, uh, it uh, sure *seems* to be a legal mission! Apparently they summoned him to the phone in the middle of the battle—now how in *hell* did that little fruitcake pull *that* shit off?"

My heartbeat slowed as wary relief washed through me. *How* did *that little fruitcake pull that shit off?* I realized I had not drawn a breath in several minutes and quickly gulped air into my depleted lungs and swiped at my brow gratefully, thinking my nerves couldn't take much more of my lieutenant's shenanigans.

"Turn up the speakers on the alternate radio and put it on the Red Platoon operational frequency," Major Crystal directed in exasperation.

Captain Nichols tuned in the frequency and the speakers jumped to life.

"Roger, Sugar Bear, I have a visual on your primary target, but not my secondary target," Captain Benedict transmitted. "Do you have a firm fix on the position?"

"Roger, Sly, the little dumb bastard drew me a nice straight line with his tracers," the lieutenant replied.

"Roger, Sugar Bear, stand by," Captain Benedict advised. "Dandy, make another run to try and draw his little buddy out."

"Dandy, he was near that little rise off to your left there the last time I was out here," the lieutenant advised.

"Oh, sure, just swing on back through there again and wiggle my ass so he can shoot my tail feathers out," Captain Everett complained. "I nearly pissed myself when the big boy opened up and sent those basketballs whizzing by!"

"Be a sport, Dandy, all we need is a few rounds from his little pal," Captain Benedict soothed. "Sugar Bear, climb and relocate to the east to get the sun behind you. Set your time to target for thirty seconds. Lead with your rockets and pooper and then raze him with the minis when you go by. Got that?"

"Hot damn! Taking fire! Taking fire!" Captain Everett's frantic call jumped out of the speakers at us. "I'm hit. I'm hit!"

"Roll right, Dandy, roll right!" Captain Benedict called. "I've got a fix on him. How bad are you hit?"

"I-I think I'm okay, Sly" Captain Everett answered, obviously shaken. "Several rounds hit me, but my gauges are steady, my controls are solid, and I'm still flying."

"I think I just shit my pants!" his copilot cut in with a nervous chuckle.

"Dandy, if you're flight-worthy, go into a holding pattern south of us and stand by," Captain Benedict ordered. "Sugar Bear, where the hell are you? I can't see you."

"I'm hiding up here in the freaking sun like you told me to do, Sly," the lieutenant replied. "You're not *supposed* to see me, and I hope that little bastard with the big cannon can't see me either. I'm thirty seconds out on target, waiting for you to get your shit together."

"Roger, I'm coming around now," Captain Benedict affirmed in a strained voice. "Are you sure about your time to target?"

"Well hell, Sly, I didn't exactly make a practice run on him or anything, but it's the best I can estimate," the lieutenant replied.

"Roger, get your wits about you," Captain Benedict ordered. "We've got one chance to get this right. On my count, begin your attack. Good luck, Sugar Bear."

"Let's kick some gook ass, Sly!" the lieutenant replied.

"You two assholes be careful now," Captain Everett cautioned.

"Roger that, Dandy," the lieutenant answered. "We can't afford to lose another bird—Dean Six has about cornered the market on my damned flight suits!"

"Five – Four – Three – Two – ONE! *Rolling hot!*" Captain Benedict advised.

"*Yee HAW!* Rollin' with you, Sly!" the lieutenant yelled.

The swish of rockets leaving their tubes emitted from the speaker before the transmission ended. The radio was utterly silent now as we stood in the tense operations room. The thirty seconds of silence became almost unbearable as I stared out the window at the crowd in my hangar hovering around their own speakers as we inside held our breath.

The lieutenant's voice jumped out at us in the hush. "I got him! I got the bastard! Look at those secondary explosions!"

"*Mayday! Mayday!* I'm going down! Going down!" Captain Benedict yelled. "I'm flame out and going down!"

"I'm coming around, Sly!" the lieutenant called. "Did you get the little gun?"

"I'm locked on you, Sly!" Captain Everett called. "Oh shit! Taking fire! Taking fire! Get him off me, Sugar Bear!"

"I'm rolling on him now, Dandy!" the lieutenant called through the grinding roar of his miniguns. "Oh *hell* yeah, you little slant-eyed piece of shit—*your ass is mine!*"

"Didn't you hear the Mayday call? Launch the heavy lift rescue, goddamn it!" Captain Nichols yelled, sending his ops sergeant scrambling for the field-phone.

"Sly's down safely, Sugar Bear!" Captain Everett reported. "I'm flying cap over him now."

"Roger, I think the little gun is neutralized, Dandy," the lieutenant answered. "He's not firing back at me. I'm going to make another run on him for good measure; you keep Sly covered, okay?"

"Roger that," Dandy transmitted. "They're both out and waving at me. Sly appears to be taking a piss as we speak."

We waited for several minutes, silence again engulfing us as we listened intently.

"Red One-Seven, this is Big Bird. Your flight ops daddy called and gave me your approximate location and frequency. Whatcha got goin' on out there, buddy?"

"Roger, Big Bird," the lieutenant answered. "We're just having a little fun in the sun out here at Go Dau Ha, over."

"Roger, One-Seven, and Go Dau Ha yourself, Snake boy," Big Bird chuckled. "Can we join the party?"

"Roger, Big Bird. Come on out," the lieutenant answered. "We've got a Snake down in good condition and need an extraction. Area is unsecured, but Red One-One and I are flying cover, over."

"Roger, One-Seven, ETA is ten minutes. We've got Little Bird with us to snatch the crew, and I've got a recovery team on board for the Snake. We'll need twenty minutes on site, over."

"Roger, Big Bird. We're close on fuel, so don't jack around," the lieutenant replied.

"You just keep the bad guys at bay and we'll get your crew and Snake outta there, One-Seven," Big Bird responded.

"Consider it done, Big Bird, and thanks for the rapid response," the lieutenant called.

"That's what us dull old transports are all about, One-Seven—to clean up the mess you glory boys make," Big Bird radioed back.

"Roger, Big Bird, somebody's got to do the dirty work," the lieutenant bantered happily.

"There you have it, One-Seven," Big Bird agreed.

The downed Cobra was out in fifteen minutes, slung under the belly of the giant Chinook. Little Bird picked up Sly and his copilot in their slick, and Dandy and the lieutenant escorted them home. Both hovered to their ramps as the crowd in my hangar surged toward them in an excited mass. The Chinook dropped Sly's wounded Cobra off near our hangar as the slick deposited him and his copilot on the pad. When the lieutenant opened his canopy and dropped down to the pavement, the assembled group rushed at him in a cheering mob. Ellen flung herself into his arms as Cherrie stood silently watching. Linda rushed to embrace Captain Everett as he dismounted, and Sandra clung to Sly as he wrapped one arm around her and raised the other in a clenched-fist victory salute to the lieutenant and Captain Everett. In the ensuing melee, Major Crystal slunk off in a huff without directing me to have any of us report to him.

"How'd you get that mission called in?" I shouted in the lieutenant's ear when I could get near him in the mass of bodies.

He grinned as he draped his arm around Ellen. "They owed me a favor, Captain. When I called, they were more than happy to oblige us. Why?"

"Major Crystal got wind of it from somebody at the club last night and came out here specifically to bust our ass. He even called Go Dau Ha to confirm it was a legit mission."

The lieutenant laughed. "I guess clean living pays off, don't it, Captain? I'd love to have heard that conversation."

"Judging by Major Crystal's side of it, it wasn't very pleasant. That was too close for comfort."

The lieutenant scowled. "I had a feeling it'd be a good idea to cover our ass in case anything went wrong— I'd love to know who the skunk was that ratted us out!"

My after-action report read: "In the ensuing engagement on this date, Captain Everett's aircraft took six rounds through the fuselage without sustaining serious damage. Captain Benedict's aircraft took four rounds through the fuselage, one of which severed a fuel line causing the engine to fail and forcing an emergency power off autorotation, executed without further damage incurring to the aircraft due to pilot's exceptional skills. Maintenance judges both aircraft will be flight worthy within two days." After I signed and filed the report with flight ops, I went directly to the Dean lounge by myself and quaffed down two straight shots of raw tequila.

When we assembled at the club that evening, we discovered Mad Hatter had bolted a pilot's armored seat high up on the wall and wired an old aviator helmet without the inner headbands into the stereo so that it would broadcast over the speaker system. As our rowdy victory celebration progressed, he crawled up into the seat, strapped himself in, and placed the helmet on his head, where it wobbled around in a hilarious fashion.

The festive roar of the club subsided expectantly as he spread his arms. "Ladies, Gentlemen, and Razorbacks! Henceforth any aviator in our brotherhood who engages the enemy in combat will be strapped into this hallowed hot seat so that he may share his stimulating tale with those assembled in order for us lesser mortals to draw inspiration from his daring deed. At the conclusion of his yarn our hero will then down a flaming Drambuie to cleanse all the bullshit left hanging in the air."

The assembled crowd received this new ritual with wild enthusiasm and Lieutenant Sharpe, already prepped with round after round of booze from his adoring audience, was borne forthwith upon the shoulders of the drunken mob, strapped into the chair, and the helmet placed on his head amid chants of "*War Story! War Story! War Story!*"

"Well, there I was," he proclaimed in a slur as the group quieted. "Just me and the four hundred gooks I had cornered." The crowd cheered enthusiastically. "I was all alone because one of my wing men had wandered off to the south to get his bearings as he waffled around in a most odious cloud of gas released by his copilot. My other wing had landed in a rice paddy at a most inappropriate time, apparently for the express purpose of playing with his dong." A chorus of applause rose as Sly and Dandy grinned and shook their heads. "Needless to say, I held my position and single-handedly pressed home the attack through the huge glowing orbs whizzing by my head erupting from the steady hammering of the cannon trying to bring me down in flames. Alas, being the staunch pilot I am, I pressed home my attack until I had exhausted my rockets and miniguns, sending the varmint to hell in a great billowing ball of fire. But being ever resourceful, as well as handsome and debonair, I searched out the second enemy position and again attacked, even though out of ammo. I proceeded to land on top of the rascal's head and do a pedal turn, thereby screwing the tyrant into the ground as he screamed in agony. I then flew out victorious as his buddies fled in terror. And I swear this to be the truth as I know it to be!"

Amid the feral cheering, Mad Hatter handed a Drambuie up to him with the top lit in blue flame. The lieutenant lifted the drink in a toast to us, downed it, and breathed out a gush of flames as the horde roared approval. The crowd then transported Sly on their shoulders and placed him up in the chair, where he strapped in.

"Well, there I was," he began amongst the cheering. "There were actually six hundred gooks. I knew from the outset I would have to carry the whole mission because I had two inexperienced greenhorns for wingmen. One of them was out to the south flying in circles after his copilot's premature bowel movement, and the other was lost somewhere to the east in the sun. I attacked both positions simultaneously in a fiery roar of rockets and miniguns, destroying both sites in one daring, graceful dive. But alas, during the attack the enemy put up a fierce barrage of counter fire, whereupon one lucky round killed my engine. With no other options open to me, I auto-rotated into a convenient field to await Big Bird's extraction, where I was forced to keep the enemy at bay by pissing at them. Unbeknownst to me at the time, Sugar Bear arrived on the scene, late as usual, and made a belated gun run on both destroyed sites, thereby receiving all the credit for my victory. And I swear this to be the truth as I know it to be!"

A flaming Drambuie made its way up to him amid gleeful cheers, where he toasted the crowd, tossed it back, and spewed flames from his mouth amid thunderous applause. Dandy was next strapped into the chair and fitted with the helmet.

"Well, there I was," he began, holding his hands out to calm everyone. "As the designated target in order to facilitate the attack, I personally counted eight hundred gooks as I flew by and scouted the position, taking intense fire the whole time. My copilot thought there were a thousand, so for accuracy's sake, I flew by a second time to recount them. On the second pass, my copilot experienced a huge gastric attack, whose noxious fumes temporarily incapacitated me. When I regained consciousness, I found myself somewhere to the south. I immediately flew back to the target and found Sly standing in a field fondling himself and Sugar Bear flying around in circles, obviously lost as usual. Upon seeing me, the enemy fled in terror, destroying their guns in place to prevent me from capturing them. And I swear that to be the truth as I know it to be!"

When presented his flaming Drambuie, he downed it, blew the flames out in a huge fireball, unstrapped himself, and promptly fell out onto his face to another round of jovial cheers.

I somberly raised my glass in toast to the three of them as they reseated themselves around my table. "To a good mission."

"To a good mission!" they chanted solemnly, hoisting their glasses.

"Do you guys do that sort of thing often?" Cherrie inquired tentatively as Ellen slid into the lieutenant's lap. "I mean, it sounded so graphic and scary over the radio."

"Hell no," Dandy assured her. "Most of the time it's boring as hell, but Sugar Bear tends to liven things up a bit for us. That gun we took out today's not something we ordinarily fool around with."

Cherrie turned to the lieutenant. "So why did you do it?"

He shrugged. "Because it was there."

"But you could have gotten killed!"

He studied her in wry amusement. "That's what made it interesting."

"Is your life so unimportant to you?"

"It's not about living or dying; it's about the thrill of battle."

"It just seems like such a … I don't know, such an *empty gesture*, especially since the war is almost over."

He grinned. "Do you want to play shrink with me, darling? That might be intriguing."

"Pardon me for being a third wheel here!" Ellen simpered as she slipped off the lieutenant's lap. "The heat radiating between you two is stifling!"

Cherrie flushed. "Ellen, I … I *assure* you I—"

"Enjoy, *darling*," Ellen tossed over her shoulder as she wandered over to the next table and slid onto the lap of the lieutenant's copilot. "Just keep in mind he's not the committing type!"

"She's right," the lieutenant counseled. "That needs to be understood upfront before we play the doctor game."

"I-I don't want to play doctor with you, and I didn't mean to imply I was interested in you *personally*,"

Cherrie sputtered. "I just find it hard to comprehend what you do."

Sly smirked. "Give me odds, Dandy?"

Dandy shrugged. "Time frame?"

"Inside three days?" Sly challenged.

"Two to one?" Dandy bargained.

Sly nodded. "For five?"

"You're on," Dandy acknowledged.

"What are you betting on?" Cherrie asked, looking from one to the other.

"Just ignore them," the lieutenant advised as he glared at them.

"You should go to her," Cherrie encouraged, refocusing on Ellen. "I didn't mean to cause a problem. I was just trying to understand. I'll go talk to her if you'd like."

"For what purpose?"

"T-To try and smooth things over with her …"

The lieutenant glanced over his shoulder at Ellen, who was laughing with Skeeter. "She appears to be just fine to me."

"But I don't want her upset with me," Cherrie argued.

"You touched on a nerve with all the talk of dying. She hates violence in any form, especially when she thinks it's taken so lightly."

"Then why *do* you take it so lightly?"

He grinned. "Now we're back to playing doctor, darling. Best we don't go there until we know each other a whole lot better than we do now."

She sat back in exasperation. "I don't understand any of you, or what you do, or even what just happened here tonight."

"You will in time," the lieutenant assured her. "You're still a newby to Nam."

She frowned. "Nothing I've seen or heard since I got here makes any sense at all!"

"You have to be a little crazy to understand this place. You're not there yet. In the end you'll learn it don't mean *nothing*."

She stood. "Please excuse me; I'm going over to talk to Ellen."

As she hurried over to Ellen's table, Sly chuckled. "All this damned foreplay between you two is getting tiresome, Sugar Bear."

"*You* need to mind your own damned business," the lieutenant retorted.

"He's just teasing," Linda soothed.

"But he's right," Sandra coached from Sly's lap. "It's obvious to everyone you're attracted to each other."

"*Everyone* needs to mind their *own* damned business," the lieutenant insisted.

"You guys lighten up," Linda scolded Sly and Sandra. "They'll find their own way, for heaven's sake!"

"Are you kidding me?" Sandra demanded. "These guys are so eaten up with themselves they couldn't find their own way in broad daylight with a flashlight!"

"That's part of their charm," Linda insisted, laughing. "If they weren't so damned arrogant they wouldn't do what they do. They may be crazy as hell, but you've got to admit it's interesting to see what they'll do next."

"*I'm* not crazy!" Sly insisted.

Sandra patted his cheek. "Of course you're not, honey-buns. I meant everyone else *but* you, silly."

I yawned. "Folks, if you'll excuse me, it's my bedtime."

I left them to their weird debate, grateful the day had ended well for us and that no one had been killed.

123

After dashing off a short note to Nancy, I tumbled into bed promising myself I would keep a tighter rein on my lieutenant in the future ... especially since it was blatantly obvious Sly and Dandy weren't going to be of much help in that department.

CHAPTER 9

Three days later, called unexpectedly from our hangar to the flight line, Sly, Dandy, Sugar Bear, and their copilots received the Air Medal for Valor for their attack on the anti-aircraft site, courtesy of Colonel Masterson, who put them in for the decorations with a glowing report of the operation to the corps commander. A surly Major Crystal pinned the medals to their chests and departed immediately after the ceremony with the briefest of handshakes extended to each of them.

That afternoon an aircraft in Sly's section took battle damage from ground fire and limped home with the pilot hit in the ribs and requiring hospitalization. That night we prepared the "hot seat," poured liquor down the copilot, and strapped him into the chair devoid of cheer out of respect for the wounded pilot.

"Well, there we were," he began in the hush and proceeded to tell his story of flying support for an ARVN unit in the Ho Bo Woods, where they took thirteen hits from small-arms fire. When he finished, I settled in at a table with Sly, Dandy, Linda, Sandra, and Cherrie. Intent on boosting morale in the glum atmosphere, Mad Hatter proposed a toast to our six pilots who received decorations that morning.

"Join us, Sugar Bear," Sly ordered curtly

Sharpe, seated next to us at a table with Ellen, his copilot Skeeter, and several others, ambled over and sat down across from Cherrie.

"I'm sorry things are still strained between you and Ellen," Cherrie apologized.

"Things are fine between us," Sharpe replied as the two matched eyes. "She and Skeeter seem to have a thing between them now."

"And that doesn't bother you?" Cherrie demanded.

"Why should it?" Sharpe inquired.

"Well … you and Ellen … I thought—"

"I don't have any tomorrows," Sharp injected. "She understands that completely."

"I-I don't get it …"

"There's only one thing you need to understand, darling … it don't mean *nothing*," he replied with a shrug of his shoulders.

"I've stomached about all of this I can stand," Sly swore. "You two are disrupting my harmony here."

Sharpe smirked. "Afraid you're going to lose your five bucks to Dandy?"

"Are you scared?" Sly inquired, arching his eyebrows.

The lieutenant shrank back in mock apprehension. "*Terrified*, actually!"

"Do you enjoy acting like an imbecile?" Sly taunted.

"Do you enjoy acting like a meddlesome old washwoman?" Sharpe challenged.

"You two need to get it on and get past this foolishness!" Sly scoffed.

"*You* need to mind your *own* damned business!" Sharpe bristled.

"It *is* my business when it disrupts my environment," Sly countered.

"What are you two talking about?" Cherrie asked uneasily as they glared at each other.

"We're talking about you and Sugar Bear, cupcake," Sly replied caustically. "So what's it going to be? Make up your damned minds so the rest of us can have some peace and tranquility around here! You two need to dispense with all the silly eye games and such."

"Is *that* what you and Dandy were betting on the other night?" Cherrie demanded, eyes narrowing. "You were wagering if Sugar Bear and I were going to *get together*?"

Sly grinned. "Not *if. When.*"

Cherrie turned to the lieutenant. "And you knew they were laying wagers on us?"

Sharpe shrugged. "I don't pay much attention to their silly asses."

"Are you playing some sort of game with me?"

"I don't have the patience for games," he countered. "Do you?"

A captain I vaguely knew approached and paused at our table.

"Captain Hess?"

"Uh, yes?" I answered, still focused on Sharpe and Cherrie as they played their peculiar eye game while the rest of us watched in hanging suspense.

"I'm gun qualified and I'd like to transfer to the Red Platoon."

I reluctantly shifted my attention to him. "Why do you want to join the Razorbacks?"

"You guys are the classiest act in Nam," he replied.

"Sit down and have a drink," I invited, pleased with the opportunity to ease the tension settling like a cloud of vapor over our table. "This is Sly, Dandy, and Sugar Bear. These pretty ladies are Linda, Sandra, and Cherrie."

He parked his thick built, dark curly-haired with a prominent mustache self in a chair and swept the group with solemn brown eyes. "I'm Michael Forbes. I don't mean to crash your party."

"No problem, Michael, our party has unfortunately degenerated into something resembling a conjugal crisis," Sandra replied dryly. "Hi, I'm with Sly."

"And I'm with Dandy," Linda added. "Welcome. Maybe you can bring some sanity to this wacky group."

"Hi," Cherrie chirped with a gracious smile as she extended her hand. "I'm in limbo waiting for Sugar Bear to get his act together."

"Glad to meet you," Forbes greeted uneasily. "I don't mean to be tactless, but I understand you lost one of your pilots today. I'd like to be his replacement. I out-rank Dandy here, but Sly's got two months on me. If you'll have me, I'd be delighted to serve under Sly so I don't upset the leadership balance of your teams with Lieutenant Sharpe here."

"What do you mean you're waiting for me to get my act together?" Sharpe challenged as he glared at Cherrie.

"As I recall, the bet was within three days," she replied coolly. "By my reasoning, today is the third day. Right now I'm trying to decide which side of midnight to put my money on."

Sharpe leaned toward her, eyes narrowing. "Are you propositioning me?"

Cherrie pursed her lips thoughtfully. "I'm a tad old-fashioned for that, so maybe we could start out holding hands and see how it goes—I'm only offering you this opportunity because it's my official *Be Kind to Cretins* day."

"Sounds like silly foreplay foolishness to me," Sharpe chided.

Captain Forbes leaned forward in an attempt to gain the lieutenant's attention as he stared at the two of them cautiously. "Uh, if Captain Hess finds me acceptable, what would I need to do to get a couple of those fancy flight suits?"

"If the Chief finds you acceptable, the flight suits are part of the package, Captain," Sharpe replied, still eye-locked with Cherrie across the table. "How much hand holding do you have in mind, *Toots*? Time is short over here."

"Do you have any candles?" Cherrie inquired sedately. "It takes lots of romance and soft music to move me beyond the hand-holding stage."

"Define *romance*—and what *kind* of music?"

"I like to feel special, and I simply adore classical piano."

"I can see you're going to be a lot of trouble," Sharpe groused.

"Oh, but I'm sooooo worth it," she cooed.

Sharpe leaned back in his chair, still holding Cherrie's eye. "Sly, do you have any candles I can borrow?"

Sly drew back indignantly. "Why, hell no!"

Cherrie dipped into her purse and extracted several long tapers. "I figured as much, so I brought my own."

Sandra punched Sly in the ribs. "Why don't you have candles, you brute?"

Captain Forbes looked at me hopefully. "Well, Chief, what do you think about me joining the Razorbacks?"

Linda turned to Dandy. "Do *you* have any candles?"

Dandy scowled. "Geeze, Sugar Bear, now look at what you've started!"

I glanced at Forbes, distracted somewhat as Linda punched Dandy in the stomach. "Uh, it's up to Sly, I guess."

"Okay by me," Sly replied as he dodged another blow from Sandra. "Do you have any candles we can borrow?"

Captain Forbes hesitated. "Uh, no, no candles, sorry."

"Here, you two can borrow one of mine until these louts buy some of their own." Cherrie passed a candle to Sandra and Linda before turning back to the lieutenant. "Do you have any wine, or do I need to bring *that* as well?"

Sly looked at Sandra fearfully. "Oh, shit!"

Dandy beamed. "I do! I've got wine! I've got a whole case!"

"Can I borrow some?" Sharpe begged.

"Me too?" Sly chimed in hopefully.

Dandy stood. "Sure, let's go!"

Forbes watched them apprehensively as they trooped out in a pack. "Uh, what just happened here, Chief?"

"I'm damned if I know!" I swore.

"Well, since I'm one of you now, may I speak my mind?"

"Sure, go ahead."

"You've got a nutty platoon here, Chief."

"Thank you, Mike," I said graciously.

"Um, please don't take that the wrong way, Chief ..."

"Oh, not at all," I reassured him.

"… because I really *do* want to fit in with you guys." He looked toward the door with a frown. "At least I *think* I do …"

Major Crystal approved the reassignment the following morning after grilling Captain Forbes extensively on his personal reasons for desiring reassignment to the Razorbacks. Sly conducted his refresher training, and Dandy gave him a check ride. Both reported him to be an excellent pilot. Rumor had it that when the Yellow Platoon leader discovered he had lost another one of his prized pilots to the Razorbacks, he threw his hands in the air and lamented, "Damn! Another one just flew the coop on me!"

So Forbes became Coop. At the lieutenant's insistence, I placed him over the section the lieutenant had formerly led. Coop would not accept the assignment until Sharpe himself assured him it was okay. Coop was right—I did have a nutty platoon when a captain had to have a lieutenant's permission to be in charge of him.

The lieutenant and Cherrie seemed an overnight success. When I saw them the next evening at the club they were snuggled so closely together I wondered why they bothered to waste two chairs when one would have sufficed.

Over the next week I received three more requests for transfer from the Yellow Platoon. Major Crystal approved them all reluctantly after a thorough grilling, seemingly unable to accept the fact that we were now the toast of the Deans.

Actually, we were the pride of III Corps as mission after mission, sortie after sortie our stock rose with the advisers in the field. Decorations came down on a regular basis as they gratefully sang our praise and filled the channels with tales of heroism displayed by my men.

Major Crystal officially preened when he received credit for such outstanding support, but privately gnashed his teeth in frustration over Sharpe's continued refusal to cower like a normal second lieutenant in his presence. He steadfastly refused to recognize Sharpe individually for any of the glory he brought to the Deans, and seemingly despised him even more when prominently heralded in the forefront of laudatory reports pouring in from the field. The lieutenant just as openly loathed Major Crystal with every fiber in his body. I became convinced the two must have been mortal enemies in a former life. The only good part of the bad situation was that they did try to stay out of each other's way as much as possible—which appreciatively kept me from being squished in the middle.

It all started innocently enough, but then what didn't where the lieutenant was concerned? On this day he and Coop had their aircraft on the hot pad in the suffocating heat waiting for a mission. At approximately 1400 hours flight ops called for an immediate launch in support of an ARVN unit in contact near Trang Bang and they were off in less than two minutes.

I sat in my cramped office cubbyhole in the hangar absently monitoring the two radios screening our internal platoon transmissions and the flight operations channel while I reviewed some maintenance forms with a transistor radio playing softly in the background. As I hummed along with the tune the flight operations transmitter squawked.

"Red One-Niner, Dean Ops, over."

"This is One-Niner, Ops," Coop answered.

"Your mission is an abort, One-Niner. Return to base. Unit has broken contact, over."

"We're almost there, Dean Ops," Sharpe injected. "Why don't we just buzz 'em and see if we can stir something up?"

"Negative. Abort the mission and return to base, over."

"You're no fun, Ops, you big bully," Sharpe responded sullenly.

"Mission terminated, returning to base," Coop confirmed.

My radio for internal platoon communications squawked as I flipped a page in the maintenance log and turned the volume up on my music.

"Hey, Coop, I'm going to buzz that water buffalo down there," the lieutenant called.

"Why do you wanna screw around with a poor dumb animal, Sugar Bear?" Coop asked complacently.

"Because he's just asking to have the shit scared out of him by the biggest vulture he's ever seen. He's way too serene looking and thus I feel compelled to add a little excitement to his dull life."

"I'll throttle back and wait for you," Coop called lazily as I hummed and licked my fingertips to turn another page in my maintenance log.

"Roger, Coop, rolling hot!"

Coop chuckled. "You better not be hot, Sugar Bear!"

"Just a figure of speech, Coop. I've got him in my sights now. *Ta-ta-ta-ta-ta*," the lieutenant stuttered, mimicking his machine guns firing. "*Jesus Christ! The son of a bitch just shot me!*"

I lurched up so quickly I spilled my coffee and turned my music off with one hand as I reached for the volume control on the platoon radio with the other.

"Quit screwing around, Sugar Bear," Coop answered.

"I'm hit, Coop! I'm telling you the bastard just shot me!" Sharpe yelled.

"The water buffalo? Are you crazy, Sugar Bear?"

"Not the goddamned water buffalo, Coop, the bastard riding in the cart behind it! He just shot the shit out of me!"

"Cart? You didn't say anything about a goddamned *cart!*"

"Didn't I mention the water buffalo was pulling a cart?"

"*Christ*, Sugar Bear! How bad are you hit?"

"Everything's working and my gauges are steady, Coop, but I took several rounds. I'm coming around to blast his ass. I can't believe that impertinent son of a bitch shot me!"

"Roger, I'll call for mission clearance, Sugar Bear," Coop advised.

"Make it quick, Coop, he's heading for the wood line now," Sharpe reported as the other radio tuned to flight operations squawked.

"Dean Operations, Red One-Niner, over."

"Red One-Niner, this is Dean Ops, over."

"Roger, Ops, Red One-Seven has taken enemy fire at coordinates Golf Zulu 187436. Small arms—bird hit—preparing to engage, over."

"Stand by, Red One-Niner," flight ops answered.

"Tell Ops we ain't got all day, Coop!" the lieutenant urged. "He's getting away!"

Captain Nichols's voice came over the operations net. "That is a negative target, Red One-Niner. Disengage."

"Say again, Ops?" Coop demanded.

"That is a negative target," Captain Nichols repeated firmly. "That is a pacified area, One-Niner. Disengage."

"Dean Ops, this is Red One-Seven," Sharpe called. "I just took fire and several hits from your *pacified area.* My target is now racing for the woods. There's nothing friendly about him, over."

"Red One-Seven, you are in a restricted fire zone. If you took fire, it was most likely friendly fire, over."

"Roger, Ops. Be advised I'm taking *friendly fire* and *returning the same,*" the lieutenant sang bitingly.

The platoon radio crackled to life. "Coop, cover me, I'm *rolling hot!*"

"Red One-Seven, check fire!" Captain Nichols yelled into his mike. "Red One-Seven, do you read me, over? Red One-Seven, this is Dean Ops! Check fire! Do you read me, over?"

"Sorry, Dean Ops, you're coming in garbled and stupid," the lieutenant called.

The platoon internal radio squawked. "Sugar Bear, pull out! Do not engage! Sugar Bear, do you hear me?" Coop shouted. "Goddamn it, Sugar Bear! Red One-Seven, get your ass back up here with me *right now!* That's an *order! Shit!* You've just screwed up to the max, buddy!"

"*That* stupid little asshole just screwed up to the max, Coop," the lieutenant argued self-righteously. "Who'd he think he was, shooting me like that? You'd think his momma would've taught him better!"

"Red One-Seven, Dean Ops! Red One-Niner, Dean Ops!" the ops radio squawked in frustration. "Somebody talk to me, goddamn it!"

Coop's resigned voice came over the operations net. "Dean Ops, Red One-Niner. Target destroyed, over."

"*What?*" Captain Nichols screamed in frustration. "I ordered you to *check fire*, One-Niner! I told you it was *not* a target! *You did not have clearance to fire in a pacified zone*, over!"

"Roger, Ops, I, uh, don't think Red One-Seven got the transmission clearly, over," Coop replied sheepishly.

"One-Niner, return to base and report to operations immediately," Captain Nichols ordered.

"Roger, Ops, returning to base, over," Coop affirmed.

The platoon radio cranked up again. "Sugar Bear, you've just fucked up big time," Coop advised.

"*Me?* He wants to see *you*," the lieutenant reasoned. "Sounds like *you're* going to get your ass chewed, Coop."

"This is *not* a joking matter," Coop insisted. "You fired up a pacified area and there's probably gonna be hell to pay for it."

"Coop, when a son of a bitch shoots at me, I shoot back," the lieutenant insisted. "I don't give a holy damn if some REMF back in ops has a problem with that! That bastard punched holes in my beautiful little Snake, and that's the last time he'll ever pull that shit on me!"

"Sugar Bear, you're giving me a headache," Coop replied. "Don't talk to me anymore. I've gotta figure out a way to cover your ass."

"My ass is just fine, Coop," Sharpe retorted. "Worry about something important."

"I said don't talk to me anymore," Coop ordered. "I gotta think!"

After a short pause the lieutenant again keyed his mike. "Hey, Coop?"

"*What*, Sugar Bear?"

"There's a great song on the ADF. Have you got it tuned to the Armed Forces Network? Coop? Hey, Coop? Okay, damn it! So *be* pissed then!"

The lieutenant, Coop, and I stood rigidly in front of a furious Major Crystal's desk as Captain Nichols finished his briefing.

"What have you got from the field concerning this breach of a pacified zone, Captain Nichols?" Major Crystal asked as he fixed the lieutenant with a hard stare.

"Sir, one of the civilian social workers there claims the villager involved in the attack was a solid ally of the South Vietnamese government and a prominent member of his council. He insists the man in question was on his way to market. I contacted the nearest ARVN outpost with an American adviser and requested their assistance. They've dispatched a patrol to investigate and will render a formal evaluation of the incident."

"Lieutenant Sharpe, what do you have to say about this?" Major Crystal asked.

"He fired on me, Major, and I fired back."

"How is it you were close enough for him to fire on you, Lieutenant?" Major Crystal asked.

"I felt there was something suspicious about him, so I flew down to observe him."

Major Crystal looked at him speculatively. "What was he doing to arouse your suspicion, Lieutenant?"

"He was acting nervous, Major."

"You could tell he was acting nervous from two thousand feet up in the air, Lieutenant?"

"I've got eyes like an eagle, Major," the lieutenant answered, nonplused.

Major Crystal turned to Captain Nichols. "What damage did Lieutenant Sharpe's aircraft sustain, Captain Nichols?"

"There were three puncture holes in the undercarriage, Sir."

"Bullet holes, Captain?"

"They … *appeared* to be bullet holes, Sir."

Major Crystal stared at him intently. "But they *could* have been made by some other instrument after landing?"

Captain Nichols hesitated. "I … suppose that's possible, Sir …"

"Are you implying I punched holes in my aircraft to fake an attack on myself, Captain Nichols?" the lieutenant demanded.

"Lieutenant Sharpe, you will address me alone," Major Crystal barked. "If there are questions to be asked, *I* will ask them. Is that clear?"

"That is clear, Major. But I would caution Captain Nichols not to jump to conclusions or make derogatory inferences to my honor," the lieutenant responded.

"My apologies, Lieutenant Sharpe," Captain Nichols replied. "I did not mean to make an inference one way or another. I meant only to report the facts, and the facts as I currently know them to be are that you conducted an attack without proper authorization, against my direct order to abort the attack, and ultimately may have killed an innocent farmer bound for market. Have I misstated anything in those facts, Lieutenant?"

The lieutenant turned to face him. "Captain, it is not a *fact* that I may have killed an innocent farmer. I took fire and sustained battle damage to my aircraft. I retaliated against an enemy who initiated an attack on me."

There was a knock on the door and the XO poked his head in. "Sorry, Sir."

"Yes, Captain. What have you got?"

"Sir, I just got a call from Corps. The ARVN contingent has secured the target area."

"Thank you, Captain." The XO departed, and Major Crystal looked back to Sharpe with steely eyes. "Lieutenant Sharpe, did you hear the order to abort the mission?"

"Yes, Major, I did."

"Why did you not follow that order, Lieutenant?"

"Time was short, Major. The cart was moving rapidly toward the wood line and I didn't feel Dean Ops fully understood the situation. I had no doubts that it was Vietcong since I had just taken hits from the man. I had the enemy in my sights and I eliminated him."

"But you *heard* the order, Lieutenant?" Major Crystal demanded.

"I heard the order, Major," the lieutenant affirmed.

"Lieutenant, as a disciplinary measure for your failure to follow a legal order, you are hereby grounded pending an investigation of this incident. You will report to the airfield each day and perform duties as assigned under Captain Nichols until further notice. I intend to place a formal letter of reprimand in your official conduct file. As to the incident in question, you may face further disciplinary action as the findings of the investigation dictate. Do you have any questions?" After a silence, Major Crystal turned to me. "Captain Hess, Lieutenant Sharpe is temporarily reassigned to Captain Nichols for ground duty as directed."

My heart sank with the knowledge that Major Crystal and my lieutenant's petty feud had finally come full circle. "Yes, Sir."

"Sir, may I speak on the lieutenant's behalf?" Coop demanded.

"This matter is closed pending the results of the investigation, Captain Forbes," Major Crystal replied. "You are all dismissed."

We saluted and walked out to congregate around my jeep.

"Lieutenant, for the record, I think you screwed up," Captain Nichols advised. "You should have waited for mission clearance."

The lieutenant hopped into the back of the jeep. "If I had waited for mission clearance he would have gotten away, Captain. I did what I had to do. Now who's going to buy me a drink?"

I climbed in with Coop, and we drove to the O Club. After we settled in at a table with drinks, I studied the lieutenant gravely. "How sure are you the fire actually came from the oxcart?"

He looked me in the eye. "I saw the muzzle flashes and took the hits, Captain. How sure is that?"

"What about you, Coop?" I asked.

"Chief, I was at two thousand feet and a mile away with the target to my rear. I didn't see or hear anything. But I did see the holes in Sugar Bear's aircraft after we landed. I goddamn well guarantee you they were bullet holes and that he didn't punch them in there himself."

I sighed. "I hope the ARVNs find a weapon in that cart. You should not have been down there screwing around in the first place, Lieutenant!"

He smiled smugly. "Found me a bad guy and sent him to hell, though, didn't I now? That can't be all bad in the overall scheme of things."

I sighed. "Lieutenant, I hope we can prove it beyond a doubt, otherwise Crystal's going to have your ass *and* your career. I've tried to warn you about this silly little squabble you two have going on. You can't win."

"As long as he plays by the rules, I can," he insisted. "I engaged an enemy soldier today and I destroyed him. That's why we're over here."

We had a party that night. The men carried the lieutenant to the hot seat, where he told his war story and drank the flaming Drambuie. I toasted him along with the others, but with misgivings since I was certain Major Crystal would not give him any benefit of the doubt whatsoever and that if given the chance he would most certainly destroy the lieutenant. I was also concerned about what the lieutenant might do in retaliation if Major Crystal did what I feared he was going to do.

For all of his fun and sincere goodwill there was the occasional flash of a darker side to Lieutenant Sharpe that troubled me deeply.

CHAPTER 10

Things quickly went from bad to worse.

When the lieutenant reported to Captain Nichols on the third morning of his grounding he was put in charge of a group of Vietnamese laborers hired to do menial tasks around the airfield, in this instance supervising the workers as they filled sandbags and repaired the unoccupied, unused bunkers around the boundary of the airfield.

Since the airfield was located in the interior of Long Binh it was inconceivable we would ever face an attack there because the enemy would first have to penetrate the outer defenses to reach us. In addition, no one seemed to have a clue as to who was supposed to man these bunkers if in fact we ever did come under attack, but regardless, we had our own perimeter within the larger perimeter and the lieutenant and his coolie labor force were making repairs there. The task was hot, tiring, thankless, unnecessary, boring and … my grandmother always said an idle mind was the devil's workshop.

On this day I observed the lieutenant's crew chief trudging down to the far end of the runway with a PRC 25 radio on his back. Curiosity got the better of me, so I drifted down that way to see what was going on. From a distance I saw Dandy, Mad Hatter, and the lieutenant working around the rear end of a small vehicle with a flat cargo platform used to transport supplies short distances, which we referred to as a "mule." I watched in puzzlement as Dandy and Critter placed old 2.75 rockets on the rear frame of the vehicle and wired them into place, vaguely recalling these rockets, normally fired from our former Charlie models and now slated for disposal, were temporarily stored in one of the bunkers at the end of the airfield where the lieutenant was making repairs.

I watched the lieutenant hoist a jeep battery up on the bed of the mule and Mad Hatter twist the wire ends of the rockets together while observing that the explosive end of the rockets were removed and only the long, slim bodies containing the fuel remained. I anxiously recalled that when electrically fired these cylinders were capable of reaching something like Mock 2 in about two seconds of burn time. My curiosity increased as I saw them push the mule out onto the end of the runway and point it toward the far end, after which the lieutenant climbed up into the seat and grabbed the steering wheel. With startling clarity I suddenly realized what they intended to do as the lieutenant called into the handset of the PRC radio.

"Tower, Red One-Seven, requesting clearance for departure."

"Uh, roger, uh, Red One-Seven, you, uh, are cleared for takeoff, over," the startled control tower responded as they searched frantically for the phantom aircraft.

I started screaming. "*NO! NO! NO!*"

Dandy touched the ends of the wires from the rockets to the terminals on the jeep battery as the lieutenant looked up at me running toward them waving my arms and grinned. Loud *swooshes* erupted into giant flames shooting from the rear of the mule and an instant later the vehicle was tearing down the runway in a boiling cloud of white smoke as the lieutenant hung on for his life.

An instant later the control tower, thinking a jet had attempted to land on the short runway and was disintegrating in a fiery crash from one end to the other, punched the crash alarm sending the siren blaring and the rescue teams scrambling for their vehicles. At the far end of the runway the mule flew off the end of the asphalt, climbed a small earthen crash ramp, and launched into the air with the lieutenant spiraling spread-eagle up after it.

I drew up beside Dandy, Mad Hatter, and Critter panting for breath. "*Are you guys freaking crazy?*"

"Aw, shit," Mad Hatter mused speculatively as we watched the lieutenant and the mule soar into the air in a giant streak of smoke and flame. "I think I miscalculated the number of rockets we needed."

"I bet he's really gonna be pissed," Dandy observed as the lieutenant and the mule arched back to earth and disappeared into the marsh at the far end of the runway as the hapless rescue teams scurried around in a confusing tangle looking for the crash site.

"*You've killed him!*" I gasped.

Mad Hatter fanned the smoke from his face with his palm. "Well hell, on the positive side, Dean Six will probably decorate us …"

The rescue teams regrouped and scurried out to the road in a swarm to search the outer perimeter, frantically looking through the smoldering grass for the wrecked aircraft. Dean Six's jeep roared up a few minutes later and he leaped out and ran into the flight ops building. I turned and trudged in that direction filled with despair.

The lieutenant, Mad Hatter, Dandy, and I stood in a row in front of Major Crystal's desk. The lieutenant, looking terrible with his head wrapped in bloody bandages and his flight suit soiled, scorched, and in threads, slouched over a pair of crutches looking at the major with his nose in the air in order to peep out through the swollen slits of his blackened eyes. The rest of us stood rigidly at attention intently studying a spot on the wall behind Major Crystal's desk. It occurred to me I'd had occasion to study that very spot many times lately. My foremost thought was that this could have waited until after the emergency room completed *all* their tests, not merely the certification that the lieutenant's life was not in any *immediate* peril.

Major Crystal stared at him calmly. "So you were bored, Lieutenant?"

"That's right, Major. I was pulling a joke on the control tower," Sharpe replied in a hoarse whisper through battered lips below tufts of cotton sticking out of his nostrils giving him the uncanny appearance of a disheveled walrus.

Crystal nodded thoughtfully. "Did they laugh, Lieutenant?"

"I don't think so, Major. You see, it didn't turn out right ..."

"What would you do in my position, Lieutenant?"

"Ground me until my leg and back get better, Major, and warn me not to do it again," he recommended.

"You are grounded until your leg and back get better, Lieutenant," Crystal ordered softly. "And I warn you, don't do that again."

"Yes, Major."

"Now get the hell out of my office, Lieutenant!" he screamed, slapping his palm on his desk as we flinched. "Not *you* three! You stay here!" he ordered as we tried eagerly to make our escape with the lieutenant. "Sit down," he snapped, which caused some confusion since there were only two chairs. Dandy and I ended up with the chairs while Mad Hatter stood timidly off to the side.

"What have I got here?" he asked, his voice painfully dejected. "Have I got *three* captains who can't control *one* little goddamned second lieutenant? What's wrong with this picture?"

I cleared my throat. "Well, Sir, I—"

"I *sure* as hell don't understand how you can let a *second lieutenant* lead you around by the nose and pull the *shit* on you he does and *you* just let him get away with it! One of you *explain* that to me, *goddamn it!*"

"Well, Sir, he—" Dandy started.

"And *you* two actually *helped* him pull this stupid stunt!" Major Crystal accused as he glared at Dandy and Mad Hatter. "You could have *at least* ensured he *killed himself* in the process, but *noooooo*, you can't even get *that* right, can you?"

John W. Huffman

"Sir, uh, it probably wouldn't have been so bad if we'd used two rockets instead of nine," Mad Hatter explained rationally. "You see, Sir, I didn't carry the decimal—"

"Captain Hess, *get these two out of my office!*" Major Crystal screamed. "Get them out of my sight! I can't stand looking at them anymore. You severely disappoint me, gentlemen! *Severely! Disappoint! Me!* Now get out!"

When we reached my jeep, the lieutenant was perched in the back smiling his swollen, twisted grin as he peered at our ashen faces through puffy eyes.

"Got your asses chewed, didn't you?" he taunted gleefully as we climbed aboard.

I spun the wheels getting out of there. "Just whose idiotic idea was this?"

"Critter's," the lieutenant replied.

"*Critter?* Your crew chief?"

"Now, Sugar Bear, you know he tried to talk you out of it," Mad Hatter insisted.

"Yeah, but he *didn't* talk me out of it, so it's *his* fault," the lieutenant reasoned.

"Actually, I think its Major Crystal's fault," Dandy injected. "If he hadn't grounded you, you wouldn't have been bored and you wouldn't have found those rockets, therefore none of this would have happened."

"That's a very good point, Dandy," Mad Hatter agreed affably.

I clenched my jaw. "You think this is *funny*, don't you? He almost *killed* himself in that stupid stunt and *you two* should have *known* better! Major Crystal was pretty lenient under the circumstances."

"Captain, please don't defend that jackass," the lieutenant injected. "He's a solid asshole to the core who's jerked me around since the first day I got here."

"Most of your trouble with him is self-inflicted," I argued hotly. "You put yourself in the positions you get into without his help, thank you very much, so that's not jerking you around."

"Oh yeah?" he challenged. "Then why hasn't he informed me of the results of the investigation and restored me to flight status?"

"The investigation is still ongoing," I insisted.

"With who, Captain?" he demanded. "The report was given to Major Crystal the day before yesterday."

I slammed on the brakes and turned to face him. "What?"

"The day after the 'incident' Corps sent down a report generated by the ARVNs that secured the site. It stated they found one dead ox, one dead Vietcong, one destroyed oxcart, and recovered five AK-47 rifles, two hundred rounds of 7.65 ammo, and ten 61-millimeter mortar rounds."

"How do you know this?"

"I have my sources, Captain. The real question is why hasn't Major Crystal shared this information with us? I call that jacking me around in a big way!"

"That's a serious accusation, Lieutenant," I warned.

"Damn, Captain, read it for yourself." He pulled a crumpled sheet out of a zippered pocket and thrust it at me. "It's a little battered thanks to Mad Hatter's miscalculations on rocket propulsion, but I think you can still read it."

I read the short report, checked the heading, date, and signature, and then read it again.

"This is dated two days ago—where'd you get it?" I demanded.

"Details, Captain, details. If you don't mind, I need that back, and I'll ask you to never discuss me having it with anyone outside of the four of us."

Mad Hatter and Dandy each read the report and then handed it back to the lieutenant, who placed it back in his pocket. I put the jeep in gear and continued on to the compound as the implications of the report sank in.

When we reached his room, we helped the lieutenant out of his destroyed flight suit and he hobbled naked to the shower point as we sat in his room. Cherrie, Ellen, Linda, Sandra, and four other nurses had joined us when he hobbled back, still naked and bleeding from newly reopened wounds. He lay on his bed with a towel spread across his groin as the women tried to outdo each other pampering him. As they worked, Mad Hatter graphically relayed the incredible, if somewhat sordid, launch of the Army's version of the space program to them, but they weren't amused.

The lieutenant was too sore to move, so that evening's party evolved to his room with the crowd spilling outside around his door and everyone bringing their own booze. At one point there were over thirty-five men and nurses gathered around as he held court from his bed. Cherrie finally ran us off so he could get some rest, and I drifted back to my room near midnight to write a disturbing letter to Nancy outlining the distressing events.

The next morning I went to the orderly room with some half-baked plan to confront Major Crystal with the fact that the investigation had exonerated Sharpe. As I waited to be ushered into his office the Red Cross delivered a teletype emergency message for me—my darling wife had delivered a healthy six-pound, eleven-ounce son the day before. I rushed out, drove to the MARS station, and waited two hours to place a call to the hospital. The static-filled connection was almost inaudible, and each of us had trouble remembering to say "over" after our part of the conversation, but it was still one of the most supremely joyous moments of my life to know my wife was doing well and I had a new son to go with my adorable daughter.

Everyone celebrated with me that night and Sharpe seemed especially happy for me. The next morning when I returned to the orderly room I was ushered into Major Crystal's office.

"Congratulations, Captain Hess. A son to carry on his name is the high point in a man's life. I have three daughters myself, but we keep hoping."

"Thank you, Sir. Nancy really had a hard time with this one. I'm just thankful the two of them are healthy."

"How is that fruitcake lieutenant of yours doing, Captain?"

"Actually, that's why I'm here, Sir, I—

"Have you got something on him?" he interrupted eagerly.

"Uh, Sir, I'm actually here to find out how the investigation is going. I thought we would have heard something by now."

"These things take time, Captain," he replied airily. "We'll just have to be patient and allow it to run its course, won't we? But I wouldn't get your hopes up too high on nailing him."

"Then you think he may have been justified in his attack, Sir?"

Major Crystal glowered. "He wasn't justified in disobeying a direct order, no matter what the outcome of the investigation, Captain. Do you agree?"

"To a point I do, Sir. But in combat there are sometimes extenuating circumstances that should be considered and factored into the overall equation—"

He scowled. "What's your point, Captain Hess?"

"Sir, if it should be proven the man he attacked was the enemy it would seem he was justified in attacking him, therefore we wouldn't be justified in punishing him for it."

Major Crystal waved his hand dismissively. "Yes, yes, Captain, I see your point." He steered me to the door with his palm on my shoulder in a fatherly gesture. "You just keep that little bastard under observation until we catch him at something. Understand, Captain?"

I went back and sat with the lieutenant for a while in his room, where I ranted and raved in frustration about the situation.

"Don't worry about it, Captain," he soothed. "I can't fly for a week or so anyway. He can't hide that report longer than that."

Feeling somewhat better after his applied logic, I rushed back to my room to write Nancy a long, tender letter expressing all of my love and admiration for the newborn son she had given me.

The following morning Major Crystal summoned me to his office, where I found him at his desk with a bandage covering his head and a sling supporting his left arm. From his half-stooped position, he motioned painfully at two men sitting before his desk.

"Captain Hess, this is Mister Hall and Mister Miller, from the Criminal Investigation Division. They would like to question you about Lieutenant Sharpe."

My heart pounded. "Lieutenant Sharpe, Sir?"

"Someone tried to assassinate me last night, and damned near succeeded. They fired three shots at me as my driver dropped me off at my quarters. One bullet struck me in the arm, one grazed my head, and one lodged in a Zippo lighter in my breast pocket above my heart. They have asked me for a list of disciplinary problems in my unit. As you would expect, I put your lieutenant at the top of the list."

"Captain Hess, do you know where Lieutenant Sharpe was at approximately 2400 hours last night?" Investigator Hall asked without preamble.

My mind raced with the implications as I recalled what the lieutenant said about the major paying a price he couldn't fathom if he didn't play by the rules. "I believe he was in his room. He was injured in an accident two days ago and is still recuperating."

"Do you know for a fact he was in his room, Captain?" Investigator Miller asked.

"I visited with him until about 2200 hours before I turned in for the night. There were several people with him when I left."

"Who were those people, Captain?"

"Let's see, Captains Benedict, Everett, Forbes, and Harding; Warrant Officers Miles, Sanders, James, and Warner; and four nurses I know only by their first names—Linda, Ellen, Sandra, and Cherrie. There were others wandering in and out periodically."

"That's quite a crowd for an injured man," Hall observed. "Do you think Lieutenant Sharpe is capable of making an attempt on his commanding officer's life?"

"I … would certainly hope not," I said fearfully, lying through my teeth.

"How would you describe the relationship between the lieutenant and his commanding officer, Captain?" Miller asked.

"They don't get along very well," I acknowledged.

"Can you be more specific, Captain?" Miller pushed.

I hesitated. "They ... seem to rub each other the wrong way ..."

"Can you think of anyone in this unit, or outside of this unit for that matter, who would want to harm Major Crystal?" Hall demanded.

I drew a ragged breath as my stomach convulsed in knots. "Offhand ... I can't imagine anyone wanting to kill one of our own, especially our commander."

"Do you know anything of your lieutenant's past, Captain, specifically about his first tour of duty before he became an officer?"

"Uh, no ... he never talks about it."

"His enlisted records are sealed, Captain, which is curious. We do know there was some controversy regarding his last tour of duty in Vietnam, but we don't know specifically what was involved."

"I know he's highly decorated," I replied. "But he's never discussed it with me or anyone else as far as I know."

"Is there anything that comes to your mind that might help us in this investigation, Captain?" Miller asked.

My stomach did flip-flops, but I made no reply.

"Captain, if anything occurs to you later that would help our investigation into this incident, please contact Agent Hall or me directly. Thank you."

I saluted the major, rushed back to our quarters, knocked on the lieutenant's door, and barged in without waiting for an invitation, relieved to find him lying on his bed with no one else present.

"Hi, Captain, have a seat," he invited. "You look a sight. What's up?"

"Did you leave this room last night?"

His eyes narrowed. "Why do you ask?"

"Just answer me! Did you leave this room for any reason?"

"I took a shit and a shower, does that count?"

"Who was here with you?"

"At different times most everybody. Where is this leading, Captain?"

"All night? Were there people here with you all night?"

"Cherrie ran everybody off about 2300 hours, as I recall. She thought I needed some rest since everyone stayed until after midnight the night before."

"But Cherrie stayed with you all night, right?"

"No, she left when everyone else did. She has the graveyard shift this week. What's the deal, Captain?"

"So you were here by yourself from about 2300 hours on? Did anybody come by and talk to you or see you after that?"

"As I recall, I went to bed and slept until morning—what the hell's going on, Captain? Did somebody pop Dean Six or something?"

My blood ran cold. "Was it you?"

He sat upright in his bed. "Are you shitting me? Did somebody *really* nail that bastard, I hope?"

"You didn't answer my question, Lieutenant. *Was it you?*"

He studied me coolly. "If it was, do you think I'd admit it, Captain?"

I trembled under that awful stare. "Is there *anybody* who can give you an alibi for last night after 2300 hours?"

His swollen lips eased into a smile. "Not that I know of, Captain—so did they kill the son of a bitch or not?"

"You and I never had this conversation, Lieutenant."

"He must not have played by the rules, Captain," he taunted as I opened the door. "What do you think?"

I left quickly with my emotions in turmoil. I honestly couldn't say I knew he had done it, but I honestly couldn't say I knew he hadn't done it either. In our American system of justice that was supposed to mean he was innocent until proven guilty beyond a reasonable doubt by a jury of his peers—but I was sure no jury would ever see the look I had just seen either.

I went back to my room and threw up my breakfast in great shuddering heaves, unable to purge the waves of nauseous fear coursing through me or shake the awful sense of liability clinging to my subconscious. I tried to write Nancy, but my hand shook so hard I finally wadded the paper up and threw it into the trash.

CHAPTER 11

The investigation ran its course over the next few days. I had no further discussions with the investigators or the lieutenant about the incident. After questioning him extensively, the CID turned to other potential suspects who may have had a motive to harm Major Crystal, but no direct evidence materialized, and the matter slowly faded into the background. That didn't stop virtually every man in the unit, including Major Crystal, from thinking the lieutenant did it, but it was a whispered rumor none dared say aloud. I was distraught when the sordid incident only added to the lieutenant's growing myth, unwilling to accept the possibility that someone I had grown to respect was capable of such a heinous act.

A week after the event Sharpe received his medical clearance to fly. After a lengthy session with a reluctant, hostile Major Crystal, who finally revealed the results of the attack on the farmer in the oxcart, he reinstated the lieutenant to flight status. The following day I attended a ceremony in which he along with five other members of the Razorbacks again received air medals for valorous actions. At the conclusion of the awards ceremony, almost as an afterthought, Major Crystal promoted Sharpe to first lieutenant, an act that noticeably repulsed him but one in which he had no alternative since it was a Department of the Army mandate. Afterward I observed the date on the promotion orders—almost two weeks earlier—a petty insult on the commander's behalf that had to sting, but one the lieutenant seemed to ignore.

Our mission fell into a routine of flying several sorties a day in support of the ARVNs, in which our esteem with the advisers in the field grew with each operation as my pilots tried to outdo each other in their support of them. We took the occasional hit here and there, but with no major battle damage suffered to our aircraft and only one man slightly injured. Again, oddly, a Zippo lighter placed in his flight suit pocket spared the man serious injury. The enemy round penetrated the Plexiglas windshield striking the pilot-gunner in the right side of his chest and impacting against the lighter with only a huge bruise resulting. The standing joke became that Zippo needed to hire us for their commercials.

The leading contender for the "top gun" award was the lieutenant, followed closely by Sly, with Dandy in third, and Coop in fourth place. It was a hotly contested race for a couple of weeks, but of course the lieutenant soon changed all that in his normal controversial style. I had come to expect nothing less.

The mission came in at 1000 hours one morning with a special request for Sharpe personally. He and Dandy launched their respective aircraft to support an ARVN outpost in the Iron Triangle that was under siege. To monitor the mission I went to flight ops, whose radios had a greater range due to their signal tower. Captain Nichols, at my request, switched his standby radio to my platoon frequency so I could screen the action directly since pilots rendered only post-mission reports on the operations frequency.

Dandy's voice came over the operations net. "Dean Ops, Red One-One, over."

The dispatcher keyed his transmitter, "Red One-One, Dean Ops." He picked up a grease pencil and moved to the glass-covered map on the wall in anticipation of a location report, which he tracked continuously to give a starting point for search and rescue in case contact was lost with an aircraft.

"Red One-One has target in sight, will call mission complete, over," Dandy reported.

"Roger, Red One-One, call mission complete. Dean Ops, out," the specialist replied as he marked the new location on the map.

Immediately the platoon radio cranked up. "Panther Six, Red One-One, over."

"Red One-One, Panther Six, over," a voice answered.

"Roger, Six, you've got a couple of hungry pigs approaching your location, over."

"Roger, Red One-One, always delighted to see the Razorbacks. We have targets to our south and our east. We've been taking sustained small-arms and mortar fire since early morning. Intel believes an attack is imminent, over."

"Roger, Panther, any reported anti-aircraft positions for us to worry about? We have this aversion to getting our tail feathers plucked out, over."

"Roger, Red One-One, there's a reported .51 cal. site to our east and a .30 cal. site to the south. We've taken fire from both of those positions in our compound in the last hour, over."

159

"*Ouch*, Panther, who have you guys pissed off down there, over?" Dandy teased.

"I'm sure they're something you can handle, One-One. Do you have One-Seven with you?"

Dandy chuckled. "Roger, Panther. I had to bail him out of jail for you, but he's wandering along behind me so he doesn't get lost."

The lieutenant keyed his radio. "Panther, this is One-Seven. Appreciate you finding me some playmates. Happiness is a minigun and a few gooks to play with, over."

"You're a man after my own heart, One-Seven."

"That's all well and good, Panther, but do you have any daughters I can meet?"

Panther Six chuckled. "Actually, I do have a daughter I'd like you to meet someday, so be careful up there now, you hear?"

"Roger that, Panther. Dandy, why don't you swoop on down there and see if you can draw some fire and pinpoint those two gun sites for me," the lieutenant suggested.

"Uh, I've got a better idea, Sugar Bear. *You* swoop on down there and find them for *me*," Dandy countered.

"But I'm *elite*, Dandy," the lieutenant argued. "I was requested *personally*. You always save the best for last."

"Not when I outrank you," Dandy replied. "You go."

"You're out front," Sharpe protested.

"*Go!*" Dandy ordered.

"Red One-Seven is rolling hot, albeit under severe protest. *Yee haw!*" A silence ensued. "He's eating me up, Dandy! What're you doing, picking cockleburs out of your ass?"

"I've got him now," Dandy called back grimly. "Roll left, Sugar Bear!"

"About goddamned time!" the lieutenant grumped.

"Rockets away! Take that! And that! And *that*, you little villainous cur!" Dandy called merrily as he dove with rockets swooshing from his pods.

"*You little villainous cur?*" the lieutenant responded. "Don't embarrass me now, Dandy! As a certified bad ass, I've got an image to uphold with those good people down there!"

"Your little certified bad ass better get that son of a bitch off me, *now!*" Dandy yelled.

"Roll right, Dandy!" the lieutenant yelled, followed by silence. "*Woo wee!* What a pretty sight! Fry in hell, you bastards!"

"Sugar Bear, that was a tad lower than the old manual calls for," Dandy counseled.

"Sorry, Dandy, nobody ever gave me the old manual to read," Lieutenant Sharpe replied. "I just look for the whites of their eyes, buddy. Now let's go get the big boy."

"Lead the way, Sugar Bear."

"Awww, are we going to do the *rank* thing again, Dandy?" the lieutenant whined.

"Compliments of the U.S. Army—you be careful now, you hear?"

"One-Seven is rolling hot!" The tension in the lieutenant's voice was palpable, a good indication he'd apparently figured out a .51 caliber was no joking matter. A silence ensued. "Well, I didn't entice him, so it's your turn, Dandy," he called cheerfully. "Maybe he likes candy-asses better than bad-asses."

"Thanks a lot," Dandy called tightly. "Rolling hot!" A silence. "I'm hit! *Mayday! Mayday!* Going down!"

"I'm on him!" the lieutenant yelled. "Turn toward the compound, Dandy!" A long silence prevailed. The flight ops radio crackled. "Dean Ops, Red One-Seven, over."

"Roger, Red One-Seven, Dean Ops, over."

"Red One-One is down next to the Panther compound. Fifty-one site destroyed. One-One and gunner are running toward the compound. We need Big Bird for recovery, over."

"Roger, One-Seven, launching Big Bird, over."

"Roger, Dean Ops, I'm returning to Trang Bang for hot rearm-refuel. ETA one-five minutes. Request you launch the back-up birds on the hot pad until recovery is complete, over."

"Red One-Seven, Panther Six, over!" the platoon net crackled.

"Roger, Panther, do you have my little darlings safe? I'm en route for hot refuel and rearm, over."

"We're under full-scale attack, One-Seven! Enemy in the open!"

"Roger, Panther, turning back to you now! Get my pilots inside your compound, over!" the lieutenant instructed.

"They're in the moat around the compound, One-Seven! The fire is too intense to bring them inside, over!"

"Roger, Panther, ETA three minutes, over."

The ops radio crackled. "Dean Ops, Red One-Seven, returning to target; fuel and ammo low. Get me some Snakes out here *pronto*! One-One is pinned in the moat beside the compound. Do you copy, over?"

"Roger, Red One-Seven. The hot pad has been launched, ETA twenty minutes, over," Dean Ops replied.

"My god, all the gooks in the world are down there," the lieutenant yelled. "Red One-Seven is rolling hot!"

A full five minutes passed as we listened to the hiss of the radio before the platoon radio crackled to life. "Panther Six, I'm out of bullets, buddy, and down to fumes in my gas tank. I've got to break station and run for the nearest base at Trang Bang. I'll be back in three-zero minutes. Dean Ops has launched some new Snakes to help you, ETA one-five minutes, over."

"Roger, One-Seven, hurry back or I'll never get the chance to introduce you to that beautiful daughter of mine. Tell your new birds to kick in the afterburners, situation desperate."

"Roger, we'll expedite, over."

The ops radio cranked to life. "Dean Ops, Red One-Seven, situation critical. Recommend you launch two more Snakes. I'm off target and heading for Trang Bang for rearm and refuel, over."

"Roger, One-Seven. Big Bird is minutes away. What do you want him to do, over?"

"Tell Big Bird to go back home for now, Ops. He can't recover anything in that mess. Our One-One bird is shot all to shit now anyway since it was in the open between the attacking enemy forces. I've taken several small-arms hits, but everything is steady, over."

Captain Nichols grabbed the mike from the specialist and keyed the microphone. "Red One-Seven, this is Dean Ops. If your bird has sustained battle damage, set it down at Trang Bang until we can recover per our standard operating procedures, over."

"Negative, Dean Ops. As I said, everything is steady. Unless something falls off, I'm returning to target after hot rearm-refuel, over."

"That's a million-dollar aircraft you're putting in jeopardy, Lieutenant!" Captain Nichols replied angrily.

"Shut it down at Trang Bang like I instructed you to do! Do you understand?"

"Damn, Captain, go ahead and make an appointment with Dean Six," Sharpe replied bitingly. "This might be a million-dollar aircraft, but that adviser back there on the ground is priceless and my first priority! As long as this bitch can fly I'm going back, over!"

"Goddamn him!" Captain Nichols screamed as he slammed the mike down and turned to me. "I'm going to court-martial that little son of a bitch if it's the last thing I do! Do you have any control over your men at all, Captain?"

"He's under *your* mission control!" I sizzled as the two specialists looked fearfully from one of us to the other. "*You're* the one who has the problem with him!"

"*You order him to shut down!*" he yelled at me.

"Once they're off the ground, you have operational control," I shouted back. "*You order him to shut down!*"

"Dean Ops, Red One-Two, over," Sly's voice called.

The specialists grabbed the mike off the desk. "Red One-Two, Dean Ops."

"Red One-Two is on target. Will call mission complete."

"Roger, One-Two, call mission complete."

The platoon radio hissed. "Panther Six, Red One-Two, over."

"Red One-Two, glad to see you. Situation desperate. Enemy in the open. Red One-One has crashed outside our compound. The pilots are pinned down in our moat. We're being hit on all sides with a full-scale ground attack. Two anti-aircraft sites have been eliminated by previous attacks. Give us some relief, over."

"Roger, Panther, you have the first team here now!" Sly sang out merrily. "Coop, I'm going north. You take the south. Rolling hot!"

"Roger, Sly, rolling hot!" We waited through several minutes of silence. "Holy shit! Where'd all those gooks come from? *I'm hit! I'm hit!*" Coop's voice screamed as a crescendo of fire came over the transmission in the background. "My gauges are flickering, Sly! I'm heading out of the shit now!"

"Roger, Coop! Make it to a safe area and put her down, over."

"Roger, Sly. Good luck, buddy. I'm wobbling outta here."

The operations radio hissed. "Dean Ops, Red One-Niner. *Mayday! Mayday!* I'm hit and losing gauges. Heading one-eight-zero from the target area. Need Big Bird, over."

"Red One-Niner, Dean Ops. Launching Big Bird to one-eight-zero of target. Can you make it down safely, over?"

"Dean Ops, turbine is still spinning, but vibrations are getting worse. I'm looking for a field, over."

"Roger, One-Niner, find a soft spot and set her down, over."

"Dean Ops, Red One-Seven, target inbound, ETA one-five minutes, over."

"Roger, Red One-Seven, ETA to target one-five minutes, over."

"Red One-Two, taking hits! One-Two, taking hits! Gauges fluctuating! Turning north for safe zone. *Mayday! Mayday!*"

"Roger, Red One-Two, going down north, three-six-zero degrees of target, over."

165

"So much for the *first team*," the lieutenant called dryly. "Dean Ops, Red One-Seven, can you send me some *good* pilots? I can't do this shit all by myself, you know."

"Red One-Seven, hot pad has launched. We have three Snakes down, one south, one north, and one by the compound, over."

"Hell, I know where the Girl Scouts are, Ops. I guess I'll just have to kick these sons of bitches' asses all by myself."

The platoon radio blared on. "Panther Six, Red One-Seven, over."

"Red One-Seven, Panther Six, over."

"Red One-Seven ETA to target one-zero minutes, over."

"Roger, One-Seven. Situation critical, over."

"Not to worry, Panther," Sharpe replied. "I'm going to get that intro to your daughter from you personally, so hold on for me, buddy."

There were eight agonizing minutes of silence before the operations radio blared.

"Dean Ops, Red One-Seven is guns on target. Will call mission complete, over."

"Roger, Red One-Seven, call mission complete."

The platoon radio immediately cranked to life. "Panther Six, Red One-Seven. Looks like you've pissed off the devil down there. I ain't never seen so many gooks in my life. I'm rolling hot with a full load. Let's send these bastards to hell!"

By my watch six minutes of silence ensued before the radio again came to life. "They're pulling back, One-Seven! They're pulling back!"

"About time, Panther, all I got left is a couple of pooper rounds. I'm dry on rockets and minis."

"That was unbelievable, One-Seven. Incredible!"

"Roger, buddy, but I'm flat out of firepower now. My second team should be ETA in zero-five. I've got to bail on you, my gauges are going crazy. Good luck and don't forget your promise. How old is your daughter, anyway?"

"Roger, One-Seven, she's, uh, five. You're gonna have to wait a bit for her."

"Uh, thanks, Panther. I'll catch up with her in my next life. Call me when you have some more playmates."

"Roger, One-Seven, and many thanks."

"The pleasure's all mine, Panther. Red One-Seven, out."

The fast movers, or Air Force jets, arrived before our other two Razorbacks got there and pounded the retreating enemy force. Two Big Birds picked up Coop and Sly and their shot-up aircraft. In the late afternoon a slick snatched Dandy and his copilot from the ARVN compound, where they had finally found a safe haven after cowering in the moat during the attack. They were returned to the Dean base after their Cobra was declared unsalvageable and destroyed in place. Lieutenant Sharpe, after taking seventeen hits in his aircraft, nursed it home under its own power.

All three aircraft required extensive second-echelon maintenance before they would see combat again. It had been a hard day for us, with one aircraft destroyed and three out of action for weeks—virtually a third of our fighting strength lost in one single engagement. But thankfully none of my pilots was injured, which was of the most interest to me.

CHAPTER 12

The party that night got out of control early, and no one showed any inclination to bring it back to any semblance of sanity. After the obligatory war stories from the hot seat and rousing cheers and flaming Drambuies, we settled drunkenly around our tables with our contingent of nurses.

"You guys really are crazy," Cherrie accused merrily. "Don't you ever say anything nice about each other?"

The lieutenant smirked. "I'm an eagle surrounded by turkeys—what else is there to say?"

"What's an ARVN compound?" Linda asked.

"It's a small earthen triangle with a moat around it filled with bamboo stakes that holds about two hundred men," Dandy explained.

"They put these tiny little outposts out in the middle of a rice paddy and hope they'll be attacked so we can destroy them with air and artillery," Mad Hatter added. "Without us they're buzzard meat."

"How many enemy soldiers were really attacking them today?" Sandra asked. "I know it wasn't the ten thousand you claimed in your war story."

Coop shrugged. "More than I've ever seen before—maybe six or eight hundred."

Linda was awestruck. "There were two hundred ARVNs and you guys against all of them?"

"Uh, allow me to correct you, Linda," Sharpe interjected. "It was two hundred ARVNs and *me* against all of them. My buddies here checked out when they saw what we were up against."

"Checked out, my ass!" Dandy huffed. "*You* crawl in a ditch in the middle of no-man's-land between a thousand pissed-off armed men! My asshole was so puckered up I couldn't even shit on myself. It's an experience I don't want to repeat."

"*Aw, did 'im have to cup 'is little palms over 'is ears to block out all the horrid noise?*" Sharpe jeered.

"I admit I got my ass busted on the first pass," Coop allowed, scowling at the lieutenant. "After that I sat in a field waiting for a ride home. It would've been nice if *someone* had warned me what to expect."

Dandy chuckled. "The last I saw of Sly, parts of his aircraft were flying every which way."

"They shot my canopy off," Sly groused. "My eyes were burning so bad from the wind I couldn't see a damn thing. I was trying to fire in so many directions at once I forgot where I was going."

Cherrie turned to Sharpe. "Weren't you scared?"

He profiled for us. "I got a little nervous when these assholes ran out on me. But like the ace pilot I am, I rose to the occasion when the moment called for it."

Dandy stuck his finger down his throat and crossed his eyes. "*Barf!*"

"Were you frightened, Sly?" Sandra asked.

"Yeah, darlin', I was. After I crashed, I knew Sugar Bear was going to get a higher body count than me and *all* the glory. That scared the hell out of me!"

Linda turned to me, laughing. "Captain, you have some weird men in your platoon."

I shook my head sadly. "They gave me all the nut cases. It hardly seems fair, does it?"

Cherrie hugged the lieutenant. "Everybody got shot down but you. You're so lucky."

"It wasn't luck, sweetheart, I'm just *good*. But I'll admit flying with the amateurs Chief here surrounds me with does tend to make me look better than I actually am on occasion."

"*BARF!*" Sly, Dandy, and Coop chorused together.

Cherrie laughed. "Are you guys ever serious?"

"Only about something as sexy as you!" Sharpe devoured her neck as she squealed and fought him off.

I sat back proudly, listening to them tease, trade barbs, boast, profile, and gloat after such a trying day knowing I had the best there was in Nam. Sharpe was their natural leader and I but their figurehead, but I didn't resent it in the least and was only grateful I hadn't lost any of them.

The next morning we were summoned to Major Crystal's office. Sly and I got the two chairs while the lieutenant, Dandy, and Coop stood loosely off to the side. The major read Captain Nichols's report to himself as we watched in suspense, knowing he knew every word of it by heart before we entered his office.

Major Crystal looked up at me expectantly. "Captain Hess, this report looks fairly straightforward to me. The only question I have between your report and the one from flight ops is why you did not address the peculiar situation outside the norm that also occurred. Could you please elaborate on that issue?"

"I'm not sure of the peculiar situation you are referring to, Sir," I replied, trying to make direct eye contact to encourage him not to pursue this.

He lowered his head to the after-action report. "But, Captain, I am led to believe you *are* aware of the situation," he said, refusing to meet my eyes. "I am led to believe you were present when Captain Nichols ordered, let's see, uh, Red One-Seven, it says here, to land at Trang Bang and shut down due to reported battle damage to his aircraft. Is that not so?"

"Oh, *that* situation, Sir. Right. Well, Sir, I'm not sure it was an order, exactly. Captain Nichols was concerned for Red One-Seven's welfare. But the pilot assured him that everything was fine and that he was capable of resuming his mission. The situation was critical at the time, Sir, and I think it admirable that the pilot was willing to risk his life and—"

"*And* one of my million-dollar aircraft for his own selfish ends," Major Crystal finished. "Is that what you mean to say?"

"That's not at all what I meant to say, Sir," I reasoned. "There was about a ten-minute gap in the fire support after Red One-Niner and Red One-Two went down before our next two aircraft arrived on station. The enemy was swarming all around the compound. Red One-Seven had just refueled and rearmed and was less than—"

"Red One-Seven?" Major Crystal pretended to read the report as if he were unsure of the facts. "Is that the same aircraft that had sustained previous battle damage and was ordered to shut down?"

"Sir, I—"

"Isn't this the second time this same pilot has refused a direct order from flight operations in a controlled mission environment, Captain?"

"Well, Sir, I believe he was exonerated the first—"

"We seem to have a trend developing here, Captain. Two times that pilot has been given a direct order, and two times he has ignored the direct order given. Does that appear to be a trend to you, Captain?"

"Major, I—" the lieutenant began.

"Excuse me, Lieutenant Sharpe; I believe I was addressing your platoon leader, not you!"

"Yes, Major, but—"

"Then don't speak until you are called upon, Lieutenant."

"Major, I feel it important that—" the lieutenant tried again gamely.

"Lieutenant Sharpe, get out of my office," Major Crystal ordered softly. "You obviously do not possess the required military courtesy and skill to be in the presence of your commanding officer. Your platoon leader will see to it that you are properly coached in the correct military etiquette to use in the presence of your commander in order to perform as a disciplined soldier instead of a barbarian. Now get out."

The lieutenant drew himself up and saluted. Major Crystal ignored him. Sharpe held his salute as the two battled wills.

"I told you to get out of my office, Lieutenant. *Now get out!*" Major Crystal shouted.

Sharpe dropped his salute and departed without comment.

Major Crystal sank back in his chair. "Captain Hess, your impertinent lieutenant is grounded until the investigation of this matter is complete. It is my intention to court-martial him for disobeying a direct order."

I sighed. "Sir, please, don't take this action."

"Perhaps I have misjudged you, Captain Hess. You seem to have lost your way where your subordinate is concerned. Have you lost control, Captain?" He raised his head and looked me in the eye, his stare cold and bland. I knew instantly that my ass was on the line too, right along with the lieutenant's. "What is your opinion, Captain Benedict?" Major Crystal asked, still staring at me menacingly.

Sly drew himself up. "You're making a mistake in grounding Lieutenant Sharpe, Sir. What he did was praiseworthy under the circumstances."

Major Crystal's stare did not shift from me. "And your opinion, Captain Everett?"

"I wouldn't advise you to take this action, Sir," Dandy replied. "Under the dire circumstances out there, what he did was very brave and probably saved the whole ARVN compound from being overrun. It certainly bought them the necessary time to get the fast-movers in on target."

"And you, Captain Forbes?" Major Crystal asked without shifting his gaze from my face. "Do you share the same misguided views as your two fellow officers?"

Coop nodded. "Yes, Sir, and furthermore, if you attempt to court-martial Lieutenant Sharpe over this, I'll be the main defense witness for him. You're wrong, Sir, and I won't support it."

"Get out of my office, Captain Forbes," Major Crystal ordered.

"It's my pleasure, Sir."

When Coop departed, the major stared at Sly, Dandy, and me thoughtfully. "Gentlemen, what we have here is a rogue lieutenant who needs to be brought under control."

Sly snorted in disgust. "Sir, may I be excused as well?"

Major Crystal glared at him. "By all means, Captain Benedict. Get out."

"Sir, I request permission to be excused as well," Dandy stated firmly.

"Get out, Captain Everett."

The major looked at me coolly, daring me to leave. God, I wanted to. I wanted to spit in his eye and storm out of the room, but someone needed to try to salvage this abominable situation before it got completely out of hand, and there was only me left.

"Well, Captain?" he challenged coldly.

"Sir, I've tried to support you from the beginning. I've tried to run interference between you and Lieutenant Sharpe from the first day. In this instance, I feel I owe you my best advice and counsel, which you have called upon me to give. In my honest opinion, you're making a mistake here, Sir, one that could have far-reaching repercussions."

"You know, don't you, Captain Hess?" He stared at me intently, accusingly. "You know he tried to kill me, don't you?"

"No, Sir, I don't!" I protested. "I assure you if I did, I'd prosecute him to the full extent of the military code of justice! But any suspicions you may have concerning that incident should not be factored into this current—"

"*Captain*, your lieutenant plays in shades of gray when the world is black and white. He either *did* or *did not* disobey a direct order on two occasions. As his commander, I have a duty, a *moral obligation*, to uphold the standards of the Army. This man threatens the very code of conduct that we as an institution hold dear. He must be held accountable for his lack of discipline."

"Sir, this man is so simple he's scary. You unnecessarily complicate him when you compare him with normal men. He doesn't conform to conventional reason or judgment. He's almost animalistic in his desire to seek combat. He's a warrior who thrives on battle. To the best of my knowledge, he has never crossed the line of right and wrong, but if something gets in his way, he'll do everything in his power to move it aside. It's not a personal thing with him; it's a necessary thing. Sir, the fact is he doesn't put a lot of value on his own life and virtually none on those who oppose him."

"Are you implying he's a threat to me personally, Captain?"

"I'm trying to say, Sir, that you have nothing to gain by pursuing this vendetta against him. If you are right in your suspicions, you are only inviting a possible retaliation on his part. Neither of you will benefit from that. Don't do this, Sir. You're making a mistake."

"Get out of my office, Captain Hess."

"Yes, Sir." I saluted and departed with a heavy heart and a weary soul.

I'm ashamed of my next actions. I fugitively watched Lieutenant Sharpe. When he was in his room, I staked out his closed doorway until long after I knew Dean Six had retired for the night. The rest of the time, I kept him near on some pretext or another or accompanied him in some fashion everywhere he went. I was sure something was going to happen ... and I was determined to prevent it.

Two days later I was summoned to Major Crystal's office and instructed to bring Sharpe, Sly, Dandy, and

Coop with me. I arrived nervous and jittery since nothing good ever happened when the major and the lieutenant were thrust together. The executive officer directed me into the commander's office and instructed the other four to wait in the orderly room. After I reported, the major introduced me to the corps commander seated in one of the chairs.

He stood and greeted me with a warm, strong handshake. "Captain, it's a pleasure to meet the most distinguished platoon leader in my corps of operations. What you and your men have accomplished is nothing short of remarkable. The reports I receive from the field are filled with gratitude and praise for the heroics of your pilots. I wanted to meet with you personally and tell you to keep up the good work."

I was acutely aware of Major Crystal scowling at me from behind the general. "Thank you, Sir. My men are some of the best, and it is to them that the credit goes."

"Indeed, Captain. I appreciate your humility, but a singular group of men is an unorganized mob without proper, effective leadership. To that end, the credit goes to you and your commander here. I've brought along some awards for your most recent mission. I'd be honored to personally decorate your men with them, if you would allow me the privilege."

I swallowed as Major Crystal rolled his eyes to the ceiling. "Sir, it would be my honor for you to recognize my men for their valor."

He turned to Major Crystal. "Could we have the men brought into your office?"

"Yes, Sir." Crystal opened the door, motioned curtly to my four pilots, and stood back as they entered single-file and lined up expectantly in front of his desk at attention. All wore grim expressions, appropriately braced for the worst, having been conditioned to believe that only adverse things occurred when summoned to Crystal's office.

Major Crystal stood off to the side as I made the introductions. "General, allow me to introduce Captain Benedict, Captain Everett, Captain Forbes, and First Lieutenant Sharpe."

"Please, Captain, use their call signs," the general instructed. "That is how I get my reports and how I have come to know them."

"Yes, Sir. This is Red One-Two, Sir; Red One-One; Red One-Niner; and Red One-Seven."

"Red One-Seven?" he noted as he shook each man's hand. "It is indeed a pleasure to meet you, Lieutenant. The stories I hear about you are almost mythical. I'm led to believe that many of my field advisers request your support by name. How does that make you feel, son?"

"I'm honored, Sir. The advisers in the field are some of the finest men I've ever worked with. They have one of the toughest jobs imaginable. It's a pleasure to be of service to them. They're my heroes."

The general beamed. "Well said, Red One-Seven. I fully share your view of them. It would be my pleasure to pass your remarks along to them, if I may. They are certainly fans of yours, as well."

"I would be honored by such a gesture on your part, Sir," Sharpe replied.

"I'm going to ask your platoon leader to assist me while your commander reads some citations I have brought with me. It's not often I have the opportunity to decorate men who have so gloriously distinguished themselves on the field of battle."

Major Crystal cleared his throat and began reading. Dandy was first with an award of the Air Medal for Valor, with a credit of 22 confirmed kills in the engagement at the Panther compound. Sly was next, presented with the Air Medal with Valor and accredited with 59 confirmed enemy kills. Coop received the Air Medal with Valor with credit for 12 confirmed kills. Lastly, Lieutenant Sharpe, with each citation read aloud by Crystal's trembling voice, received the Air Medal with Valor for the destruction of the two anti-aircraft sites and then the Vietnamese Cross of Gallantry with credit for an astounding 176 confirmed enemy kills in the battle.

"Gentlemen, you and your copilots, who will receive identical awards presented by your commander at the next scheduled unit awards ceremony, have accounted for a combined total of 269 confirmed enemy killed out of a total of 553 enemy dead. You almost single-handedly turned back a major enemy attack that would have overrun and destroyed the compound. My congratulations to each of you. Lieutenant Colonel Bishop, whom I believe you know as Panther Six, has asked me to personally extend his gratitude and heartfelt thanks, especially to you, Red One-Seven, who I understand would not quit the battlefield even when your aircraft had exhausted its fuel and ammo and taken numerous enemy hits. He thinks most highly of you, son. He's a mighty fine soldier himself. He, uh, did ask me to give you a personal message. Although it's cryptic, he said you would understand. He said, and I quote, 'I would be most appreciative of an autographed picture of you and your Snake for the little lady in waiting.'" He smiled hesitantly. "I *think* I got that right."

Sharpe laughed. "It would be my pleasure, Sir. I'll arrange for that to happen."

The general turned to Crystal. "Major, it's been a pleasure visiting with you and the fine men serving under you. I hold them in high regard, as I trust you do as well. I look forward to visiting with you again in the future. Thank you, gentlemen." He shook hands again with each of my pilots and me before Major Crystal escorted him out to his sedan.

"Now *that's* a soldier!" Sharpe exclaimed after they departed.

"Why'd you get a bigger medal than us?" Dandy demanded.

"'Cause *I* did all the work!" he retorted. "What'd you expect?"

"This might change things now in the major's mind," I offered hopefully.

"Yeah, it's hard to execute a bona fide hero, even if he *deserves* to be shot," Sly agreed nastily.

We snapped to attention as Major Crystal reentered the office, plopped into his chair, and studied us under scowling eyebrows. "Lieutenant Sharpe, you are returned to flight status effective today. Now get out of my office. *Not* the rest of you—stand your ground!"

Sharpe saluted the major, who ignored him.

Damn, I seethed as we shuffled around after his departure. *Why does he always get off so easy and the rest of us have to stay and eat shit?*

"That son of a bitch is like a cat," Major Crystal observed. "He's got nine lives."

"He's a hell of a good pilot," Sly defended.

"Sir, I appreciate you reinstating him to flight status," I added, sounding like an ingrate. "We've been deluged with requests for him from the field."

"Sir," Coop added, "he can be aggravating at times, but if you could've seen him in action against—"

We all jumped when the commander slammed his palm down on his desk. "*You just don't get it, do you? Get out of my office, all of you!*"

We had a hell of a party that night. Afterward I slept the whole night through for the first time in days.

CHAPTER 13

With my new state of mind, I scarcely questioned the lieutenant's theft of a UH-1H helicopter from the ARVNs. When my attitude changed is uncertain to me. I don't recall a dramatic mind-set adjustment, so it must have been a gradual, evolving situation. I simply woke up one morning and realized I was somehow different, and upon further analysis, I rather liked myself better. My values were simpler and more straightforward. Little things were important to me now. I trusted the big things would take care of themselves, and therefore of little concern to me. I no longer judged my pilots by my own relatively conservative standards, thereby enjoying their excesses and seeming idiocy more, oftentimes with some envy for their blithe lifestyle of raising hell for the sake of raising hell because every mission they flew could be their last.

I stoically accepted that our country had deserted us and no longer wanted to acknowledge our sacrifices, that our own commander was only interested in covering his ass and climbing the ladder of success, and that the very Vietnamese people we were trying to help were only interested in what we could give them next. I knew in my heart the war was now a forlorn lost cause, and as such suffered the guilt of being a part of our nation's failure. Despondently, I accepted we were a forsaken group without definitive direction, operating under sparse, ineffective supervision, with no realistically attainable goals. It was clear to me that the only justifiable end to our ordeal was a distant rotation date with which to escape this madness upon our eventual return to the "real world."

I also recognized that in this pool of darkness Lieutenant Sharpe was our beacon of light and no longer attempted to question his reasoning as he led us into a fantasy world where anything was possible and the end justified the means. I stood abysmally silent while he continued to transform the Razorbacks into the elite of III Corps, acutely aware that he didn't give a damn about yesterday or tomorrow and lived only for today and every ounce of enjoyment he could squeeze out of it.

"The way I see it, Captain, you need this as a command-and-control bird," he explained as I stood in the hangar looking at the pilfered aircraft.

"Um, exactly what am I expected to command and control, Lieutenant?" I asked dourly.

"Good point, Captain. But you could also use it to keep your flying skills up to date since you never transitioned into guns."

"Um, won't the ARVNs miss it?" I suggested lamely.

"Not really, Captain. It was parked in Vung Tau waiting to be delivered to them, so they've never had it to miss, and furthermore, once you sign this requisition form it'll be dropped from their inventory altogether."

"But then won't our depot in Vung Tau notice it missing?" I pressed.

"They'll assume they transferred it to the ARVNs, Captain, don't you see?"

"Um, no, not really—so then why do I need to sign this requisition form?"

"Oh, don't worry about that, Captain, it's a phony anyway. We just need to slip it into their records for appearances."

"With *my* signature on it?"

"It's no big deal. You requested a bird, and the depot gave you one, right? Who would ever question it?"

"Major Crystal might."

"Hell, Captain, he doesn't know how many aircraft he has and will never even notice one more sitting around out here."

It all sounded perfectly logical and, in comparison to the fifteen Cobras we had already heisted from the ARVNs, a relatively minor undertaking.

"So why am I *really* doing this, Lieutenant?" I asked as I reluctantly signed the phony requisition form.

"Actually, Captain, we need this bird to fly us back and forth to our new villa in Vung Tau since the Cobras can't carry passengers," he advised as he whisked the form out of my hand.

My alarm bells jangled. "New villa?"

"Here's a picture of it." He thrust a color photo of a huge two-story stucco mansion with accompanying stone walls surrounding it and another picture showing an ocean view stretching to the horizon with a beautiful white beach and palm trees. "We'll build a helipad right here." He pointed to an area inside the courtyard. "It's about six clicks from Vung Tau itself, but I've worked out a trade agreement with the Rest and Recuperation Center NCOIC to ferry us back and forth if we want to go into town. Oh, and the place comes with a full complement of servants to cook and clean and—"

"*Lieutenant* ... you can't be *serious?*"

"As serious as a heart attack, Captain."

"W-Where did you get a villa? D-Did you *trade* something f-for it?"

"Details, Captain, details, but basically, we don't own it; we just get the use of it in return for ensuring its security."

My blood pressure did its jumping-off-the-charts thing. "*What?* That's not a secure area! How are *we* going to ensure its security when we can't even ensure our *own* security right here in our own damned base camp?"

"That's the easy part, Captain. We agree not to shoot up the villa next door if they agree not to harm ours."

"W-Why would the villa next door want to harm *this* villa?"

"Well, they don't necessarily want to harm it, Captain, but that's subject to change when we arrive on the scene."

"How so, Lieutenant?"

"Frankly, Captain, it's rumored the villa next door belongs to the local Vietcong district commander, so I suggested a sort of conditional truce with him while we house-sit our villa until the owner gets back."

"The *Vietcong* own the villa *next door?*"

"So they say, but no one knows for sure, of course. By the way, he's putting together a welcoming luncheon for us to sort of break the ice."

"Are these the *same* VC we spend our days trying to *blow their shit away?*"

"Actually he's upper echelon, Captain, not the riffraff we normally face. As I said, supposedly he commands the whole southern region."

"C-Co-Commands t-the w-whole s-southern—"

"Did I mention the villa's fully furnished, with eight bedrooms and a huge ballroom with a bar?" he continued, admiring the photograph. "I took the master bedroom for myself. I figured that was only fair since I put the deal together. You, Dandy, Sly, and Coop have private bedrooms as well. The other three bedrooms are for the rest of the pilots on a rotating basis. Oh, and this building out back here is the servants' quarters, and the one beside it is a four-bedroom guesthouse we can use for the NCOs and enlisted men. It's perfect, Captain."

I grasped a maintenance stand next to me and sank down on the steps. "You n-negotiated a-a *truce* with the e-*enemy*?"

"Well, in a manner of speaking, Captain."

"I-Is-that *legal*?"

"I didn't negotiate it *personally*. That would have been pushing the legality issue a bit, so I had someone do it for me. But it's binding. We don't go shooting up their villa and they don't bother ours."

"*W-W-We're going to jail!*"

He beamed. "Aw, no one's going to jail, Captain! If we play our cards right, no one will ever be the wiser. Now if you'll hop aboard your new Huey, I'll fly you on down there and give you a tour of the place. It's only about twenty minutes away."

I clutched at his sleeve. "Tell me you're *joking*! You *are* joking, right?"

"Come along, Captain, or we'll be late for our luncheon engagement."

187

He took my arm and steered me up into the copilot's seat of the newly stolen C&C aircraft as Sly, Dandy, Coop, and Cherrie hopped in back. Twenty minutes later we circled the area so he could point out various landmarks before setting the aircraft down on the beach next to "our" new villa. As we climbed out and the blades coasted to a stop, three Vietnamese men approached us, two of them carrying AK-47 automatic rifles. Sly, Dandy, and Coop tensed as they reached for their weapons.

"Easy, guys, let me handle this," Sharpe soothed.

The unarmed man in the lead greeted him. "Hall-o, G.I., welcome you to my beach, yes?" He shook hands with the lieutenant as his two companions eyed us coldly with their rifles slung on their shoulders.

"Hello to you," the lieutenant replied. "It is good to meet you. I trust we will be good neighbors."

"Yes, yes, that is good. Important to be friends when we here in this place, I think. I hope it possible to do some trading as well. Maybe some whisky and American cigarettes? Is very hard to obtain, you see."

From inside the aircraft the lieutenant pulled a box that contained four cartons of cigarettes and a bottle each of whisky, gin, and vodka. "I brought you a sampling of my goods."

"I thank you so very much, yes. This is good. I have prepared a meal to welcome you and your esteemed guests. Please, you come with me, yes."

We dumbly followed him and Sharpe for a hundred yards and entered the villa next to ours, a grand two-story stucco affair with huge windows, where we sat around an enormous table and ate a multi-course meal as the two guards stood outside on the patio watching us suspiciously. Sharpe and the Vietnamese talked nonstop as the rest of us sat mute other than for the occasional comment on the food or the grandeur of the place. After lunch we took our departure after much bowing and good wishes, and as soon as we cleared the place, collectively expelled our pent-up breath.

"Sugar Bear, tell me we didn't just have lunch with the enemy!" Sly demanded.

"Technically he's not the enemy here, Sly. You guys need to remember that when we're down here and act accordingly."

"This is the *craziest* damned thing I've *ever* seen," Dandy moaned. "I only came along because I thought it was a joke you were pulling on Chief here!"

Coop nudged Dandy as we entered the courtyard of our villa. "You owe me five bucks, ducky! I don't doubt *anything* this crazy little lieutenant says!"

"It's beautiful!" Cherrie exclaimed, staring up at the magnificent structure before us.

The door opened as we approached and some twelve Vietnamese men and women rushed out to line up for our inspection as an older, distinguished man waited expectantly.

"Bien, right?" Sharpe greeted.

"So good to meet you, honored guests," the man responded, bowing. "I Ty Son Bien, but please, justa call me Bien."

He introduced each of the servants as they bowed to us, but the gibberish of their names was meaningless, and then clapped his hands to send them scurrying back off to work. Sharpe and Cherrie held hands like newlyweds as we followed a cordial Bien on a tour of our new home.

We entered through high double doors into an entranceway that fed into a huge room with curved staircases on each side. A large bar covered with mirrors lined the far end, with sofas, chairs, and tables arranged around large groupings of greenery. A game room to the right held a billiards table, a Ping-Pong table, and various other tables with chess, backgammon, and such. On the other side of the great room we found a large library, but unfortunately most of the books were written in French, so they wouldn't be of much use to us. Several overstuffed chairs with reading lamps and a long worktable were spaced comfortably around the room.

Through large double doors at the back of the great room we entered into a long dining room with engraved teakwood table and chairs capable of accommodating some twenty people. Against the wall teakwood cabinets held crystal, china, and silverware. Beyond was a large kitchen with stoves, coolers, and food-preparation counters. Upstairs Sharpe assigned us our private bedrooms, each with a private bath, claiming the master suite for himself as Cherrie blushed at the mirrors on the ceiling over the high, overstuffed bed. Double French doors led out onto a balcony with a full view of the ocean. The floors throughout the mansion were gray slate with large oriental rugs spaced about in an opulent display. I decided if I ever got rich I wanted a place just like this—though I figured the odds of me getting a four by ten dank cell in the military prison complex at Fort Leavenworth were far better.

"Who owns this place?" Cherrie asked in awe.

"A Frenchman who owns several rubber tree plantations over here," Sharpe answered.

"So what's the deal? The *real* deal?" Sly demanded.

"We're sort of caretakers while he goes back to France for a few months. We'll rotate our platoon through here on a regular basis to ensure no one loots the place."

"And the gooks next door?"

"We stay on our side of the beach; they stay on their side. We don't screw with them; they don't screw with us. This area is neutral."

"Do you actually *trust* them?" Dandy demanded.

"He's got more to lose than we do, and he hopes to do a little trading with us on the side," Sharpe replied. "We can trust him as far as that, I guess."

"I'm going to have a weapon with me every damned minute," Coop allowed as the others mumbled their agreement.

"Suit yourself, but remember your manners," Sharpe cautioned.

"And just how in hell do you propose we slip ourselves and our men out of Long Binh and down here on a regular basis?" Dandy demanded.

"Easy," Sharpe replied. "I've got copies of three-day in-country R&R passes to Vung Tau for the five of us stamped with Major Crystal's signature on file in the orderly room. The only things missing are the dates, which will appear if the need should ever arise. As for the other officers and men, the captain here can put them in for three-day passes down here in the Vung Tau R&R center on a rotating basis."

"H-How did you get Major Crystal's—"

"Now, Captain," Sharpe warned. "All you need to be concerned with is that it's *legal*, right? And I guarantee you his signature is legit."

"But we won't be in the R&R Center in Vung Tau," I insisted. "We'll be *here* instead!"

"Got that covered too, Captain. The R&R Center has this place listed as an annex, so in essence, we *are* under their control."

"How can this *possibly* be an annex?" I demanded.

He sighed. "Enough already, Captain. Suffice it to say the commandant of the R&R center signed the authorization—albeit maybe without knowing exactly *what* he was signing. In fact, I understand he was led to believe he was signing for a building next door to their compound that they in fact already own, but nevertheless ..."

Sly started at him in wonder. "And how did *that* come about?"

Sharpe grinned. "I agreed to give his NCOIC the concession on all the whores we'll need to keep our enlisted men and NCOs happy down here."

I shook my head to clear my befuddled brain. "I'm sorry, Lieutenant ... and I know I'm probably going to regret asking ... but exactly how did you manage to engineer this feat?"

"You *really* don't want to know, Captain."

"Just the short version, Lieutenant," I insisted. "And preferably devoid of any details that might result in court-martial actions against me."

He grinned. "Okay, Captain, the short version: It seems this Frenchman needed to return to France on an urgent matter for an extended period and of course was very concerned about his property being looted in his absence. He had one of his people approach MACV about providing some form of security on his behalf while he was away. MACV turned him down cold, of course, since they're not in the business of providing such service to a foreign national's private property. When I learned of this, I had one of my sources approach the Frenchman's emissary on an unofficial basis and suggest he make the premises available for our private use, which in turn would afford him the security he sought. Pure genius, huh?"

"Can I *please* have a shot of *tequila*, Lieutenant?" I begged.

CHAPTER 14

The lieutenant, Sly, Dandy, Coop, and I, along with a group of seven nurses, broke in our new home in style by spending two glorious days eating like royalty, lying on the beach, and drinking like fish—with our weapons within easy reach. Our neighbors weren't seen after dropping by to visit the lieutenant on the first day, where several cases of liquor and cigarettes exchanged hands.

We quickly settled comfortably into our indescribably crazy setup and happily adapted to the situation in spite of the oddity of it all. After the initial visit we were soon rotating our men through the villa under a heavy cloak of secrecy. The lieutenant strung two lines of rocks on each side of the villa leading down to the ocean and prohibited the men from crossing these boundaries when they were on the beach. Each man doled out five dollars per visit, which paid for Bien and his staff to cater to their every whim as well as for all the whores, food, and liquor they wanted. He further instructed them never to discuss our mission or give anything but their first names or, more preferably, nicknames to any of the staff or their women companions.

I personally found it inconceivable that so many people could keep something of this magnitude hush-hush, but indeed the Razorbacks and selected nurses who accompanied us kept our hidden paradise strictly confidential. Even I never mentioned the villa to Nancy, though I never slept with any of the nurses or the Vietnamese whores, which in itself was probably the only virtue I had left at this point, but one I was proud of considering the many temptations surrounding me.

If the lieutenant was my platoon's de-facto leader, I was their father figure, a role I accepted with some trepidation. I listened to their personal problems and attempted to give them tidbits of wisdom and the moral strength to carry on in what all viewed as an increasingly foolish venture in Vietnam. The one thing I did not understand was how my pilots could so eagerly seek combat with its inherent dangers to their lives in what was so clearly a lost cause. The nearest I ever came to understanding this phenomenon was on one of our visits to the villa a few weeks later as we gathered around a fire built on the beach.

On this occasion I sat in my own melancholic state staring into the flames, my thoughts longingly of home and Nancy as the surf broke gently nearby below the twenty billion stars lighting the sky overhead in an awesome display. I morosely studied the group around me, taking in Dandy and Linda cuddled together in blissful rapture, whispering and giggling in the near darkness on the edge of the firelight. Cherrie sat with her back to the lieutenant, his arms draped loosely over her shoulders, her eyes dreamily content. Sly lay flat on his back with his head in Sandra's lap while she played with his blond curls in tender twists. Coop held a toasted marshmallow up for Sara's tentative nibble. I surveyed another fire a short distance away partially illuminating my enlisted men and NCOs with their Vietnamese women as a transistor radio tuned to the Armed Forces Network softly played popular American songs nonstop—while we sat peacefully within one hundred yards of the Vietcong Southern District commander's villa basking under his personal protection.

My thoughts shifted to Buzz, one of our warrant officer aviators seriously wounded three days before and now in a hospital in Saigon fighting for his life. An attack of acute remorse swept over me as I considered that only the day before his aircraft went down he had approached me about a letter he received from his wife requesting a divorce. Maybe I should have grounded him due to the psychological anguish he was suffering. Maybe if I had been more attuned to his mental state of mind he wouldn't be in his present dire condition.

"Do you realize how insane all of this is?" I blurted out angrily as the guilt worked through me.

Heads lifted, eyes questioning.

"Are you trying to make a point about something, Captain?" Sharpe asked.

"Hell yes, I'm trying to make a point!" I retorted. "I don't think Buzz is going to make it!"

"You underestimate him, Captain," Sharpe replied. "He's tougher than you think."

I heaved a sigh, praying my inadequacy in counseling Buzz on his marital matters was not a contributing cause to his seeming lack of will to live. "Or maybe it's everything to do with us being over here, especially with our country's indifference to us back home. I mean, it appears Buzz is going to die for nothing! I don't understand how you idiots can go out day after day looking for combat! Nobody cares if you kill a hundred gooks or a thousand, or worse, if you get killed yourselves in the process! It's not going to change one damn thing! It just doesn't make one damned bit of sense to me!"

"I think you need to get laid, Captain," Sharpe teased as the others chuckled nervously. "You're wound *way* too tight."

"I'm sorry—I don't know where that came from," I muttered. "I shouldn't trouble you guys with my dark thoughts."

"Chief, you might be looking for answers that don't exist," Coop suggested. "But they're questions we've all probably asked ourselves at one time or another. For the hell of it, let's see what some of our answers are." He stared thoughtfully into the flames. "I'm here because my country sent me. I really don't want to be here because I think the war is lost, and I sure as hell don't want to die over here even though I know that's a possibility. But since I am here, I'd prefer the time pass quickly. Ergo, I watched this crazy lieutenant transform this platoon into a mighty fine outfit, and you guys having more fun than your fair share, so I figured as long as I'm here, I might as well join up with you and enjoy it. Dandy, you go next."

Dandy shrugged. "Hell, I don't want to be here either, mainly because I agree this is a lost cause. It hurts because our country seems to be against us. I'm a Razorback because the lieutenant here had some pretty flight suits and I wanted one. I guess I stay around to see what he's gonna do next to entertain us. I never think about dying. Sly?"

"I wanted to fly Snakes, and Sugar Bear promised to get some. I love the feel of the aircraft when my rockets and miniguns are firing. I love the noise and the danger. I get high on the adrenalin of combat. I don't think I'll die over here, and the folks back home can just kiss my ass. This war may be lost, but we didn't lose it, they did! Chief?"

I frowned, wondering how to put my thoughts in context. "I honestly tried to get out of this assignment. I'm ashamed to say I tried to use Nancy's pregnancy to get a deferment, which would have cut my time left in the Army short enough that I wouldn't have had to come at all. Once I was committed to come over, with no way out of it, I was determined to serve my time with the least exposure to combat as possible. Just do my job and by all means stay out of harm's way. Just get back home safely to my wife and kids and get out of the Army.

"Lieutenant Sharpe tricked me into becoming the platoon leader for the Razorbacks. I was sure they would disintegrate within a few weeks anyway, so no big deal. Today I want to see as many of you as possible go home alive. I live in terror with every mission you fly. I cringe when I hear the citations read about what you do out there. If the lieutenant would let me, I'd quit this job today because I care so deeply about each of you it tears my heart out when one of you gets hurt, like with Buzz right now. I'm not mad at the people back home. I'm mad at the press for what they've done to us as a people. And I'm mad at the Army for their muddle-headed policies in fighting this war. I'm mad at the self-serving politicians who have sold us out. The folks back home have been duped. Someday I'm certain they'll come to see that. Lieutenant?"

Sharpe stared into the fire. "Hell, I'm here for purely selfish reasons—to kill as many of these communist bastards as I can. And while I'm about it, to raise as much hell and have as much fun as possible."

Cherrie shivered. "That's pretty cold and diabolical."

"It is what it is," Sharpe replied.

She turned to face him. "Are you saying you enjoy killing these people?"

"I get a certain amount of satisfaction from it."

"H-How could you possibly get satisfaction from taking another person's life?"

"That's a subject best left unexplored because you could never understand it."

"Try me," she challenged.

"Okay, darling, try this on for size. The simple fact is I was in the Infantry at the beginning of the Vietnam buildup when we were all patriots and our country still united as a people. I soldiered with some of the finest men who ever served our nation. Our unit got caught in a trap up in War Zone C that our idiot commander walked us into, and most of those men got massacred in the huge battle that followed. They hit us with five human wave attacks. They overran our position and the fighting became hand-to-hand. Some of the enemy soldiers got through our line and attacked our aid station to our rear. They shot every one of our wounded as they went through us. I lost the best friend I've ever had, a man like a brother to me, as he lay wounded on the ground unable to defend himself. They shot him in the eye. They shot him for no good reason at all. I swore on my own life that I would avenge his death. That I would kill as many of these bastards for him as I could. I would kill them for no reason, as they killed him. I intend to fulfill that pledge as long as this war lasts."

"But the war is almost over," she argued. "Killing them now won't change any of that."

"Maybe it'll help me sleep better. You see, they made me a sergeant afterward. I led a squad and then a platoon of the best infantry in Nam. My men believed in me and in what we were doing. Then my commander sold me out on a bogus mission into Cambodia. They sent me home in disgrace. I spent years cleansing my record by rising up through Officer Candidate School and Flight School and pulled every string I could to get back here in order to atone for my friend and all the others who won't go home on their feet."

"Why do you think killing more of these people will chase away your demons?"

"Because I'll know I took a measure of sweet revenge for those who died for nothing over here."

"You're saying you need to kill in order to heal your-self?" she asked, incredulous.

"Something along those lines," he agreed.

"So when you finally got back over here and discovered the war was basically over you decided to start your own war? My god ... t-that's so scary ... I mean that's really ... *crazy scary*!"

He shrugged. "So be it."

"If you don't give a damn about yourself, what about these men you've assembled around you—are you saying you're just using them for your own selfish ends?"

"With the exception of the captain here, they're all volunteers," he replied. "They're free to transfer out of the Razorbacks and go their own way anytime they want."

"What about me ... what am I supposed to do when you get yourself killed playing your pathetic little deranged revenge game?"

"Go on with your life, I assume," he replied.

"So I'm just part of your good time and mean nothing to you beyond that?"

A cold silence engulfed us as we waited uneasily in the flickering firelight.

"*Answer* me!" Cherrie demanded. "Do I mean *anything* to you?"

He held her stare. "I told you up front I had no tomorrows."

"You selfish, self-serving bastard!" she swore as she scrambled to her feet, slapped his face, and ran to the villa.

"That was pretty damned heartless," Sara accused.

"Living a fantasy is one thing," he replied. "Living a lie is another."

"What's the difference?" Sara demanded.

"A fantasy is merely make-believe," he explained. "Everyone knows it and enjoys it as a means of escaping reality. A lie is an ugly deception meant to be taken as the truth."

"That doesn't make sense," she argued.

"Do any of you honestly believe this moment here tonight is reality?" he asked softly. "Are we really sitting here in the middle of a war zone under the protection of our acknowledged enemy in a million dollar villa? Does anybody here believe this is *real?* Do you believe that it will be here tomorrow or the day after? This is a *fantasy*! Enjoy the moment while it lasts. But love is a truth, meant to be carried over into the morrow. It becomes a lie if you have no tomorrows to give it and you know it and let it stand in the place of truth."

"How morbid!" Sara scolded as she stood and followed Cherrie back to the villa.

Coop laughed. "Uh, have we helped you work things out here, Captain?"

I laughed in an attempt to bring some levity back to the group, wondering how in hell I had inadvertently opened Pandora's box. "Actually, I think I'll just wander on down to the ocean there and throw myself in."

"Who's for a drink?" Sharpe asked as he stood and turned to the villa. We dusted off the sand and followed him in a troubled group.

Cherrie stayed in the bedroom that night while Sharpe got us all drunk in the great room below. He slept on the couch and the next morning departed on the early flight back to Long Binh before she woke up. The rest of us straggled back with our hangovers in early afternoon, with Cherrie still clearly angry.

That night at the club the lieutenant approached her as she sat at our table with the other nurses. "Are you still upset?"

She glared at him. "I have nothing to say to you, you sick son of a bitch!"

"Can we talk it out?" he offered.

"I've heard everything you have to say," she declared as we shifted in uneasy embarrassment. "Leave me the hell alone."

"As you wish," he replied and settled into a chair across from her, where he ignored her ignoring him while the rest of us pretended they weren't ignoring each other.

Later, when she asked a man from an adjoining table to dance, the lieutenant politely bade us good night and walked out as they gyrated together on the dance floor. Out of the corner of my eye I saw Ellen hurrying out after him.

With his departure Cherrie proceeded to get plastered as everyone skirted around her cautiously. She was still the lieutenant's girl until he said she wasn't, so extra care was exercised by all not to take advantage of her in her drunken, emotionally reckless condition. Eventually I poured her into my jeep with the help of two nurses, and we drove her back to her room and put her to bed sometime after midnight.

The lieutenant flew two sorties the following day and took heavy ground fire in the last encounter, resulting in nine hits to his aircraft. When maintenance reported it would be down two days for repairs, he departed for the villa that evening. I was in my room writing about all of this craziness to Nancy when there was a knock at my door and Cherrie barged in with tears streaming down her cheeks.

"I can't believe he would humiliate me like this!" she wailed. "How could he run off like that?"

"Uh, Cherrie, I thought you made it pretty clear to him last night you weren't—"

"He knows better!" she sobbed. "How could he *do* this to me?"

"I think the two of you need to talk this thing out," I mumbled and grabbed a clean washrag for her since I didn't have a handkerchief handy.

She wiped her red-rimmed eyes and blew her nose. "He's the most ruthless son of a bitch I've ever known. I can't believe I let myself fall in love with him. He doesn't care about anybody but himself. You heard what he said. He *uses* us!"

"I don't think he meant it exactly that way."

"I can't stand thinking of him with another woman! You've got to fly me to the villa tonight."

"We don't have any landing lights at the villa," I explained. "We couldn't land."

"I'll go crazy if I spend another night without him!" she wailed. "And if he gets up with someone else I'll kill myself!"

"I-I don't think anything as drastic as that is necessary ..."

She collapsed into sobbing convulsions. "Have you got anything to drink?"

So I got her drunk, which was pretty easy in her emotional state, and she soon passed out on my bed. I sat in the chair and slept as best I could and awoke stiff and sore the next morning. To my utter humiliation, Dandy, Sly, and Coop, on their way to the airfield, paused to give me a questioning look as she departed.

"This isn't what it seems!" I mumbled feebly before ducking back into my room.

Finding the lieutenant that afternoon to explain things before he heard about it from someone else was easy. He and Ellen were skinny-dipping in the surf in front of the villa when I landed. After shutting down the aircraft, I rushed down to the water's edge. They walked out naked to meet me, laughing as I quickly turned my back to them. They walked past to their blanket and clothes, forcing me to turn quickly seaward again.

When they were dressed, I turned to Sharpe. "I need a word with you in private."

"I'll get us a drink," Ellen offered cheerfully and set off for the villa.

I quickly told the lieutenant everything that had happened the night before, emphasizing that I had slept in the chair as Ellen returned with the drinks and handed one to the lieutenant.

He took a sip. "Captain, I appreciate all of this, but I don't understand the necessity of you rushing down here to tell me."

"What's the problem, love?" Ellen asked.

"The captain had Cherrie in his room last night and wanted to tell me before someone else did."

"Please don't make it sound that way," I begged. "I wouldn't want people thinking ..."

He shrugged. "Captain, it's of no concern to me anymore what she does or who she does it with."

"Well, you, uh, the two of you, uh, I just thought ..."

"She's a sweet girl. We had a good time together for a few months, and then she blew me off. It's no big deal."

I shuffled my feet in the sand. "She's pretty distraught. She threatened to ... well, kill herself if ... well ... if you got up with another woman ... I don't think she really means it, of course ... but ... look, I'm not trying to interfere in your personal life or anything and ... and I've obviously misjudged the situation ... I made a mistake coming here."

"Not at all, Captain," Ellen reassured me. "Cherrie is hopelessly in love with him." She turned to the lieutenant. "Why don't you fly back with the captain and talk to the poor girl before she does something stupid?"

Sharpe scowled. "Am I beginning to bore you?"

She laughed huskily. "Actually, there's a cute little warrant officer sitting at the bar who looks lonely and I just happen to know the cure. You go on back and comfort Cherrie. I'll catch up with you later."

"Damn, Captain, my ego can't take much more of this rejection crap," the lieutenant growled as he stalked off toward the villa. "You're a little slut, Ellen!" he yelled over his shoulder.

"That's why you love me," she called after him gaily. "I'll sure miss the mirrors, though—and you know where to find me if things don't work out, sweetie!"

I shifted uncomfortably. "I-I didn't mean to … well … the truth is … I feel rather awkward for interfering and … and what I'm trying to say is I … think what you just did was very classy and unselfish."

She turned to me with haunting eyes. "Don't be concerned for me, Chief, because there was nothing classy or unselfish in what I just did. Sending him back to Cherrie is the only way I can hold him. He'll break her heart in the end, many times over most likely before she gives up on him completely. She will never understand he is truly the son of Lucifer. Oh yes, I know this to be true because I've danced in his withering heat, tasted his erotic passion, and marveled at his boundless lust as the fires of hell burned in his eyes. His draw to my dark side is stronger than I've ever felt with another. But lucky for me, it also frightens me. I'm wise enough to know no one woman will ever hold him, and content with the precious little he's capable of giving. I will always love him, for he owns my heart, but I will never give him my soul. Do you understand what I'm saying, Chief?"

"I-I, uh, no …"

She stood on tiptoe to kiss my cheek. "It doesn't matter. Now go take my love to see Cherrie, and always look out for him as best you can and he will allow." She hurried away wiping at her cheeks and disappeared into the villa.

I returned to my aircraft and started the blades turning as the lieutenant climbed into the back with his bag and a fresh drink. I flew us back to Long Binh with my mind in a complete turmoil, longing for the security and comfort of Nancy. After landing I waited for the lieutenant to shower and put on a fresh flight suit before escorting him to the bar. We were on our third drink when Cherrie and the other girls trooped in.

"Welcome back, you son of a bitch," she flared, causing me to dribble my drink down my chin as she and the others settled in around our table. "How was your trip?"

Sharpe's eyes glinted. "It was just fine, darling, right up to the point where the captain here made me come back to rescue you from the depths of despair."

She glowered. "I can't believe you would treat me this way!"

"You dumped me and wiggled your little ass around the bar like a tramp. What did you expect me to do?"

"I assure you there were a lot of men who enjoyed seeing my little ass wiggle around the bar while you were off with your little whore Ellen," she yelled. "Don't try to deny it either! I've already heard she was at the villa with you, asshole!"

His eyes narrowed. "Leave Ellen out of this."

"She's a whore and a tramp!" she spat at him.

"I didn't fly back here to listen to this crap!" he seethed as he stood.

It would be an understatement to say every ear in the place was tuned in to this situation. I shuffled uncomfortably as Dandy, Sly, and Coop grinned and Linda, Sandra, and Sara glared.

"Sit your ass back down, Sugar Bear," Linda ordered. "And you listen to me, Cherrie. Either you want the bastard or you don't, but enough of the games, okay? You're making a fool of yourself."

"You've been squalling two days now because he's not here," Sandra added. "If you're waiting for him to eat shit because you broke up with him, you're on the wrong track."

"You got that shit right," the lieutenant allowed, still standing.

Sara glared at him. "You missed her as much as she missed you, so don't pretend you didn't. Now why don't the two of you quit being stupid and make up?"

Dandy laughed. "What is this—love by committee?"

"You stay out of this," Linda advised. "It's a girl thing."

"Well, by god, I think it's a guy thing too," Sly argued.

Sandra turned on Sly. "And what the *hell* would a *guy* know about a *woman's* feelings? Especially *you?*"

"Hey, this is about *them*, not *us*," Coop urged. "Let's not get caught up in their problems."

"It *is* about *us* too," Sara snapped. "You guys are just too *dumb* to know it!"

In an instant three different arguments broke out around the table as the lieutenant and Cherrie glared at each other in the middle of the verbal free-for-all. I stared at them in wonder, thinking, *God, what I wouldn't give to have my sweet, even-tempered little Nancy here right now*, as I observed Sandra splash her drink into a sputtering Sly's face and Sara kick Coop on the leg. Coop folded over and grabbed his shin as Dandy ducked a roundhouse right from Linda, who fell onto the floor in a heap when she missed. I watched in amazement as the three women attacked my three hapless aviators in a frenzied tangle, whereupon the club manager appeared and righteously threw us out of the club, which I figure had to be a first in the Dean lounge's history, considering some of the shenanigans that had occurred there over the last couple of months. But fighting wasn't one of the things he would tolerate, the manager explained as he herded us to the door while the four furious, combative women jointly called him a living piece of shit and made heated, unflattering references to his parentage.

I left the yelling mob outside the club and headed to my room as the battle raged on behind me with all eight of them blustering and cussing in a livid frenzy.

Incredibly the next morning I saw all four girls leaving the rooms of my pilots, each giving loving kisses before they hurried off to the hospital for their day's duties as my men hurried to the airfield to fulfill theirs. Go figure.

As an aside to all this, Buzz lived but unfortunately would never fly again due to his injuries. Regrettably, his wife divorced him while he was in the hospital recovering from his injuries and quickly remarried her new beau. No amount of counseling on my part seemed to ease his pain on either account.

CHAPTER 15

Life was wine and song for a glorious week … but my lieutenant seemed to have a real aversion to peace and harmony. Like the eye of a stationary hurricane, he could wreak more havoc around him in two minutes than the rest of us could collectively clean up in two weeks.

In this instance, Major Crystal called me to his office to inform me that the commissioned officers of the Razorbacks were invited to a large, prestigious party held in honor of the new commander of Long Binh. He further informed me through thin lips that First Lieutenant Sharpe specifically was to appear at the party.

"Lieutenant Sharpe?" I inquired anxiously.

"Apparently the little bastard is viewed as something of a myth to the command group with his thus-far-amassed nine Air Medals and Vietnamese Cross of Gallantry. The bigwigs would very much like to make his acquaintance and get to know him better—All-American hero that he is and all."

Major Crystal and I both observed a long pause over this prospect before he eventually sucked in a deep, exasperated breath.

"Captain, I warn you, if he embarrasses me in *any way* I will personally see to it that you serve the rest of your time in the Army shoveling horseshit in a stable somewhere in Bum-fuck, Egypt, wherever the hell that is," he threatened as I swallowed nervously.

Later when I informed the lieutenant, his response was straightforward.

"Fuck them bunch of REMFs, Captain. I'm not going to no damn party where I've got to stand around all night with my little pinky sticking out making chitty-chatter about inconsequential bullshit. I'll pass."

"It's not that simple," I explained patiently. "You see, it's sort of a command appearance."

He scowled. "A what?"

"The thing is, they want you there personally. They've got this really weird image of you being some sort of a superhero or something and they want to meet you. It seems you're something of a legend to them, and as such, an honored guest."

The scowl softened to a radiant beam. "Yeah? A legend? An honored guest? Well, hell, why didn't you say so? At least they've got *some* taste. Will there be any broads there or do we need to bring our own?"

"Uh, it's not exactly a *date* thing, you see. I mean it's not really even a party, although I'm sure all the civil service secretaries and such will be there. But you don't get drunk or anything like that. You just sip your wine and talk real nice and quiet, and then when it's over, you go somewhere else and do the real party thing."

The scowl flashed back. "Fuck them then. I'm not going. The only time a man should have to drink wine is to get laid. If they want to meet me so bad, bring them on down to the Dean lounge and introduce them."

I quickly fell back to plan B.

"Bullshit," Dandy argued. "There ain't no way I'm going to be held accountable for Sugar Bear at a bigwig shindig like that. Are you crazy, Chief?"

Sly shook his head. "Same here, Chief. I'd do about anything for you, but not something like that under those circumstances. Sorry!"

"Count me out too," Coop allowed. "That's just plain asking for trouble."

I smiled complacently. "Okay, let me put it to you in a way that will help clarify the issue a bit for you. If I end up shoveling horseshit out of some stable in Bum-fuck, Egypt, wherever the hell that is, *my* primary responsibility will be supervising *you* three assholes— and I warn you—we will have the *cleanest* stables in Bum-fuck, Egypt. Do I make myself clear?"

Dandy pursed his lips thoughtfully. "Well, that certainly puts a new perspective on it."

Sly nodded appreciatively. "There's four of us and only one of him—as long as we don't let him out of our sight ..."

"It *could* be done, I suppose, under the right circumstances," Coop speculated cautiously. "Are we allowed to sedate him beforehand?"

And so the big night arrived. Brightly lit lanterns illuminated the parade field next to the headquarters building, with all unit flags flying proudly. Music played amongst the three big tents spread around the area. Men and women mingled, laughing gaily in a pleasant atmosphere of decorum and grace. Waiters carried multiple glasses of champagne on silver platters amid long tables of food sending tantalizing aromas wafting around us. Our group marched casually into this mass of tranquility with Sly on one side of the lieutenant and Dandy on the other, their shoulders pressed against his, as Coop crowded his heels in a reserve mode.

So far, so good, I congratulated myself as I led the way. *He's here. Now if we can get him to greet the new commander and then get him the hell out of here fast we might survive this fiasco.*

Major Crystal appeared from out of nowhere with a nice-looking young blond on his arm to confront us with narrowed eyes. "Gentlemen, so glad you could make it. Allow me to introduce my special friend, Miss Candice Freemont. Miss Freemont, this is Captain Hess, my Red Platoon leader; Captains Benedict and Everett, two of his most distinguished pilots; and of course, Captain Forbes there in the rear. Enjoy your evening, gentlemen."

"Which one of you is Red One-Seven?" Miss Freemont asked.

"That would be him, Ma'am," I indicated the lieutenant sandwiched between us as Major Crystal grimaced. "Lieutenant Sharpe, may I present Miss Freemont. Ma'am, Lieutenant Sharpe, or as you know him, Red One-Seven."

The lieutenant bowed. "My pleasure, Ma'am, and may I say that lovely dress nicely accents the sparkling sapphire blue of your eyes."

She flushed. "Oh, thank you, Lieutenant. It's so hard to get decent clothes over here. I'm afraid this thing is quite old, but I try to make do. You are so charming. I don't know what I expected. From what I hear of your aerial heroics, I imagined you to be something of a seven-foot-tall wild man eating raw meat, I suppose." She tittered in mortification. "Please forgive me, I'm only teasing."

He smiled knowingly as he held her eyes. "Thank you, Ma'am, but my keepers here flog me regularly to properly subdue me before allowing me out in public, and alas, they feed me only *cooked* meat, though I do prefer it *rare* and on the *tender* side ..."

Now, how he made *that* sexy and intimate I'll never know, but in the one instant she giggled and blushed, and in the next, the major scorched us with a withering glare before whisking her off.

Dandy exhaled a sigh of relief as Miss Freemont looked back over her shoulder and waved happily. "One down and one to go. Now where's this new asshole commander? Let's introduce them and get the hell out of Dodge!"

"Am I allowed to have *one* drink?" the lieutenant demanded.

"*NO!*" the four of us replied in unison.

We wandered around for a few minutes trying to look like we belonged there with the lieutenant snatching at every tray that passed near us as the four of us blocked him off. We found the formal receiving line under the biggest tent, fell into a long procession of eager officers waiting their turn to greet the new commander, and patiently shuffled forward in a tight cluster, eager to finish our assigned task and escape with our hides intact.

Unfortunately, Sharpe was pissed by now, and that was never a good thing.

As we drew nearer, I checked my uniform, adjusted my gig line, and smoothed my hair amid the jostle of bodies and silently rehearsed my spiel. Two introductions away from the commander I felt a tug on my sleeve.

"What?" I demanded in a tight whisper over my shoulder.

"He's gone," Dandy whispered back.

"*What?*" I turned sharply to stare into the bleak faces of Sly, Dandy, and Coop. "Where the shit did he go?"

"He was here one minute and gone the next!" Dandy explained as we looked in every direction at once.

The adjutant smiled proudly as the pack shuffled us forward. "General, allow me to introduce the pride of the 120th Aviation Company, the Razorbacks. Sir, this is the platoon leader, Captain Hess, who will make the introductions of his distinguished pilots."

"It is my pleasure to meet you and your men, Captain." The general grasped my hand firmly and shook. "My briefings have been filled with praise for you and your platoon."

I panicked. "Thank you, Sir. It's my honor to present to you, Sir, uh, Captains Benedict, Everett, and Forbes. We're honored that you invited us to your ceremony and are honored to serve under you. It's an honor to be here tonight and we're ... just honored that you invited us, Sir. It's truly an honor."

"Thank you, Captain. The *honor* is all mine," the general replied. "Is Lieutenant Sharpe in attendance tonight?"

"Uh, yes, Sir, of course ... uh, he is ... uh, here somewhere ..."

"Please give me the pleasure of meeting with him after I get out of this infernal receiving line, if you will," the general directed. "I'd like to spend a few minutes with him."

"It would be my hon—uh, *pleasure*, Sir. Thank you, Sir."

I wiped the sweat from my brow as we moved beyond the commander and turned on my three hapless captains, who were in the process of swabbing their own brows.

"About one more '*honor*' back there and I was going to faint, Chief," Dandy swore.

"Which one of you lost that son of a bitch?" I demanded.

The three of them pointed to one another simultaneously. *"He did!"*

"Okay, split up," I ordered grimly. "The first one to find him, drag him out of sight and kill him!"

Coop pointed. "There he is!"

We turned hastily in the indicated direction and saw a very pissed Major Crystal rocking back and forth on his heels and toes with his arms crossed and his head down as a glowing Candice Freemont laughed effusively at something the lieutenant said as he sipped his champagne. As we gaped, I noticed the son of a bitch even had his little pinky extended daintily from his glass.

"Go get him!" I ordered.

Sly drew back. "Uh, Chief, I think this is *your* mission."

"Definitely a *Chief* mission," Dandy concurred.

"No doubt about it," Coop agreed. "I *knew* we should have drugged him!"

"What do we do?" I pleaded.

"Flee," Coop advised.

"With great haste," Dandy proposed.

"And hide," Sly counseled.

The adjutant banged a silver utensil against the side of his crystal goblet as he stood on a small raised platform next to the general. Everyone quieted and moved around them in an expectant cluster. Miss Freemont hooked her arm through the lieutenant's and guided him toward the assembling group as Major Crystal tagged along behind scowling.

The adjutant stepped back as the general cleared his throat. "Ladies and Gentlemen, please allow me a moment of your time. I am indeed honored to serve as your new commander. I have spent the last week becoming acclimated to the heat." He paused while everyone laughed. "And, of course, becoming familiar with our operations here in Vietnam. It is a pleasure to watch the professionalism with which you go about your daily tasks. Without each of you, we could not move forward and accomplish our mission. There is no discernible way I can recognize each of you or give you the appropriate individual attention to express our nation's gratitude for your endeavors. Your accomplishments for the most part go unrecognized, but nevertheless are critical to our war effort here. As a representative of each of you individually, I have chosen to identify one among you who exemplifies your dedication. I am informed that this is one we can all look to as the epitome of our own devotion to duty, one who best represents what we stand for collectively, and one whose actions speak for the valor of all.

"I would ask that the commander of this man come forward and join me up here to honor this individual, for as the commander, he is the role model for this man's unselfish devotion to duty. Major Crystal, would you please join me up here for this occasion? Thank you, Commander. Please hold your applause. Next I would ask that Captain Hess come forward and join me, for this is the man who provides the day-to-day leadership and direction to these young men who risk their all in our pursuit of liberty for these unfortunate people in this troubled land."

I climbed up onto the platform with quaking legs avoiding Major Crystal's glazed eyes.

"Thank you, Captain. And now for the man who carries our torch of freedom so highly, who stands on the threshold of battle on a daily basis with a brave heart and a resolute mind, please welcome the soldier who has been decorated with nine individual Air Medals for Valor and the Cross of Gallantry, First Lieutenant John Joseph Sharpe, our immortal *Red One-Seven* of the famed *Razorbacks*. Give him a hand!"

The lieutenant mounted the stage and shook hands with the general amid thunderous applause as I squirmed and ignored Major Crystal's glare. As I listened to the ovation, I was so proud of the lieutenant I could burst, even though I feared someday I might have to court-martial him and have him shot. But he *was* something special and *did* represent what we were, both good and bad: the skillful warrior and the selfish opportunist. He was striking as he raised his hands in victory up on that stage amid wild cheering and chants of "*Speech! Speech! Speech!*" and ugly in what he casually hid offstage unbeknownst to them. At least I hoped it was unbeknownst.

Being in the Razorbacks, I was of course aware of some of the fame and incredible rumors that surrounded our famous lieutenant, but I had no real appreciation of him as seen by others until this most frightening moment. The lieutenant grinned and raised his clenched fists, bringing on another thunderous round of cheers and applause. I watched in bewilderment as he milked the moment to the fullest extent and then held out his palms to quiet them. *Oh my gawd,* I thought in horror as Major Crystal clenched his jaw and turned white with apprehension, *now he's going to speak!*

"Ladies and Gentlemen, fellow soldiers and dedicated civil servants of our armed forces, the commander of Long Binh said it correctly. It is *you* he chooses to recognize and honor. He has graciously singled me out as a most humble representative of *you* and the daily sacrifices you make. I join with him in that endeavor. This small platform cannot possibly hold all of you, so I stand up here with the general, my commander, and my own special role model, Captain Hess, to thank *you* for what you do on a daily basis to keep us flying and fighting in the name of freedom and democracy. It takes ten of you to keep one of us in the field. It takes *all ten* of you doing your job every minute of the day to bring us home *safely.* For that, I am grateful to each of you, for truly, *you* are the unsung heroes of this conflict. Each of you has earned my deepest, most profound respect and gratitude. From the bottom of my heart, *I thank you!*"

The son of a bitch could have run for president and garnered every single vote under that tent that night. They mobbed him after he stepped off the platform, erasing any hope we had of keeping him under control as they inundated him with handshakes, pats on the back, and hugs and kisses from the women as the four of us trailed along looking for an opportune moment to mug him and duck out of there.

He leaned over in the milling throng eagerly awaiting their chance to greet him and whispered in my ear. "These REMFs ain't so bad, Captain! And they're gullible as hell! We might find some real opportunities here." He winked knowingly as my heart pounded fearfully.

The champagne flowed freely as the lieutenant basked in the adulation heaped upon him—right up to the moment he disappeared. One minute he was laughing with Miss Freemont and several of her civilian coworkers, and the next he was gone. Unfortunately, so was Miss Freemont. And even more unfortunately, Major Crystal wasn't.

He stood an inch from my face as Sly, Dandy, and Coop studiously ignored the horrendous ass chewing I was receiving. "She is a-a *personal* friend of mine, Captain! She is a-a somewhat *innocent* and *naive* young lady. She is my *companion*. For the *evening*, I mean. If that *despot* of yours corrupts her or in any way causes her *grief*, I will hold you and your *inept little cronies here* personally responsible! Do I make myself perfectly *clear* on this matter? Now you *find* them before it's too *late*!"

And we did find them. But not before it was too late.

Long after the party was over, and long-long after the four of us had searched every square inch of the terrain around us, to include under a foot bridge crossing over a small creek, we retired dolefully to the Dean lounge. There just after midnight the lieutenant and a very rumpled but serene Miss Candice Freemont strolled in arm-in-arm. We stared at them dully as the lieutenant grinned.

"Hey, guys, here you are. We've been looking all over for you. Hope it's not too late for a nightcap. Captain, I need to borrow your jeep to see Candice home, if you don't mind."

I nodded listlessly.

"Great, order me a bourbon and Coke, and I'll be back in five minutes." He led her out with his arm around her waist.

A long silence prevailed before Coop finally sighed. "The son of a bitch was in his room with her the whole time. I say we kill him."

"We better do it tonight," Dandy allowed. "Because I expect Dean Six will probably kill *us* tomorrow."

Sly flashed an admiring grin. "I can't believe he stole the major's girl. Can you believe he did that shit?"

Fifteen minutes later the lieutenant hurried in, picked up his drink, downed it in one long draught, and motioned for another. "Damn, Major Crystal sure doesn't have a sense of humor, does he? By the way, he wants to see you first thing in the morning, Captain." He took his new drink from the tired bartender and chugged it down as well.

"Where did you see Major Crystal?" I asked.

"Outside Candice's room parked in his jeep in the dark. I didn't see him until I was leaving. What's his problem anyway?"

My left eyelid twitched, possibly the forerunner of an oncoming stroke. "What exactly did he say, Lieutenant?"

"Oh, hell, I don't know, Captain. He was yelling so much he wasn't making a whole lot of sense so I thought I'd give him some time to collect himself so he wouldn't make a complete fool of himself. Hey, those REMF parties are pretty neat. When's the next one?"

"Did Major Crystal request I bring you with me when I meet with him in the morning?" I asked.

"Actually, he said he never wanted to see me again because I disgust him. That was right before he started yelling for me to come back because he wasn't through with me yet. I don't think he knows for sure what he wants."

"Lieutenant, are you aware that Major Crystal and Miss Freemont have a *personal* relationship?" I demanded.

"Did he imply such, Captain? She said he was smothering her to death and that she had explained to him she didn't date married men."

"Do you realize what's going to happen if Cherrie gets wind of this?" I demanded.

"Oh, I told her about Cherrie and she's cool with that. We agreed to keep things strictly recreational between us and low key. I don't blame the major for being hot for her. She's some woman, for sure."

I struggled up wearily. "I'm going to bed."

Coop sighed. "We need to find a priest to administer us last rites."

"Dandy, Sly, can I buy you guys a drink?" the lieutenant offered. "Or are you going to be party poopers too?"

Dandy waved him off as he limped toward the door. "Good-night, Sugar Bear."

"I'm tempted to stay and hear all about Miss Candice," Sly called over his shoulder. "I'd love to know if she's worth dying for!" He followed us out emitting a weird, high-pitched gurgle that passed for laughter.

"Hey, guys, what's your problem?" the lieutenant called after us. "Have I missed something here?"

CHAPTER 16

I waited in the orderly room for over an hour the next morning before being informed by the XO that Major Crystal wasn't feeling well enough to meet with me. I scampered out of there like a cat with its tail on fire. When I arrived at the hangar, I found a crowd clustered around my tiny little office listening to the platoon radio.

"Red One-Seven is down, Sir," my NCO informed me grimly. "We just heard his Mayday call. He was on fire and you could hear his copilot screaming in the background. It was the most awful sound I've ever heard!"

I crowded my way into the room. "Who's out there with him? What brought him down?" I reached for the radio and turned up the volume.

"Red One-Niner is on target with him, Captain. Red One-Four and One-Zero have scrambled from the hot pad and are en route. He was hit by a 23 mike-mike. I've never heard of one of those this far south."

My heart froze. "What's a 23 mike-mike, Sergeant?"

"It's a 23-millimeter, radar-controlled, anti-aircraft gun from World War II that fires exploding rounds and creates huge clouds of flack. They're used extensively in North Vietnam against the Air Force jets but are unheard of down here!"

"Shit!" I groaned as I keyed the mike. "Red One-Niner, Red Six, over."

"Red Six, Red One-Niner, over," Coop answered.

"Give me a SitRep, over."

"Roger, Six, situation is not good. One-Seven went down in a ball of flame. I see no movement around the wreckage. He was burning all the way to the ground. I'm down under five hundred feet just to the south. There's a big boomer somewhere to my north that won't let me climb higher. I've called for backup. When they get on station I'll try to land and check things out if I can. Things are pretty hairy around here right now. That's one nasty gun." Coop's voice broke near the end, conveying his concern for the crew. "Six! I hear small arms fire coming from the area, but it's not directed at me. Somebody's raising hell down there! It might be one of our pilots. Where are my other birds?"

"Red One-Niner, this is Red One-Zero. We are ETA to target in one-five, over."

"Roger, One-Zero, come in low and from the south, buddy. We've got a boomer to the north. You don't want to get in his crosshairs. We've got heavy small arms fire to the northern part of the wood line beyond the burning aircraft. I can't wait one-five if I'm going to help them. If I lose radio contact, look for me in that area, over."

"Roger, One-Niner. Be careful, buddy."

The operations radio crackled beside the platoon radio. "Dean Ops, Red One-Niner, over."

"Red One-Niner, this is Dean Ops, over."

"I'm low over the target area. The Red One-Seven bird is burning with no activity around the wreckage. Backup birds are one-five out from target. I have nondirectional small arms fire from the northern wood line. It's possible our pilots are engaging the enemy. I'm going to make a low recon to see what gives, over."

Captain Nichols's voice came over the ops radio. "Red One-Niner, hold your position. I don't want to risk another aircraft unnecessarily, over."

"Dean Ops, do you sorry fuckers buy these aircraft out of your own pocket?" Coop's angry voice responded. "If that's our pilots down there they need help. Do you fucking copy, over?"

Captain Nichols's subdued voice responded. "Uh, roger, One-Niner, proceed with caution. I was only concerned for your safety, over."

The platoon radio crackled again. "One-Zero, I'm going to talk to you, buddy, so you can track me until you get on station. I'm below five hundred feet heading three-six-zero from the burning Snake, looking for the source of the small-arms fire, over."

"Roger, One-Niner. We're monitoring. Talk to us, buddy," One-Zero responded.

"*Ouch*! Taking fire! Taking fire! I'm hit! I'm through the area and turning south with guns armed. Gauges are normal and no funny sounds. I think I'm all right, just some skin punctures. I'm firing rockets and the pooper now." We heard the swish of rockets leaving their tubes and the steady thumping of the 40-millimeter firing in the background. "I'm back across the field now and coming around to the north for another run. I see someone running into the field! It's one of our pilots!

He's kneeling and firing into the wood line. I'm going hot!" He continued to key his mike and we could hear his miniguns churning in a long roar. "I'm through the area and turning for another run. Rockets away! I'm running west to east now, west to east along the wood line, taking small arms fire." There was a pause. "I'm coming around east to west now, east to west. Our pilot is on the far side of the field waving at me. I think he wants me to come down and get him. I'm going down when I finish this run." There were several minutes of silence. "We're outta there! I've got Sugar Bear hanging on my skids below me! I'm heading south looking for a safe drop zone for him. I'm about a hundred feet in the air hovering slow so I don't shake him off, over."

"Roger One-Niner, ETA zero-five, over," One-Zero called.

"Roger, One-Zero, I'm two clicks south of target. I'm hovering down now to drop Sugar Bear off! He's blowing me a kiss!"

"Red One-Niner, this is Big Bird. Your Dean Ops launched us out to help you. I've got my slick sidekick in tow. I hate to intrude on a tender moment with you and your Sugar Bear, but we're approaching you from the east. If you'll move that souped up super Snake out of our way, we'll extract your little love buddy down there and be back in time for lunch, over."

"Did you call me your *sick* sidekick?" Little Bird demanded indignantly. "And that Sugar Bear better not try to kiss *me* or I'll leave his ass on the ground. What's the deal with these Razorback guys blowing kisses each other and all? I thought they were supposed to be bad-asses. I hope the Department of the Army doesn't get wind of this."

"We're just a loving bunch of guys, Little Bird, regardless of what the enemy propaganda says about us," Coop responded. "You're one pretty sight. If you'll get on down there and snatch up my partner the drinks will be on the Hogs tonight, little buddy!"

"Is he asking me out on a date now, Big Bird?" Little Bird protested.

"You guys leave my Little Bird alone," Big Bird scolded. "He's sorta shy."

"I'm off with your Sugar Bear and headed back to base, you barbarians," Little Bird retorted.

"Roger, Little Bird, ask Sugar Bear where his copilot is, over," Coop called.

We waited tensely.

"One-Niner, sorry, buddy. The copilot didn't make it out of the aircraft. You didn't tell me this was Red One-Seven we had on board. He's pretty torn up about his copilot, so I won't ask him for his autograph, over."

"Thanks, Little Bird," Coop replied. "Get One-Seven home. We'll clean up here."

I turned away from the radio with my heart grieving over our first death in the platoon, Skeeter's loss a heavy burden to bear.

I listened to the radio chatter as they circled low over the downed aircraft and determined there was nothing they could do about the smoldering wreckage with the incinerating body of the copilot within. My three aircraft made numerous gun runs on the northern section of the woods, but the enemy had apparently fled. Spoiling for a fight, they begged Dean Ops to allow them to remain on target, but Captain Nichols was adamant that they return to base and not risk another aircraft.

Sharpe was stone cold sober when he took the hot seat that night to give an account of the action as the men hung their heads in sorrow. He proposed a toast to Skeeter at the end, and every pilot in the room, to include the Green and Yellow Platoons, drank flaming Drambuies to his memory. Sharpe climbed down from the chair in the heavy silence and threw his empty glass against the wall, shattering it. The rest of us smashed our glasses in the same spot, ensuring no other toast would ever be drunk from that sacred container in honor of our fallen comrade.

I thought I had seen every side of the lieutenant, but this night I saw another. The only way I can describe it is *poisonous*. It wasn't fierce anger, nor sadistic, but there was no doubt in my mind he was going to hurt someone—and derive pleasure from it. Near the end of the evening he looked at Sly and uttered the simplest statement I'd ever heard him make, but one carrying deep meaning.

"He's *mine*, Sly."

Sly nodded. "I'm with you."

"Count me in," Dandy agreed soberly.

"And me," Coop whispered.

"Make it legal," I urged as the four of them clinked their glasses together across the table.

The ARVNS recovered the remains of our copilot, consisting of scorched dog tags and a few pieces of charred bone, the following day. I wrote a long, heart-felt letter to Skeeter's mother, crying as I sealed and mailed it.

We held a memorial service in our hangar the next afternoon. Every pilot and maintenance man at the airfield attended. A chaplain read scripture and several of the pilots gave testimonials to our fallen comrade. A soldier played Taps with the bugle's sad notes echoing in the emptiness around us. The lieutenant wore a haggard look. I knew he was blaming himself, analyzing the mission, trying to determine what he could have done differently.

The answer was nothing. It was a typical ground-support call. Everything had been routine until the big anti-aircraft gun opened up on them. One of the rounds took the aircraft's nose off, engulfing the gunner's compartment in flames and killing the copilot before the crash. Sharpe made it out of the wreckage with his stubby little automatic rifle and encountered the enemy in the trees. There he fought in a kill-or-be-killed venue until Coop's daring rescue. As I studied him now with his head bowed in grief, I could only imagine what he was feeling—or worse, thinking and planning.

The tale of Sharpe's escape by clinging to the bottom of Coop's aircraft skids quickly became another chapter in the saga surrounding him. It took a lot of daring on Coop's part and genuine guts on Sharpe's part, but when someone pointed that out admiringly, Sharpe simply looked at him and asked, "What was my alternative?"

I knew then capture had never been an option for him. That summed him up entirely, as a soldier and a man.

The war had come home to us with our loss. In many ways I suspected we would never be the same. I knew I never wanted to write another one of those letters to a mother back home.

Sharpe underwent a thorough flight physical, as required by Army regulation following any crash, where it was determined he'd suffered a whiplash to his neck at impact. Medically grounded for ten days, he took a second physical to regain flight status. I had been dreading this moment for I knew he was not a forgiving man—nor a patient one.

Although there was little left to surprise me about him, he surprised me. I knew he had spent the previous ten days resting and recuperating from his injuries by alternately entertaining Cherrie and Candice at the villa to speed along his convalescence. I also knew Mad Hatter had flown him in my C&C aircraft to Ton Son Nhut Air Base and three outlying ARVN compounds for visits. I suspected he was pulling a plan together, but still didn't see it coming.

Early that morning I made my way to the flight operations room as per my usual routine, where all sorties are controlled and the Deans' missions approved. Each pilot was required to file a flight plan for each mission and personally visit flight ops each day to update his map from the operations board to ensure adherence to controlled airspace. This simple operation was effective and generally worked flawlessly.

I checked the large map on the wall covered with glass, as per our unit SOP, where special lighting made the different colored marks drawn on the glass glow, with red designating no-fly zones to avoid, such as the 23 mike-mike site that shot down the lieutenant and killed his copilot. I noted the red circle covering a five-mile radius that had previously encircled the area was missing and now encased in green, depicting a free-fire zone of known enemy activity, which allows a pilot to engage anything in the area without question. I naturally assumed the anti-aircraft gun had relocated or been destroyed. This area was now currently only one of two free-fire zones on the map. I routinely cleared four aircraft to calibrate their weapons into this area and filed the flight plans.

Calibrating the weapons systems of our Cobras was a routine mission normally required after an aircraft had its weapons removed and reinstalled for any reason, such as battle damage or second-echelon maintenance. I expected these four aircraft, returned to us over the last few days, to recalibrate their guns after reinstalling the weapons systems. The designated duty pilots drew these missions as routine assignments to fly out, expend their ordnance in a live-fire exercise, and adjust their weapons if necessary when they returned in order to correct any misalignments. A special sighting mechanism used to adjust the weapons after installation made this operation only a verification of the procedure prior to facing a combat situation.

I then mapped out several areas circled in yellow warning pilots to use caution when flying through the zones for a variety of reasons, such as recent enemy activity or ground fire taken. Lastly, I carefully studied the blue circles outlining pacified or friendly areas where pilots were not allowed to engage without direct approval from operations or in extreme situations if taken under fire, such as the lieutenant encountered when he buzzed the oxcart and ultimately destroyed it in the previous controversial encounter.

My first indication that things were not as they should be was when I returned to my hangar and noticed a large number of maintenance personnel loitering near the door to my small office where the radios were located. That many men suddenly finding small tasks to perform within such a small area was odd, I thought abstractedly as I settled in my chair and listened to Red One-Seven, One-One, One-Two, and One-Niner call Dean Ops for mission clearance to depart for the weapons test. When Dean Ops routinely approved the mission, the men edged closer grinning and nudging each other. An eerie premonition swept over me—Sugar Bear, Coop, Dandy, and Sly all on *standby* together? *Not likely!*

"What's going on, Sergeant Hays?" I asked quietly.

"They're going after that gun, Captain," he replied somberly.

A nauseous twist dug into my midsection. "The gun isn't there anymore. It's a free-fire zone now."

He grinned. "How convenient, Sir."

I reached for my hat amid a flash of hope that Sharpe's plan was flawless and, please, please God, *legal.* "I'm going to flight ops to cancel the mission!"

He grabbed my elbow. "Sir, Mad Hatter is standing by with your C&C aircraft. You have about four minutes to get off the ground. You need to observe the weapons test in the free-fire zone. Hurry, Captain." He steered me toward the door.

"What's going on, Sergeant?" I demanded.

He handed me my flight helmet. "Go, Sir, or you won't get off the ground. They may need you."

The turbine on my aircraft was already turning as I crawled up into the copilot's seat filled with anxiety, strapped in while Mad Hatter completed his preflight check and called for taxi clearance. At the runway he received mission clearance to the free-fire zone and the tower cleared us for takeoff. As we climbed into the sky, Dean Ops went off the air.

When Mad Hatter could not activate his flight plan with Dean Ops, per unit SOP in such a situation, he automatically switched to Ton Son Nhut Air Control for flight tracking.

When he'd finished his transmission, I keyed the intercom. "What's going on here?"

He glanced at me. "Hard to say, Chief, but if I was a betting man, I'd lay money on one of the electrical transformers leading to the airfield failing."

"We have emergency generators for backup at flight ops," I reminded him.

He leveled off at two thousand feet. "Those diesel generators can be balky at times. It could take several hours for the electrical transformer to be switched and approximately as long to get a diesel mechanic if the generator won't start. But not to worry, we're in good hands with Ton Son Nhut, Chief."

I switched to private intercom to cut out the crew chief and door gunner. "Okay, I want to know what's going on, and I want to know now, damn it!"

"Take it easy, Chief. Everything's under control."

"You've got ten seconds to tell me *everything* or I call this mission off."

"Sugar Bear arranged for flight ops to be off the air for this mission, Chief. That way they can't interfere. He wanted everything nice and legal."

"How did he manage that?"

"He said that wasn't our concern. You know how he is about protecting his sources. He just assured us it would happen."

"Go on," I insisted. "What about the no-fly zone being converted to a free-fire zone?"

He chuckled. "All I know is that a flight alert bulletin came down from the Air Force during the night changing the no-fly zone around the 23 mm site to a free-fire zone. Nice touch, huh? Who knows what the Air Force was thinking."

I imagined Captain Nichols initialing the routine flight alert and placing it in the post-it box, one of the specialists then routinely erasing the red circle and redrawing it in green after checking for Captain Nichols's initials signifying approval. No one had questioned any of the standard operations that morning. Everything was routine … and very legitimate. How Sharpe had arranged it was the only question—which could explain his visit to the Ton Son Nhut Air Force base, where he had extensive connections as proven by the silver flight suits he obtained—but it didn't explain the visits to the three ARVN outposts. Obviously, there was still more to come.

"What did Lieutenant Sharpe do when you flew him to the ARVN outposts?"

"Drank coffee and visited, as far as I know, Chief. The crew and I waited on the pad."

"If you're holding anything back on me—"

"Easy, Chief, you know what I know, I swear to you. I know those goofballs are going after that gun, but I haven't been briefed on the whole plan yet. We'll get the details when we land to refuel. Fair enough?"

We continued to the free-fire zone in silence as my mind swirled in dizzy circles. As we drew near the area, Mad Hatter keyed his mike.

"Red One-Seven, this is Red One-Five, at your service. I have a baffled and very inquisitive Red Six on board, over."

"Roger, Mad Hatter, go into a holding pattern south of the target area, over," he instructed.

"Roger, we'll hold two clicks to the south," Mad Hatter acknowledged. "Call if you need us, buddy. Good luck."

"Dandy, are you in position?" Sharpe called.

"Roger, Sugar Bear, I'm to the west at five hundred feet, over."

"Sly?"

"Roger, Sugar Bear, east at five hundred, over."

"Coop?"

"South, five hundred. Let's roll. You be careful now, Sugar Bear."

"One-Seven is two thousand and turning north. ADF is tuned and systems are armed. Guide on me."

Mad Hatter put us in a holding pattern to the south at three thousand feet. Sharpe's aircraft was to our front a thousand feet below us. Dandy, Sly, and Coop's aircraft were on the deck slightly higher than tree level converging toward the center of the free-fire zone from different directions. Sharpe was obviously the bait. Mad Hatter turned up the volume on our automatic direction finder, a receive-only radio normally used for navigation over which Morse code electronic signals transmitted from the towers. A needle on the gauge located on the dash of the helicopter pointed in the direction of the signal received, giving a directional readout on the 360-degree azimuth indicator around the circular face of the instrument.

"What are they doing?" I asked over the intercom.

"Sugar Bear talked to his Air Force buddies about these guns. The ADF will supposedly pick up their radar signals and the indicator will give us a direction. Once they lock onto him we'll have several different readings. When we draw them out on a map it'll tell us where the gun is at the point they intersect on the map. Pretty ingenious, huh?"

Over the receiver a distinct *beep* occurred and the needle on the ADF fluctuated.

"He just pinged me," the lieutenant called. "Be ready."

A second *beep* and then a third sounded with a corresponding jump of the directional needle. Then the needle swung rapidly as the audio rang out in our headsets. *Beep–beep. Beep–beep–beep. Beep–beep–beep–beep.*

"He's sweeping me but hasn't locked on yet," the lieutenant called.

Beep-beep-beep-beep-beepbeepbeepbeepbeepbeepbeep. The ADF needle settled down to a steady direction.

"He's got me! Lock in! I'm out of here!" the lieutenant yelled.

I locked the azimuth in and marked a prominent terrain feature under us on the ground as Sharpe's aircraft dove in a hard descending left turn. Above and behind him black puffs of smoke erupted from the anti-aircraft fire trying to shred him with exploding shrapnel.

"*Yee haw*, that was close!" he called. "Let's get back to Trang Bang and compare notes."

We landed, hot refueled, and shut down as the other four aircraft refueled and then set down. The pilots climbed out to gather around us.

Sharpe grinned. "Welcome, Captain!"

"We're not going to get away with this," I warned.

"Why not?" he challenged. "It's a free-fire zone and all perfectly legal."

"Promise me that before Dean Six has us shot you'll tell me how you pulled this off."

"Not a chance, Captain. Okay, guys, give me your locations and readings."

Each pilot gave him a spot on the map and a compass reading. When he was finished plotting our four lines, they all crossed at a specific point on his map.

He sat back on his heels. "Got you, you little son of a bitch. Now you're going to die. We'll come in from the east at five hundred feet with separation between aircraft of one hundred meters each. These are our four checkpoints." He quickly circled four points spaced a hundred meters apart on his map, one for each of them. "Captain, you circle in this area to the south in case one of us goes down. I'll pop up to a thousand feet and drop my load on their head. You three pop up behind me after I've got them ducking for cover and rip their guts out while they're rattled and confused. Any questions?" There were none among the grim faces surrounding him. "Let's go!" Each headed for his aircraft and we were soon under way to our assigned locations.

"Give me a position check," Sharpe called.

"One-One at check point one and holding," Dandy called.

"One-Niner at check point two and holding," Coop called.

"One-Two at check point four and waiting," Sly called.

"One-Five at check point five and holding," Mad Hatter beside me called.

"Roger, I'm at check point three and holding," Sharpe reported. "On my count, five, four, two, one! *Rolling Hot!*"

"You left out *three*, dumb ass!" Dandy called. "One-One, *Rolling Hot!*"

"Hope the sucker shoots better than he counts!" Sly called. "One-Two, *Rolling Hot!*"

"*Ta*-Da *Ta*-Da *Ta*-Da! One-Niner, *Rolling Hot!* Lead us to the shit, Sugar Bear!"

From our vantage point Mad Hatter and I watched the four aircraft streak toward the center of the target skimming the trees. They climbed in sync to five hundred feet, and the lieutenant's bird kept climbing higher before tottering and nosing over in a graceful dive. Rockets streaked downward as smoke boiled out behind him. His miniguns and pooper fired as the other three aircraft popped up above him in unison expending their rockets, miniguns, and 40-millimeter cannons. The area in front of them exploded into a flaming ball as their combined firepower chewed up the thick jungle and threw debris into the air in fury. I don't think the enemy knew what hit them, or even knew that an attack on their position was imminent. Some probably died with their mouths open wondering what was happening. The four Cobras flashed across the area as secondary explosions erupted, billowing smoke and debris into the sky.

"Pepper them on your way back across and let's get the hell out of here," the lieutenant called, and the four of them popped up at the end of their initial run, turned gracefully, and dove in a flashing plummet.

"One-One, *Rolling Hot!* Die, you fuckers!"

"One-Two, *Rolling Hot!* Burn in hell!"

240

"One-Niner, *Rolling Hot*! Eat shit, gooks!"

"One-Seven, *Rolling Hot*! This is for Skeeter, you bastards!"

With rocket pods blazing, followed by miniguns and the poopers, the area below them imploded into balls of flame and smoke, ripping the area to shreds for two hundred square yards as they streaked back to the south. Huge secondary explosions backlit them as Mad Hatter turned and followed as they streaked past.

"Anybody hurt?" the lieutenant called.

Dandy laughed. "In a routine weapons test?"

Coop chuckled. "My weapons calibration is fine."

"Sugar Bear, will you marry me? I think I'm in love," Sly called happily.

When we landed, our platoon swarmed around to lift our pilots out and carry them on their shoulders to the hangar as Captain Nichols stared out in puzzlement from the flight ops window. Within minutes the flight ops generator mysteriously started and a short time later the transformer kicked on, restoring electrical power to his radios. The men of our platoon closed the hangar doors and secretly toasted us with flaming Drambuies in a cheering mass.

CHAPTER 17

Odds are we would have gotten away with the operation altogether if our ARVN adviser buddies hadn't been so impressed they submitted us for awards. The lieutenant had arranged, during his mysterious visits to their bases, for them to launch a three-pronged joint operation immediately after the attack. They converged from different directions and swept through the battered zone on the heels of our assault, where they found the destroyed anti-aircraft gun, seventy-one dead bodies, and took some forty or more wounded prisoners. Putting us in for the awards was a bit awkward to explain since no mission had been flown other than a routine weapons check into a designated free-fire zone.

Captain Nichols had briefed Major Crystal, who had me standing in front of him now in his office. "So explain how this happened, Captain," he demanded.

"Well, uh, Sir, I guess you could say we were just lucky. We were testing four of our aircraft when Lieutenant Sharpe came under fire. The others were able to quickly react to the situation."

He stared at me as I squirmed. "Were you aware that there was a misprint on the flight alert from the Air Force that changed the no-fly zone to a free-fire zone?"

"No, Sir," I answered truthfully, desperately wanting to wipe at my sweat-beaded brow. "I naturally assumed the gun had left the area. We were pretty lucky, all things considered."

"And the Dean operations power problems, Captain?" He let the question hang in the air as he watched me intently.

I swallowed. "Uh, well, Sir, everything was working fine when we took off. After we were airborne we were unable to raise flight ops, so naturally, per our SOP, we switched to Ton Son Nhut Air Control and continued our mission."

He formed a pyramid with his palms before him. "Don't you consider all of this rather convenient, Captain?"

"Actually, Sir, it was all pretty *inconvenient* at the time. We were damned lucky we didn't get one of our aircraft shot up."

He placed his palms together under his chin. "You've crossed over, haven't you, Captain?" he asked softly.

"Sir?"

"You're on the lieutenant's side now," he accused. "He's corrupted you. I'm not sure I can rely on you anymore, Captain Hess. And that's unfortunate. I had come to think a great deal of you, to view you as one of my best officers. Am I mistaken in my judgment of the situation?"

I shifted uneasily, certain I looked as guilty as I felt. "Sir, I regret you feel that way. I consider myself a loyal and dedicated officer under your command and try to fully support you to the best of my ability." *Liar, liar, pants on fire!* my conscience whispered nastily.

Major Crystal arched his eyebrows. "How did Lieutenant Sharpe pull this off, Captain Hess? I'm just dying to know."

"I don't understand the question, Sir. I have him outside, per your instructions. Would you like to ask him that yourself?"

He smiled scornfully. "No, Captain. I would rather talk to that wall behind you—it would give me more information and offer a higher level of intellectual discourse. You may go now, and take your lieutenant with you. Take these with you as well," he directed as I turned to the door. He tossed a pile of ribbons with medals onto the desk and slid a stack of papers next to them. "These are the awards and citations. Please see that they get to the right people." He turned in his chair to stare out the window in contemptuous dismissal.

I collected them up and hurried out. On my way past Lieutenant Sharpe, I jerked my head for him to follow as I charged out to my jeep in a building rage. The lieutenant slid into the jeep as I fired it up and took off sharply, jerking his head back.

"Easy, Captain," he soothed. "What's the problem?"

"That no-good, dirty, rotten, evil, son of a bitch!" I yelled.

"Wow, Captain! Want me to set you up with Candice so you can screw his girl too?"

That got me laughing, and the more I laughed the funnier it got, until we were both bellowing at the thought. I pulled over to the side of the road gasping for air, wiped the tears out of my eyes, and took several deep breaths.

"Tell me about it, Captain," he urged, "since you've seen fit to cheat me out of my own pleasure of spitting in his eye."

I handed him the citations. "He's not stupid. He knows we pulled one over on him and he's pissed. The dumb advisers put us in for awards, bless their hearts, and he found out we weren't even on a mission. He threw these at me and told me to get them to the right people. For him to insult my men like that is inexcusable. Asking me to distribute the awards instead of him presenting them himself at an official ceremony is an insult to all of you who earned them. I'll never forgive the rotten bastard for that."

"Aw, don't worry about it, Captain. We didn't do it for the medals anyway."

"That's not the issue," I argued, unable to shake the anger. "It's an insult to me personally and every man in my platoon. I refuse to have my men and their valor degraded like this by that asshole."

The lieutenant leafed through the stack. "Well, hell, since you feel that way about it, let's rub shit in his face and have our own ceremony at the airfield. I'll get the corps commander to present them if it means that much to you. That should really piss him off."

"I'd love to pull off something like that!" I swore. "What an asshole!"

"Give me a couple of days and I'll set it up. If you don't mind, Sir, I'd like to pull these six out."

"What six?"

"Seven of these Air Medals are for me, which would be a little bit of an overkill, so let's just have one of them awarded."

"Let me see those!" I demanded. Sure enough, seven of the awards were for the lieutenant with various dates and events. My face flushed with heat as I realized Major Crystal had been deliberately withholding the awards from him over a prolonged period.

"I'm so sorry," I apologized, mortified.

"Aw, screw it, Captain. That makes sixteen of the sons of bitches now. It's getting a little awkward. Every time I go out there and blow somebody's shit away they write me up. It's getting ridiculous, to tell you the truth."

"Don't you *dare* say that, Lieutenant Sharpe," I scolded. "The advisers ask for you by name on the toughest missions because they know they can depend on you. Don't *ever* degrade yourself like that again. Do you understand me?"

He shrugged. "Since it's come down this way, I'd still prefer to just slip these six off to the side. I don't particularly want to be awarded seven Air Medals at once. It kind of defeats the purpose and would lessen the impact of the awards the others receive."

"We can spread them out over time," I suggested.

He smirked. "No, Captain, I plan to get more anyway. You'd never catch up. I need you doing more important things than spending all your time in awards ceremonies decorating me and making speeches about how wonderful I am."

"Can you tell me now how you pulled that mission off?" I begged.

"In time, Captain," he replied. "When it becomes a non-issue, until then you need your deniability."

He was right, of course. Deniability had served me well today with Crystal, even if the curiosity was killing me.

True to the lieutenant's word, the corps commander flew in two days later and presented the awards to us at the airfield in a special ceremony. The fun was watching a humiliated Major Crystal come roaring up halfway through the ceremony when Dean Ops called him to report what was occurring.

The men and I—yes, I got put in for an Air Medal with V too, thank you very much, even though I had been slinking around way to the south out of harm's way like the coward I am— were thrilled to be decorated by the corps commander himself. From the speech he gave, I think he rather enjoyed it as well. Major Crystal visibly shamed by the ceremony only added to our jubilation.

"How did you manage that?" I asked Sharpe afterward.

"Details, Captain, details," he answered. "You need to focus on the bigger picture."

Now that everyone knew what we had done, although they couldn't for the life of them figure out how we had done it, we were free to celebrate the event properly. The rascals went out of their way to crucify me from the hot seat to the approving roar of the others.

"So, there I was," Sharpe began. "Just me and a thousand gooks. Chief was hiding up there behind this cloud about eleven-teen miles away to the south and ..."

"And so, with fifteen hundred gooks shooting at me," Sly explained. "I called Chief Hog, hoping to get some support. Now calling him took a while, 'cause he was so far to the south of the target we had to radio-relay messages through half the Dean fleet ..."

"Well, these two thousand gooks threw down on me," Coop reported. "I was virtually all by myself because Red

Six had taken the others back somewhere near Saigon for a conference you see, and …"

"Red Six took out his binoculars to follow the action …" Dandy reported.

The worst part came when I drunkenly tried to drink my flaming Drambuie. I didn't have much practice at this war story business—mainly because I never got my ass shot at—and therefore I missed my mouth. Honest. The syrupy liquid clung to my face in a ball of flames, singeing my eyebrows and the front portion of my hair before those around me smothered the flames out by dumping their drinks on my head. Thereafter I looked ridiculous for a couple of weeks with patches of my hair missing. Some of us just aren't cut out to be heroes.

Nancy was proud of my medal but filled with apprehension at my appalling, reckless disregard for my personal safety in putting myself in harm's way to begin with. I didn't tell her about the flaming Drambuie part, or even of how it ultimately turned out to be the most dangerous segment of the whole operation for me.

Nancy was still the conservative sort, even if I was becoming somewhat wild and crazy.

Things were fairly tranquil a few days later when Major Crystal summoned the platoon leaders to his office. On this occasion an extra chair was brought in so all three of us could sit down.

"Gentlemen," he beamed as he waved a letter at us. "I have been selected by the chief of staff to host a surprise birthday party for the commander of Long Binh. This is truly an honor. I'm going to make it the most special party of his life! This is the type of thing where I can stand out from my peers and I don't intend to let the opportunity pass me by," he gloated as we stared at him uneasily.

"We've only got five days to get ready for this event, so I expect your full dedication in pulling it off. This will be a top secret operation. No one outside of the XO and us four are to know the details. This will be an elaborate party. Spare no expense! I want the entire Yellow Platoon hangar cleared out and groups of your men put to work cleaning and decorating. I want tubs of champagne, cases of wine, and tables of food. I've prepared the full menu personally. Here is a list of your assigned tasks." He handed out sheets of paper as we looked over our responsibilities dubiously.

"I've ordered a huge banner that will stretch all the way across the hangar with the slogan '*Happy Sixty-fifth Birthday, Old Man!*'" He paused to chuckle at his pun, as most commanders in the Army were affectionately known as the 'Old Man' by their subordinates. "I plan to fly in a special band from Ton Son Nhut Air Base. The dress will be formal. The guest list will be hand-carried to the select officers on the list in order to maintain secrecy. Gag gifts will be presented by the commanders of each unit in Long Binh."

He leaned forward to ensure he had our undivided attention. "Gentlemen, this will be *the* social event of the year. Pay for everything you need and turn in the receipts to me. I will submit the final bill to MACV for reimbursement from discretionary funds available to them. I emphasize that *no* expense is to be spared! I again caution you about the confidentiality of this event. It absolutely *must* be a total surprise. Now get going, gentlemen, you've got a lot to accomplish in a very short time!" He rubbed his palms together in anticipation.

We didn't ask why. We were soldiers. Soldiers do as they're told as long as it isn't illegal, immoral, or fattening. We're trained to follow orders, not challenge them. My single overriding thought at the time was my men and I had a hell of a lot more important things to do than throw a stupid birthday party for a damned general—but then again—not mine to question why.

Thus the next five days became a beehive of activity as we and our poor soldiers ran every which way under Major Crystal's personal guidance. We were near exhaustion when we put the last touches on the festive event—three big truckloads of flowers and confetti to spread around in colorful arrangements after we had transformed the hangar into a grand ballroom, featuring a wood dance floor covering the cement in front of the raised bandstand. Every square inch of the hangar was spotless after we relocated all of the aircraft, tools, and platforms into the cramped hangars of my Red Platoon and the Green Platoon.

What we and three hundred of our exhausted soldiers accomplished in five days was miraculous, I thought as I proudly viewed the tables of food and cases of spirits spread out in a magnificent display amongst the flowers sprinkled liberally about. The banner went up last in order to preserve the secret until the very last minute.

I turned in my receipts to Major Crystal and he happily wrote me a personal check for over twelve hundred dollars. My bill was the lowest of the three. From his office I hurried back to my room to shower and change into my formal attire before rushing back to the hangar. Our guests arrived punctually, as is the custom in the military, and we soon had several hundred men and women standing around waiting for the big man to arrive for the surprise of his life.

But the big man didn't arrive at the appointed hour. Major Crystal paced at the entrance to the hangar as everyone else waited patiently inside. A half hour later we three platoon leaders clustered in the small hangar office around Major Crystal as he placed a frantic call to the chief of staff, who, according to the letter, was supposed to bring the general to the event at the specified time.

"Sir, we're ready," Major Crystal reported anxiously when the chief of staff came on the line. "Everyone is here and waiting. When can we expect you and the general to arrive, Sir?"

"What are you talking about, Major?" the chief of staff's faint voice inquired from the receiver.

"Sir, I'm talking about the general's surprise birthday party."

"Do what?"

"The general's party, Sir."

"What fucking general's party, Major?"

"*Our* general, Sir."

"Are you drinking, Major?"

"Uh, no Sir."

"Then would you kindly explain what the fuck you're talking about?" the chief of staff demanded impatiently.

"You directed me to throw a surprise birthday party for the general's sixty-fifth birthday today, Sir," Major Crystal explained. "You said to keep it a secret and that it would be paid for out of discretionary funds from MACV. Everyone's here waiting. Your directive said you would bring the general to the hangar at 1900 hours sharp."

"Major, I've never written such a directive," the chief of staff replied irritably. "I don't have the faintest clue as to what the shit you're talking about."

Things sort of drifted downhill from there.

"But, Sir, your directive said—"

"Are you fucking *deaf*, Major? *I said I never wrote such a directive!*" the chief of staff bellowed. "In the first place, the general is in Saigon at MACV for a briefing and will not return until the day after tomorrow. In the second place, the general's fucking birthday is eight months away. In the third place, the general is fifty-five years old, not *sixty-five* years old. And *lastly*, there is no such thing as a *discretionary fund* at MACV, especially for such frivolous fucking expenditures as a fucking birthday party!"

"But, Sir, your directive—"

"Are you *crazy* or just plain fucking *stupid*, Major? Goddamn it, I *did not write a goddamned*—I'm on my way down there, Major! I want to see this goddamned directive!"

Major Crystal hurriedly dispatched his XO to retrieve the letter from his office. A few minutes after the chief of staff came storming into the hangar the XO returned.

"Sir, I couldn't find the letter!" the XO reported nervously as the chief of staff glared at the two of them and we platoon leaders crouched together in the corner trying not to draw attention or get caught in the crossfire.

"It was on my desk!" Major Crystal insisted.

"Sir, I looked everywhere and checked every piece of paper on your desk three times," the XO assured him fearfully. "I went through every drawer twice. The letter is not there, Sir."

"Go back and look again, damn it!" Major Crystal ordered.

"Yes, Sir," the XO replied as he hurried for the door.

We huddled with Crystal and an outraged chief of staff in the small office in the hangar as the guests waited restlessly. Minutes later the XO called back.

"Sir, I assure you, I tore your whole office apart," he reported. "There *is no letter*!"

"I'm losing my goddamned patience here," the chief of staff warned menacingly.

"But, Sir," Major Crystal pleaded, "I swear I had the letter with your letterhead and your signature on it directing me to do this. Ask my captains here." He turned to us in desperation. "You saw it! Tell him!"

The chief of staff turned to us as we cowered. "Well, damn it, did you see this phantom document or not?"

The Yellow Platoon leader shifted nervously. "Uh, well, Sir, I never actually *saw* it ..."

The Green Platoon leader swallowed painfully. "Sir, I, uh, saw a letter in the Major's hand that he claimed, uh, err, was from you, but I can't say that I actually *read* it, Sir."

My stomach clutched when he fixed his beady little black eyes on me. "Uh, no, Sir, I never actually saw it either, but the major *did* have a letter in his hand when he gave us his instructions, so I naturally assumed ..."

The chief of staff turned back to Major Crystal, who cowered under his scornful glare. "So you can't find this bullshit so-called directive from me authorizing this, Major? And *nobody* seems to have seen this document except for *you personally*? Is that the situation here?"

Major Crystal visibly shrank back. "Sir, I'm sure we'll find it! I *know* we will!"

The chief of staff drew a deep breath. "Well, Major, it appears you've got yourself a party that's going stale on you. I suggest you inform them the general is unable to make an appearance—*and since you've got the whole goddamned base dressed up and standing around with their fingers up their asses, let them party!*"

Major Crystal wiped his forehead with trembling hands. "D-Do you want to tell them, Sir?"

"Are you fucking *nuts*, Major? *I'm* not having anything to do with this fiasco. Good night!" He stormed out the door without a backward glance.

Poor Major Crystal climbed up onto the platform with the beautiful bunting and gay flowers, mumbled that the general was unable to attend because of pressing business in Saigon, and ordered the band to strike up to officially start the party.

And a hell of a party it was after it finally got started. Word quickly spread that it was all a hoax and peels of laughter broke out spontaneously around the ballroom, adding to the gaiety of the event as Major Crystal slunk away shamefully to spend the remainder of the night searching for the mysterious missing letter.

It was one of the best military balls I've ever attended. Everyone turned it loose, the food was excellent, the champagne flowed freely, the music blared, and the party roared on until the wee hours of the morning.

The only clue I ever got—and believe me, I never asked for another because I flat out did not want to know—was when the lieutenant waltzed by with Candice, leaned over, and winked at me.

"I throw a hell of a party, don't I, Captain?" He waltzed off roaring with laughter as Candice floated in his arms in enchanted rapture.

The major never found the letter. Captain Nichols made an attempt to take up a donation to help offset some of Major Crystal's expenses, but since the enlisted men and warrant officers had been worked to death preparing the party and had not even been invited, less than four hundred dollars was collected against the nearly thirty-eight hundred dollars he had reimbursed to us platoon leaders. I don't know what he spent on his own beyond that.

Every man in the unit, including Major Crystal, believed the lieutenant had pulled the hoax. By this point no one even questioned his culpability in such issues, but of course he never actually admitted it. Nor did he ever actually deny it.

CHAPTER 18

The prank was the talk of the base camp as a sheepish Major Crystal kept a low profile and the lieutenant maintained his usual buoyant spirit.

But things got ugly quickly a couple of weeks later as I stood at my desk reviewing maintenance logs, which is not my favorite pastime. I was standing because the lieutenant was lounging in my chair with his feet propped up on my desk talking to Candice on my landline. Call me petty, but he could annoy the hell out of me at times, and this was one of those times.

The platoon radio crackled. "Red Base, Red Alternate, over," a panicky voice called using the code for the villa. I reached around the lieutenant's sprawled form to grab the handset as he murmured sexy suggestions in Candice's ear and chuckled in a low, husky tone.

"Alternate, this is Base, over."

"Roger, Base, we need One-Seven down here immediately! One of the Victor Charlies just shot one of our men, over," the tremulous voice reported.

The lieutenant grabbed the mike out of my hand as he hurriedly brushed Candice off and hung up the phone.

"Alternate, this is One-Seven, SitRep over?"

"Flesh wound to the arm, One-Seven. Things are tense around here right now and everyone is armed."

"Roger, Alternate, keep everyone calm until I get there. ETA two-five minutes, over."

"Roger, One-Seven. Please expedite."

The lieutenant rushed out the door. "Let's go!"

We fired up my C&C bird and were airborne in minutes with the lieutenant pushing the aircraft for all it was worth as I called flight ops to file a flight plan. He flew us straight in, flared at the bottom, and plopped down hard on the pad, cutting switches and shutting down radios with both hands as the blades coasted to a stop. He jumped out and ran for the door of the villa with me dogging his heels. Several of our men, armed with rifles, crouched behind the compound wall peering over the top as we passed. Inside the great room one of our men lay on a sofa with a bloody bandage on the upper part of his left arm. Several others, along with an anxious Bien and members of his staff, crowded near.

Sharpe inspected the man's wound quickly. "What happened?"

The soldier grimaced. "I stepped across the line to retrieve our volleyball and the son of a bitch shot me."

Sharpe scowled. "The *whole* story, Specialist, and don't leave anything out!"

A sergeant in the group hovering around us spoke up. "It started this morning during a trading session with the gooks, Lieutenant. Specialist Green here and the gook got in an argument over a carton of cigarettes; you know, shoving and yelling at each other."

"The bastard owed me for another carton that he hadn't paid me for," Green insisted. "I told him he had to pay me what he owed me before he got any more cigarettes."

"Bullshit, Sir," another of the men spoke up. "Green here tricked the man. He acted like he was selling him the new carton, but after he got the money, he claimed it was for the first carton and wouldn't give the gook the new carton unless he paid him again in advance. The gook tried to grab it from him, Green shoved him, and then both of them went at each other. We had to pull them apart."

"Hell yeah, I tricked him," Green acknowledged. "That was the only way I was gonna get my money for the first carton."

"What happened then?" the lieutenant demanded, his lips thin, eyes angry.

"Later on we were playing volleyball," a third man volunteered. "The ball went out beyond our line on the beach. Green ran after it. The VC he argued with snatched his rifle off his shoulder and ripped off about five rounds at his feet, sort of like a warning. One of them ricocheted up and hit him in the arm. Everyone ran for cover after that."

"Have there been any other shots fired by either side?" Sharpe asked.

"No, Sir, Lieutenant. We called you immediately."

"Give me the carton of cigarettes," he directed. Someone thrust a carton of Marlboros at him and he turned to the door as I hurried after him. "You might want to wait here, Captain," he advised as he strode purposely toward the VC villa. "This could be a little hairy."

My heart pounded. "I'm going with you."

As we approached the villa several men appeared in front of us with AK-47 rifles. Two more slipped in behind us as another blocked our path at the entrance to the compound.

Their VC chief walked out as we waited. "Hall-o, Lieutenant. So good to greet you again, I think."

Sharpe nodded curtly. "We have a problem. I need to hear your version."

"Yes. You man of few words. That is good, I think. Your man cheat my man. Your man cross the line. My man fire warning at him. It silly accident, I think."

"My man said your man owed him money and would not pay his debt."

"My man say your man take his money and not give him cigarette. Your man must to give him the cigarette. That is how it must be."

Lieutenant Sharpe held up the carton of Marlboros. "Your man must pay if he wants the cigarettes. *That* is how it must be. From this day forward no credit will be given for trades. All transactions will be cash and carry."

"Because so you say, Lieutenant? This my beach, yes? I make the rule. You must to follow the rule. *That* how it must to be. Your man must give my man cigarette."

Sharpe pointed his finger at him. "You and I had an agreement. There would be no shooting. If we had a problem, we were to talk it out. You have broken the truce."

"You have lot, how do you say, nerve, Lieutenant. You must be crazy, I think, yes. You stand on my beach and accuse my man and insult me. I think you go now before there is big trouble. You tell your men do not cross my line. That my rule. Must be obeyed. You tell your men do not cheat my men. You go now, Lieutenant. I lose patience with you."

Sharpe extended the box of Marlboros to him. "Here is the carton of cigarettes your man claims my man cheated him out of. Your man owes my man money. I expect you to ensure your man pays my man."

"It no longer one cigarette. Now your man must pay my man two cigarette. That my rule. You pay before your men use beach again. You go now. You bring two cigarette by four o'clock today and all be well, yes?" He walked back to his villa without a backward glance.

The lieutenant turned back to our villa as I hurried to stay abreast of him and again went to Green as most of the men followed us inside, leaving only a couple outside to watch the enemy compound.

"Specialist Green, does this man really owe you any money?" he demanded. "I need the absolute truth now."

"Sir, I swear to you he does. Tommy here can verify it. I'm not the only one that's been cheated. They bum, borrow, buy on credit, and then don't pay their debts. They even deny they owe us. Ask around, Sir." Several other men grumbled in agreement.

"Okay, you men pack up," Sharpe directed. "I want all of you out of here until we can get this sorted out. Green, your story is that you were hit on the way back by a stray round fired at our aircraft. That is your story and it will not change. You will leave on the first flight and go to the hospital. Captain, we'll need to make two flights to get all of our men out of here. You and I will return at 1600 hours with the cigarettes and try to calm this thing down."

We took the first group of men back, refueled, and flew back for the last load. When we returned, Dandy, Coop, Mad Hatter, and Sly waited expectantly in my office with a map spread out.

Sharpe studied the map. "Okay, here's the plan. Mad Hatter, you and Chief will hold in this area here. Be prepared for an extraction if one of us goes down. Dandy, you'll take the north; Sly, the south; Coop, the west. I'll come in from the sea on the east. Come in low and hover about three hundred yards out and fifty feet up. On my command, we level the joint. Hit them with the rockets first, then the 40-millimeter cannons, and finish them off with the minis. Leave nothing standing."

"I thought we were going to negotiate with them," I protested. "You said we were going to meet with them at 1600 hours to smooth this thing over."

"I deliberately led them to believe that, Captain. It's important to make them think we're going to bow down to them. In case you didn't notice, Bien and the others were listening to everything we said. The VC commander knew our intentions within minutes. Or thought he did."

"Is this really necessary, Lieutenant?" I demanded fearfully.

"Unfortunately, it is, Captain. The goodwill is gone. Once we start paying tribute to them it will never end and the price will continue to increase. There's no turning back. That has been their game for thirty years. Besides, Sir, they broke the truce. They shot one of our men. At 1600 hours today they'll have a good-sized crowd around to watch him humiliate us. I'm going to bust their ass big time. It was fun owning a villa, but it's over. Now it's back to reality."

"We'll never get mission approval for this," I warned grimly.

He tapped the map spread out before us. "We'll call off for this free-fire zone here up to the north in five-minute separations. We'll slip around to the south and fly to the villa instead. Make sure you call in your phony checkpoints to Dean Ops. We can't have any slip-ups." He sighed. "I'm ashamed to admit it, but we've got to hide the fact that we're going to kill a bunch of VC. What has this war come to?"

We departed singly for our phony destinations, periodically calling in bogus checkpoints as we circled around in the opposite direction, timing our real checkpoints to the phony ones. Mad Hatter and I circled high in the air off to the west as their four birds dropped down on the deck and slipped toward the enemy villa. At precisely four o'clock they appeared simultaneously on all four sides of the villa, hovering menacingly as the startled VC grabbed their weapons and scrambled for cover. The VC chief rushed out, looked at the four Cobras, turned toward the lieutenant's aircraft hovering straight out in front of him on the beach, and waved his arms over his head signaling he wanted to talk.

"*Too late, you little slope-eyed piece of shit*," Sharpe grunted over the platoon net. "On my command of three! Ready! One, two—*FIRE!*"

His first rocket caught the VC chief flush in the chest and streaked through him in a gory flash, lifting his body in the air and tossing it backward before exploding at the front door of the villa. All four Cobras expended their rockets in hammering sequence as the villa disintegrated before them in billowing eruptions of swirling death. If the VC got off a single shot they didn't hit anything. It was ugly and utterly devastating. My stomach convulsed at the brutality. Bitter bile rose in my throat as I watched limbs ripped from the hapless men caught in the fiery roar of the crossfire. I couldn't

263

find my breath as bodies were flung about in gyrating death dances amid the destruction which seemed to go on forever.

I sat high in my aerial perch mesmerized as my mind unwillingly recorded the pounding rockets blowing great chunks of mortar into the air amid eruptions of fire and smoke, bringing down the walls of the villa and collapsing the roof. Next the poopers danced throughout the wreckage in blistering strings of explosions raising great clouds of dust as shrapnel turned the whole area into a zone of death before the miniguns chewed the remaining pile of rubble in shimmering, dancing spurts, finishing off anything still remotely clinging to life. One Cobra was a lethal weapon; four in a square represented destruction on a colossal scale.

When it was finally over they slipped into the air to trek homeward, calling in their phony checkpoints as Mad Hatter and I followed meekly after them. No one said a word. There was nothing to say. We drifted in one at a time, landed, and congregated in my office, still silent. The lieutenant was the last to join us. My platoon sergeant called us out into the hangar, where every man in the platoon stood with a glass of Drambuie. He handed each of us a glass of the liquid from a table before him. The lieutenant lit his drink with his lighter before lifting the glass to the assembled men.

"Razorbacks! To the mission that was never flown, to the enemy who never died, and to the war story that can never be told!" He downed the flaming shot and breathed out the fire. We and the other men followed his lead with our unlit shots.

"Let this day never be spoken of again," he ordered, slamming his shot glass down on the table and breaking it into pieces.

Coop slammed his glass down next to the lieutenant's. "Never again!"

"Never!" Sly intoned as his glass shattered against the table.

"Never!" Dandy swore, thrusting his glass down.

"Never!" I vowed, smashing my glass.

The platoon sergeant slammed his glass down, and the men walked forward one at a time to break their glasses on the table while intoning "Never more!"

After the last man finished the pledge, Sharpe nodded in satisfaction. "I'm going to get drunk and then get laid."

Dandy, Sly, Coop, and Mad Hatter followed him out in an agreeable mob. That sounded good to me too, so I trailed along behind them—but not to get laid.

Thus, sadly, our beautiful villa was lost. And tragically, the Vietcong commander of the southern region and fifty or so of his palace guard were sent to hell over a single carton of Marlboros. And principle, I suppose.

Thankfully there weren't any advisers around to put us in for medals, so the incident was never brought to light. I assume the ARVNs took the credit, if any was ever taken, since there were no American cobras in III Corps other than ours and all of ours were accounted for on that day up north on a free-fire range. I could attest to that because I was there with them. Major Crystal was right: I had turned and could no longer be trusted. My loyalty was to the lieutenant now.

I awoke with a start in the wee hours of the morning to a screeching melee of hysterical discord. As the clamor reverberated across the RMK compound I rushed out in my underwear, pistol in hand, not knowing what the hell was going on, and stopped to stare in amazement at the sight of two naked women screaming and fighting as the lieutenant, also naked as a jaybird, valiantly tried to separate them. Half-dressed men appeared around me to watch the two wildcats enthusiastically whacking the hell out of each other and whamming the hell out of the lieutenant in the damnedest catfight one could imagine, their initial alarm slipping to grins and outbursts of gleeful mirth.

I rushed over to Dandy, Coop, and Sly standing together observing in delight. "Don't just stand there!" I besieged. "Separate them!"

Sly turned to me incredulously. "You want *us* to get in the middle of *that*, Chief?"

"If we don't do something, they'll kill him *and* each other!" I insisted, giving him a push in their direction.

"Why do *we* always get the shit details!" Sly complained. "Dandy, you take Cherrie, I'll get Candice! Coop, you grab Sugar Bear!"

Sly and Dandy rushed in to grab the two furious women as Coop graciously rescued the lieutenant. Afterward the two hissing felines tore the lieutenant's room apart as they dressed, with Sly and Dandy still keeping them physically separated while Coop hid the lieutenant out in his room. After Cherrie stormed off to the hospital, I gave Sly my jeep to drive Candice back to her quarters, and then hurried with Dandy to Coop's room to confront the lieutenant.

"What the *hell* was *that* all about?" I demanded as Coop worked with a bottle of alcohol and a rag to cleanse the ugly fingernail slashes across the lieutenant's cheek, chest, and back.

Sharpe looked up at me with one eye swelling shut and a prominent knot growing on his forehead. "Well hell, Captain, Cherrie had the late shift tonight, so I invited Candice over. How the hell could I know Cherrie would decide to slip into my room when she got off duty, undress in the dark, and hop in bed with us?"

"You need to go to the hospital and have those wounds looked at," I advised.

He grinned crookedly around puffy lips. "You want *Cherrie* or one of her *friends* to look after me after all that? I'd rather take my chances with Coop playing doctor on me."

With the situation somewhat under control, I returned to my room to rehearse my explanation of the fracas to Major Crystal, which I was certain I'd be called upon to do the following morning.

The lieutenant looked like hell the next day with his right eye puffed up, a knot on his forehead, his lips swollen, and raw tiger slashes on his cheek. The man loved living on the edge. Things were strained around the club that evening, but thankfully, Cherrie didn't make an appearance.

A few days later I was sitting at my desk reviewing maintenance logs and monitoring my radio as the lieutenant and Coop flew a routine support mission in support of the ARVNs.

"Rolling hot, Coop!" the lieutenant called.

"Watch the area to the left, Sugar Bear," Coop counseled. "I took heavy fire on my last pass. *Oh Shit! Mayday! Mayday! Red One-Seven is down! Red One-Seven down!* Coordinates Zulu 7549. Grid 7549! *Red One-Seven down!*"

My heart pounded as the Dean Ops radio squawked. "Roger One-Niner, understand grid Zulu 7549, aircraft down! Launching Big Bird! Sit rep, over!"

"Situation not good, Ops. I'm over the area now and can see broken limbs and such where he went in, but it's so thick down there I can't see his aircraft. Get me some backup out here fast!"

"Roger, Red One-Niner, launching hot pad now! Keep us posted, over!"

"Roger, Dean Ops, will do!" Coop answered.

I listened intently to the sparse radio calls as Coop continued to suppress the area in search of the lieutenant's downed aircraft. When the other aircraft arrived, he flew to Trang Bang to rearm and refuel as they circled over the crash site until an ARVN contingent could reach the area and conduct a ground rescue operation. After almost an hour of anguished suspense, Coop called his report in to ops.

"Dean Ops, Red One-Niner."

"Red One-Niner, Dean Ops."

"Roger, Ops, the ARVNs have found Red One-Seven's wrecked Cobra after fighting a brief encounter with the enemy to reach the crash site. They report it as destroyed with no sign of the crew other than their flight helmets on the ground beside the wreckage, which gives some indication they may have survived the crash. I'm keeping the rescue teams on station until dark. We will refuel in relays while the ARVNs continue their search, over."

"Roger, One-Niner, keep us posted. Ops, out."

I sat glumly waiting as the crowd outside my door listened and speculated quietly amongst themselves, imagining Coop and his team circling over the site, patrolling from the air like angry hornets as the ARVNs searched the heavy jungle from the ground. A seemingly interminable time later Coop again called ops.

"Dean Ops, Red One-Niner."

"Red One-Niner, Dean Ops, over."

"Roger, Ops, darkness is moving in on us. The ARVNs are setting up a night defensive position and will continue sweeping the area at first light. Red One-Niner is returning to base."

"Roger Red One-Niner, understand returning to base, out."

When I entered the club later that night, Coop was inconsolable. When a halfhearted attempt to get him in the hot seat failed, the group of solemn pilots gathered around our table to hear his broken account of the incident.

"It was about as bad as it could be," he informed us gravely. "Sugar Bear was pulling out at the end of his run when a volley of ground fire hit him. He was low and in the worst possible position when his engine failed. He didn't even have time to get off a Mayday call!"

"But you said they found their helmets outside the aircraft, right?" Bingo asked gravely from the encircling pilots.

Coop nodded. "That's what the ARVNs reported."

"Then they're alive!" Blue Skies insisted. "I say let's drink a flaming Drambuie to them for luck!"

The bartender quickly set up the rounds and each man in the bar drank to our two pilots. Afterward they dispersed to cluster quietly around tables in small groups as an oppressive, strained atmosphere settled over the place. I took my own dark mood back to my room to compose a heartrending letter to Nancy detailing the horrible events of that day, ending with the summation that if anyone could have survived the crash, I believed the lieutenant could. It was as optimistic as I could get since I feared deep in my soul they were gone.

The following morning I officially listed Lieutenant Sharpe and his copilot, Hawk, as missing in action. I felt I was signing a lie as I scratched my name on the bottom of the report. I didn't believe for a minute the lieutenant would ever allow himself to be captured, so I assumed he and Hawk were probably dead. Even so, I couldn't bring myself to face the unimaginable.

That evening we sat in a sober group in the club staring into space with little to say. What could we say? Our leader was gone, leaving us in a vacuum.

Cherrie was a mental, sobbing wreck. Implausibly, Candice came in later, and the two clung together, united in their grief as Ellen sat dry-eyed with them, unseeing, saying nothing. Dandy, Sly, Coop, and Mad Hatter sat silently twiddling their glasses, drinking little in the suffocating gloom surrounding us.

Cherrie stayed in the lieutenant's room alone that night, desperately trying to recapture the essence of him amongst his things. I arranged for Linda and Sara to drag her out the next morning so that, as per our unit SOP, I could reluctantly inventory and pack his and Hawk's personal effects for storage and eventual shipment back home. It was the single hardest thing I'd ever done. Dandy, Sly, and Coop refused to help as Mad Hatter and I performed the odious task.

The airfield seemed lifeless that day as we mindlessly sat around and fidgeted, trying to occupy ourselves, but unable to accomplish anything as we breathlessly awaited the results of a second massive search conducted by air and ground rescue teams. Every man in the company with the exception of Major Crystal attended the debriefing late that afternoon in our hangar when the search was finally called off. A chaplain led us in prayer for our two pilots, followed by spontaneous eulogies given by officers, warrant officers, NCOs, and enlisted men alike in an impulsive outpouring of affection in the heavy silence of the hangar.

Afterward everyone seemed to want to mill about and tell funny stories about Hawk or the lieutenant as we tried to laugh and fight back the tears, most recalling some of their crazier shenanigans. Over twenty nurses and fifteen Air Force personnel attended the official service the following afternoon. Most of them did not know Hawk but talked about the lieutenant with great reverence, unwilling to let him go. I went off into my office alone, closed my door, and stared at the wall, unable to let either of them go as well.

That night I wrote another long, distraught letter to Nancy, who I'd kept posted about the lieutenant throughout my tour—with a few exceptions, of course, wherein I finally admitted for the first time that I thought I'd lost the finest soldier I'd ever known. I then wrote the lieutenant's mother and Hawk's wife, expressing my condolences and offering a prayer to each that they would eventually return safely to us. Filled with grief afterward, I couldn't bear the thought of being alone, so I went to the club to be with the others, but it was like a morgue in there with everyone sitting around listlessly, so I left without finishing my drink and returned to my room, unable to stand their grief or hide my own.

Soon Sly came by and lingered at the door trying to make conversation. Dandy joined him, and then Coop. Linda, Cherrie, Sara, and Ellen came by as a group, all hanging out and talking quietly, each lost and not knowing what to do any more than me.

The lieutenant had filled our lives, and now we didn't know how to act in the empty void he left behind. Soon others joined us and my small room overflowed with people. I herded them back to the club, where every Razorback stayed until the manager ran us off at 0300 hours. Before we left, we each drank another Drambuie to our lost pilots. Even the girls joined us in our prayerful toast. Cherrie and Ellen slept in my bed that night while I slept in my chair.

I was helpless watching them congregate to me looking for guidance and comfort. I was as miserable as they were. I needed someone as much as they did. Near dawn I wrote another letter to Nancy, the only person I felt I could express myself to even though she was half a world away. I knew we had to let go. But how?

The next day Dandy got shot up but limped home in a running landing. There was some gaiety at the club that night with his hilarious war story, but it faded quickly as we settled back to staring at each other afterwards.

I couldn't stand it anymore. "We've got to let them go," I announced grimly. Everyone stared at me defiantly.

"*Missing* is not *dead!*" Sly insisted angrily.

"I won't believe it until I see their bodies," Dandy agreed.

"We all know Sugar Bear would die before he'd allow himself to be captured," Coop stated quietly, defining what we all secretly feared.

"He's out there somewhere," Ellen vowed, her voice breaking. "A-And he's *hurt*. I can *feel* him."

Coop folded his arms around Cherrie as she collapsed against him sobbing. "Ellen, we've searched everywhere. If he were on the ground, the ARVNs would have found him. If he were alive, he'd signal us overhead. Either he's a prisoner of war or—"

"We can't give up on them!" Ellen argued. "Not until we know for sure! If they're prisoners, how long will it be before they tell us?"

"They'd never tell us," Mad Hatter replied. "Some of our men have been POWs for years and they still won't confirm it, even when we have pictures of them in prison."

"He's out there hurt and needs our help!" she insisted tearfully.

"Out there where?" I asked softly. "The area was searched thoroughly. We have to let them go. This is not doing any of us any good. Lieutenant Sharpe would be the first to tell us we need to move on."

"Would *he* give up on one of *us*?" Sly demanded. "*Hell no*, he wouldn't! We can't give up on him either, damn it!"

"Not until he saw our dead bodies," Dandy insisted. "I'll believe it only when I see his, not before!"

"I'm not giving up on him until I know for sure he's …" Sly hesitated, unable to finish the dreadful thought.

"Until his body is found or it's confirmed he's a POW, I'll believe he's alive and out there trying to find his way back home," Dandy agreed.

"He's *out* there, *believe* me," Ellen pleaded. "It's spooky, but I can *feel* him. And he's hurt. I can feel that too."

"Goddamn it, I can't stand this anymore," Sly snarled. "Captain, we've got to look for them ourselves. Tomorrow! First thing in the morning! And we've got to get the advisers to help us. We've got to mount our *own* search-and-rescue mission. We can't give up on them until we know ourselves."

"Fine, Sly," I agreed, with misgivings. "We'll do that if it'll make you feel better. But you know it will be ground that's already been thoroughly searched. Those advisers don't know them personally like we do, but they care about the lieutenant almost as much as we do. He was their hero. Believe me, they've looked high and low for them. They feel like they owe it to him. They're as upset as we are. Guys, I don't want to give up any more than you do. I just don't know anything more to do that we haven't already done. Somehow we've got to put this behind us and get on with our lives."

"Do you guys want to do a flaming Drambuie for them?" Mad Hatter asked.

"No! Not until I *know* they're dead," Sly swore.

"Let's drink to them and send them our prayers," Ellen pleaded. "Maybe it will bring them luck. If we believe strongly enough, all of us together, it might help him if they're still out there somewhere."

"Bartender! Drambuies all around," Dandy called.

And so we drank a toast, offering our spiritual encouragement to our lost crew.

"Come home to me," Cherrie whispered as she set her glass gently back on the tray.

Sly set his glass on the tray. "Tell me where you guys are, Sugar Bear. I'll come get you, man, even if it's in Hanoi."

Dandy added his glass to the others. "Red One-Seven, you and Hawk get your asses back here or tell us where you are. Sly and I'll come to you guys. Just tell us where to look, man, and we'll be there."

Coop lifted his glass. "But for fate it could've been me out there instead of you, Sugar Bear. Here's to you and Hawk's safe return." He downed the liquid and set his glass on the tray carefully.

"Feel the love of all these people for you," Ellen pleaded as she set her glass on the cluttered tray. "Absorb the faith we're sending out to each of you tonight. Find the courage and the strength to come home to us."

Linda set her glass on the tray as tears trickled down her cheeks. "We miss each of you, and we'll never give up hope for you. If you're lost and hurt don't give up on yourself."

Sara set her glass on the tray. "Come back to us if you're still alive. I really do love you, Lieutenant Sharpe, as the others here do, even if you are the most exasperating jackass I've ever known."

Everyone laughed except for Cherrie as Mad Hatter put his glass down. "Sugar Bear, if you don't hurry home, Dean Six will trade all our pretty little Cobras for slicks and make the Razorbacks fly ash-and-trash missions. We need you, man."

I firmly placed my glass on the tray. "Lieutenant, if you and Hawk are out there, you find your way home to us. And that's an order, goddamn it!"

We looked at each other, drawing ragged breaths, wiping at stray tears.

John W. Huffman

Cherrie nodded. "That felt good."

"Yes, it did," Coop agreed. "We needed that."

Sly nodded. "So now we've agreed to believe and not give up on them."

Dandy nodded. "I'll drink to that!"

It felt so much better to believe than the alternative of accepting them as dead. We ordered drinks all around, closed the bar down again that night, and stumbled out in a drunken mob. Ellen and Cherrie again slept in my bed while I propped up in the chair, figuring that if the lieutenant didn't get back soon I was going to have to get another room.

We did go out the next day and again fly the whole area around the crash site, crossing and criss-crossing in our search grids. We found nothing. Four ARVN compounds joined us from the ground and again searched every inch of the terrain thoroughly. They found nothing. Our two pilots had simply disappeared. Tired and disappointed, but with the matter finally settled to our own satisfaction, we turned homeward with heavy hearts, having put the matter to rest.

CHAPTER 19

A grim Captain Nichols summoned me to flight ops in mid morning, pulled me into his office and closed the door.

"Grab an aircraft and fly to Hotel Six at Ton Son Nhut. I'll have a jeep waiting there to drive you to the hospital in Saigon. Two pilots are en route there now by dust-off chopper. They're both American. They've got to be our pilots. One is dead and one is in bad shape. That's all we know. Carry three pilots with you for positive verification of the dead pilot if he *is* ours."

I ran for the door. Mad Hatter got my bird ready as Dandy, Coop, and Sly rushed to join us. We flew directly to Hotel Six, our VIP base on the outskirts of Ton Son Nhut Air Base, and crowded into a jeep for the two-block drive to the hospital.

An orderly escorted us to a small office, where a major wearing medical corps brass waited. "You made good time. I'd like you to identify the dead pilot first, if you don't mind. The other one is still in the emergency room undergoing treatment." He led the way down a series of halls to the morgue.

"Where did they find them?" I asked.

"From what I've been told, one of the pilots walked up to an ARVN compound shortly after daylight this morning carrying the dead pilot on his back. He's been unconscious since he arrived here."

The major led us into a cool room with low lights and multiple stainless steel tables, pulled a sliding tray from a wall with a sheet-draped body on it, and waited for us to settle in around it. "It's not a pretty sight, gentlemen. He's been dead in the severe heat for several days." He lifted the sheet and pulled it back.

I blanched, stepping back quickly from the darkly blotched, swollen body with its open eyes staring blankly. "That is our pilot, Warrant Officer Harold Hanks," I confirmed in a choked voice, bleakly realizing the lieutenant was still alive, at least for the moment.

"I will need all of you to make a positive identification and sign affidavits. Is there any one of you who has any doubts as to his identify?" the major asked.

We shook our heads and followed him numbly back to his office, where each of us signed the forms. Congregating in a waiting room, we then sat or stood around for almost three hours with little to say, partly in grief for our dead pilot and partly in concern for our lieutenant, who was fighting for his life in the emergency room. At last we were ushered into a single room, where a man lay on the bed covered to his waist in a sheet with IVs attached to each arm. Insect bites and welts covered his battered, almost unrecognizable face, chest and arms. Traction devices suspended by cords attached to pulleys gripped his head and both legs. His breath came in ragged gasps around a plastic tube taped to his lips below a bandage encasing his head. After staring at him for a few minutes we were quietly motioned out and back to the major's office.

"Well?" he asked.

"That is First Lieutenant John Joseph Sharpe of the 120th Aviation Company," I confirmed. "Is he going to be all right?"

"A lot will depend on how strong he is and if any infection sets in," the major replied. "We won't know for sure if he has any brain damage until he regains consciousness. That hopefully will be sometime tomorrow when the sedation wears off."

"What's wrong with him?" Dandy asked.

"Exposure, dehydration, a concussion, and multiple bruises from the crash. He's got some slipped disks at the base of his neck and in the small of his back. We won't know if there is any nerve damage for a few days. It obviously didn't help his injuries to carry the body of your other pilot around. The concussion also worries us. Until the swelling in his brain goes down we won't know how serious that is."

"Will he be able to fly again?" Sly asked.

The major shook his head. "His injuries are extensive and certainly serious. I expect he'll be medically discharged and shipped home if he pulls through this. He's a very lucky man. He wouldn't have lasted another five hours in his condition. I don't know how he made it as far as he did under the circumstances."

"Can we visit him tomorrow?" I asked.

"Captain, it's a day-by-day thing," the major cautioned. "When and if he regains consciousness he will need to see familiar faces and talk to people he knows. That is the only way we will initially know what memory loss he may have suffered."

We thanked the major and walked the two blocks back to Ton Son Nhut in a silent group, flew back to Long Binh, where we briefed Captain Nichols and completed his incident reports. I went to Major Crystal's office alone to report to him, where he instructed me to conduct a memorial service for my warrant officer and dismissed me without comment on the lieutenant.

At the club that night we briefed all the other pilots. There was little gaiety after giving his prognosis, but a great deal of relief that he was at least alive. We formally drank the flaming Drambuie to Hawk, smashed our glasses against the wall, and spent the remainder of the evening talking quietly, trying to give encouragement to each other.

The biggest problem we faced was in deciding which of us would return to Saigon the next day. Obviously I was going because I was boss. Nobody doubted that Cherrie was going because she was officially his "first girl." Sly was going and offered to kick anybody's ass who disagreed. I detailed Dandy to set up the memorial service the following afternoon for Warrant Officer Hanks and assigned Coop to help him. That left Mad Hatter by default. With that issue settled, we drifted into silence, drank sparingly, and retired around midnight in order to be refreshed the next morning.

We spent a long day at the hospital, but the lieutenant did not recover consciousness. Late in the afternoon we returned to the airfield and attended the memorial service for our warrant officer. Lots redrawn that night dictated Cherrie, Sara, Sly, Dandy, and Linda would return with me to the hospital the next morning.

When we arrived we were informed the lieutenant was semiconscious and that we were not to tire him. We slipped into his room quietly to cluster around his bed, finding the tube removed from his mouth and only one IV remaining attached to his left arm, but the traction devices still attached to his head and arms. Cherrie lifted his limp hand and held it as we stared down at him fearfully. His eyelids fluttered and partially opened.

He looked around weakly at us encircling him, settled his gaze on Cherrie, and moistened his lips as we all leaned forward. "Did-anybody-bring-booze?" he whispered hoarsely and then tried to smile.

The girls began crying as we guys swallowed the lumps in our throats. The lieutenant closed his eyes and went back to sleep.

The next morning we found him feebly conscious. With the IV removed, only the traction devices remained suspending his head and legs from the pulleys and cords. He appeared agitated by all the restrictions to his movement, which we took as a good sign.

"I'm hungry," he complained by way of greeting us.

Cherrie kissed his battered lips tenderly. "You're not allowed solid food yet," she soothed as tears glistened in her eyes.

"That sucks," he whispered. "How about a bourbon and Coke then?"

We laughed as we settled in around him with Linda, Ellen, and Cherrie trying to outdo themselves attending to him.

Dandy, Sly, Coop, Linda, Sandra, Ellen, Cherrie, and I fell into a rotating routine visiting with him. On the eighth day, I sat off to the side as Ellen sponge-bathed him as he lay strung up helplessly. His condition had improved dramatically, I noted, turning away in embarrassment as his manhood leapt upward under her tender, cleansing strokes administered during the bath, thinking he obviously didn't have any nerve damage.

"Captain, could you please wait outside?" Ellen suggested.

"Sure," I agreed readily, not wanting to cause him any discomfort in the unfortunate circumstances.

"And Captain, please guard the door for us." She smiled seductively as she began unbuttoning her blouse.

I hurried out into the hall as the heat rose in my face, closed the door, and pressed my back to it. I stood there like a dummy, trying not to listen to the cooing sounds coming from within. Naturally, the doctor and head nurse appeared within minutes with clipboards in hand.

"Uh, you can't go in!" I spread my arms out protectively, barring their entry into the room as they drew up in surprise. "Come back later!"

The head nurse cocked her head. "What?"

The doctor looked up from his chart. "Move aside please, Captain."

"No! You can't," I pleaded desperately, just about dying of humiliation as the head nurse stiffened in alarm as she tuned into the sounds emitting from the room.

"What's going on in there, young man?" she demanded sharply. "Who's in there with him?"

"A nurse!" I gasped in panic, still barring the door with my spread arms. "She's, uh, giving him a bath!"

The doctor chuckled. "Well, I guess we could come back later then—when he's finished with his, uh, *bath*!"

"Well I *never*!" the head nurse swore as she followed him down the hall to the next room. I slumped weakly against the door, thinking that *I never* either.

The next day Coop flew Cherrie down alone to visit with him. That night we gathered around our table at the club as usual, eager for a report on the lieutenant's progress.

"Captain, Sugar Bear's doing just fine," Coop assured me with a leer. "Believe me, he got the bath of a lifetime today."

"I don't want to know anything about it," I protested as Cherrie blushed and punched him in the ribs. Ellen smirked at me knowingly while Cherrie beat at Coop good-naturedly.

The next day Sly and Sandra flew down to visit with him. That night at the club, Sly leaned over to me and grinned. "Chief, Candice flew down with us today. Sandra and I spent an hour in the hall guarding the door for them." He winked as Cherrie watched us suspiciously from across the table.

"I don't want to hear anything about it!" I protested.

They removed the lieutenant from traction a few days later. A week after that, he was transported back to our hospital in Long Binh. The bawdy crowd in his room became a problem that evening, and we were thereafter required to visit in groups of no more than two at a time with visiting hours strictly enforced. The fourth day after he arrived back in Long Binh, everyone stood in a cheering mass when Cherrie triumphantly pushed him into the club in a wheelchair.

"Barkeep! Jim Beam and Coke!" he called jubilantly as everyone mobbed him.

He spent another week in the hospital and two weeks on outpatient status. He then went before a medical flight evaluation board and received his conditional flight clearance. Sly administered a check ride and reported to the board that he was flawless in his flight skills. When the board readmitted him to unrestricted flight status the following day, we threw the biggest party in the Deans' history, where he held court over his loyal subjects in his normal, aristocratic manner. In the ensuing brawl they eventually carried him protesting to the hot seat and strapped him in to tell the war story we had waited six weeks to hear as we hunched forward in anticipation-charged silence.

"Well, there I was," he began. "Facing about five hundred VC. Coop made a run on them and missed them so badly they ... were laughing so hard they ... couldn't shoot back at him and then I ... crashed and ... the next thing I knew ... I was in the hospital in Saigon." He bowed his head as everyone laughed nervously.

"I-I honestly don't recall much about the operation," he began again softly, head still bowed. "My worst fear is that I may have inadvertently killed Hawk."

Total silence ensued. "I remember pulling him from the aircraft. I remember hearing the enemy soldiers around us. Hawk was alive then. I promised him I would get him home safe. He wanted me to leave him there ... to try to escape on my own. I couldn't do that. I remember covering Hawk and myself with leaves to hide us. I remember doing that several times, it seems, but things are sort of hazy. I remember thinking I had to get us out of there somehow. I hung on to that thought ... that I had to get us out of there. Hawk had a wife and ... and I had to get him home safely. I couldn't allow him to be captured. *I had to get him home*," he insisted fiercely as tears slid down his cheeks.

The tension in the room was gripping as each of us tried to visualize what he had gone through out there.

"I … don't know when Hawk died. I may have … hidden him from the ARVNs trying to find us … because I thought they were Vietcong. He might have lived … if I hadn't hidden us from them. I just don't … know for sure.

"There was a point … one night I think, I'm not sure, but it was dark I think … when I couldn't go on anymore. I had fallen down with Hawk on top of me and … I couldn't get back up again. I … dreamed of you back here as I lay there. I could almost feel you … it was like you were talking to me, encouraging me to get up … to keep going. I crawled my way up and kept walking. I had to come back … and bring Hawk with me. I don't remember anything after that. They said I walked up to an ARVN compound. I guess I did that. And that's … the truth as I know it to be," he whispered miserably.

As I watched him up there in that chair fighting his emotions, I suddenly knew the terrible doubts and guilt he carried inside himself. I recalled the night we had decided to believe in him again and sent out our messages of faith to him with the unbroken glasses. Had he somehow heard our prayers? It was eerie.

Mad Hatter stood and began clapping deliberately, keeping time with his right foot stomping the floor. Sly stood and clapped in rhythm to his stomping right foot with Mad Hatter. Then Dandy and I and every man in the room stood as the applause and stamping boots grew thunderous.

The lieutenant lifted his head. A quiver of a smile worked its way across his face as tears clung to his cheeks. He nodded in gratitude for our understanding, for our forgiveness, if it were called for. The flaming Drambuie was ceremoniously presented to him as we clapped and stomped. He quaffed it down and blew out the flames in a roar. We cheered as a horde of men pulled him down from the chair and sat him back at our table. He wiped at his eyes as Cherrie, Ellen, Sara, Sandra, and Linda engulfed him in a throng of hugs and kisses, smothering him with affection as they cried with him. Hell, I had tears in my own damned eyes.

Sharpe came back with a vengeance. The ARVN advisers welcomed him back with cheers on the radio when they heard his famous Red One-Seven call sign. Belatedly the VC paid dearly as he swooped and tore into them with unabated fury. Within weeks he was put in for six Air Medals, carrying his total count to twenty-two. Sly was second in the unit with eleven, and Dandy and Coop had nine apiece. The lieutenant became even more of a legend, if that was possible, and an instant celebrity wherever he appeared, which he took as his sacred duty to exploit at every given opportunity. He filled the following weeks with adventure, but his biggest crash occurred with as little warning as the first.

We platoon leaders were summoned to Major Crystal's office on that fateful morning.

"Gentlemen, please have a seat," he directed. I was odd man out on the two chairs and stood casually off to the side. "It is with great pleasure that I inform you that a cease-fire to the hostilities in Vietnam is imminent. Peace accords are being negotiated in Paris at this very minute which will bring an honorable end to this sad little conflict. Congratulations! *We have won the war!*" No one moved or spoke as he beamed at us.

This man really is an imbecile, I mused silently in wonder.

The Yellow Platoon leader cleared his throat. "What does that mean, Sir?"

"I received orders this morning. Every man with less than ninety days left on his tour in Vietnam qualifies for early rotation back home. The rest of us will move to Saigon and quartered at Ton Son Nhut Air Base to operate out of Hotel Six, our new home base."

I mentally did the math. I had been in-country eight and a half months, some thirteen days short of the early out. "Sir, Hotel Six is not big enough to house all of our aircraft," I advised despondently.

Major Crystal smirked. "We'll be turning all of our Cobra aircraft and all but twelve of our Hueys over to the ARVNs in the next week. The Deans will become a detachment instead of a company." He smiled as my stomach sank for the second time in as many minutes.

He spent the better part of an hour giving us the logistics of the move to Ton Son Nhut and the particulars of the ARVN transfer of material. As of this minute, our guns would stand down and we would fly no mission outside of VIP or support. On the one hand, I was grateful that it was finally over. On the other, I wished someone else could be the one to inform my lieutenant. I found him at the airfield and pulled him aside.

Before I had a chance to speak, he smiled sadly. "From the look on your face, Captain, I'd say it's official.

We're all a bunch of REMFs now, right? Well, fuck them then and so be it. You need to put me in the advance party to Ton Son Nhut so I can get the best shit for us." He stared longingly out across the airfield at his beloved Cobras.

I found my voice. "I'm sorry …"

He shrugged. "Aw, don't worry about it, Captain. I'm working on a deal to get out of the Army in a couple of months to fly for Air America anyway. I knew this day was coming."

I could easily imagine him being part of such a renegade group as Air America, the CIA mercenary air force operating in Cambodia, Laos, and Vietnam well known for their extremely hazardous missions and high rate of casualties.

"Please don't do that, Lieutenant Sharpe."

He grinned. "That's where the action is, Captain. I wouldn't last long as a REMF anyway and you know it. They'd be trying to put me in jail in no time. When do I depart for Ton Son Nhut? I'll have everything set up when you arrive."

He trudged off with his head down without waiting for a reply.

CHAPTER 20

The next few days were a blur of activity. I pulled eighteen-hour shifts attending to all that was required of me and was in the last group to leave Long Binh for Ton Son Nhut. Coop met the rotation criteria and happily headed home, as did most of the other Razorbacks in my former platoon. Cherrie, Ellen, Linda, and Sandra transferred to the hospital in Saigon two blocks away from us, while Sara rotated back to the States. Candice was still at Long Binh but would be stateside within a week.

The lieutenant, Sly, Dandy, and Mad Hatter met me at the helipad at Hotel Six. I was all out of sorts, having watched my whole world turned upside down as our tight-knit family scattered to the winds. Saying goodbye to my men had been difficult. Not going back with them to Nancy and the kids was unbearable. I was tired and grouchy as the four of them helped load my gear into the back of a three-quarter-ton truck, rationalizing gloomily that now I was just a pilot again and didn't even merit a personal jeep.

"I'll show you your official residence," Sharpe informed me as he climbed behind the wheel.

I crawled into the passenger side as the others hopped into the back and we lurched around some side streets before he parked in front of a two-story barracks-type building.

"Follow me, Captain."

Sharpe led the way as we climbed to the second story and walked around the far end to the most inconvenient room available. He threw open the door expectantly and I walked inside to look around, finding a shambles roughly the size of my former room. I sat down on the squeaky bed and sniffed at the damp, dry-rotting, lumpy mattress in dismay.

"This is your official room, Captain," Sharpe advised. "You need to remember where it's located. If you're ready now, I'll show you where you're really going to live." He grinned as Dandy, Sly, and Mad Hatter cracked up in laughter at my dejected expression.

We climbed back into the truck and drove several blocks to an area that held some small houses near the Air Force officers' club. Sharpe pulled into the drive of one of the cottages with a well-maintained yard and a screened porch.

"This is your new home, Captain." He opened the door to a spacious two-bedroom, two-bath palace with a small kitchen and a large living room tastefully deco-rated and gracefully furnished. "The one next door is mine. Dandy and Sly are on the other side of me. Mad Hatter lives with you. We have hooch maids to do all the cleaning and laundry. They'll even prepare meals for you. I've managed to get a jeep for each cottage and they'll be here tomorrow."

I looked around with some trepidation. "Who lived in these houses?"

"Air Force generals and bird colonels, Captain. But they're all gone now."

"Does Major Crystal rate one of these?"

He grinned. "Uh, not really, Captain. He's got one room in the field grade officers' quarters, but he did get a private bath, I understand."

I laughed and shook my head. "How did you swing this, Lieutenant?"

"Details, Captain, details. You need to focus on the bigger picture."

I hesitated, remembering the dark, dank room back at the barracks. "Lieutenant, I'm no longer your platoon leader. I don't deserve this kind of treatment anymore."

He arched his eyebrows. "Captain, as much as you'd like to be rid of me, you're still my boss."

"What do you mean?"

"With Captain Nichols and the XO rotated home, you are now the second in command of the detachment. Your new job will be as the flight operation's officer of the Deans, or what's left of us. Congratulations, and oh, by the way, I took the liberty of stocking your bar." He opened a double door on one wall to reveal a hidden wet bar filled with glasses, liquor, and a small refrigerator for beer. "Welcome home, Captain."

That evening Sharpe invited us over for dinner at his cottage, which was identical to ours but with the living room set up specifically for entertaining. A moderate-sized teakwood bar with mirrors and bar stools occupied one side of the room. The other side held a long teakwood dining table with upholstered chairs and a china cabinet outfitted with delicate chinaware. Two sofas, with matching overstuffed chairs, and a coffee table were in the center, and a stereo perched against the far wall between the two bedrooms with private baths.

Linda, Sandra, Cherrie, and three other nurses joined us for dinner, which consisted of three-inch steaks cooked to perfection by a Vietnamese on the grill outside, baked potatoes, salad, and apple pie topped with ice cream. It was the best meal I had eaten since arriving in Vietnam. We soon had a free-swinging party going, dancing to the stereo and drinking shots from the exotic, well-stocked bar until I happily passed into exhausted oblivion.

I awoke the next morning in Sharpe's spare bedroom with two of the nurses in bed with me. They were in panties and bras, but I still had my trousers and undershirt on. I slipped gently out of bed, grabbed my shirt and boots off the floor, and crept out to the living room to find Sly passed out on one sofa with Sandra and Dandy on the other with Linda, all four naked and half-covered with blankets. Through Sharpe's open bedroom door I saw him on his back with Cherrie draped across his chest, both naked and half-covered with a sheet. I got the hell out of there as quietly as I could. Back at my own cottage, I found Mad Hatter and a nurse named Debbie naked on one of the couches with no sheet or blanket covering them. I crept by them into my bedroom and closed the door, wondering what this world was coming to.

I scalded myself in the first hot shower I had experienced since coming to Nam before finally getting the temperature adjusted to my satisfaction and languishing in the unaccustomed luxury of the steaming water. I walked out naked, drying myself off, and bumped into a little brown woman standing in the middle of my bedroom. I shrieked as she covered her lips with her palms and giggled, dashed back into the bathroom and closed the door, having just met my hooch maid, I surmised, as I calmed my wildly thudding heart.

I settled into my new job at Hotel Six by throwing myself into the reorganization of our detachment. Major Crystal busied himself elsewhere in his new office with a secretary in the command building at Ton Son Nhut, which we called "The Head Shed" due to all the high-ranking officers hanging around there. I'm not sure what he did all day, only that it was some kind of a liaison job. The good news was that he seemed content to stay out of our way and didn't seem to give a damn what we did as long as he had me to hang by the balls if anything went wrong.

I reorganized our detachment into three sections of four aircraft each with the twelve UH-IH Huey aircraft. Each slick's armament consisted of a single M-60 machine gun on each side manned by a crew chief and a door gunner. The VIP Green Detachment still carried the few generals and congressmen around, the Yellow Detachment still transported the handful of colonels and celebrities, and the Red Detachment, to which the lieutenant, Mad Hatter, Sly, and Dandy were assigned, became my ash and trash detachment for all the weird missions.

The Red Detachment's primary role was to fly resupply missions to the advisers in the field, a mostly thankless and boring job. The lieutenant and my captains asked for assignment there, along with their fellow pilots left over from the Razorbacks. I should have known better. I can be dumber than a brick at times.

The first indication I had that things were not as they should be was when the lieutenant and Sly brought their new Hueys back to Hotel Six shot all to hell. On their first mission they had managed to destroy half of the Red Detachment. Thankfully nobody had been killed. I walked around the two crippled birds trying to determine if they were salvageable, while Sly and the lieutenant stood together reflectively viewing the damage.

The lieutenant grimaced. "I forgot how slow these sons of bitches are, Sly."

"And big," Sly added in disgust. "I felt like a blimp up there."

"We haven't got any goddamned firepower," the lieutenant vowed hotly. "How're we going to keep their heads down with two piss-ant machine guns? We've got to get us some minis!"

"*Heeelllooooo!*" I yelled. They turned to me in puzzlement. "Were you two dumb asses *actually* trying to make a gun run with these slicks?"

"Gun run?" Sly asked, feigning innocence.

"Captain, we were just flying along when these gooks started taking pot shots at us like they were somebody special," the lieutenant complained. "We were defending ourselves, weren't we, Sly?"

Sly nodded piously. "Oh, indeed, purely self-defense."

"*Two* of my birds are *completely* destroyed," I argued. "What are you going to do when you get the *other* two torn up with your foolishness?"

Lieutenant Sharpe drew himself up. "Aw, the birds aren't the problem, Captain. I'll get you two more before the end of the day from the ARVNs. But these things are *dangerous*. We almost got *killed* out there!"

"It was *probably* because you were out *screwing around* and not doing your *proper mission*," I declared. "You were *supposed* to be flying *supplies*—not looking for a *fight!*"

He flushed. "Well hell, they started it! Bastards shot at us first. We might officially be REMFs, but we don't have to be chicken shits too."

"That's right, Chief," Sly agreed. "We're allowed to protect ourselves, aren't we?"

"Protecting yourself means fighting your way *out* of something," I argued, "not going back and *jumping* on them. Now how did this happen? You were both supposed to be in different locations to begin with."

"Well, this adviser wanted to do a flyover to check out an area they're going to be operating in tomorrow, so I flew him around for a quick look," the lieutenant explained. "Then he wanted to take a closer look at something he thought he saw, so I buzzed the trees for him, and these jackasses started shooting me up. I called Sly, and we met up and dropped off the adviser and then went back out there to see if they still had a problem with us."

"Which apparently they did," I challenged. "We're not supposed to be *looking* for trouble, guys. *Our* war is *over*. We won … or whatever … but it's *over*. Don't you *get* it?"

The lieutenant shrugged. "Come on, Sly, let's go get the captain two more birds so he'll calm down a bit."

I watched them saunter off, sadly wondering how we could have possibly lost this feud over here with warriors like that on our side? An hour later they flew two more Hueys in and their crew began repainting the numbers on the tails to camouflage the fact that they'd been stolen from the ARVNs. Not that anybody gave a damn anymore, but old habits die hard.

The next day I happened by the Red Detachment birds and slowed my pace as something nagged at my subconscious. I stopped, turned around, and walked back to the lieutenant's bird for a closer look. The crew chief and his gunner hurried up carrying two heavy boxes and set them on the floor of the aircraft as they grinned at me happily.

"How do you like 'em, Captain?" Critter asked proudly.

I looked at the two M-60 machine guns closely. Or at least they were once M-60 machine guns; I wasn't sure what they were now. "What is this?"

"They're baby minis, Sir," Critter explained. "Lieutenant Sharpe used to be an Infantryman, remember? He figured out a way to modify them. We test-fired them this morning and boy, they work great."

"Please explain what it is I am looking at," I requested calmly as ten pounds of lead settled in my stomach uncomfortably.

"Well, here's the deal, Captain. The old guns fired 750 rounds a minute. But the barrels melt down if you fire them too long. So the lieutenant, he sawed the barrels off to about six inches, so now they can't melt down. You can fire them as long as you want to. And look here, Sir," he directed eagerly, opening the feeder mechanism and lifting the top. "What he did was, he went in here and double-sprigged the feeder mechanism. That increased the rate of fire to 1,100 rounds a minute. Then he got these old minigun belts and attached them to the side of the gun, so now we can fire 4,000 rounds without stopping to reload. Ain't that just the neatest thing, Captain?"

I was growing ill. Sharpe just wasn't going to give up this war.

"And look here at what else he rigged up for us, Captain!" Critter turned to the boxes they had brought over and lifted out one of the containers, a jar with a grenade inside.

I stared at it in puzzlement as I reached for it.

"Easy, Sir, it's sort of volatile if you drop it," Critter cautioned.

I snatched my hand back quickly, instantly deciding I didn't want to hold it after all.

"You see, Captain, the lieutenant took an ordinary hand grenade and screwed the blasting cap off because it takes four and a half seconds to explode once the handle is released. That's too long to do us any good. So then he screws in a smoke grenade-blasting cap, which ignites in half a second after the handle is released. Then we pull the pin, without releasing the handle, and slip it into these jars. When we toss the jars out, they break when they hit the ground and *BOOM*, we've got us a bomb. Now ain't that neat, Captain?"

"Critter, where is your lieutenant?" I deliberately used an unassuming voice so as not to alarm him.

"Oh, he's out going around to all the mess halls trying to scrounge up some more of these jars, Captain. They're hard to come by. They've got to be just the right size, you see, or you'll blow yourself up."

"Yes, well, thank you for the briefing, Critter. Tell Lieutenant Sharpe I'm looking for him when you see him."

Critter nudged the door gunner with his elbow as I wobbled off on quaking legs. "I bet Captain Hess is gonna decorate the lieutenant again or something for this!"

I had the uneasy feeling that I was beginning to identify with Major Crystal somewhat now. The lieutenant presented a different perspective from the command angle. I knew I should try to stop him, but I also knew I couldn't. I had ninety days left in Nam. Eighty if I milked the out-processing time. Seventy-three if I counted the R&R time I had coming to me.

Let's see, I thought, counting on my fingers, *the lieutenant only flies every other day now, so if I divide seventy-three by two, that means he only has approximately thirty-six and a half chances left to drive me insane or have me put in jail.* The odds were not what I'd hoped they'd be.

"Sir?" a crew chief asked as I passed him mumbling to myself.

I waved him off. "Nothing, Specialist, carry on." *That's not a good sign, walking around talking to myself. I'm already beginning to slip. I've got to get a grip on myself—for Nancy and the kids' sake!*

The next day I sent the lieutenant and Dandy out in different directions. The lieutenant and his crew hitched a ride back home with Dandy after leaving his aircraft smoldering back in a rice paddy, where he had ditched it with its hydraulics shot out.

"Geeze, Captain, I'll get you another aircraft," he insisted. "There's plenty of them around!"

Dandy stood off to the side shaking with suppressed mirth as I glowered like a father to a reticent son. "It's *not* the aircraft, Lieutenant! It's *you* and your *crew*! I don't want to see any of you killed or maimed this close to the end of this thing."

"Well, hell, me either, Captain," he agreed indignantly. "If you'd get us some decent fighting aircraft—"

"*Goddamn it, Lieutenant! The fucking war is over!*" I yelled. "The mothers back home don't want any more body bags shipped to them with their sons in them!

They want us to stop fighting and risking our lives in a lost cause! *Why can't you understand that?*"

He glared at me. "It's *not* a lost cause, Captain. If I kill one more gook it'll be worthwhile. The ones I'm killing now are not about winning or losing this war. I kill them because they don't deserve to live. I kill them for the fun of it. And if one of them gets lucky and kills me, I hope he enjoys it as much as I did."

"What about your *men*, Lieutenant?" I demanded. "Are *they* doing this for the fun of it?"

"My crew are all volunteers. They can choose not to fly with me. I always ask them before we do something out of the envelope of the mission. If one man doesn't want to go, then we call it off. You'll have to ask them why they're willing to do it." He turned to his copilot, gunner, and crew chief standing a short distance away and motioned them over. "Captain Hess wants to talk to you. Be straight up with the man. I've got to go get us a new bird." He walked away with his shoulders slumped as his crew looked at me warily.

"Do you men realize this war is all but over?" I looked each one in the eye. "Do you realize if you get killed or seriously injured over here now doing something stupid it will be a total waste of your lives? Why are you doing dim-witted shit like this?"

"I wanna fly with the lieutenant, Captain," the gunner insisted. "I don't wanna fly with anybody else."

"Why?" I demanded.

"'Cause he makes things exciting, Sir. He ain't afraid of those gooks. He'll kick their ass. I paid his old gunner fifty dollars to trade places with me."

I turned to his crew chief. "And you?"

299

"I was Lieutenant Sharpe's crew chief on the Charlie models, Captain. And I was his crew chief on his Cobra, even though I couldn't fly with him anymore. I was so happy when we had to give up the Cobras so I could fly with him again I didn't know what to do. I've been offered two hundred dollars by another crew chief to trade places and I won't do it."

I turned to his copilot. "And you?"

"To tell you the truth, Captain, I won the right to fly with him in a poker game. Every copilot in the Red Detachment is waiting for me to fuck up so they can replace me. I've got the ride of a lifetime with the lieutenant and I'm not giving it up to nobody."

"And all of this excitement is worth your life?" I asked.

"We're soldiers, Captain," Critter replied. "This is what we're trained to do—to fight. I joined the Army to fight. I'm just sorry our country sold us out."

"Me too, Sir," the gunner agreed.

I sighed. "You're good men. You keep yourselves and your lieutenant out of trouble, do you hear me? He's sort of crazy, so I'm putting it on your heads to keep him within sane limits. Do you understand what I'm asking of you?"

The copilot grinned. "Yes, Sir, you can count on us!"

"We got him covered, Captain," the gunner reassured me.

Critter laughed. "We'll keep the butterfly net handy, Captain!"

"Good. You men be careful now and keep a close eye on him."

I walked away as Dandy moved along beside me. "What do you think, Dandy?"

"Leave him be, Chief. He's enjoying himself and he's not nearly as crazy as you think."

"Like *you* would know crazy?" I demanded. "You're about as nutty as he is."

He heaved a sad sigh. "I sure miss our old unit and our Cobras, Chief. It was all so much fun, with the flaming Drambuies and war stories and all. Sugar Bear gives us that. He makes war fun. We're at the end of an era. It's all kind of sad when you stop to think about it …"

CHAPTER 21

The next few days were sort of anticlimactic—I mean that in the context that the lieutenant didn't get anybody killed, any of my aircraft all shot to hell, or of equal significance, not implicate me in any heinous crimes he may have committed, which could only be viewed as a relatively successful period. Two months, three weeks and counting until I returned to the land of the Big Mac, I reminded myself happily.

Out of abject boredom, I agreed to join Sharpe and his band of gypsies at the Air Force officers' club that night. I could accuse him of many things, but boring was not one of them. We sat around a large table in a festive mood drinking and enjoying each other's company. Linda, Cherrie, Sandra, Debbie, Ellen, and three other nurses I didn't know soon joined us. A good Vietnamese band played American songs from the stage as we sang along with them. Across the room a group of Navy pilots on temporary duty assignment to Ton Son Nhut were equally loud and boisterous. One of the Navy pilots approached Cherrie at our table.

"Excuse me, pretty little lady, would you like to dance?"

Cherrie politely pointed to Sharpe. "No, thank you, I'm with him."

"Sorry to hear that, darling." He turned to Ellen. "How about you, little lady?"

Ellen, obviously annoyed at being his second choice, pointed. "I'm with him also."

The Navy pilot turned to Sharpe with an insolent smirk. "Since you've cornered the market on all the women, would *you* like to dance?"

"No, Swabbie," Sharpe answered. "But thanks for asking. It just saved me the trouble of kicking your ass since for a minute there I thought you were after my women, but now I see you little sailor boys like men too."

The sailor's smirk faded. "Are you Air Force pilots?"

Sharpe glanced up at him. "We don't have enough class to be Air Force fast-movers. We're Army rotor-heads."

The sailor puffed out his chest. "I'm with the Navy."

Sharpe's eyes narrowed. "I can tell."

The sailor held his proud profile. "How so?"

"You're well fed, your fingernails are clean, your flight suit is pressed, your hair is trimmed, and your manners are atrocious. It all adds up to a boy trying to be a man, a jet-jockey imitating a real pilot, and a rear-echelon mother-fucker pretending to be a warrior."

The Navy pilot puffed up indignantly. "You and I need to step outside."

"That's the whole problem with you distinguished little flyboys," Sharpe replied as he stood. "You think you can choose your battlefield—but *combat* is where you *find it*!" He caught the Navy pilot flush on the jaw

304

with a roundhouse right that sent him stumbling backwards across a table and crashing to the floor in a heap of glasses and chairs.

"Therefore, Swabbie, you've always got to be prepared for battle *whenever* and *wherever* you find it!" He sat back down, ignoring the rush of Navy pilots scurrying over to help their fallen comrade up from the litter and back to the bar area.

Sly grinned. "Damn, Sugar Bear, that was rude."

Dandy frowned. "I agree, your etiquette is appalling—you *should* have let him throw the first punch since he's technically our *guest* here."

"You pack a mean wallop for such a little shit," Mad Hatter added admiringly.

"You're going to get us thrown out of here," I admonished as the manager stood frowning at us as members of his staff cleaned up the mess on the floor.

"See, I told you he was exciting!" Cherrie gushed to the three new nurses staring at the lieutenant with dubious expressions.

"Oops, here comes trouble," Ellen warned as one of the other Navy pilots eased up to our table cautiously.

"Excuse me … I believe we got ourselves off to a bad start. May we buy you a drink?" he inquired politely.

Sharpe glanced up at him. "Why?"

He smiled contritely. "One of the gentlemen at the bar just told us who you are."

"And that would be?"

"Red One-Seven. We thought you were a myth. We'd like to apologize to you."

Sharpe shrugged. "Join us, then, and buy us *all* a drink."

They crowded around our table introducing themselves, shaking hands, and drawing up chairs wherever they could fit in as they ordered rounds for us. The pilot Sharpe had punched sat warily on the opposite side of the table from him with a growing lump on his jaw. As was his custom in the company of his admiring fans, especially ones who were footing the bar bill, Sharpe let us do the talking as he sat silently preening and soaking up their adoration. We were soon having a roaring good time with the Navy men, with each of us trying to outdo the other as we told stories about the lieutenant, making some up as we went along, embellishing others as the situation dictated. What the hell, it was harmless entertainment and the drinks were free.

The only awkward moment occurred when Sly slipped up and told the story of Sharpe getting laid three days in a row while he was in traction in the hospital. Dandy and I had to quickly hustle Cherrie off to the side as she worked herself into a proper tirade over the fact that she hadn't *visited* him three days in a row. We eventually convinced her it was just something Sly made up for the sailors and she reluctantly agreed not to beat the living shit out of the lieutenant right there in front of the Navy boys since that predictably would have spoiled his whole image thing and dried up our free liquor supply.

I don't recall exactly when the carousing got out of hand. I was quite tipsy by that point, but I think it started with the flaming Drambuies. The Navy salts were completely enthralled with the story of us sending our prayers out to the lieutenant in the jungle, and of his having thereby gained the strength to continue. As Ellen told the story most of the women wiped tears from their eyes and the Navy sat appropriately spellbound.

"What's a flaming Drambuie?" one of them asked in the emotional silence that followed.

"It's a custom inspired by the lieutenant," Mad Hatter explained. "When a pilot gets shot up he has to sit in the hot seat and tell his war story. Then he drinks the sacred brew and blows flames out of his mouth to seal the hallowed covenant."

"Can you show us how it's done?" another of the pilots requested eagerly. So of course, Sharpe had us do it as they watched in wonder.

"Incredible! Can you teach us how to do that?" pleaded the pilot Sharpe had punched. "We'll make it our custom too, if you'll allow us the honor?"

And so the practical application began after the Navy ordered a round of flaming Drambuie for everyone. Several rounds in fact—it *does* take a bit of practice coupled with a lot of nerve. By the time they perfected the art the inside of the club resembled a steel factory as *whooshes* of flame spouted out everywhere amid the smell of burnt hair permeating the air from singed eyebrows and smoldering heads among the Navy guys from their mishaps.

Since we now had a large audience to entertain, which had gathered around to watch the festivities, a new challenge was initiated by the Navy called *carrier landings*.

The Navy pilots lined up three tables end to end against one wall. They left a six-inch gap and lined up six more tables with the first three. The basic idea was that six men, three to a side, would take one man in a running start and propel him down the line of tables on his stomach with his hands behind his back grasping a sawed-off broom handle. The man would slide rapidly down the first six tables toward the wall and hook his toes in the six-inch gap at the last three tables to stop before careening headfirst into the wall. They normally splashed the tables with Wesson cooking oil to ensure a slippery surface, but since the club manager insisted he did not have any Wesson oil to lend us, we improvised with ketchup, mustard, and mayonnaise. It wasn't pretty, but it was a darned effective lubricant.

We attacked the "carrier deck" time after time in a drunken tangle of bodies. Sly and the lieutenant were the only two Army types successfully able to snag the stopgap with their toes, albeit even then only after several attempts. The Navy guys did it almost every time. The rest of us, to include the Air Force pilots who had joined in by now, beat our silly brains out on the wall every time we went skidding down the deck. I had knots all over my head when the manager of the club finally threw us out.

We walked home in a drunken, boisterous mob. Two of the new nurses stayed at my place that night, on my couch of course. I woke up with one of them snuggled up to me in my bed after she had apparently gotten cold during the night and joined me, but nothing had happened.

Of that, I was fairly certain.

A few days later I became a bona fide hero by earning my second Air Medal as Sharpe claimed his twenty-third in an incredibly brave, unselfish, and daring operation. My personal contribution to the event is questionable since I was so scared my mind was fuzzy, and I freely admit I had my eyes shut tight most of the time.

On this occasion, the ARVNs saw fit to give Sharpe and his crew an award of their own, which was the equivalent of our Silver Star, for the mission flown in support of them the day they got their hydraulics shot out and crash-landed in the rice paddy. Although it was an ARVN medal and ARVN ceremony, they invited Major Crystal to the event and protocol stated that he, as the detachment commander, should attend as a courtesy. I knew from the outset I was going in his place since the major would probably throw up on himself if he had to commend the lieutenant for being a hero again.

In any case, I had not flown for some time myself, so on the day of the event I scheduled myself as Sharpe's copilot, intending to get a little "stick" time and shake some of the rust from my flying skills. After all, it was to be a short flight to Tay Ninh Province to pin the medals on my illustrious crew and then a quick trip back home. No big deal—unless you failed to factor in the lieutenant of course—which, even after all I'd learned, I somehow naively failed to do.

The routine flight to Tay Ninh produced a little drama from the beginning and set the tone for the rest of the day. Sharpe allowed me to do the flying, but complained about my altitude, swearing he and the crew were getting nosebleeds from the lack of oxygen. I thought five thousand feet was comfortable and definitely safer than the customary one thousand feet they normally flew, also figuring nothing short of a SAM missile could reach my precious little buns a mile high in the sky with the earth far below so scenic with its tiny squares. Even the fluffy white clouds below us were strikingly picturesque.

As I flew serenely along humming to myself to drown out the carping of the crew, Sharpe reached over and shut down my engine. Yep, just flipped the master fuel switch and turned that sucker off—right over the biggest patch of jungle in the world.

I came unglued.

My first task was to get my eyeballs back in their sockets and my heart out of my throat. I also reasoned the warm, odorous mass suddenly appearing in the seat of my pants would just have to wait until I got the confounded engine restarted again, by-golly.

Now, restarting a turbine engine while you're falling out of the sky like a rock is no easy task. It takes concentration and a very definitive set of procedures performed efficiently and flawlessly in sequence. There is no room for error and no second chance. Miss a step and you have to start at the beginning and go through the whole process again. Given that the process takes about two minutes, and from five thousand feet we had about two minutes and ten seconds before we hit the ground like a ton of bricks and made a big hole in it, you can imagine the concentration required of me. What's more, I had to accomplishing this feat with the lieutenant and his crew screaming over the intercom *"Oh my god! We're gonna die! We're gonna die!"* at the top of their lungs as they laughed uproariously. Weird people the lieutenant and his crew.

Nevertheless, being the superb pilot I am, I pulled the procedure off without a hitch and fired that turkey up again to pull out of the plunging dive with just the tiniest bit of leaves and limbs from the treetops clinging to the bottom of the aircraft. I actually think Sharpe was somewhat disappointed because he had to pay off five-dollar bets he'd made during the plunge to the crew chief and the gunner, who obviously had more faith in me than he did. Afterwards he scout's-honor-promised he wouldn't do it again if I didn't go above a thousand feet. Screw the damn VC—I kept that puppy at about nine hundred feet the rest of the way to Tay Ninh, hoping like hell the ARVNS would let me actually fasten the medal to his chest and that it would have a great-big-old pin on the back of it.

We landed, the ARVNs did a big ceremony with the crew, made a lengthy speech in Vietnamese about them as we stood in the dizzying heat, and then performed a pass in review with their soldiers as a show of respect. Unfortunately, a Vietnamese general pinned the medals on, so I didn't get the opportunity I'd hoped for. Then we had tea and crumpets with the general and his staff, during which we all grinned and nodded a lot, acting like we each knew what the other was saying. I had to grit my teeth and agree about eleventeen times during the social event that, yeah, the lieutenant was just one hell of a great, brave pilot.

Finally, they trucked us back to our aircraft to depart for our base at Ton Son Nhut, where we shook hands, bowed, and saluted our hosts again at the helipad. As this was occurring, I noticed a flurry of activity at the top of Nui Ba Dien, or Black Virgin Mountain just to the north of Tay Ninh.

This mountain is sacred to the Vietnamese for reasons unknown to me, but in essence we did not bomb it or use artillery against the known VC entrenched in its tunnels and caves. However, we did have a Green Beret post on its very top, some twelve hundred feet up. This small garrison was normally composed of six or seven

Americans and about a hundred Vietnamese soldiers. Since the VC controlled the entire mountain except for this small outpost, the only entry or exit to the site was by helicopter via a single ten-by-ten-foot landing pad capable of holding one aircraft at a time located on top of the mountain.

From our vantage point about five miles away, we could see ARVN aircraft flying in circles around the top of the base camp, which appeared to be under attack. We climbed aboard our aircraft, got the rotors turning, and were preparing for takeoff when a jeep came roaring up.

An American bird colonel dismounted and rushed up to my window. "Are you Red One-Seven?" he yelled up at me from where he stood on the skids by my door.

I shook my head and pointed at Sharpe beside me. The colonel rushed around, opened the lieutenant's door, and climbed up beside him as Sharpe removed his helmet to confer with him. I leaned in their direction, but the noise of the turbine engine drowned out their conversation as the colonel waved his arms around in excitement. Sharpe nodded in agreement and the colonel hugged him before jumping back down and closing the door.

Sharpe strapped his helmet back on as I keyed the intercom. "What's up?" I asked complacently as I lifted the bird up into a smooth hover, admiring my deft touch on the controls.

"He's got a couple of wounded Americans he wants us to pick up on our way back and drop off at the hospital in Saigon," he answered casually. "Since it's on our way, I told him we'd be glad to do it."

"Sure thing," I readily agreed, grateful to be of service to them in such a noble fashion. "Why didn't he just call for a dust-off? That would have been faster."

"Well, he sort of did," he explained. "But the first dust-off got shot up trying to extract them and now the other one is refusing to go in at all."

A heavy lead weight sank into the vat of jell-o in the pit of my stomach as I climbed jerkily into the air, my control touch suddenly askew as I absorbed this troubling bit of information.

"Climb to two thousand and fly to Nui Ba Dinh," he instructed.

"The *mountain*?" I gasped as beads of perspiration sprung out on my brow and my hands shook on the controls. "Are you *crazy*? They're *shooting* at each other up there!"

"One of their men is critically wounded," he explained patiently. "He won't make it if we don't get him to a hospital immediately."

My heart pounded in earnest. "He won't make it if we do a barrel-roll down the side of that mountain in a ball of fire either!"

"We're his only chance," he replied.

"You *promised* you wouldn't get me killed," I reminded him pointedly.

"I haven't broken my promise yet, have I?" he argued.

"Well no, not *yet*," I whined.

"Listen up, guys," he continued over the intercom, addressing the crew. "This is a volunteer mission. It's going to be extremely hairy. I can drop you off and pick you up on the way out if you'd like?"

"Hey, Mike, do you hear anything?" Critter asked the gunner.

"Just a lot of static, Critter," the gunner replied.

"Okay, Mike, I'm gonna take a nap now," Critter advised. "Wake me up if anything exciting happens."

"Like if Sugar Bear turns off the engine again or something?" Mike asked gleefully.

Critter giggled. "Yeah, like that. I don't wanna miss the Captain peeing on himself again."

Mike snickered. "Pee? He's on my side of the bird and it was a lot smellier than *pee*."

Sharpe grinned. "Okay, Captain, my crew has lost their radios, so I'll have to carry them with us since I don't have time to land and explain things to them. Your call?"

Nancy and the kids flashed before my eyes. "I … can't hear you either," I stuttered. "Just be careful!" I leveled off at two thousand feet and pointed the nose toward the top of the mountain as he dialed in a new frequency on the radio.

"Rocky Top, this is Red One-Seven, over," he called.

"Red One-Seven, this is Rocky Top. You just got a cheer from my WIAs when they heard your call sign. They're real fans of yours, over."

"I'm a fan of theirs. They do all the dirty work, I just get the glory."

"Flat Lander Six heard you were in the neighborhood and went looking for you. He said if anybody could do this, it would be you, over."

"I appreciate his confidence. SitRep, over."

"We've been under attack for most of the day. Clouds are moving in from the west. I have three WIAs, one critical code red. We can run them out to the pad and dump them on board in less than a minute to limit your exposure if you give us enough warning. We've had one bird shot up already. The other refuses to come in."

"Roger, I'm circling over you now at two grand. Give me about two minutes to get in position. I'll call my times down to you. Get your litter teams ready and have your men lay down a heavy base of fire. We'll only get one shot at this because it looks like there are clouds moving in on you fast, over."

"Roger, Red One-Seven, and God bless you, over."

Sharpe took the controls from my trembling, sweat stained palms and I tried to relax as my stomach did flip-flops. I'd never in my life wanted to be as far away from a place as I wanted to be away from Black Virgin Mountain at that moment, this not being a good day to die in my humble opinion. *God, please don't let me throw up or be proven a coward*! I prayed reverently.

"You're not going to throw up or be proven a coward, Captain," Sharpe replied, laughing. "Just tighten your seat belt and hang on, this shit's going to be fun!"

I blushed, realizing I had spoken over the intercom without thinking. "W-What do you want me to do?"

"Just sit there and enjoy the sights, Captain. If anything happens to me, be prepared to take the controls. Okay, guys, I want maximum firepower coming out of those peashooters of yours for psychological effect. Don't shoot into the compound and watch out for friendlies around the pad. Let's not kill some of our own trying to save them."

"You just fly this sweet baby, Sugar Bear," Critter chided. "Me and Mike know our job."

It was somewhat comforting to hear the edge in his voice—apparently I wasn't the only scared-shitless-fraidy-cat on board.

"Rocky Top, One-Seven is four minutes out and counting, coming in east to west, over."

"Roger, Red One-Seven, our litter teams are at the edge of the perimeter. May God be with you, over."

"He's always with me, Rocky Top, as I endeavor to smite the forces of evil in His holy name and vanquish the wicked from His eminent domain. Three minutes and counting, over."

"Roger, Red One-Seven, the ground fire is picking up down here."

"Aw, screw them, Rocky Top, the little fuckers can't shoot worth a damn. Two minutes out, over."

Bullets zipped by us as I flinched and tried to shrink my six-foot-two-inch frame into the approximate size of a Barbie doll, wishing I smoked so I could have a Zippo to place over my heart and hide behind. I jerked as a round penetrated the hull of the aircraft. Then another struck it and another. I was certain every gook in the world was shooting at us now, and that each of them was aiming directly at me. Another round hit us and then two quick holes appeared in my Plexiglas showering needle-thin slivers of plastic across my face visor and chest.

"One minute out, Rocky Top," Sharpe called calmly. "Looks like the party's heating up and they intend to give us a warm welcome, over."

Another round ripped through the windshield and then another impacted in the nose of the aircraft causing one of the gauges on the console to burst out of its socket trailing smoke from the jagged hole as the spent bullet ricocheted between Sharpe and me as I sat petrified. Suddenly the pad to our front disappeared in the edge of a cloudbank sweeping over the top of the mountain, engulfing it in white billowing foam.

"Breaking off, Rocky Top, Red One-Seven is breaking off the approach. I just lost you in the clouds, buddy, over."

"So close, Red One-Seven. Thanks for trying." The dismay in his voice was gripping, signaling his code red was certain to die now.

Sharpe turned the aircraft away from the mountain and the firing stopped as we flew out of range. "Don't sound so gloomy, Rocky Top," he chided. "This is just a temporary setback."

"Negative, Red One-Seven," the voice replied in despair. "Once the clouds come in they stay until morning. There's nothing you can do now, but we appreciate you trying. My code red says he'll see you in the hereafter and thank you personally, over."

"Bullshit, Rocky Top. Tell your code red I'm not through yet. Do you have any trip flares around your perimeter?"

"Roger, One-Seven. Why?"

"Strike one and throw it onto your helipad, over."

"Roger, standby, over."

"What are you going to do, Lieutenant?" I asked nervously.

"If I can see the flare through the clouds I can use it as a beacon and hover down to the pad," he replied.

I came close to hyperventilating at the thought of going back down there again, especially in that swirling, milky fog. "We're over *twelve hundred feet* in the air! We don't have the power to *hover* at that altitude!"

"I think I can stair-step down to it," he replied grimly.

"You *think* you can?" I gasped.

"Red One-Seven, flare is out, over."

"Roger, Rocky Top, making a run on it now." He nosed the aircraft over and skimmed across the top of the clouds with our skids touching them.

"I see it, Sugar Bear, off to the left there," Critter called in excitement as a tiny glowing yellow spot appeared in the white mass covering the mountaintop.

"Rocky Top, get those men back down to the pad and keep the flares burning. Red One-Seven is on approach and three minutes out, over."

"Roger, One-Seven, you're one nutty dude, but we love you for it. Litter teams are on their way, over."

Our airspeed dropped and the aircraft shuttered as Sharpe dropped the nose and then flared it back up, dropping slowly through the clouds in quick little jerks as he focused on the glowing yellow spot. We dropped down, down, down into the pearly whiteness as my heart clutched. The aircraft shook violently as he pulled maximum power trying to slow our descent, using all fifty pounds of the available torque, but our rate of descent continued to increase rapidly. *We're going to crash!* I realized in horror.

A dirty gray-black shape slid by my window—the crest of the mountain. We hit hard and bounced. Sharpe fought the controls trying to steady the aircraft as we pitched up and spun around, almost toppling over as we came to a wobbly stop. *We're still alive!* My terrified mind grasped as I sucked air into my paralyzed lungs.

Instantly the VC sought to remedy that situation by firing through the clouds at our rotor clatter, the rounds zinging around us, striking the aircraft with sharp thuds. Blurred, ghoulish men appeared out of the ghostly mist, thrust three stretchers in our cargo bay, and then disappeared back into the murky white void. Sharpe pulled all fifty pounds of torque as the aircraft strained to clear the pad, but it didn't have enough power to lift off with the additional weight of the three casualties at that altitude. I hunkered down waiting to die as the firing increased in tempo and rounds impacted against the aircraft with greater frequency.

"Fuck it! Hang on!" Sharpe yelled over the intercom as he pushed the nose forward grimly.

I gaped in shocked disbelief as the aircraft rose up on the toes of the skids, slid over the side of the mountain in an abortive running takeoff, popped out into the air, and dropped rapidly downward. I'm fairly certain I screamed, but with all the battle noise and turbine whining, blade chopping confusion erupting around us no one seemed to notice. He nosed it over further as we plunged down in an attempt to gain airspeed at the expense of altitude. I grew dizzy with the disorientating rush through the swirling white fluff. *We're going to die*!

I tensed for the crash into the side of the mist-covered mountain, anticipating the explosion to follow as brush snatched at our skids—and unbelievably, looked into the startled eyes of a VC with an AK-47 rifle as we flashed by. Miraculously the blades suddenly caught air and we dove out and away from the mountain. A heartbeat later, we popped out from the bottom of the cloud layer and streaked away from the mountain as the gunner and crew chief whooped victoriously and shook their fists at the VC behind us.

"Flat Lander, this is Rocky Top! Red One-Seven just bought the farm! He's crashed into the side of the mountain, over!"

"Negatory, Rocky Top!" Sharpe responded cheerfully. "That's VC propaganda, old buddy, and their reports of my untimely demise are greatly exaggerated, as the well-known Samuel Clemens once said. Red One-Seven is airborne and heading to Tay Ninh with your WIAs.

We're going to have to land there and put your men on the dust-off though, my little bird's shot to pieces and stressed out from the over-torque. I'm afraid she's seen the last of being a great bird of prey, over."

"Red One-Seven, if you're not a ghost I'm talking to, that was the most indescribable thing I've ever seen! Now I've got my own Red One-Seven war story to tell—but I'm afraid nobody will ever believe me!"

"We aim to please, Rocky Top," the lieutenant chuckled. "We've got to stay one up on our competitors trying to hone in on some of this grandeur because we aim to hog it all for ourselves, over."

"Red One-Seven, to you and your crew, we up here on Rocky Top pledge that someday, somehow, someway, we'll show our true appreciation for what you just did for us! We'll never forget it, over."

"You've already showed me, Rocky Top, with the way you guys are hanging in there against the Victor Charlies. Red One-Seven, out. Flat Lander, Red One-Seven, over."

"Roger, Red One-Seven, this is Flat Lander. I've been monitoring you on the radio with Rocky Top. The dust-off is standing by to transfer our casualties. I don't know what just happened up there, or how you pulled that off in the cloud cover, but I want to express my gratitude along with Rocky Top's. I'll never forget what you and your crew did for us today."

"Aw, shucks, Flat Lander, you're embarrassing us," the lieutenant replied. "Just help me explain to my boss why I got another one of his birds all shot to hell. He gets grouchy about things like that. I'm a real sensitive kind of guy and it hurts my feelings when he yells at me."

Flat Lander chuckled. "I'll speak to your boss personally, One-Seven, and even have the MACV Commander chat with him if you'd like."

"Would you, Flat Lander? I'd greatly appreciate it. He's sitting here beside me right now and he's so pissed he won't even talk to me."

I keyed my transmit button. "Flat Lander, this is Dean Five. I'm not talking to him because I swallowed my tongue back there and I think I'm sitting on it after I shit it back out. For the record, the only thing sensitive about him is his imagination. Right now I'm so happy to be alive I'm going to kiss him when we land. But after that I intend *yell* at him for a very, very long time before I *kill* him, over."

Flat Lander laughed. "Roger, Dean Five, thank you for the insight. Could I persuade you to just maim him a little this time around? That man's the greatest pilot I've ever known."

"Roger, Flat Lander, I'll take your suggestion under advisement. You wouldn't think he's the greatest pilot for long if you had my job. He goes through about four of my aircraft a week."

"Roger, Dean Five. You have my sympathy there. I'm on my way to the pad now with some cold beer for you guys to help take the edge off, over."

After we landed on the narrow asphalt strip at Tay Ninh I sat stoically staring out at the shimmering heat waves as the lieutenant shut down the aircraft. I listened mechanically as he called for Sly to ferry us back home. I listlessly watched the colonel drive up in his jeep, and Sharpe join him to walk around our aircraft to inspect the damage. Critter opened my door and tugged at my arm inquisitively.

I virtually fell out onto my knees because my legs seemed incapable of functioning properly and lowered my body down to kiss the ground. A stray, mangy old yellow dog hurried over to me spread eagle on the ground, tail wagging furiously, and licked my cheek, his nose comfortingly cold against my skin. I hooked my arm around the cur and hugged him to me affectionately thinking him to be the finest dog I'd ever seen. I rose to my knees cradling the dog to my chest as litter teams rushed up to remove the wounded from our cargo bay to transport them to the dust-off chopper idling behind our aircraft. One of the men stretched out a bloody hand as they set his stretcher on the ground beside me.

"Are you Red One-Seven?" he inquired in a half dazed, weak voice.

I nodded at the lieutenant standing a short distance away talking to the colonel.

The man smiled as he collapsed back onto his stretcher. "He ain't as big as I thought he was," he whispered. "Tell him I said *thanks*. Will you do that for me?"

I nodded wordlessly as they lifted him up and trotted to the dust-off. I sniffed at the fragrant, dung-infested aroma wafting out from the rice paddy beside the airstrip, thinking air never smelled sweeter. I gazed reverently at an ox cart ambling by on the road outside the wire, the old papa san guiding it wrinkled with age and stooped by years of thankless toil, finding him the most handsome man I'd ever seen as I absorbed the exhilaration—the rapturous high—of being alive. Coming so close to death so many times in such a short span gave new meaning to life. Everything seemed sharper and filled with meaning. I felt wiser, stronger, and … *humble.*

I closed my eyes. "Thank you, Lord. Thank you for this gift of life."

Critter stared down at me suspiciously. "Are you alright, Captain?"

I lifted my head to the marvelous blue sky framed by magnificent cotton patches of white and smiled. "I've never been better, Critter. Life is beautiful. I never knew how beautiful."

"Hey, Lieutenant," Critter called. "I think the Cap's in shock or something. Better take a look at him. He's acting all weird, man."

Sharpe and the colonel approached me still on my knees clutching the mangy dog to my chest. "You alright, Captain?"

I smiled up at him. I loved this crazy little lieutenant. "Sugar Bear, I wouldn't take anything in the world for what I just went through—but I never want to do it again either. You know what I mean? Does that make any sense to you? It makes perfect sense to me."

He thrust a brown bottle at me, the sides coated with droplets of beaded water. "Here, Captain, have a beer. It'll help you regain your perspective."

The colonel extended his hand to me as I knelt before them. "Thank you, Captain, on behalf of myself and my men. That was quite a feat your team pulled off back there. I counted twenty-seven hits in your aircraft. I don't know how you kept it flying."

I set the dog down, clasped his hand, and used his bulk to pull myself to my feet, still shaking all over. I fought the urge to laugh, to bellow, scream, and run in circles. I was alive! I tilted my head to drink the cold, bitter beer in deep droughts, not lowering the bottle

John W. Huffman

until it was drained, thinking it the best-tasting beverage I'd ever put to my lips.

The colonel and Sharpe walked off shaking their heads as Critter handed me another bottle. I took it and sought out the shade on the side of the aircraft to lower myself down from my wobbly legs to wait for Sly, listening to Sharpe and the colonel talk shop about the Infantry. This was indeed the most gorgeous, exhilarating day I'd ever lived. I looked back up at Black Virgin Mountain, so pretty now in the distance with its fluffy cloud covering, trying to recall the sheer terror I'd experienced there roughly a quarter of an hour ago. I watched Sharpe and the colonel shaking their heads sadly over the fate of the war as the crew calmly stripped their beefed-up guns off the side of the aircraft, marveling at how it must feel to do this on a daily basis. They were so nonchalant—just another day at the office, it seemed.

I was suddenly awe-struck by my lieutenant. I understood for the first time his courage and dedication to these men in the field he thought of as brothers. What would he do without a war to fight? He loved war. He lived for the adrenalin highs of the danger, the sheer thrill of defeating his sworn enemies in mortal combat. He was a battle junkie, and it really didn't matter to him the war or the cause. It was frightening.

He would definitely join Air America and become a mercenary. *If* he lived long enough to get there.

I had a sudden flash of sympathy for them … thinking if they only knew what was coming their way.

CHAPTER 22

I sat at my desk in flight ops suffering under a massive hangover from the previous night's celebration.

As I reviewed the day's mission requests, I turned to the window reflectively to watch the lieutenant and his crew busily mounting their illegal guns on the aircraft he'd just stolen from the ARVNs, knowing I'd never feel the same about things as I had before that incredible mission. I was sure the letter I'd written to Nancy rambling on incoherently about discovering life's real meaning and the secret of happiness being in one's inner soul would convince her I had slipped over the edge. In any case, I damn sure wasn't going to fly as the lieutenant's copilot again. *That* near-death experience had made me wiser in many ways.

I turned back to my desk and idly studied a routine mission request to fly a USO show around to several outlying areas in III Corps, musing to myself that the quality of the shows had diminished greatly over the last year with the drawdown of American troops. From the brief review I held in my hand, this one appeared to be near the bottom, featuring three men in their early fifties and one female in her early forties. Claude Deals and Susan Wheels headlined the act entitled *The Wheels and Deals Comedy Show*, accompanied by musicians Dan Blackmon and Ray Schuler as their backup. Their old style vaudeville troupe apparently sang silly jingles and told off-color jokes. Though most likely fashionable in their era, I had never heard of them. Like many of the performers we got here at the end of the war effort they had in all probability, in a burst of nostalgia, decided to give their dated road show another shot after being off stage for years and signed up for the USO tour to polish their act. From the dated posters of that era, the woman had once been a real doll and a hot star when she was in her twenties. Oh, well, whatever, I mused. The mission called for one aircraft for four days with overnight billeting for the flight crew at each of the four locations where they were to perform. I routinely assigned the mission to one of my yellow detachment crews and moved on.

That afternoon their personal USO escort and gofer, Second Lieutenant Brown, who was responsible for arranging all of their travel and lodging accommodations during their stay in Vietnam, introduced them to me at the pre-mission briefing.

Susan flashed her heavily make-up burdened lashes provocatively. "Oh, Captain, I'm *so* afraid of flying— would you be so kind as to assign your *best* pilot to little ol' me?"

I smiled graciously. "Ma'am, I assure you all of my pilots are professional and capable."

She sniffed testily, displaying a trace of bitchiness around her wide, brightly colored red lips. "I *said* your *best pilot*, Captain. I want Red One-Seven."

I blinked. "Red One-Seven? Uh, I'm afraid that's not possible, Ma'am. You see, Lieutenant Sharpe doesn't fly VIPs. He's assigned to—"

Her eyes narrowed. "*Captain*, please don't make this *awkward* for me. I had dinner with your general last night—he's such a *sweet, dear* man, and a *personal friend* of mine—and *he* said if I needed *anything* at all I was to give him a call. Do I *need* to make that call, Captain?"

"Ma'am, you don't understand … um, why do you specifically want Lieutenant Sharpe to fly you?"

She smiled coyly as she did the eyelash thing again. "He's *all* we've heard about since we got here. They say *he's* the *best pilot* in Vietnam. That's who I want to fly *me*, Captain, so *do* please be a *dear* and *give* him to me."

"Ma'am, please understand, Lieutenant Sharpe is a combat pilot, not a VIP pilot. There's a big difference between—"

She stamped her foot impatiently. "*Where* is your phone, Captain?"

"Ma'am, please …" I hedged.

She turned to Lieutenant Brown standing behind her watching uncomfortably. "Harold, *dear*, please be a *good* boy and get the *general* on the phone for me."

I sighed. "Give me a moment, Ma'am, and I'll see what I can do." I hurried out to the flight line, where I found the lieutenant painting the new numbers on the stolen aircraft under Critter's watchful supervision.

"That looks like shit, Sugar Bear," Critter fumed as I approached. "You need to stick to flying." He turned to me. "Captain, can't you find something for him to do before he screws up my bird?"

The lieutenant continued to smear paint around as I paused at the base of the platform he was standing on, noting his numbers did resemble something out of kindergarten. "Lieutenant, I need a word with you."

He didn't miss a stroke. "Damn, Captain, can't you see I'm busy right now. I can't stop in the middle of this or the paint will dry. What's up, anyway?"

"I need to assign you to a VIP mission for four days to fly a USO show around."

He continued painting. "Fuck no. I'm not a VIP pilot. Give that pussy mission to the girls in the Yellow Detachment."

"They asked for you personally," I pleaded. "They've got some silly notion you're the best pilot in Nam."

"Well, they got that shit right," he replied without a pause in his strokes. "But I'm still not flying their silly asses around. I'm not a goddamned taxi driver."

"The woman is threatening to call the general if I don't let you fly her," I persisted.

"Woman?" he paused to look down at me with some interest. "What's she look like?"

"Uh, she's about forty something, but not too bad-looking for her age."

"Sorry, not my type." He turned back to admire his handiwork. "How does this look?" It looked like hell.

Critter sighed in disgust. "Don't quit your day job, Sugar Bear!"

"Is that your final word?" I threatened. "I don't think she's bluffing about calling the general."

"Fuck her. What General is she calling anyway? I thought most of them had already run out on us."

"Ton Son Nhut," I replied.

He scowled. "Well fuck him too; he's an Air Force dick—he can't tell us what to do."

"No, but he's real pals with the MACV Commander," I warned.

He wiped his paint-stained hands with some old rags. "Tell the bitch I'm busy or that I got shot down or something."

I trudged back to flight ops rehearsing my story. When I walked through the door Susan-the-drama-queen was in my office on my phone sending the makings of a gigantic headache pulsing through me.

"Oh, *General*, that's *so* kind of *you*! I *do* hate to be a *bother*, but you *did* say to *call* if I needed *anything*," she cooed in her best imitation of a sexy voice. "Well, I *will*, General. Yes, I *will*, and thank you again. You're *such a dear*, taking the time out of your busy schedule to help *little ol' me* with my *silly* little *problem*. Yes, General, he *just* walked in. Would you like to speak with him? Here he is, General, and thank you again, you *sweet* little *thing*, you." She flashed me her best go-to-hell look as she tossed the phone to me triumphantly and stalked out of my office.

I put the receiver to my ear. "Captain Hess?"

The general's voice was cautious. "Captain, is Miss Wheels in a position to hear us?"

I turned to observe her out in the lobby waving her arms indignantly at Lieutenant Brown. "Uh, no, Sir."

"Captain, I would like for you to do me a small favor and give her that damned pilot she wants so badly, that-that Lieutenant whoever."

"Uh, Sir, Lieutenant Sharpe says he would prefer not to fly that mission."

"Captain, I don't give a *damn* what the lieutenant would *prefer* to do or *not do*. Just tell him to *fly* the *damned mission*."

"But, Sir—"

"*Obviously* we're not communicating effectively, Captain," he advised sweetly. "Let me be perfectly clear on this issue. If I have to talk to that crazy woman again I'm going to make you and that arrogant little lieutenant of yours my special pet project and dedicate myself to seeing just how *fucking miserable I can make your careers and your lives.* Does that clarify things for you, Captain?"

"Perfectly, Sir, perfectly, I'll attend to it personally, Sir."

"Goodbye." He hung up on me.

Susan smirked as I walked back out to the lieutenant and his crew chief, who were in the middle of another argument.

"Sugar Bear, why don't you just stick to flying this damn thing, okay?" Critter wailed. "Let *me* work on it! That's the second time you've dropped an oil sample bottle in one of my transmission sumps. It'll take me an hour to fish it outta there."

"Well, hell, Critter, I'm just trying to help," the lieutenant protested. "The little wire thing-a-ma-jiggy was loose. Here, I'll help you dig it out."

"If you *help* me, it'll take *two* hours to fix it. Go help Sly's crew chief, or Dandy's. Go help the Yellow Detachment or somebody else you don't like very much."

"You don't have to be so pissy about it," the lieutenant sulked. "It's just a little bottle."

"A *little bottle* that'll *kill* our ass," Critter spat back in disgust. "It'd eat the transmission out of this thing in a skinny minute. Then the rotor would stop turning and we'd become a rock a thousand feet up in the air. Even *you* can't fly a rock!"

"Excuse me," I called up to them. "I hate to interrupt your psychosomatic discussion on the basic aerodynamics of rotorcraft, gentlemen, but I need to speak with you, Lieutenant."

Critter raised his arms to heaven. "*Thank you, Jesus!* By all means *take* him, Captain, *please!* If he helps me anymore we'll *never* get this crate off the ground again! We'll spend the rest of our tour fishing little bottles out of my oil sumps!"

The lieutenant climbed down off the top of the helicopter in a huff. "One of these days I'm going to get me a crew chief that ain't so damn picky about his precious little aircraft! What's up, Captain?"

"You're going to fly the VIP mission."

He shook his head adamantly. "Bullshit, Captain— we've done been through that."

"The general feels differently. He basically said you and I would pull latrine duty for the rest of our lives if you didn't. He isn't kidding."

"Fucking generals!" he swore vengefully as he kicked the side of Critter's aircraft. "Why can't they just leave well enough alone? He ought to be out playing golf or something instead of trying to tell us how to do our jobs! No wonder we're getting our ass kicked over here!"

I smiled sweetly. "Would you please come with me, Lieutenant Sharpe, and meet the Army's distinguished guests that you are going to fly around for the next four days?"

He bitched every step of the way to flight ops.

"Miss Wheels, this is Lieutenant Sharpe, call sign Red One-Seven," I introduced graciously when we entered the flight ops room. "It took some doing, but we were finally able to clear his heavy schedule and make him available to you during your stay with us. Lieutenant Sharpe, may I present Miss Susan Wheels and Mister

Claude Deals, of the famous Wheels and Deals USO show. And this is Dan Blackmon and Ray Schuler, who are part of their act."

The lieutenant nodded, scowling.

"Oh, he's so *handsome!*" Susan gushed. The lieutenant's scowl lifted noticeably as she clasped her hands together. "No one told me how *gorgeous* he was. He's just *adorable!*"

"I'm pleased to make your acquaintance, young man." Claude shook hands with him. "We understand you're quite the hero around here."

The lieutenant preened modestly in his best awe-shucks true hero fashion. "There's nothing heroic about doing your job."

I stifled a grin, observing he had exploitation written all over him now as Dan and Ray shook his hand and offered their praise as well.

Susan smiled winningly at him. "I had to call the general *directly* to get you, Lieutenant. You must be in *great* demand. I *simply* would have *no other* pilot fly me but *you.* How many medals do you have?"

"Uh …" He looked at me blankly for help.

I arched my eyebrows innocently.

His own knitted together as he scowled back at me. "I don't rightly know, Ma'am … I've never counted them."

She fluttered her eyelashes. "*Brave, handsome,* and *modest.* I bet you *just kill* the *ladies!*"

He gave me a '*you've got to be kidding me,*' look. "Uh, if you'll excuse me, Ma'am, I need a word with the Captain here." He walked straight into my office without a backward glance and closed the door.

Susan tittered girlishly. "*Bye,* Lieutenant! We'll see you in the morning, *dear.* You *sleep tight* tonight, you *hear?*"

332

I saw them out the door and walked into my office where Sharpe sat in my chair behind my desk with his feet propped up on the top and his hands clasped in his lap.

"Which fucking general?" he demanded hotly. "I'm going to make a gun run on his hooch tonight!"

"It's only for four days," I soothed. "Sometimes you've got to take the salt along with the sugar."

He stared at me darkly. "One good hammer-head stall with a left pedal spiraling dive and I'll have that bitch puking all over Critter's bird."

"Now don't do anything foolish!" I urged. "You might give that old Claude gent a heart attack or something."

His eyes narrowed speculatively. "Okay, Captain, what's in this for me if I pull your ass out of the fire with that general?"

I smirked righteously. "Actually, *your* ass is in the fire as much as mine."

He shrugged indifferently. "Doesn't count."

"Why doesn't it count?" I demanded.

"'Cause *I* don't give a shit and *you* do."

I wrung my hands. "What kind of a deal do you want?"

"I'll fly your pussy mission with that *dinky-dou* bitch, but I get one mission of my choice in the future," he offered.

"No stalls and puking?" I countered.

He nodded reluctantly.

"Absolutely perfect manners and smooth-as-silk flying? No gun runs or buzzing water buffalo? Absolutely nothing out of the ordinary, just regular stuff like sane pilots do day in and day out? Nothing weird? Your word on it?"

He scowled. "You're driving up the price, Captain. *Two* missions of my choice!"

"One!" I countered.

He swung his feet off my desk and stood up. "*You* fly the bitch then."

"What kind of missions?" I hedged.

"*Any* two missions of my choice," he demanded.

"Okay, any two *approved, legit* missions that come *legally* through my flight operations," I agreed reluctantly. We shook hands on it as I mutely recalled my grandmother once telling me to never cut a deal with the devil because he cheats like hell.

But realistically, where could the harm lie?

The next morning the lieutenant stormed into my office. "Bullshit, Captain, I'm flying my *own* bird with my *own* crew!"

"I assigned you a Yellow Detachment aircraft because *your* aircraft is *stolen*, has an *illegal* gun system on it, and stands out like a sore thumb with its *crudely painted numbers*!" I argued.

"No one will notice the numbers unless they look real close," he insisted.

"So what happens if someone takes a picture of the USO troupe with your stolen aircraft with the illegal gun system and crudely painted numbers in the background? You could end up in jail for ninety-nine years if somebody important sees it."

He scowled. "Okay, I'll fly the Yellow bird then, but with *my* crew!"

"*Your* crew isn't properly trained to handle VIPs, and besides that, they *look* like a band of *vagabonds*," I explained. When he crossed his arms and glared at me, I sighed. "Okay, damn it, at least get them in clean flight suits with fresh hair cuts, and I want to *personally* inspect and brief them before you depart!"

Later, when I threatened his crew about their language and manners around civilians of the genteel persuasion and such, they stared at me like I was nuts—especially when I also warned them that if they let their crazy lieutenant do *anything* out of the ordinary I would hold them equally responsible for his actions.

They didn't like that part worth a damn and wanted to debate what was *ordinary* and what wasn't. *I* didn't like *that* part worth a damn.

In due course, I serenely waved them off late that afternoon bag and baggage for their mission, and with them launched and headed in roughly the right direction to their first destination, settled back for a peaceful four days. That lasted until 0900 hours the next morning when I took the call over a landline from their liaison officer, Second Lieutenant Brown.

"Um, Captain Hess, we've got a problem, Sir."

"What's the problem, Lieutenant?"

"Mister Deals, Sir. He wants a new pilot."

My stomach gripped. "Why?"

"Sir, he feels your Lieutenant Sharpe is stealing his show."

"And how is my lieutenant stealing his show, Lieutenant?"

"Well, it's sort of hard to explain, Sir."

"Give me your best effort, Lieutenant," I encouraged.

"Well, Sir, don't tell anybody I said this, but, uh, their show is, uh, sort of *dated*, Sir."

"Dated?"

"Yes, Sir. It's like from the forties or something … and just kind of … well, *boring.*"

"So how does that affect my lieutenant, Lieutenant?"

"Well, Sir, he seems kind of popular. When the men found out who he was, they kind of flocked around him, talking to him and all, and a few of them even asked for his autograph and wanted to have their pictures taken with him and his crew. Honest to god, Captain."

"Okay," I replied placidly, stifling a yawn. "I'm still waiting for the problem here with my lieutenant, Lieutenant."

"Well, uh, Claude, uh, Mister Deals, he thinks the lieutenant is getting more attention than they are. He thinks it might be better if they have a different pilot, Sir. That is, if you wouldn't mind, Captain. He doesn't want to put you to a lot of trouble or anything, he says."

"Lieutenant, please remind Mister Deals that Miss Wheels went directly over my head to the general to get that particular pilot and that there's nothing I can do about it now."

"Yes Sir. I'm aware of that. The general told me if I ever put a call through to him and put her on the phone again like that, he would personally chain me to the next thousand-pound bomb the Air Force dropped on Hanoi."

"Yes, well, I wish I could help you, Lieutenant, but my hands are tied on this issue."

"Well, uh, I have a suggestion then, Sir."

"Which is, Lieutenant?"

"Have your lieutenant use a different call sign so they won't know who he is, Sir."

"Why don't you suggest that to Lieutenant Sharpe, Lieutenant Brown?"

"Uh, I did, Sir."

"And …?"

"We were flying at the time and I was on the intercom, and, um, he told me to go piss up a rope, Sir. Then his crew chief asked, 'Do you want me to throw his ass out, Sugar Bear?' and the lieutenant, he said, 'Hell yeah, throw his ass out!' But the copilot talked them out of it after a big argument and all, Sir."

"That's reassuring, Lieutenant, because I'm fairly certain we have a strict policy in place in regards to throwing people out of our aircraft," I assured him, stifling my laughter. "But of course, I don't always know *everything* that goes on out there in the field."

"Uh, okay, Sir, I guess that's all I have for now."

"Sorry I couldn't help you, Lieutenant."

"Yes, Sir. Goodbye, Sir."

The next morning at 0900 hours, I took another call from Lieutenant Brown.

"Sir?"

"Yes, Lieutenant."

"Things are kind of getting out of hand, Sir."

"How so, Lieutenant?"

"Claude got real mad at our next stop because Susan grabbed Lieutenant Sharpe and got all the attention from everyone crowding around him and he didn't get any attention at all. He pretended to be sick that night, but he wasn't really sick. He was trying to embarrass Miss Wheels, see, and let her know he was the main attraction. He told me he was going to do that, but for me not to worry, because he would come in later and save her. He just wanted to teach her a lesson, you see, and—"

"Lieutenant Brown, I don't mean to cut you short here, but my only interest is in the aviation side of this mission," I reminded him sternly. "The performance end of it is up to you and whoever you report to."

"Yes, Sir. I'm coming to that part. Well, Susan, she pulls Lieutenant Sharpe up on the stage with her that night when Claude didn't show up, and she and they put on this real funny show. See, they were talking and flirting and just saying real suggestive things to each other, and everyone was laughing and stomping their feet and all. They even had me laughing. But now Claude refuses to go on stage at the next stop unless he gets a new pilot, and Susan won't go on to the next stop without Lieutenant Sharpe to fly her, and she even wants him to do the same show with her again tonight onstage. So what do I do, Sir?"

"Lieutenant, what does your boss say?"

"He told me to handle it, Sir," he replied meekly. "But I don't know how to handle it, Sir. I was hoping you could help me."

"Lieutenant Brown?"

"Yes, Sir?"

"Handle it."

"Yes, Sir. Goodbye, Sir."

On the third day, I got a call from the XO at the previous night's stopover.

"Captain Hess, this is Major Ferguson, the Executive Officer of Song Bay."

"Yes, Sir. How can I help you?"

"I have seventy American servicemen and four hundred ARVNs here in my little outpost, and your unit has done more for our morale in one night than I've been able to accomplish in the last six months. I want to personally express my gratitude and say that anytime you want to send that crazy crew of yours back up this way again it would be greatly appreciated."

"Uh, that's ... that's ... uh, thank you, Sir, I'm ... uh ... glad to be of service to you ..."

"With men like that under your command, I know you must be proud. They've flown missions for us before and we've always had the greatest respect for their courage, but meeting them in person was an experience. That Red One-Seven's a real wildcard."

"Um, yes Sir, he's … um, definitely, uh … one of a kind …"

"Many thanks again, Captain, and good day to you."

"Yes, Sir, and thank you, Sir!" I hung up the phone wondering *now what in the hell was that all about?* Apprehensive tremors fluttered in the pit of my stomach when I realized he hadn't even mentioned the USO show. When Lieutenant Brown called two hours later from the next location, I kicked my office door closed as I grabbed the receiver off the cradle.

"Lieutenant Brown, what happened last night?" I demanded.

"Sir, it was just crazy," he replied. "Everything kind of got out of hand before I knew it. I told you I didn't know what to do, Sir. But it turned out just great."

"Okay, good, so tell me everything that happened."

"Well, Sir, when we got to our overnight location, everybody started fussing and feuding right off the bat."

"My crew, Lieutenant?"

"Oh, no, Sir, all the USO people. Your crew was just fine."

"Please continue, Lieutenant."

"Well, Sir, Claude starts yelling at Susan that she's a used-up has-been and that now he remembers why they broke up their act twenty years ago. And Susan starts yelling at Claude that *he* was the used-up has-been that couldn't even get *it up* anymore. And Claude yells back at her asking why would he want to get it up anymore with her as an inspiration because she was about as *sexy* now as a dried-up fig and—"

"Lieutenant?"

"Uh, yes, Sir?"

"Where is this heading?"

"Well, Claude locked himself in his room and wouldn't come out. And then Susan locked herself in her room and she wouldn't come out. And then—"

"Lieutenant Brown, *what about my crew?*"

"Oh, well you see, they put on the show with Dan and Ray, Sir. And it was great. The men loved it. It was hilarious, Sir."

"A show? What kind of show?"

"Well, Sir, they took these four chairs up onstage and set them up like where they sit in the aircraft. You know, with the pilot and copilot side by side, and the crew chief and the gunner facing to the side with their backs together. They pretended they were in their helicopter and were talking to each other as they flew different missions. They were shooting their machine guns, which were really broom handles, and all. And Dan and Ray were adlibbing with their music as they acted out the different scenes. It was just hilarious, Sir. Do they really do that kind of crazy stuff in combat, Sir?"

"*Nothing* about that crew would surprise me, Lieutenant Brown," I replied dryly.

"Oh, and they had this one scene with you in it, Sir. The copilot was playing your part, and Lieutenant Sharpe, he reaches over and cuts off the engine and—"

"*I get the picture, Lieutenant*! But everything ended well, right?"

"Oh, yes Sir. They saved the day for me. Those soldiers just loved those guys. I heard them talking all around me saying they never realized how funny they were."

"Yes, they're quite the comedians."

"Even the episode in the bunker was hilarious, Sir, with Susan and Lieutenant Sharpe, and it had everyone laughing so hard they couldn't talk. Captain, I got to know—did Lieutenant Sharpe *really* cut off your engine or was he just making that up? Of course I know you probably didn't *really* pee on yourself and all, but it was *so funny!*"

"*What* episode in the bunker with Lieutenant Sharpe and Susan, Lieutenant?"

"Oh, that, well, Sir, when we first got there they briefed us on emergency procedures we were to take if we come under attack. Basically we were to run to this big underground bunker and wait inside until they told us we could come out. Anyway, about an hour after the show was over the camp took some mortar rounds and everybody goes running to the bunker and jumps inside. Somebody turns on this red overhead light and there's the lieutenant and Susan buck-naked."

"*What!*"

"Yes, Sir, and Susan starts yelling for everybody to get out, but of course nobody was in any hurry to leave with mortars dropping all around us and all. Anyway, she starts trying to put on her clothes and the first thing she does is grab the lieutenant's underwear and put them on. And then she had to take them back off to put her panties on, and the whole time she was yelling for everybody to turn around and not look at her, but it was so crowded in there nobody could turn around, I mean, not that they were really trying that hard or anything. You should have been there, Sir. I just can't describe how funny it was."

I sighed. "How many men saw them like that?"

"Oh, there were about thirty or forty that ran into the bunker, including me, Sir."

"And what was my lieutenant doing all this time?"

"He was just laughing like crazy with the rest of us and trying to help Susan get her clothes on. It was the wildest thing I've ever seen. Susan made us leave there first thing this morning. That's why I'm so late calling you. I mean, she wanted us out of there at first light because she was so embarrassed that half the camp saw her naked."

"What is the situation with your USO show now, Lieutenant?"

"Oh, hell, Captain, nobody is talking to anybody, but I don't care. I've got the best road show in Nam with your crew. They're more entertaining than the bunch I brought with me, that's for sure. The others can just stay in their damned old rooms for all I care."

"All right, Lieutenant, keep things together for one more night and I'll see you when you get back here tomorrow."

"Yes, Sir. No problem. I've got a handle on things now. I'm having a ball."

"Yes, it certainly sounds like it, Lieutenant. You hang in there."

"Yes, Sir, Captain. Don't worry about a thing. I've got everything under control."

"Goodbye, Lieutenant."

"Goodbye, Sir."

They flew in the next day around noon and deposited the USO troupe on the VIP pad before hovering out to their parking revetment. When the USO foursome breezed through my lounge and out the door without a word, I summarized the Wheels and Deals USO show was now again defunct.

Lieutenant Brown stopped long enough to pump my hand and tell me how great an experience it had been for him, and that he had taken pictures of my crew during their performances and wanted my assistance in getting the photographs autographed when they were developed, before rushing happily out after his disintegrating USO troupe.

A few minutes later the lieutenant strolled in. "Hey, Captain."

"I gather from some of your fans you guys are in show business now?"

He scowled. "What an experience! That VIP shit makes combat look easy. I'm not going to be so hard on those Yellow Detachment pussies in the future if all show-biz people have egos like that!"

"It never occurred to me you and your nutty crew would steal the spotlight from a USO show."

"We saved the day, Captain!" he protested. "That had to be the most rotten act I've ever seen in my whole life. We just livened things up and had some fun with the grunts in the field."

"I understand your love life became something of an issue as well?"

He scowled. "Now don't go there, Captain—I went above and beyond the call of duty there! The old broad was suffering a complete meltdown after the things that Claude dude said to her and I was just trying to boost her confidence a little. How was I to know the dinks would pick that exact moment to heave some mortars our way?"

"What a charitable endeavor," I sneered.

"Just keep in mind I held up my end of the bargain," he argued.

"But as usual, with questionable methods and debatable results," I pointed out. "Under the circumstances, I propose *one* future mission of you choice."

"I'm too tired to argue with you, Captain," he allowed as Ellen hurried in to my visitors lounge and embraced him. "It's a deal if you'll also throw in the next two days off—I need some *serious* downtime after *that* crazy mission."

"Four days is like forever, love, I'm so glad you're finally back!" Ellen cooed, tugging him toward the door. "Come on, darling, Cherrie is expecting you for dinner, so we've only got a few hours to get you a hot bath and loosen you up a bit!"

CHAPTER 23

Though we were increasingly focused on the ongoing Paris negotiations, my first indication that things were not what they seemed on the peace accord side was early one morning when an abrupt flood of requests for command and control missions began pouring in. Within minutes, it seemed every ARVN outpost in our III Corps sector was under siege and the commanders in the field in desperate need of aerial platforms to observe and direct the furious battles taking place.

With only four Red Detachment aircraft to cover over twenty mission requests, I quickly pulled low-priority missions from the Yellow Detachment and sent them out while covering their missions with the Green Detachment. Within an hour, I had all ten of my flyable aircraft in the air, with double crews working on the remaining two aircraft down for maintenance to get them airworthy. I was busy juggling requests, attempting to double up some and piggyback others, while consciously sending my less experienced Yellow Detachment pilots into the safer zones and my experienced Red Detachment combat pilots into the more hostile areas, when the radio squawked and things suddenly got worse.

"Mayday! Mayday! Mayday! Red One-Seven going down south of Song Bay!"

I hurried over as the specialists keyed his transmitter, quickly evaluating that Song Bay had a small ARVN outpost with American advisers that could possible be of assistance to us.

"Roger your Mayday call, Red One-Seven!" the specialist transmitted. "Launching Big Bird to vicinity of Song Bay, over!"

"Negative, Ops!" Sharpe responded. "The area's saturated with boomers! I'm down a couple hundred yards east of the ARVN outpost—we'll make a run for it! Red One-Seven out!"

"Roger, One-Seven, Dean Ops, out," the specialist responded.

"Try to raise Song Bay on the radio and alert them one of our aircraft is down!" I instructed. "Ask them for assistance in recovering our crew!"

"Dean Ops, Red One-One," Dandy called before he could transmit. "I've taken numerous hits and trailing smoke. I'm attempting to make it to Trang Bang with gauges fluctuating, over."

"Roger, Red One-One, understand you are making an emergency landing at Trang Bang," the specialist responded. "Do you want Big Bird launched for recovery, over?"

"Not a good idea, Ops—there are anti-aircraft guns everywhere out here—will advise further after I'm on the ground, over!"

"Roger, One-One, Dean Ops standing by, over."

"Captain," my operations sergeant gasped as he rushed up to me. "I've got reports over the landline that Red One-Five just went down somewhere near Tay Ninh, Red One-Two crashed at An Loc, and it appears we've lost Yellow One-Zero in the vicinity of Loi Kia!"

I turned to the wall map where one of my men was frantically plotting locations as the reports poured in. Sly was down at An Loc north of Song Bay, the hamlet next to where Lieutenant Sharpe was down. Both outposts straddled Highway 1, long considered the primary invasion route for the North Vietnamese Army. Mad Hatter was down near Tay Ninh, which was due west of us guarding the Parrot's Beak and blocking the main Ho Chi Minh Trail leading from Cambodia into our III Corps area of operations. Dandy was down northwest of us at Trang Bang, which was along the main VC re-supply route into our area of operations. Warrant Officer King from the Yellow Detachment was down at Loi Kia to the south of us, which guarded the intricate river networks of the Mekong Delta.

I stood frozen in the middle of my operations room with my heart thudding and my wits scattered, realizing we were under siege on a massive scale in what was obviously a major thrust against the South Vietnamese capitol of Saigon, briefly recalling a conversation a few days earlier as we sat around a table at the officers' club.

"The rumors are rampant that a cease-fire is imminent," Cherrie advised happily. "We could all be going home soon."

"It's a sham," Sharpe argued. "The North Vietnamese are just using the negotiations to move their forces into position for a major attack on our outlying positions."

"Why do you think that?" Cherrie asked.

"Because the sons of bitches are too quiet," he insisted. "They're lying low, waiting. We haven't been shot at in so long it's spooky."

"I don't know if they're planning an attack or not," Mad Hatter observed. "But I do know our intelligence gathering capabilities are so screwed up from our downsizing nobody would know if they were."

"Why would they want to attack us now?" Linda argued. "They should be happy we're leaving. In a few months we'll be out of here. It doesn't make sense to attack us now."

"Oh, they want us out of Vietnam alright," Dandy allowed. "But they also want to humiliate us like they did the French. If they do hit us now we'd be just like the Frogs were at Dinh Bin Phu."

Sharpe nodded grimly. "I agree. After a year of withdrawals, we've evolved into a few scattered outposts with a handful of advisers clustered around in small support groups. From over five hundred thousand American troops in-country we've dwindled down to fewer than thirty thousand now, with no combat units among us. We're in the perfect position to get our ass kicked. But then again, we haven't done anything else right in this war, so why should we expect anything different now?"

I realized in alarm that in less than half an hour I had lost every aircraft in the Red Detachment and half of the Dean's flyable assets. Fleeting panic swept over me as I watched my small staff desperately trying to shift aircraft around to launch search and rescue missions, make frantic calls to pinpoint crash sites, and simultaneously handle pleas for nonexistent aircraft from the beleaguered outposts fighting desperately to stave off the onslaught.

"Dean Ops, Red One-Seven, over!" I snapped out of my trance and snatched the transmitter from the specialist's hands, my heart pounding. "Red One-Seven, this is Dean Ops, over!"

"Roger, Ops, Red One-Seven inbound with a WIA. Request a replacement door gunner for immediate turnaround to Song Bay, over."

"Red One-Seven—I thought you were down, over!"

"Roger, we bummed a ride with an ARVN bird back to their holding compound and picked up one of their aircraft. Get me a door gunner, Chief, and be quick about it, over!"

I found the utter calm of his voice soothing and shook the cobwebs from my addled brain as I turned to my ops sergeant. "Get a volunteer gunner to fly with Red One-Seven! Have him standing by the pad!"

Sharpe set down minutes later and I watched a medical team pull his gunner off the aircraft, who had a flesh wound in his leg, and the new volunteer gunner scramble aboard before he was off again without even shutting down. I watched him climb into the air and turn north to Song Bay, growing despondent. How could he and his crew show such resolve and courage under the circumstances? As I stood there glumly, a Green Detachment aircraft flew in to drop off Dandy and his crew. I jumped up on the skid to direct them back out to search for Mad Hatter and his crew as Dandy ran over to me.

"I need an aircraft, Chief!" Dandy demanded as they departed.

"We don't have any aircraft left," I replied.

"Then give me your jeep and driver to transport me and my copilot over to the ARVN compound while my crew grabs some lunch."

"How are you guys getting all these aircraft from the ARVNs?" I demanded.

"Ask Sugar Bear, Chief, he's the one who cut the deal."

As my driver whisked Dandy and his copilot off in my commandeered jeep, my operations sergeant rushed up to me.

"Captain, Red One-Seven is down again!"

"What! He just flew out of here not more than fifteen minutes ago!"

"Sorry, Sir, I'm just the messenger."

"Damn it!" I screamed in frustration. "Any word on the crew?"

"No, Sir, we just got the mayday call and then lost contact."

I hurried back into the operations room trying to calm my rattled nerves as a growing sense of desperation settled over me. Minutes later an ARVN aircraft dropped Sly and his crew off on the helipad.

"I need a backup aircraft!" Sly demanded as he rushed into the operations room.

"We don't have any," I replied.

"Then I need your jeep to give me a lift over to the ARVN holding area to get one!"

"Dandy has already got my jeep and is on his way over there to get one for himself," I replied. "How in hell do you guys keep stealing aircraft from the damned ARVNs anyway?"

"Ask Sugar Bear!" he directed as he rushed out.

My returning Green Detachment aircraft dropped off Mad Hatter and his crew, who linked up with Sly in a truck he scrounged up from somewhere and they set out together for the ARVN compound without even coming into the operations room.

"Dean Ops, Red One-Seven is inbound requesting a replacement copilot on standby for immediate turn around!" the radio squawked.

I took the mike. "Red One-Seven, we received a report you were down again, over!"

"Roger, Ops, I'm in another ARVN bird. My copilot is seriously wounded—I need a medical team standing by with ambulance, over!"

"Roger, One-Seven, I don't know where you're getting all these aircraft from, but beware we're running out of crewmembers for them as well, over."

"Understand, Ops, just get me a warm body to fill the seat for ballast if nothing else, over!"

A Green Detachment pilot volunteered to fly as his copilot and was standing by minutes later when a medical team extracted his unconscious copilot, his midsection a bloody mess, and rushed him off to a waiting ambulance as Sharpe and his patchwork crew immediately headed back out to Song Bay in his third aircraft of the day.

As I watched this thinking it madness on a massive scale, one of my ops personnel extended the phone to me.

"Sir, there's a Mister Lambert on the line. Maybe you can make sense of what he's saying."

I took the phone. "Captain Hess here?"

"Captain Hess, I need to get a message to Lieutenant Sharpe. Can you help me?"

"He's in the field in and out of radio contact, but I'll try. Who are you, and what is your message?"

"I run the ARVN aircraft holding compound here in Saigon. Please inform him I've only got one flyable aircraft left, but I can get several more flight-ready by morning if he needs them."

"Uh, okay, I'll relay the message to him when he checks in," I replied, perplexed.

"I appreciate your assistance, Captain. You guys have put such a heavy call on my available assets I'm just trying to stay ahead of you over here."

"Um, could I send a crew over to get the one aircraft you have available now?" I asked tentatively, hoping he wouldn't remember my name when the criminal investigators came calling.

"Sure thing, Captain, I'll have it fueled and ready. Tell Lieutenant Sharpe to get up with me as soon as possible with an estimate of his future requirements."

"Yes, I will, and thank you, Mr. Lambert."

I turned to my operations sergeant. "Round up a crew from the Red Detachment and have my driver ferry them over to the ARVN holding compound to pick up a Huey they're holding for us."

"Yes, Sir, and where is the ARVN holding compound, Sir?"

"Damned if I know," I replied. "But apparently my driver does!"

At dusk, my exhausted pilots began straggling home, almost all of them with battle damage to their aircraft. Sharpe was the last to make it back, with thirteen bullet holes in his aircraft, after logging twelve hours of flight time, being shot down once, shot up twice more, and losing two of his crewmembers.

I wrapped things up in flight ops and hurried to Sharpe's cottage late that evening, where I found Mad Hatter, Debbie, Sly, Sandra, Dandy, Linda, Ellen and Cherrie already assembled, each looking as shell-shocked as I felt.

As the girls worked briskly in the kitchen, Sharpe limped out of his bathroom with a towel around his waist, his damp hair tousled, and sporting a large purple bruise on his left arm and shoulder.

"You okay?" I asked.

"A little tired and banged up, but I'm fine," he replied as he moved behind the bar and poured us a drink. "It's a slaughterhouse out there, Captain, and we've got nothing to fight the anti-aircraft guns with. They're knocking us out of the air as fast as we take off."

"We're almost out of aircraft and crews anyway," I replied grimly. "By the way, I got a strange call today from someone named Lambert who works at some ARVN aircraft holding compound requesting I inform you that they only had one flyable aircraft left, but that he could get more ready by tomorrow if you needed them. What was that about?"

"He's referring to all the aircraft we're turning over to the ARVNs parked in a holding compound he manages," he explained. "When we need one, we give him a voucher."

I shook my head in wonder. "We stand down and give them our aircraft, which they put in a holding area, and we then steal them back again by giving them a *voucher* for it?"

He nodded. "That's about the gist of it, Captain. The ARVNs pay a storage fee to a civil contractor until they take control of the aircraft. When we steal one of the aircraft from the ARVNs, who probably don't know they own it in the first place, and don't give a damn in any case, their government then pays the storage fee, and in turn passes it on to our government for reimbursement."

"How much is this storage fee?" I asked.

"Runs about two hundred dollars per aircraft."

"Who signs the vouchers?"

"Major Crystal, of course, he's the only one authorized to sign them."

I stared at him in shock. "How do you get him to do that?"

"His civilian secretary gives them to him to sign along with other authentic documents. They're in Vietnamese and he signs them without knowing what he's signing. She's best friends with Ellen's sister in MACV."

"Doesn't anyone ever question this storage thing?"

"It's paid out of Washington from some obscure accounting office. They don't know what the shit's going on over here any more than we do. Nobody pays any attention to a few hundred bucks. It's foolproof."

"What if Major Crystal suddenly refuses to sign the vouchers?"

He studied me impassively as he lifted his glass. "Then you'd need to convince him to do so, Captain, so I don't have to." He took a sip of his drink, his cold blue eyes staring into my own giving me the look I'd never wanted to see again, leaving me as disturbed as the first time.

"Alright, you guys, come get it!" Ellen called, clapping her hands to get our attention.

"If it comes to it, I'll do my best," I replied uneasily.

He smiled. "That would save me a lot of trouble, Captain. Come on, I'm starved!"

He led the way to the table containing mounds of cold cuts as I followed, realizing I was ravenous because I hadn't eaten since breakfast early that morning.

"So much for 'peace is at hand,'" Dandy observed sourly as he filled his plate.

"They set us up like chumps," Mad Hatter grated, spreading mayonnaise on bread.

"I can't believe every one of you got shot down today!" Linda exclaimed as she forked sliced meat onto Sly's plate.

"It was the most frightening day I've ever lived," I agreed grimly.

"I've never seen so many anti-aircraft guns," Sly complained. "Half of our maps are covered with red circles and no-fly zones. We've got to revise our tactics. Any suggestions?"

"Low level," Sharpe advised as he bit into his sandwich. "If we gain any altitude at all we're sitting ducks. We've got to get down to tree-top level where they can't find us."

"Then we're sitting ducks for the small arms fire," Mad Hatter argued.

"I'd rather get hit with rifle fire than 23 mike-mike or .51 cal," Sharpe countered. "We can fly different routes when we go in and out of a location so they can't set up for us. If we use speed and surprise to get past them, and fly zigzag routes instead of straight lines we've got a chance. We've got to rethink our whole scheme of maneuver. Right now they control the sky. I lost my gunner and my copilot while getting my ass fired up three times, and flew half the day without a windshield. Frankly, I'm not having a lot of fun out there right now and we're fortunate none of us got killed."

"Even with the aircraft we're stealing from the ARVNs we have a big problem with ground crews," I cautioned. "With most of our maintenance crews already sent stateside, what we've got left is precious little."

As I stood amongst them listening to them revise tactics and analyze tactical situations it dawned on me they were tired, demoralized, and a bit shell shocked, but by god they weren't beaten! I felt a sense of pride in being amongst them, a strong pull of the camaraderie they shared so easily amongst themselves. By golly, if they could face what they'd faced on this day and be willing to go out into that chaos again tomorrow, then I could damned well do my level best to support them!

"Gentlemen!" Ellen called. "Everyone go home and get some rest now!"

We turned to the door as a group, too tired to argue.

The mission requests for C&C birds were down considerably the next morning because most of the outposts were now in enemy hands. Of the previous twenty-seven we controlled the day before, only eight remained in a massive setback for the ARVNs and us. Outright defeat was suddenly a very real possibility as the enemy continued to push relentlessly towards Saigon. Reports of enemy tanks rolling south down Highway 1 poured in, with seemingly the only thing slowing their advance the civilian refugees clogging the roads before their onslaught, which also hampered the rush of ARVN reinforcements north in a desperate attempt to blunt their attacking columns.

I pulled two clerks, a cook, and a vehicle mechanic to work with my shallow pool of aviation maintenance personnel, and selected two pilots to ferry five aircraft over from the ARVN holding compound in relays.

I lost three more aircraft during the day, one each for Sly, Dandy, and the lieutenant, replacing them with three of the stolen ARVN aircraft. By midday, Sly's crew chief was gravely injured and in intensive care with a head injury, Dandy had lost his gunner to an arm wound, and Mad Hatter's copilot had a chest wound, leaving us critically short of pilots and crew. I ran a quick check, determined there were some twenty aviators in various staff positions at MACV headquarters, and placed an emergency request for volunteers to fly as copilots on a short-term basis. Four pilots showed up, two of them majors, after Major Crystal's secretary called to inform me he was unavailable to fly due to his pressing agenda. I put the four volunteers with experienced pilots in the Yellow and Green Detachments and shifted some of their experienced pilots over to the Red Detachment.

A crisis can bring out the best in people, and I was amazed at how everyone pitched in for all tasks, with officers working alongside enlisted men as everyone jumped in wherever needed without regard to rank. We regrouped that night at Sharpe's cottage to pick tiredly at our food and sip at our drinks sparingly with no humor among us. Afterwards we sat glumly around the table as the girls moved about cleaning up the debris of our meal.

"We've got over twenty anti-aircraft positions plotted on our flight board," I informed them in the heavy silence. "But the information is unreliable because the positions are moving as the NVA advances."

"We need the Air Force to put a high priority on these positions," Sharpe stated after some thought. "Captain, call up that Air Force general that put my ass on that USO mission and tell him we need a dedicated group of fast-movers to help us eliminate those sites. We can search them out and they can come in with the shake-n-bake to destroy them."

"I agree," Sly nodded. "If we pinpoint them and have the fast-movers overhead, they can do in one run what it would take us half a day to fly around."

"I'll make the request first thing in the morning," I allowed. "We sure as hell aren't going to have any aircraft or crews left at the rate we're going now, and without us the commanders in the field don't have any C&C capability."

We drifted back to our beds and slept the sleep of the exhausted. When I arrived at flight ops the following morning only four outposts remained in ARVN hands out of the initial twenty-seven, each of them cut off, surrounded, and under heavy attack.

Thankfully, the Air Force general readily agreed to give us an immediate ready reaction force of jets to respond to the anti-aircraft sites. Though rocked back hard on our heels and the situation desperate, with the dedicated Air Force firepower we were now ready to wage a counterattack. The lieutenant, Sly, Dandy, and Mad Hatter poured over my map plotting the counterattack and in effect becoming the point of the spear—four lightly armed helicopters to face an army streaking down Highway 1 and over the ARVNs like a steamroller.

Sly and Mad Hatter launched for the Tay Ninh and Trang Bang area to the northwest. The lieutenant and Dandy launched north towards An Loc and Song Bay. Over the next few hours, they pinpointed eight anti-aircraft sites for the Air Force to pound with bombs and napalm, opening a flight corridor to Trang Bang and An Loc for our C&C birds. The American advisers immediately went on the offensive with the ARVN ground and mechanized forces, during which the lieutenant was shot up and forced to crash land near An Loc. Dandy sustained heavy battle damage while extracting the lieutenant and his crew. When they returned, they immediately commandeered two more of my ARVN aircraft and launched back out again into the fray.

By days end, things were looking up for us. The heavy air power concentration and renewed ARVN ground counterattacks slowed the enemy's onrush towards Saigon dramatically. In a somewhat festive mood following our day of victories, we met at the Sharpe's cottage again that evening, where one of the nurses brought along a copy of the *Stars and Stripes* with a picture of his shot-up aircraft on the front page, along with a glowing account of his actions on the first day of the offensive. The only inaccuracy was that the article reported him as shot down three times that day, when in fact he had flown two of the aircraft home and technically not crashed. The reporter called him "Red One-Seven, the most famous and revered pilot in Vietnam" and listed his many medals won, concluding that he was "certain to add to that most distinguished inventory with his tireless heroism on this day of desperate fighting on all fronts."

He bowed majestically as we booed and jeered, and afterwards the fatigue and booze sent us staggering off to bed early, but with our pride on the rebound.

The next morning my ragtag crews set out to clear flight corridors from Trang Bang to Tay Ninh and An Loc to Song Bay with their fast-mover Air Force counterparts lurking overhead like birds of prey. They were soon in the thick of things taking out anti-aircraft sites in both directions and by evening had cleared routes to both Tay Ninh and Song Bay for the ARVN Mechanized Infantry relief units to plunge forward under the leadership of their American advisers. Sly went down in late morning, and Dandy that afternoon, each recovered by Mad Hatter and Sharpe respectively and flown home. I quickly requisitioned two more aircraft from the ARVN holding compound and dispatched a crew to pick them up as replacements.

When they returned late that evening and shut down for the day, Sharpe came directly into my flight ops. "Captain, wrap up your paperwork for the day."

"I've got too much going on to party, Lieutenant," I replied wearily.

"I've arranged for beer, barbeque, and baked beans to be trucked over here to the flight line," he replied. "Our maintenance crews are pulling twenty-hour shifts trying to keep us in the air. They're overworked and for the most part going unrecognized. I've got half a dozen nurses on their way over to set up a serving line and help feed them in an attempt to boost their morale."

As the surprised but grateful men ate, I walked around inspecting our battered birds. Sharpe's aircraft had nine 23-millimeter guns painted on its side, symbolizing anti-aircraft sites destroyed. Sly had eight on his aircraft, Dandy seven, and Mad Hatter five—a total of twenty-nine sites in two days, an almost unbelievable accomplishment in such a short time. The hidden factor was that by this deed they had given the advisers their critical C&C aerial platforms from which to mount their ground counterattacks to stem the tide of the furious onslaught from the north.

I stood overwhelmed by a sense of wonder for my tiny group, the leading edge of a Herculean effort, a lump forming in my throat. They were the pride of our nation, even though our nation had forgotten them. They were unbowed, incredibly brave, determined, and resourceful.

I knew in my heart no finer warriors had ever served a cause anywhere at any time in our history. I turned from the aircraft with the painted emblems and walked back to the group to find the men carrying Lieutenant Sharpe on their shoulders toward my jeep in a howling mob as the nurses followed encouraging them on.

"Help me, Captain, please!" Critter called. "He's got a wrench in his hand!"

"Well, hell, *you're* the one who said you needed more help!" the lieutenant protested.

"If you don't get him outta here he'll single-handedly wreck our entire air-war effort!" Critter threatened. "He can do more damage to an aircraft in five minutes than the enemy can in a week!"

"Lieutenant Sharpe!" I called sternly. "Give up that dangerous weapon and clear this area immediately. That is an order!"

The men cheered as Sharpe reluctantly handed over the wrench, and then turned back to their thankless tasks, their fatigue lightened and morale considerably lifted.

Our joy was short-lived when we lost Dandy and his whole crew the next day to a .51 cal anti-aircraft site, which turned their aircraft into an aerial ball of flame. Though Dandy and his crew were officially listed as missing in action because we were unable to recover their bodies, we knew from the after action report there was little chance any of them survived the crash. The same gun shot the lieutenant down as he flew in to search for survivors. He crashed two hundred yards from the site, where in a fit of rage, he reverted to his Infantry training, organized his crew, and attacked the gun from the ground with their CAR-15 snub-nosed automatic rifles, killing six of the enemy soldiers

361

handling the gun while destroying it. He and his crew then carried his copilot, wounded in the hip during the attack, on an improvised litter another mile through enemy lines to An Loc, where an ARVN aircraft flew them back to our base at Hotel Six.

I was down to five seasoned pilots and half a dozen inexperienced copilots when I entered the lieutenant's cottage that evening, which resembled a funeral parlor with everyone sitting numbly around grieving for Dandy and his crew.

"Please, Sugar Bear, tell me there's some hope!" Linda begged as she fell on her knees before him. "You were there with him! You saw what happened! Tell me he's not gone!"

He pulled her to her feet as she knelt sobbing before him and hugged her to his chest as tears slid down his own cheeks.

The next day our president ordered the bombing of Hanoi in retaliation for the all out attack on the south. The Navy and the Air Force flew night and day, north and south, pulverizing the enemy capital to the north and the advancing enemy columns in the south. During the day Sly was shot down and his copilot wounded. Sharpe took his aircraft out to Song Bay and lost it that evening, getting splinters of Plexiglas in his arm and cheek and twisting his leg so badly trying to get out of the burning aircraft he couldn't walk without crutches. We were out of business the next day when Mad Hatter went down at An Loc with our last aircraft. We fell back in exhaustion, crippled and nearly beaten, as the Air Force bombed the area around us into a smoldering pulp and the Navy pounded the north with everything they had.

The next day the North Vietnamese were back at the negotiating table asking for a cease-fire in an obvious attempt to regroup their decimated forces. Our stupid politicians gave it to them and our offensive operations ground to a halt with us still in control of Tay Ninh, Trang Bang, An Loc, and Song Bay, but everything else in enemy hands—a bitter pill to swallow.

In the following lull, we conducted a memorial service for our three dead pilots and visited our wounded, most of who were shipping home. I reduced the Dean Detachment in size again to eight aircraft, putting two in the Green Detachment and three each in the Yellow and the Red Detachments. We were now down to ten pilots and only half of the ground crews needed to maintain our aircraft.

We spent two weeks healing, catching up on our rest, grieving for our dead and wounded, and watching as the negotiations in Paris drug on. The enemy activity grew passive during this time as they reorganized and we waited warily. A flurry of medals came down through the system, the most notable being the Distinguished Flying Cross for the lieutenant, Sly, and Dandy, who of course received his posthumously. The lieutenant received another Silver Star for the attack on the .51 cal site, which shot him and Dandy down, and a Purple Heart for the wounds to his cheek and arm in his last crash.

And then the attacks resumed with a furious siege on An Loc and Song Bay. The lieutenant went down at Song Bay the morning of the renewed attacks, making it the seventh time in thirty days. Unfazed, he was back in the air that evening, and shot up again within the hour. In the last instance, his copilot received a light shoulder wound and his beloved crew chief, Critter, was gravely injured. The lieutenant was inconsolable that evening as we sat around his bar in a dejected group.

The next morning our president ordered an immediate resumption of the bombing on Hanoi and expanded the air raids into Laos and Cambodia to stop the troops and supplies flooding down the Ho Chi Minh Trail, but in our heavy hearts we knew it was too little to late.

CHAPTER 24

At noon, Major Crystal appeared in my office for the first time since we had been assigned to our new base at Hotel Six. "Song Bay has become untenable. I've been ask to mount an emergency evacuation of the forty or so American advisers stranded there."

I shook my head in despair. "With what, Sir? We're down to two flyable aircraft and we don't even have adequate crews to man them."

"This is our opportunity to shine," he replied with a gleam in his eye. "This request comes from the MACV commander himself!"

"But, Sir, extracting those men will take at least five sorties. Song Bay is completely encircled and under siege. Nothing can get in or out. If our aircraft go down, there are no reserves to get the crews out or to continue the rescue operation."

"We need to make it happen, Captain," he grated. "We can't let the MACV commander down. This could make or break my career! Find a way!"

He followed me out into the lounge where my few remaining pilots were clustered around in a dispirited group. "I need volunteers." Heads lifted as I explained the mission and the lack of resources. "I don't want to mislead you. This could be considered a suicidal mission," I finished bleakly.

Lieutenant Sharpe rose. "We can't leave those men out there like that. I need a copilot and a crew chief."

Captain Benedict stood as well. "Count me in."

Benedict's copilot raised his hand. "Yo, I'm with Sly."

I waited in the ensuing hush, but it was obvious there were no other takers.

"It's our chance to make a name for ourselves," Major Crystal snapped at the remaining men who sat with their heads lowered. "I don't buy the suicidal nature of this task, as Captain Hess refers to it. Surely there's one of you who has the guts to fly this mission?"

When the silence continued I drew a deep breath. "I'll fly as Lieutenant Sharpe's copilot." *Had I lost my mind? Regardless of what Crystal thought, this was indeed a suicidal mission!* Visions of Nancy and my children flashed through my mind, followed by fearful regret at my reckless impulsiveness.

"You're needed back here at base if things should go wrong, Captain," Sharpe replied in the silence. "Perhaps Major Crystal would do the honor of flying with me?"

Major Crystal turned white as his eyes flicked around the group watching him. "I-I'm not qualified as an aircraft commander. I-I'm not current …"

Sharpe's eyes narrowed. "I need a copilot, Major, not a qualified aircraft commander. You meet those specifications."

Major Crystal blinked rapidly. "B-But I'm the Commander of this Detachment. Y-You're my subordinate …"

Sharpe watched him coldly. "I need a *copilot*, Major."

It was an odd situation to have the detachment commander, a field grade officer, fly copilot for a first lieutenant in his own detachment, but there were few other options. The silence became untenable as the two stared at each other.

Sharpe smiled. "Perhaps the mission has more risk than you allude to, Major?"

Major Crystal's face turned scarlet. "Are you implying I'm afraid, Lieutenant?"

Sharpe shrugged. "I'm simply implying that a true leader leads by example."

Major Crystal's jaw clenched. "I'll fly the mission, Lieutenant! And I'll deal with your impertinent inferences to my personal integrity afterwards!"

Sharpe tilted his head in acknowledgement. "I look forward to that, Major." He turned to me. "Captain, would you please canvas the crews for volunteers for us?"

I hurried out to the crew lounge flooded with guilt, knowing I had I taken the easy way out by not insisting on flying the mission myself even though I knew if anything *did* go wrong I was in the best position to help them, but that fact didn't completely relieve my shame.

Sly's crew volunteered without pause. A crew chief named KP, and a gunner called Potshot, volunteered to be the lieutenant's crew without pause amongst the clamor of the others.

True leaders do lead by example, I thought humbly as I made my way back. *And these men's unhesitating willingness to go where their officer's led is a prime example of this idiom.*

When I entered the operations room the lieutenant, Sly, and his copilot were clustered around the large map on the wall as Major Crystal stood aloft off to the side.

"We'll use different routes in and out of Song Bay due to the heavy concentration of enemy forces laying siege to the city," the lieutenant instructed as he drew grease penciled marks on the Plexiglas covering the map. "We go in at treetop level to neutralize the anti-aircraft fire, and fly zigzag routes to avoid the ground fire. When we land to pick up the advisers, we'll be vulnerable to small arms fire. We can negate that risk somewhat by having different pickup zones on each sortie so they can't zero in on us in one specific location. I'll set up a series of different LZ's with the advisers beforehand so they can be at the right place on each sortie."

Sly nodded. "That'll also help keep the civilians off balance. The last time I flew in there the refugees were in such a frenzied state to get out we had to kick them off our aircraft to gain enough power to lift off."

Master Sergeant Morrison, my operations NCOIC, rushed up to me. "Sir, I just got a call from the ARVN compound. They've got another Huey ready for us!"

Sharpe turned to me. "Captain, get a volunteer to pick up that aircraft and fly it to An Loc. We can use it as a reserve if one of our birds is unable to continue."

I nodded grimly. "I'll fly it there myself and be on standby if you need me." Fear gripped my gut again, but my pride was partially restored.

Sergeant Morrison cleared his throat hesitantly. "Sir, we've also got some electrical cattle prods we can issue the crew to help keep the civilians in check. It'll knock them off the aircraft in a hurry, but only daze them with no lasting harm."

Sharpe nodded. "Issue them to the crew ASAP, Sergeant. Gentlemen, we'll rendezvous at An Loc for a final mission evaluation. Let's get airborne!"

I landed the reserve aircraft on the tarmac at An Loc just as the lieutenant and Sly lifted off on their first sortie after making the final arrangements with the beleaguered forces at Song Bay. I shut down the aircraft and rushed to the Tactical Operations Center to monitor the action. As I burst through the door in the sandbagged TOC the radio clattered to life.

"*Taking fire! Taking fire!*" the lieutenant barked, his voice charged with energy.

"So what's new?" Sly responded grimly. "That's a given on this mission, so don't bore me with the details!"

"*Yee Haw! Taking hits! Taking hits!*" the lieutenant responded.

"Are you're going down, asshole!"

"I'd have to gain altitude to go down lower!" the lieutenant yelled. "I just knocked the top off of a tree back there!"

"Don't zig when you should be zagging, dumb ass!"

"Thanks for the tip! *Yikes!* I just overshot the helipad! I'm swinging back around!"

"*Holy fuck! What the shit are you doing there? I almost ran over you!*"

"I *told* you I missed the helipad and was swinging back around! I think you made KP pee on himself when you came barreling over the top of us like a banshee!"

"Hell, I peed on *myself!* Like I knew where the hell you were! I'm coming around behind you, so get your ass off the pad so I can land!"

"Roger that! I'm a sitting duck here! *Taking hits! Taking hits!* I'm out of here!"

"Bout fucking time! *Taking hits! Taking hits!*"

I waited through an interminable fifteen seconds of silence.

"I'm off!" Sly yelled. "I've got civilians hanging off my skids!"

"That happens when you lollygag around!" the lieutenant chided. "Don't sweat it! They'll fall off eventually!"

"My gauges are fluctuating!" Sly reported.

"Can you make it back?" the lieutenant asked.

"I sure as hell ain't gonna land to inspect the damage! *Taking fire! Taking fire!*"

The distant thumping of rotor blades reached us in the TOC. I rushed to the door as the lieutenant's bird popped over the tree line and decelerated for landing. The bedraggled Americans on board spilled out the sides, pulling two stretchers after them. Without hesitation the aircraft lifted up, dipped its nose, and gained altitude as it circled back to the north.

"Red One-Seven is enroute for a second load!" the radio behind me crackled.

"Roger, Sugar Bear! I'm gonna have to shut down and switch aircraft!" Sly reported. "This damned thing's shaking itself to pieces!"

Sly's aircraft zipped over the trees, dipped towards the runway, and made a grinding running landing. When the aircraft stopped, the crew spilled out and ran for the backup aircraft I had flown out as the advisers tumbled out and headed off in the opposite direction. Within two minutes the backup bird's rotors were turning. I turned back to the radio as the lieutenant's voice rang out.

"Where's the alternate LZ? Anybody see it? Never mind, I see it now! The dumb asses threw smoke! Look at all the civilians scrambling that way! KP, you and Potshot get your cattle prods ready! *Holy shit! They're throwing mortars at us now!*"

"Red One-Seven, Red One-Two is airborne and heading your way!" Sly called.

"Roger, Sly! Recommend you coordinate an alternate LZ. We're beating the civilians off down here at this one. The dumb bastards threw smoke and they're swarming all over us, but the enemy fire is helping knock some of them off for us! I'm out of here with another load!"

"Roger, I'll raise their base and shoot for the third LZ. *Shit! Taking hits! Taking hits!*"

"Maybe you should be zagging instead of zigging, Magnet Ass!" the lieutenant chortled. "*Oh, fuck! Taking hits! Taking hits! Gauges going to hell! Mayday! Mayday!*"

I tried to swallow my heart as it lunged into my throat.

"One-Seven, are you going down?" Sly yelled. "Give me a location!"

"For what, you dope? Are you going to come get me?" the lieutenant replied. "I've lost partial power, but she's still churning. I think I can make it to An Loc!"

"Don't scare me like that, asshole!" Sly groused.

"*You*? Want to check out the ass end of *my* pants?"

"Red One-Two's airborne. Looks like we've still got about five advisers left down there. We're gonna need another sortie."

I ran for the door when I heard rotor blades. The lieutenant's aircraft glided over the tree line trailing smoke and eased down onto the tarmac. The turbine whined down as the troops spilled out the sides. The lieutenant and KP jumped out and climbed up to inspect the engine compartment as the blades coasted to a stop. Minutes later Sly's chopper flashed over the tree line and flared. The troops tumbled out of the cargo doors as he threw the lieutenant a salute and pulled pitch, jerking the aircraft up into the air for the last run into Song Bay.

I turned back into the TOC and snatched up the mike. "Talk to me, Sly! It looks like Sugar Bear's down for the count. You're on your own."

"When the going gets tough, the tough get going!" Sly sang out with a gleeful chuckle. "I'm swinging around to the east so I can surprise them. I've already notified the remaining advisers to relocate to the last LZ. Stay with me, Chief!"

"I'm with you all the way," I assured him as Major Crystal stumbled into the TOC, his face ashen and eyes glazed.

"I w-want t-these crews put in for m-medals!" he ordered, his whole body shaking. "Y-You take care of that, Captain!"

I bit my tongue to keep from asking him if he meant himself as well. I had no doubt he would have refused the mission if he had known what to expect, but still, he *had* flown the mission so my respect for him edged up a notch: I wouldn't begrudge him his medal if it meant recognizing my crews as well. My attention was jerked back to the radio.

"*Taking hits! Taking hits! Mayday! Mayday! One-Two's going down in the Song Bay compound!*

I snatched up the mike as the lieutenant rushed in the door. "Red One-Two, can you read me, over?" I waited a few seconds. "Red One-Two, over?"

"We bought the farm, Chief!" Sly yelled through a background of roaring carnage. We're flame out and down inside the compound. We're okay, but our bird's cooked, over!"

My heart sank as the lieutenant took the mike from my hands. "Sly, can you read me?"

"I still read you! But we've gotta get out of here fast! They're making mincemeat out of this thing!"

"Make your way to the advisers at the last LZ. I'll be there pronto, over!"

"In what, you knucklehead? Your bird is toast!"

"Naw, I was just faking it so you'd have to fly the last load out. My bird's fine." The lieutenant dashed for the door. "Let's go, Major!"

"You lying asshole!" Sly sneered. "Don't even think about putting that bird back in the air!"

"He's right!" Major Crystal shouted. "That aircraft is not flyable! It's taken too many hits! It was practically on fire and losing power when we landed!"

The lieutenant whirled around. "We can't leave our crew and those advisers out there, Major! That place is collapsing around their ears! We've got to go back for them! That bird's got one more flight in it!"

"No!" Major Crystal shouted. "We've done all we can. Don't you see that?"

"If that bitch will crank, it'll fly!" the lieutenant snarled over his shoulder as he rushed out the door. "Now let's go!"

The major rushed out after him as I picked up the mike. "Red One-Two, are you still copying?"

"I'm still here, Chief, but only because we're pinned down and can't move! What gives, over?"

"Can you make it to the adviser position at the last pickup point?"

"We can try! It can't be any worse than this position!"

"Sugar Bear's trying to get airborne to come back for you. Do the best you can. There won't be a second chance."

"That dumb son of a bitch!"

I tossed the mike on the table and ran out. The lieutenant was strapped in with the blades turning on the aircraft as KP peeped in the doors of the engine compartment.

Major Crystal stood on the skids outside the copilot's door with his helmet on, obviously engaged in a shouting match with the lieutenant. I climbed up into the cargo bay and strapped on the headphones to listen.

"Goddamn it, Lieutenant! I'm *ordering* you to shut this aircraft down!"

"Either strap in or get the fuck out, Major!" the lieutenant yelled. "I'm going back for our crew and the remaining advisers!"

"The hell you are!"

"KP! How're we looking?" the lieutenant barked as he glared at Major Crystal.

"Nothing's on fire, Sugar Bear, but the turbine don't sound so good," the crew chief reported.

"You and Potshot stay here. I don't need you on this mission!"

"This bird don't fly without me and Potshot, Sugar Bear," KP retorted.

"Lieutenant, I'm giving you a direct order to abort this mission!" Major Crystal screamed.

"KP, you and Potshot help the Major out of this fucking aircraft!"

"You men stay where you are!" Major Crystal shouted. "That's an order!"

"Grab a couple of those sandbags over there and put them in the copilot's seat for ballast," the lieutenant continued.

"Goddamn you, Lieutenant!" Major Crystal protested. "Shut this son of a bitch down!"

"Get out, Major, or I'll throw you out!"

"I'll have you court marshaled!"

The lieutenant placed his hand on the butt of his pistol in his shoulder holster. "Major, this aircraft is operational! Now get the fuck out of my bird or I'll—"

"You'll *what*, Lieutenant?" the major bellowed.

"*Goddamn it! KP! Get this son of a bitch off my aircraft before I do something stupid!*"

I tore my headphones off and rushed to the copilot's door as Major Crystal jerked his helmet off and threw it into the seat. KP and Potshot grasped him by the arms and pulled him away from the aircraft as I scrambled up into the seat and buckled in. Major Crystal pointed at me and shouted something unintelligible as I jammed his helmet on my head.

"What the fuck do you think you're doing, Captain?" the lieutenant demanded as KP and Potshot jumped aboard while Major Crystal ran around to his side of the aircraft and shook his fist up at him, again yelling something incomprehensible.

"Flying as your copilot," I replied as I fastened my chinstrap.

"We're flying straight into the jaws of hell, don't you understand that? Now get out!"

"You promised not to get me killed! I'm holding you to that!"

"All bets are off on this mission, Captain!"

"My wife and children expect you to be a man of your word, Lieutenant!"

"*Aw, for Christ's sake!*" he cursed as he pulled pitch and lifted us up off the ground, forcing Major Crystal to turn his back to us to avoid the rotor wash blasting him with sand and debris. "*I speak Chinese and I'm surrounded by fucking idiots!*"

I instinctively ducked as we climbed above the trees and turned north. Small arms fire zinged around us as my side of the windshield shattered and flew back in my face from multiple rounds striking it in loud *Whoomps!* I clawed at the Plexiglas and thrust it aside, acutely conscious of the roar chasing us through the treetops in an angry snarl of clutching death. The aircraft shuttered and swayed as the lieutenant swung it left and right in an attempt to evade the clamor beneath us. The instrument panel in front of me shattered amid puffs of smoke and arcing electrical sparks as I shivered fearfully with my stomach clenching. *Was I fucking crazy or what?*

The heavy jungle beneath us dissipated abruptly as we flashed out over a huge clearing filled with the ugly carnage of war. The ground fire tapered off somewhat, to be replaced by jarring mortar eruptions spewing black soil and debris high into the air around us as tracers swept across our front and hordes of civilians swarmed in panicked confusion seeking a safe haven in the inferno of flaming hooches and wrecked vehicles. As we descended rapidly down into the dense fog of putrid smoke reducing visibility in the chaotic disorder before us, I saw glimpses of ARVN soldiers wedged behind walls of sandbags firing indiscriminately into the dense jungle. Death clutched at us from all directions as I braced myself against the armored seat and the aircraft flared, dropping rapidly toward a large group of screaming civilians. Green fatigued men fought them away as we descended and thumped down hard. In an instant we were mobbed by the terrified throng. A woman thrust a small bundle of rags through my shattered window into my lap. I gasped as I realized it was a baby and snatched up the bundle before it rolled off my knees onto the floor, unsure of what to do with it. I looked out of my side window in horror as bullets tore through the mass of bodies engulfing us, spewing blood and gore as they shrieked in pain and fell away.

"*Go! Go! Go!*" KP's voice screamed in my headphones.

"*Is our crew on board!*" the lieutenant yelled back.

"*Yes, goddamn it! Go! Go! Go!*" K.P. urged frantically.

The aircraft lurched and staggered into the air. I looked instinctively at the torque gauge, still clutching the bundle of rags to my chest, to see the torque meter register a quivering forty-two pounds, and realized we didn't have the muscle to take off.

The nose dipped and plowed into the civilians around us, knocking them aside, as we staggered into the air, the aircraft vibrating, straining, clutching for altitude. I looked over my shoulder to see men clad in jungle fatigues flinging civilians out of the cargo doors to lighten our load as others screamed and clutched for handholds, pleading for their lives. Horrified, I turned back to the front and saw the tree line rushing at us, knowing we didn't have the altitude to clear the tops. I braced and clenched my eyes shut, waiting for death. The aircraft swept up under me with branches clutching at our skids. *We made it! We're alive!* I thought as the roar of small arms fire engulfed us again and bullets thudded into our aircraft. *This living hell's never going to end!*

We gained airspeed and hugged the treetops as the crescendo of firing chased us away. I focused on the whining turbine fearfully, which I could hear steadily losing power as the lieutenant grimly jockeyed the collective to keep us airborne. Sweat beaded my forehead.

Please, please, God, keep us up just a little longer! We're almost there! Don't let the engine fail now! Not after all we've been through! I don't want to die! I don't deserve to die!

I sobbed as I looked down at the tiny bundle in my arms. The child stared back up at me with curious, dark trusting eyes. One of its clinched fists waved as it arched its back, immune to the insanity erupting around us. Peaceful tranquility washed over me in a soothing glow. For the first time since we took off I thought of my newborn son, of Nancy and my daughter. I took a deep breath. *Fuck it*, I thought calmly. *If I'm to die here and now, so be it. I'm doing the right thing for the right reasons, so just fuck it.* I tuned out the roar around me as I cradled the child in my arms in an attempt to protect it from the bullets splitting the air around us.

The long strip of tarmac at An Loc appeared in front of us as hope surged through me. The aircraft dipped down and jolted through a desperate running landing, swaying side to side as it slid down the runway to a groaning halt. I looked down at the child in my arms as the men spilled out behind me and ran. My door lurched open and Potshot fumbled at my seat belt.

"Get out, Captain!" he yelled. "We're on fire! This bitch is gonna blow!"

I clamored clumsily out of the aircraft with my bundle of rags and trotted away with the others, clutching the child to my chest as the aircraft exploded into huge red flames, and turned with the others, panting, to stare at the billowing clouds of black smoke in wonder.

A Vietnamese medic hurried up to me and extended his arms for the child. "I take, Die Wi."

A strong sense of protectiveness swept through me. "No! Get away, I'm keeping it!"

Sly moved in front of me, grim, dirty faced, arms extended. "No, Captain. That's not right. Hopefully someday its mother will be looking for it. You've done all you can."

I reluctantly handed the child to him.

Song Bay collapsed thirty minutes later and the triumphant NVA swarmed through the city massacring the civilians and the ARVN soldiers as they fell to their knees begging for mercy. As this tragedy was occurring, we were ferried back to Hotel Six in an ARVN aircraft.

Sergeant Morrison rushed up as we entered flight ops. "Sir! The peace accords were signed in Paris this morning! We've been asked to fly a team to Song Bay tomorrow to negotiate the cease fire agreement! I've requisitioned an aircraft from the ARVNs for the mission!"

I stared at him dully as the lieutenant turned to me with a weary smile.

"Well, I guess that about does it, Captain. I reckon I'll call in that marker from the USO show now and take that mission, since it'll be the last combat mission flown in this stupid fucking war. Oh, and I want Sly as my copilot."

In my opinion, no pilot had earned that privilege more.

CHAPTER 25

The lieutenant and Sly departed at dawn the following morning with the team of negotiators. I watched them until they disappeared north toward Song Bay, the forward line of the NVA advance. When I walked back into flight ops Major Crystal was waiting in my office.

I eased behind my desk as he settled into a chair. "Good morning, Sir. What brings you out so early?"

"Captain Hess, I am here to inform you that late yesterday afternoon I filed formal court-martial charges against Lieutenant Sharpe and his crew. Lieutenant Sharpe is to be placed under arrest and restricted to his official quarters."

I stared at him in shock. "Sir, charges for what?"

"Disobeying my direct orders."

"Sir, what are you talking about?"

"I'm referring to the mission yesterday, Captain, when I ordered Lieutenant Sharpe to shut down the aircraft. He refused that order even though I repeated it several times. As you are aware, he then ordered his crewmembers to drag me out of the aircraft. I ordered them to remain in their crew compartments, but they disobeyed that order as well and physically put their hands on me. I'm going to run that renegade out of my Army for good this time, by god!"

"Sir, can we please discuss this matter before—"

"There's nothing to discuss, Captain! That bastard is looking at a dishonorable discharge and probably some hard time in Leavenworth prison. I *knew* I'd get his ass eventually!"

"Sir, I beg you, the war is *over*. There's nothing to be gained by—"

"You're basically a good officer, Captain Hess, but you're weak. It's fortunate you are not a career man, since I don't think you are suited for higher command. I'm sure civilian life is more suited to your talents. Have Lieutenant Sharpe report to his quarters immediately. He is to have no visitors outside of his selected defense attorney unless I specifically approve it. Is that clear? As for his despicable crew, they will be placed in the stockade and dealt with as well."

"Sir, Lieutenant Sharpe is on a mission," I replied as sorrow filled my soul.

"What mission? All missions are cancelled until the cease-fire is … Captain Hess, I don't *even* want to think you might have put that little bastard on the mission to *Song Bay*! Surely your judgment is not so impaired by that man that you would put him on the single most *prestigious* mission of the whole war?"

"Sir, I can think of no finer pilot to fly that mission than Lieutenant Sharpe—and for the record, I'll do everything in my power to prevent you from doing him any harm."

He stood angrily. "You are relieved from your duties, Captain Hess! Your Officer Efficiency Report will reflect your disloyalty to your commanding officer due to the regrettable stance you have taken here today."

"I *hope* to *fuck* it will make me a better civilian, *Major*, and possibly even hasten me in getting back home to be one!" I grated. "If I may be excused, I'd like to turn over my duties immediately!"

"By all means, Captain, you are excused. The sight of you has become disagreeable to me as well. Good day." He strode quickly out of my office.

I kicked the trashcan against the wall. "Sergeant Morrison!"

Sergeant Morrison rushed into the room as the trashcan bounced around in a clamor. "Sir?"

"Sergeant, you are now in charge of Dean flight operations. You are to relieve yourself with the next ranking individual that walks in the door and instruct him to do the same thing until the highest ranking son of a bitch on Ton Son Nhut is reached, or until someone else with the proper authority instructs you differently. Do you understand, Sergeant?"

"Yes, Sir—no, Sir—what do you mean, Sir?"

"Find yourself a new boss, Sergeant!"

I kicked the trashcan again, grabbed my hat, stormed out the door, and tore out of the compound in my jeep with the wheels spinning, drove directly to the hospital, and asked for Ellen. A few minutes later, she hurried down the hallway, her smile vanishing at my expression.

She rushed to me as tears sprang into her eyes. "Chief, it's not Sugar Bear, is it? Oh, god, please tell me it's not Sugar Bear!"

"He's okay, but in serious trouble," I replied grimly. "I need your help. Does your sister still work for the MACV operations officer?"

The fear left her eyes to be replaced by wariness. "What has he done now?"

"Can you get off duty and go with me to go see her right now? It's urgent, Ellen. If we don't move fast, the lieutenant's going to be in more trouble than we can ever get him out of."

"Give me five minutes!" She hurried off.

Late that evening Sly and the lieutenant returned from the mission to Song Bay. Two waiting military policemen escorted the lieutenant directly from the helipad to the anteroom of the MACV commander where Major Crystal, a colonel from JAG, and I waited. We were ushered into the commander's office by an adjutant and seated at a long conference table with a huge map of Vietnam spread on the wall, where we waited.

"What's this shit about, Captain?" Sharpe asked.

"I'll ask you to refrain from conversation until the commander arrives," the JAG officer ordered.

Sharpe looked hard at Major Crystal. "I hope you haven't done something stupid, Major."

"That will be all, Lieutenant!" the JAG officer ordered curtly.

Major Crystal smirked. "It's not *me* who has done something stupid, Lieutenant Sharpe!"

"If another word is spoken, I will separate the three of you," the JAG officer threatened.

The door opened and the MACV commander entered briskly as we all jumped to attention.

"Sit down," he ordered sharply as he deposited some papers on his desk before striding over to plop down into his leather seat at the head of the conference table. We sank back into our own chairs as he studied each of us in turn.

"What we have here appears to be a travesty, gentlemen," the commander observed dourly as we shifted uneasily under his unwavering gaze. "If what I've been briefed on in bits and pieces holds up, we're faced with a potentially embarrassing situation that will make us all look like fools. To begin with, I want to point out that at least two, if not three, commanders in the chain of command have been bypassed on this issue for it to reach my desk, and I'm still trying to figure out just how *that* happened. As such, you may consider this an informal conference in its entirety, and any discussions here kept strictly confidential. Is that clear?"

"Sir, I—" Major Crystal began.

"*Is* that *clear*, Major?" the commander demanded.

Major Crystal cleared his throat. "Yes, Sir, it is clear!"

"Colonel Ring, you have the floor," the commander directed to the JAG officer.

The colonel cleared his throat and shuffled his papers in front of him. "On yesterday's date charges were filed by Major Crystal against Lieutenant Sharpe for flying an unauthorized mission and disobeying a direct order from his commanding officer. Major Crystal also filed charges against Lieutenant Sharpe's crewmembers, Specialist Rodriguez, the crew chief, and Private First Class Henderson, the door gunner, for disobeying a direct order in regards to that mission, and further, for assaulting a commissioned officer."

The general turned to me. "Since you seem to be behind this impromptu meeting in some mysterious fashion, Captain Hess, what are the facts as you know them to be?"

I swallowed nervously. "Sir, it was originally a two-aircraft mission to rescue the trapped advisers in Song Bay.

I called for volunteers since Song Bay was under siege and I considered the mission extremely hazardous. Lieutenant Sharpe and Captain Benedict immediately volunteered to fly the mission. Major Crystal, our detachment commander, volunteered to fly as Lieutenant Sharpe's copilot. Lieutenant Sharpe's aircraft sustained battle damage on the second sortie and Captain Benedict's aircraft was my last flyable aircraft. During the last rescue attempt, his aircraft sustained battle damage to an extent that he was forced to crash-land in the Song Bay compound, which stranded him and his crew there with the last of the American advisers. Lieutenant Sharpe elected to attempt to rescue them with his damaged aircraft. Major Crystal ordered Lieutenant Sharpe to shut down the aircraft and abort the mission. Lieutenant Sharpe ordered Major Crystal to depart the aircraft so he could continue the mission alone. When Major Crystal refused, Lieutenant Sharpe ordered his crewmembers to remove Major Crystal from the aircraft. Major Crystal ordered the crewmembers to remain in their gun bays and again ordered Lieutenant Sharpe to shut down the aircraft. Lieutenant Sharpe's crew physically removed Major Crystal from the aircraft upon a second order from Lieutenant Sharpe and I replaced Major Crystal as the copilot. Based on these actions, Major Crystal filed formal court-martial charges against Lieutenant Sharpe and his crew. Of special note here, Sir, I understand I am listed as a witness to the insubordinate actions of Lieutenant Sharpe and his crew."

The general turned to Sharpe. "And your justification for these actions, Lieutenant?"

"Sir, I was the designated aircraft commander with full operational control of the mission. As such, the decision to abort was my decision, not my copilot's. When I made the decision to continue the mission and my copilot refused to fly it with me, I initially ordered him off my aircraft, and when he refused, I ordered my crew to remove him. I stand firmly behind both of those decisions, Sir."

"Hal, what is your take on this?" the commander asked, turning to the JAG officer.

He frowned. "General, this is a touchy subject. Technically, the detachment commander has full purview over all operations under his command. However, the designated aircraft commander has full mission control over the aircraft as long as it is operational. This issue has never been put to the test in a legal environment before, Sir, and frankly, a military court could rule either way due to the fact that the aircraft was running at the time and therefore, in theory, could still be construed as operational. It is an interesting legal challenge, Sir. I could argue either side of the issue with a clear conscience."

The general focused on Major Crystal. "Why did you wish to discontinue the mission, Major Crystal?"

"Sir, I elected to abort the mission because we had already lost two aircraft and our own aircraft had taken numerous hits from ground fire and was no longer flight-worthy."

"But Lieutenant Sharpe judged it airworthy and his crew was willing to continue the mission?"

"Well, Sir, their judgment, uh, as my subordinates ... I felt it was my responsibility to ensure their safety and—"

"You lost your nerve, didn't you, Major?" the commander asked quietly.

"Sir, I ... *deeply* resent—"

"Am I correct in assuming the aircraft you judged to be not flight-worthy in fact made that flight into Song Bay and rescued the remaining Americans advisers and the crew members stranded there minutes before Song Bay fell into enemy hands?"

"Sir, I—"

"Are you aware that the commander of Song Bay, who was personally on that last flight out, put the crew of that aircraft in for medals, and specifically, the pilot of that aircraft in for the Congressional Medal of Honor?"

Major Crystal's face turned white. "Sir, I fail to see—"

"Yes, you do fail to see, Major, and that's the crux of the problem here. Earlier I spoke hastily when I stated that what we had here seemed to be a travesty. More simply put—it's clearly a cluster fuck." He leaned forward. "I intend to do the talking from here on out, and then you three gentlemen can sleep on it, and I'll accept your decisions in the morning. As for further explanations or justifications, I don't personally give a damn, so spare me any more sordid reasoning. I would like to quote Heraclitus, circa 500 B.C. "'*Out of every one hundred men, ten shouldn't even be there, eighty are just targets, nine are the real fighters, and we are lucky to have them, for they make the battle. Ah, but the one, one is a warrior, and he will bring the others back.*'"

He sighed and leaned back in his chair. "Now I'm going to make you an offer, Major Crystal—drop the charges against Lieutenant Sharpe and his crew by 0900 hours in the morning and I will not prefer charges against you for cowardice in the face of the enemy. That is all, Major. You are dismissed."

We held our breath as Major Crystal stumbled out ashen faced.

"Lieutenant Sharpe, I am aware of your request submitted some time ago resigning your commission as an officer in the United States Army," the general continued. "I am led to believe you have applied for a position with Air America upon your release from active duty. I will contact the Department of the Army on this issue and request they grant your resignation as an active duty officer. I expect you will process out of the service within a few weeks. I wish you luck in your new career field. I would also like to take this opportunity to personally thank you for your dedication and service to our country. I especially would like to thank you for flying that last mission into Song Bay. My son-in-law was on that flight and I assure you he holds you in his highest regards. You are dismissed, Lieutenant Sharpe. Go with God, young man."

The lieutenant stood, saluted the general, and walked out the door.

"Captain Hess, when you return to civilian life, I want you to drop me a note explaining just how the fuck you got all of this on my desk before it got out of hand. I'm afraid if you tell me now, I'd have to court-martial you or someone dear to me. I've directed your rotation date back to the states be expedited. I wish you well, Captain. You are dismissed."

I stood, saluted, and hurried out the door, where I found the lieutenant waiting.

"Damn, Captain, you're getting almost as good at this shit as me!"

I sighed. "No one will ever be as good at this shit as you are, Lieutenant. Promise me you'll behave for just a few more days until I get my ass out of here, and then you can do whatever the hell you want to do."

He scowled. "Sure would feel nice to be appreciated…"

CHAPTER 26

I closed the journal and laid it aside, my tears long dried for a war gone wrong as I reflected back across that era. Within a week of the signing of the cease-fire agreement I shipped home a month ahead of my scheduled rotation date.

Shortly after my departure Mad Hatter died in a senseless accident in Vietnam. As I understand it, he and the lieutenant flew two aircraft loaded with nurses to the R&R facility in Vung Tau. On the flight down, the lieutenant dropped to the deck and flew his aircraft under a bridge as a lark. On the return trip Mad Hatter, not to be outdone, dropped low and flew at the bridge with the intent of doing the same. Tragically, someone, most likely the local VC after observing the lieutenant pull his stunt a few days earlier, dropped a one-inch steel cable over the side of the bridge in the interim, which sheered off Mad Hatter's rotor blades at over one hundred miles an hour, killing all aboard, with Linda and Debbie among his passengers.

Sly remained in the Army and was reassigned to the 101st Airborne Division. He and Sandra married when they returned to the States and were expecting their first child the last I heard from them.

I lost track of Cherrie after Nam. I know she was heartbroken by Sharpe's decision to pursue a career with Air America, and that they had a huge fight just before I left, after which the lieutenant again took up with Ellen.

I never heard from Lieutenant Sharpe again. I suppose that was to be expected since he zealously lived each day to the fullest and had no tomorrows.

When I returned to the states, I rushed through the processing station at Oakland, California, and dashed back home to my beloved wife, my precious daughter, and the son I had never seen. There I received the most crushing blow of my life—Nancy had filed for divorce the week before. In the lonely months I had been gone she had met a former love from her college days and their relationship had rekindled. Though I pleaded for the opportunity to give our marriage and our life together a second chance, she knew where her heart lay, and it was not with me. Shortly after our divorce, she married her former beau. They divorced within a year.

A week prior to my out-processing from the Army I was called to the White House, along with KP and Potshot, for the awards ceremony for our valiant rescue of the advisers at Song Bay. They listed me as the aircraft commander on the mission with no mention of the lieutenant in the glowing citation as the president placed our nation's highest award around my neck. The guilt of accepting that award has haunted me ever since.

After my discharge, I went back to school under the G.I. Bill and got my Ph.D. Afterwards I landed a position with the University teaching American history and specializing in the Vietnam conflict.

I rented a car at the airport, drove to the chapel, entered the foyer, and paused to sign the guestbook, where I found over three hundred signatures already posted, taking special note of a dozen high-ranking prominent names.

I entered the chapel filled to capacity, with the spillover lining the walls on each side of the pews, and walked to the table centered at the front draped with an American flag and holding a framed picture of a much older but recognizable version of the John Joseph Sharpe I knew. I removed the case from my pocket in the restless silence, extracted the Medal of Honor, and placed it before the picture on top of the flag. Moving to the side, I stood immobile during the ceremony listening attentively to five separate eulogies from key members of our government attesting to the long and honorable service provided by John Joseph Sharpe to our country.

Afterwards an honor guard gently removed the Medal of Honor from the flag before folding and presenting it, along with the medal, to a woman flanked by a teenage boy and girl seated in the front pew whose features reminded me strongly of someone, who I assumed to be Sharpe's daughter, Mary Ellen Jones. I saw a vague likeness to Lieutenant Sharpe in the boy's features and figured him to be a grandson. I stood discretely in the throng for the short closing prayer service, followed by the haunting bugle blowing taps in the distance, and a twenty-one gun salute. As I turned to depart, the teenage boy approached me.

"Professor Hess?"

"Yes?"

"My mother would appreciate a word with you, Sir, if you have the time?"

"Of course." I stood passively off to the side for over half an hour as Mrs. Jones received the condolences of the throng of attendees. When the last of them passed, she looked to me and I stepped forward.

"Professor Hess, so good of you to come. I feel a little overwhelmed with the turn out. If I had known this many people would attend I would have held his memorial service in a much larger chapel."

"Your father was a very special man," I acknowledged, my throat tightening.

"My father has two pictures hanging in his den, one of you, my mother, and him sitting in a bar, and the other of you, a Captain Benedict, a Captain Everett, and him taken years ago at some old airfield in Vietnam."

"Do I know your mother?"

"I believe you knew her as Captain Ellen Rollins. She was a nurse in Vietnam when she met my father."

"*Ellen*! Of course!"

"She passed away three years ago."

"Oh, I'm so sorry to hear that. If you don't mind my asking … how did you find me?"

"I googgled you and found you listed on the registry at the University and got your home number from information. I hope you don't mind?"

"No … no of course not."

"He never spoke of you."

"He didn't?"

"No, but my mother did when he wasn't around, and I assume he must have thought a great deal of you since you're in the only two pictures of him he'd allow my mother to display."

"What kind of accident was he involved in?"

"A helicopter crash in the mountains of Afghanistan. They said he was trying to rescue some trapped soldiers. His body was never recovered."

"That sounds like him," I replied. "Was he still in the Army?"

"Oh, no, he worked for many different organizations over the years, but I'm not sure who he was working for when it happened."

"Your mother, Ellen, was a unique lady," I said. "You favor her a great deal."

She smiled fondly. "My mother was a flower child who abhorred violence in any form until the day she died, but she loved my father with all of her heart. She followed him halfway around the world for almost five years after he left the Army, but only agreed to marry him when she was six months pregnant with me."

"That sounds like Ellen," I acknowledged, suppressing a smile.

"She was the sweetest soul I've ever known. I don't know what she saw in my father."

"I found him to be an … exceptional soldier," I replied cautiously.

"My mother said he was a consummate warrior who relentlessly sought the thrill of battle to appease the fierce inferno of his combatant's spirit."

"He made Vietnam very interesting for us," I agreed.

"She said he left you all with a strong sense of pride to help assuage your defeat over there, and that she hoped there were others like him who did the same for their comrades in arms. When I asked her what she meant, she said he allowed each of you to return home with your heads held high knowing you had stared dishonor squarely in the eye and rose above it by giving your full measure as soldiers."

"That's quite gracefully put … and very true," I acknowledged.

"I certainly didn't know that side of him," she continued. "I didn't see him often because he was always off somewhere mysterious that he could never talk about. Mainly he came home to recuperate from some unexplained injury. There were far too many of those times, but mother was always pleased to have him back in whatever shape, and always devastated when she got him all healed up so he could run off to wherever again."

"I think Ellen was probably the only person who ever really understood him."

"I don't want to give you the impression he was a terrible father, Professor. It's just that he was rarely home. He never missed calling on my birthday, or Christmas, and always sent exotic gifts. The truth is when he was around he spoiled me horribly and was very devoted to me. I don't think he ever understood it only made it more difficult for me when he went away again."

"That was quite an impressive gathering at his service."

"And they were very moving in their eulogies to my father. Obviously, he served our country with distinction in whatever endeavor he was involved in, as my late husband did."

"Your late husband?"

She smiled ruefully. "James was one of the misfits my father drug home after one of his trips. I partly married him to irritate my father, but he loved me and gave me two marvelous children before he … eventually didn't come back himself. I suppose my son John will turn out to be a mercenary as well. He worshiped his grandfather and his father and has already started flying lessons. Thank goodness, my daughter takes after my mother and me. She loves the ranch my father left us and wants to become a veterinarian."

"She's quite lovely," I replied as I studied her and John standing by the limo. "I can see Ellen in her features, and your father's in John."

She reached into her purse, pulled out the medal, and extended it to me. "I'm sure my father would appreciate the gesture, but I feel strongly he would want you to keep this."

"That was awarded to me many years ago," I replied. "But frankly, it belonged to him."

She smiled. "My father never spoke of Vietnam, but my mother told me the story of this medal."

"Then I'm sure she also mentioned your father should have received it instead of me."

"Actually, she said you were one of the few men my father respected, and that he was proud when it was awarded to you because you were one of the bravest men he'd ever served with."

"I'm … honored he would think such, but I assure you, nothing could be further from the truth."

"You don't strike me as an overly modest man, Professor," she chided.

I smiled. "I recall the first time I met your father. At the time, I experienced a strong sense of foreboding.

I suppose it was a natural reaction to someone distinctively different and rather odd. I suspect now if I had known then what was to follow I might have run. That undoubtedly would have saved me, the Army, and most certainly the Vietcong we were trying to eradicate from the Republic of South Vietnam a great deal of future anguish."

"But you didn't run, Professor, so in a bizarre way you are somewhat accountable for what followed, wouldn't you say?" she teased, a smile playing at her lips.

"No … no I didn't run … and I do admit that if I had run, I would have missed the excitement, the indescribable *distinction* your father brought to our lives as he conquered our souls and bent us to his incorrigible will. I think we are all the better for having known him. I can certainly say that categorically, none of us was ever the same afterwards."

"I don't detect any false humility in you, Professor, so I take it you honestly believe that to be true, which only makes my father's opinion of you more endearing. When I was a little girl, I once heard a dignitary say my father was a true American hero. Later I asked my father what being a hero meant. He said it meant doing the right thing when you had everything to lose. From what my mother told me you flew that mission with my father when no one else would. I also understand it was the right thing to do and that *you* had everything to lose." She held out her hand with the medal in her palm. "Please, take your medal back, Professor, and display it with pride, for I am quite certain you earned it!"

As I hung the recessed frame displaying the Medal of Honor on its blue velvet background next to the picture of my receiving it, my doorbell rang.

"*Paw-paw!*" my great grandson squealed as he rushed forward.

"Are you okay?" Nancy inquired anxiously from the front porch.

"I'm fine," I replied.

"Are you sure?"

I looked down at my great grandchild clutching my legs. "Why wouldn't I be?"

Her eyes shaded. "Connie mentioned you went to Texas to ... say goodbye to an old friend?"

"Yes ... a man I served with in Vietnam."

"She said you sounded distraught ... if you'd like some company?"

"That won't be necessary. Perhaps I could take Randy to the park and treat him to pizza and ice cream. I'll drop him off at our granddaughter's afterwards."

She wavered. "I'm sure ... you and the others did your best over there. It was all wrong to begin with. We were right to pull out. It wasn't even a *real* war."

I stared at her coldly, this woman who once was the love of my life.

"But one should never doubt that *real soldiers* fought and died in it ..." I replied bitterly.

Made in the USA
Lexington, KY
06 July 2010